perfect for you

BY SAMANTHA LEIGH

Valentine Bay Series
Ready For You
Meant For You
Perfect For You
Only For You

Aster Springs Series
Wallflower
Sunshine

perfect for you

samantha leigh

Cover design by Echo Grayce at Wildheart Graphics
Editing by Killing It Write
Proofreading by My Notes in the Margin

A catalogue record for this book is available from the National Library of Australia

ISBN: 978-0-6455703-7-3 (paperback)
ISBN: 978-0-6455703-6-6 (e-book)

To the person who told me I couldn't do this... Ha!

(Me. That person was me.)

AUTHOR'S NOTE

My books are low on angst and big on feel-good vibes, but they occasionally touch on topics that may be difficult for some readers. To access a complete list of content warnings for all my books, including *Perfect For You*, please visit my website at samanthaleighbooks.com or use the QR code below. And most importantly, take care of yourself.

1

ISAAC

"I'M SORRY, ISAAC. It's not me. It's you."

Amanda, the woman I'd been dating for three weeks, stretched a hand across the scarred timber tabletop and squeezed my wrist as she gave me a tight, apologetic smile. When she pulled back and settled her bag over her shoulder, I watched—dumbfounded—as she scooted out of our booth at The Salty Stop, Valentine Bay's best pub, and beelined for the exit.

Blinking hard, I tried to work out if my brain had screwed up the order of her words. It's not her. It's *me*?

Huh?

Making a split-second decision to follow her, I pushed to my feet just as my best mate and The Stop's owner, Will Kidd, cocked a mocking eyebrow. He stood behind the bar, serving—and flirting with—a gorgeous brunette I'd bet twenty dollars had stumbled across his playboy energy on social media and wanted to try her luck with the real thing. I flipped him the bird, and he flashed his dimples before returning to the girl.

I didn't need to explain to Will why my date had lasted less than ten minutes. He was smart enough—and my life was predictable enough—to work out I'd been dumped.

As I pushed against the heavy front door of the pub, I replayed Amanda's line in my head one more time. There was no way I'd heard her right… Right? It took a moment on the footpath outside to work out which way she'd gone, but I finally spotted a glimpse of her bouncing blonde curls as she disappeared around a corner. Excusing myself as I navigated my burly frame through the sparse foot traffic on Main Street, I hurried after her.

Amanda had reached her shiny red hatchback by the time I caught up. She was dressed in office clothes, her generous curves wrapped up in a tight white pencil skirt and tanned calves looking incredible in tall red heels.

The woman was a knockout, and I wasn't immune to the way she looked—I sure as hell hadn't missed the way her black blouse was unbuttoned just enough to reveal the slopes of her breasts and a tease of lace—but the truth was I usually dated the girl-next-door types, which is what I thought Amanda was when we met for the first time at the gym. I soon discovered she was anything but the girl next door, and I'd embraced it. Part of me took it as a sign. I'd hoped this relationship would be different from all the others. I'd hoped it would last.

I set my hand on her shoulder just as she opened the driver's side door, but she startled, and I jerked back.

"Sorry. I didn't mean to scare you, but..." I searched for something in her face. Regret, sadness, a second thought... Anything.

Nothing.

Amanda turned, a questioning lift to her brow that struck me as impatient, and then tucked her bag away in the car. She held the driver's side door open, keys jangling in one hand.

I cleared my throat and went on, feeling like an idiot, as every self-preservation instinct I possessed shouted at me to shut the hell up. "It's not you, it's *me*?"

Her mouth tightened in a one-sided smile, and she reached up to touch my arm. One hand drifted to my bicep, and she kneaded it with a wistful sigh. "You're a great guy, and I like you, but it's just not going to work out."

"Come on, Amanda." I brushed a gentle, playful punch against her arm. "We have fun together, don't we?"

Her brown eyes darted to the spot where my hand had connected with her shoulder, and her brows climbed towards her hairline. "I think we're better off as friends."

The forced smile froze on my face, then I let it fall away as I closed my eyes and dropped my head back.

"Why?" I groaned at the sky. "Why does this keep happening to me?"

When Amanda didn't slide into her car and zoom away as fast as she could, I squinted down at her. Her plump, ruby lips were pursed, and she studied me with narrowed eyes as if she were contemplating something.

"What?" I asked, running an open hand over my short, thick beard. It'd be just my luck to have food stuck to my face the moment I was getting dropped like a hot potato. "What is it?"

"Do you *really* want to know why this is about you and not me?"

"Uh…"

Fuck. Did I? The answer could ruin me for life, and yet… What if Amanda could help me unravel a riddle I'd been unable to solve for ten years or more?

Was it *really* me? It was hard to see how. I was twenty-nine years old. An all-round nice guy—and one of the literal good guys as a sergeant at the local police station. I owned my own place. I coached my niece's junior soccer team. I helped little old ladies cross the street.

I'd been an awkward, long-limbed, self-conscious teenager—six foot four by my eighteenth birthday and not done growing—but then I filled out and worked out until I wasn't awkward anymore. My beard was professionally trimmed. I dressed well enough. I smelled damn good. I could cook. Sure, nothing fancier than spaghetti carbonara or steak and salad, but I wasn't burning through takeout menus either.

So why the fuck couldn't I find someone willing to stick with me for more than a month?

"Yeah, I want to know," I said. I cleared my throat again while she gazed up at me, possibly reconsidering the wisdom of telling a giant of a man why he was unlovable. I smoothed the line between my brows and tilted up the corners of my mouth, trying for an open and friendly expression that encouraged her trust. The kind I saved for Saturday nights on duty when it was my job to convince intoxicated townsfolk that the bonfire was over and it was time to go home—preferably in peace and without their vomit on my boots.

Amanda crossed her arms over her chest and cocked her head. "Okay. You're not very demonstrative, Isaac."

I nodded before I realised I had no idea what she meant. "What?"

Amanda flapped her hands back and forth through the air. "There's no physical connection between us. No chemistry. No… No *throwdown*." She met my eyes again, and I pulled back a little from the challenge in them. "It was almost like you didn't want to touch me at all."

"I touched you," I disagreed, mirroring her posture and crossing my arms over my chest as I recalled the night that I'd held her hand in the movies.

"Not often," she said. "I'm not used to pursuing men, Isaac. I'm not interested in guys who play hard to get."

"I'm not playing hard to get!"

She frowned, a flicker of uncertainty passing behind her eyes. "You're not?"

Prickles of heat crept their way up my neck, and I thumbed my earlobe. "No. Women want to be treated well. They want to go slow and feel safe, so I don't assume anything. Ever. If a girl is interested in things going to the next level, she'll let me know."

She shook her head—just the slightest movement—and faint lines popped up on her forehead. "Yes, but a woman also wants to feel *desired*. She needs to believe you crave her so desperately that you can't wait to put your hands on her. You need to wait for her to give you the green light, of course, but it's never too early to rev her engine."

"So, you mean…" The woman may as well have been speaking Latin for all the sense I could make of her advice. "What do you mean?"

Amanda swallowed a frustrated sigh and jingled the keys in her hand again. "Flirt a little. Touch her. Tease her. *Tempt* her."

Of all the things I might have expected Amanda to say, this was nowhere on the list. I opened my hands and stared at them as though I could find an answer between the creases on my broad palms. "Not sure I know how to do that. Clearly."

A moment of uncomfortable silence passed before Amanda rose on her tiptoes to pat my cheek with an open hand. "You'll make another woman very happy one day but take my advice now. Give the good-boy routine a break, okay? Find the bad boy I know is hiding way, *way* down deep inside, and let him out to play. Often."

She left me standing on the side of the road, watching her car zip up the street, wondering if everything I ever thought I knew about women was wrong.

"Don't spend another minute worrying about a girl who puts a frown like that on your face."

I turned towards the thin yet firm voice of the woman who'd appeared at my side. By best estimates, Dorothy March was fast approaching her late eighties, though it would have been impolite to ask exactly how old she was, not least because she refused to act her age. Renowned for her no-nonsense attitude, fluoro 1980s-era tracksuits, and a cloud of hot-pink hair, Dot was a legend around town—a regular at the seniors' aerobics centre, a twelve-time lawn bowls champion, and president of the Bay's mysterious invitation-only book club.

She'd also worn out five or six husbands, a random tidbit that came to mind as her trademark bluntness cut through the daze Amanda had left me in.

"Can I help you with that?" I asked, nodding at Dot's overburdened trolley. She must have walked to Main Street to do her grocery shopping and was on her way home.

"Thank you, dear, but I'm all right. These little strolls keep me young."

I smiled a little. "If it's all the same to you, Mrs March, I'd feel better if you let me drive you home." I squinted up at the purpling twilight sky, then cut off the old woman's protest. "At least let me walk with you. It's a nice evening for it, and I could use the exercise."

Dot snorted. "You're the fittest man in the Bay. I hardly think a shuffle with me along Figtree Road is going to do you any favours." But she started up the footpath in the direction of her bungalow and didn't protest when I took the handle of her trolley and kept pace alongside her.

When we'd passed two short blocks, and neither of us had said another word, Dot looked up at me with a sideways glance. "Keep that up, and you'll wear wrinkles long before your time."

I relaxed the muscles in my jaw and smoothed the lines on my forehead, then shook my head at her small, knowing smile. "Am I that obvious?"

"Well, Isaac Greene's good mood is perhaps the most reliable thing about Valentine Bay, so yes, you're that obvious. Something is bothering you, and fifty cents says it has to do with that woman I watched drive away from you five minutes ago."

I sighed and ran an open palm across my face. "Her name's Amanda, and she dumped me."

"Ah."

A beat passed before I realised that was all I was going to get. "Ah?"

Dot shrugged. "These things happen, and there are plenty more fish in the sea. If she's walking away from you, Sergeant, there's obviously something not quite right with her."

I grunted. "More like there's something not quite right with *me*."

"Why on Earth would you think that?" Dot clucked her tongue. "Isaac, you're a catch. If Jessica and Logan hadn't found their way to each other in the nick of time, I might have been on her case to pin you down before it was too late."

I flashed Dot a wry smile. Jessica Frost was a childhood friend of mine—so was her new boyfriend, Logan

Reeve—and Jess and I were still good mates, which Dot knew very well.

Dot was Jess's next-door neighbour, as well as something of a surrogate grandmother to her, and she'd been one of Logan's biggest supporters when he and Jess were sneaking around a few months ago. Their relationship was out in the open now, and even Luca—Jess's ex and Logan's best mate—was happy the two of them had found a happily ever after with each other.

"You know as well as I do that Jess and I have never been more than friends."

Dot waved her hand. "Minor detail. Sometimes the best love affairs start with a good, solid friendship. That's how it happened with Thomas." She sighed, and her expression took on a dreamy, distracted air.

"One of your husbands?" I asked.

"Mm. Number five. After Harold died—he was husband number four—I spent most of my time reading to cope with the grief. When I ran out of books at the local library, I started taking the bus over to Scarborough Cove. Thomas was the librarian there—smart, charming"—she elbowed me slyly, then winked—"and a few years younger than me. We knew each other for two years before he worked up the courage to ask me on a date, and it still came out of nowhere—or so it seemed to me."

Her eyes sparkled in a way that hinted at youth—or at least, a younger spirit. By the time she was onto husband number five, Dot had to have been in her late sixties.

This part of her story intrigued me. "Did you really have no idea he fancied you?"

"None," she replied, deftly navigating an uneven stretch of pavement even though I had an arm out to assist. "Oh, I'd done my fair share of admiring the way he managed the stacks, of course, but he was so reserved and always a gentleman. I never dreamed he was interested in me romantically."

"So, what changed?"

"We'd been on six dates, and I'd begun to believe they weren't really *dates* at all," Dot explained. "He was so polite and hands-off that I concluded he was only interested in companionship. Then, at the end of that sixth date, he took me by the arms, pinned me against a wall, and kissed me hard enough to make my toes curl." Her smile was wide. "I was done for after that."

"I wonder what changed for him?" I mused, wishing Thomas was still alive so I could hit him up for some pointers.

Fuck. Did I really just wish for dating advice from a seventy-year-old dead guy?

"Oh, I know exactly what changed," Dot replied, not bothering to conceal her smugness.

"What was it?"

Dot watched me from the corner of her eye as she put one foot in front of the other, and I set a gentle hand on her elbow. Distracted like that, she was going to trip and break a hip.

"What's this all about, Isaac? I know I'm a fascinating woman, but I'm not used to young men expressing this level of interest in my love life."

I flushed. "I haven't had a lot of luck with women, and I've just been given some information about where things might be going wrong."

"Oh? And where's that?"

"I'm a lot like Thomas, apparently. I've got no idea how to, uh…flirt."

Dot's gaze travelled across my broad chest and heavily muscled arms. I could almost see the thoughts turning over in her brain. The same thoughts everyone had when they looked at me.

I was an imposing guy, a truth that was hard for me to forget. Most people glanced twice when I walked down the street—at six foot eight inches, it was impossible to blend in. My shoulders and arms strained even the most generously made shirts. I was a cop, which meant I walked around town with a gun on my hip half the time—gun, handcuffs, baton, uniform, the whole bit. All in all, I was the dictionary definition of *man*, but I had a front-row seat to the reality of toxic masculinity and what it could do to women. That was never going to be me.

Only now did I wonder if I was doing *too* good of a job trying not to live up to the negative stereotypes.

"What on Earth gave you that idea?" she asked.

I grimaced. "Not what—who. Amanda seems to think women want—" Suddenly remembering who I was talking to, I scratched my beard and muttered, "She thought I was playing hard to get when all I was trying to do was respect her boundaries and wait for her cue to take things to the next level."

"Ah."

"Really, Mrs March?" I asked with a pained moan. "I could use some advice or at least a hint about how Thomas finally figured out how to let you know how he felt."

"I'll do you one better than that. I'll show you."

We reached her driveway and drew to a stop, and just as I started to panic that the grandmotherly woman was going to try to kiss me, she pulled her handbag from the crook of her elbow, unfastened the clasp, and dug around in its depths. I waited, then took the bright pink business card she proffered. There was a handwritten time, date, and address scrawled across the back.

"What's this?" I asked as I turned it over to find the logo for her infamously exclusive invitation-only book club printed on the front. It was called the VBFYRRRBC, but only vetted members were told what the jumble of letters represented.

"*That* is your invitation to the next meeting of the—Well, you'll just have to come along to find out what the name is."

I quirked an eyebrow at her, equal parts amused and frustrated. "A book club? How's that supposed to help?"

Dot's thin mouth twitched as she fought a smile, and she tapped the card with one knobbly, pink-painted finger. "Trust me, dear. If you want to know what inspired Thomas to finally make his move—and make it very well, I might add—be at this address at this time. You won't regret it."

"Well, I'm not sure—"

My phone rang loudly, vibrating in my pocket, and I slid it out, frowning at the screen.

"Is something wrong?" Dot asked.

"I'm sorry. I don't mean to be rude, but I need to get this," I said, accepting the call and putting the phone to my ear as Dot waved away my apology. "David. What's the problem?"

"Probably nothing," my colleague replied down the line. David was on duty at the station, and a call to my personal line was unusual. "Just had someone call to say they might have seen someone poking around the Old Maxwell Place, and I wondered if you were home. Have you noticed anything?"

"The Old Maxwell Place," as it was locally known, was a large property owned by a wealthy family from the city. They'd bought the house thirty-odd years ago but only ever visited it for six weeks in summer and another two in winter, and not one of them had been back for at least twelve or thirteen years—ever since the Maxwells' only child graduated high school. Birdie was her name, and the memory of her tweaked a fond smile, as well as the nostalgic pang of an unrequited teenage crush.

For unknown reasons, the Maxwells had never come back to town after that last summer, and they'd never put their abandoned house on the market either, which meant that local teenagers sometimes tried to sneak in and use it for their own delinquent reasons. Since I'd moved into the house next door two years ago, there'd been fewer incidents of break-and-enter. Still a few, but not so many as before.

I guessed knowing a cop could be within metres of a crime was enough to discourage all but the most stupid kids from doing something they'd live to regret.

"I'm on my way there now," I told David. "I'll check it out."

"Do you need me to send anyone over?"

"It'll be kids, most likely," I said with a shake of my head. "No need to make it official if it doesn't need to be. I'll have a word with them and send them on their way."

"Cara and Ross are patrolling. I'll request a circuit of the street, just in case."

"Thanks, mate."

I tucked the phone into my pocket and smiled apologetically. "Sorry to leave you, Mrs March, but I've got to go."

"Trouble?"

"In the Bay?" I said with a wink. "Unlikely."

"Well, thank you for chaperoning me home, Sergeant." Dot took the handle of her trolley and glanced pointedly at the pink card still trapped between my thick fingers. "I hope to see you at our book club, but keep it to yourself, won't you? And hide that card. There are people in this town who would commit murder to get in on this action, and with all those dead bodies, you'll only be creating work for yourself."

I chuckled and slipped the card into my pocket and out of sight. "I'll think about it."

"Make sure you do. Oh! And new members need to bring cake, so don't embarrass me by showing up empty-handed. Call Maz. She'll give you a recipe for something easy and delicious."

"I'll do that," I agreed. "Now I really need to run."

I watched Dot totter up her driveway and through the front door, dragging her trolley cart behind her as I debated whether it would be faster to return to my car and drive or sprint straight over to the Maxwell house. Deciding quickly on option B, I took off at a run, putting all thoughts of Amanda and flirting and mysterious, super-secret book clubs out of my mind.

2

BIRDIE

HOLY HELL, IT was orgasmic to have a shower somewhere other than in a hotel bathroom.

I stood under the steaming, pelting water, dropped my head back to rinse away the shampoo suds, and let the warmth relax my stiff muscles. How long had I been standing there, sluicing off months—no, *years*—of planes and hotels and cigarette smoke and greasy food? Ten minutes? An hour? More? I checked the pads of my fingertips. Total prunes. Sighing, I turned off the water, stepped out into the steamy bathroom, and dried myself off.

The fluffy white towels I'd found in the hallway linen cupboard of my family's old summer house were a little musty, which surprised me. I didn't know—or care—if my parents had been to the house since I left the country the day after I turned twenty-one, but it was unlike my mother to let things gather dust. By the look of the furniture downstairs, plus the punch of stale air that greeted me when I finally jimmied open the lock on the back door, I guessed it had been years since anyone had been back to air the place out.

But what my parents did or didn't do with their properties wasn't my business, and I couldn't have cared less anyway.

I rubbed down my body, dried my long, copper hair as best as I could—ugh, I needed a haircut—then dug around in my toiletries case for a bottle of my favourite body lotion. The seal was still intact, so I peeled off the foil cap, then squirted a dollop of apple-scented cream into my palm. I may have moaned a little as I slathered the cool lotion over my hot skin. This was a level of luxury I rarely bothered to indulge in, but today I had nowhere to be and nothing better to do, so why not?

Washed, moisturised, and feeling genuinely fresh for the first time in a long time, I took a sip from the glass of chilled white wine sitting on the bathroom vanity before I ran a brush through my hair.

There. The bathroom portion of my impromptu pamper session was officially complete. My muscles were loose, my skin pleasantly flushed, and the sun had finally dipped far enough below the horizon to plunge the hall outside the bathroom door into shadow. Now, my favourite vibrator was calling my name.

Flipping open my *other* toiletries case—the one with my stash of single-woman goodies—I sorted through my toys until I found Mr Big Boy.

Hello, lover.

I switched it on to be sure the device was charged, so it took me an extra moment to pick up the subtle sounds floating up the stairs, noises that sounded like someone testing the handle on the front door.

Silencing the hum of the vibrator, I gently pushed the bathroom door to almost closed, allowing a single shard of yellowish light to spill into the darkened hallway. I held my ear to the narrow gap and tried to figure out what was going on downstairs.

A click. The sound of a handle turning. A door being pushed open. Careful, creepy footsteps on the old, creaky floorboards in the foyer.

I couldn't believe it. Somebody thought they could burgle my house *today* of all days? Even when I was a kid, it had stood empty most months of the year, and now some criminal decided to help himself to whatever he wanted within hours of my return?

Not today, Satan.

Cursing myself for leaving my phone next to the suitcase lying open on the bed in my room, I scanned the small, simple bathroom for something to use as a weapon.

Fantastic. It was going to be either the ratty, rusted old toilet brush or Mr Big Boy.

The footsteps drew closer, and my shoulders tensed as I wrapped my fingers painfully tight around my girthy electronic boyfriend. Straining to pick out the noises in the house over the thumping of blood in my ears, I listened to the quiet clunks of someone heavy on the stairs. A tall, broad figure slid into sight, pressed up against one wall and steadily coming closer. Fuck, he was huge.

Mr Big Boy, then.

"That's it," I coaxed in a whisper as I watched the shadow get larger. "A little closer, dick wad. Close enough I can get a better shot at you."

I glared into the darkness and held my breath, waiting until just the right moment before I flung open the door.

I smiled grimly as the intruder flung up a hand to block the onslaught of blinding light.

"Take this, you fucker!" I declared, surprising the guy enough that he dropped his arm and squinted at me, which was my cue to pitch reliable old Mr Big Boy directly at his head.

"Ow!" the man bellowed as the head of the vibrator connected with his face with a satisfying smack. He clapped a hand to his left eye as my valiant protector fell to the floor with a dull thud. "What the hell was that?"

"It was a hint to get out of my house, arsehole!" When the man didn't move, I slammed the bathroom door and flicked the flimsy lock. Something I refused to acknowledge as unease stirred up a burn in my stomach. "You've got three seconds before I call the police!" I bluffed in a shout that bordered on a screech.

"I *am* the police," he called back, "and this isn't your house."

I snorted, choosing scorn over panic. "Why the hell would a cop sneak into someone's house like a common criminal?"

"Because I live next door, and the neighbours noticed activity here when there shouldn't be."

Quickly, I tallied up the odds of this being the truth, and my heart rate slowed. Mr Criminal certainly wasn't trying to break through the locked bathroom door. His voice wasn't getting closer on the other side, and he spoke in the tone of someone used to calming people down. Not that I needed to be soothed. I'd built a life around staying cool under pressure.

Still... This could all be a ploy to lure me out, murder me, and steal—what? There was nothing here but dust motes and dirty linen.

"What's your name?" I demanded.

"Sergeant Greene," he replied calmly. "And what's yours?"

Sergeant Greene? Sergeant *Greene*. It couldn't be…

I cracked open the door just enough that I didn't have to shout to be heard. "Isaac?" I asked. "Is that you?"

"Uh… Yes, I'm Isaac."

"Holy shit!" I flung open the door and launched myself at him, and the giant didn't even budge as my entire weight crashed against him. I had to stretch up on my toes to wrap my arms around his neck while he just stood there, not moving, arms stiff at his sides. It felt like hugging a tree.

"Birdie?" he whispered.

I laughed at the disbelief in his voice. "Yes! Oh my God. I can't believe it's you."

I let go and took a step back, eager to get a better look at him, and what I saw had me smiling appreciatively.

Holy hell, I could never have predicted Isaac Greene would turn out like this. He'd been tall when we were kids, but it was the awkward kind of tall—all long limbs and self-conscious stooping. Not anymore, and his impressive height went well with the hard, broad chest and thick, ropey shoulders that no T-shirt could tame. Add in the trimmed, inky beard, the sharp cheekbones, and the green eyes—which, to be fair, looked a little stunned at the moment—and it was time to sell tickets because, ladies and gentlemen, this man here was what you called a masterpiece.

"What's going on?" I asked, setting my hands on my hips. "What have you been up to? Wait—you live next door now?"

Cheeks pink, Isaac cleared his throat and dropped his eyes, rubbing at his forehead as if to shield him from the view. "Uh, Birdie? You're, um… You're naked."

I looked down at my bare body. "Oh, yeah. Sorry. I forgot about that. You know, what with all the defending-myself-from-a-burglar business and all. I just got out of the shower."

I smirked at the way he obviously avoided getting an eyeful, and then he stooped to pick up Mr Big Boy from the floor. "Here's your, ah—" Isaac glanced at the vibrator, then groaned as if he'd only just realised I'd thrown a sex toy at his face. "Really, Red? Wasn't there a shampoo bottle in there that could have done the trick?"

"Thanks," I said, taking Mr Big Boy from him, grinning wider at the way my old nickname slipped from his lips like it hadn't been a lifetime since he'd last said it. "Didn't think of that, but I'll remember for next time. Hey, can you stick around? There's nothing to eat, but I had enough foresight to pick up wine on my way here. I'm good like that."

"I, uh…"

"Oh, come on. It's the least you can do, breaking into my house and scaring me senseless on my first night back in town. You owe me, Isaac. Not to mention that I haven't heard from you in years."

"What?" he sputtered, forgetting himself and sweeping his eyes my way. "*I* haven't heard from *you* in years!"

"Semantics," I replied, waving a hand. When he rolled his head back and glared at the ceiling, I added, "I'll put on clothes?"

"Still making deals, eh?" he muttered, then he turned and made his way back down the hall. "I'll meet you downstairs," he called back over his shoulder.

"Sounds good. Give me five minutes to get decent."

In my bedroom, I rummaged around in my suitcase and pulled on underwear, a pair of denim cut-offs, a baggy tee, and a thick pair of furry socks because I hated having cold feet, even in spring. Twisting my hair into a long, loose braid, I absently checked my phone for calls or messages. It lit up, and I hated the way my heart hitched at the name that flashed up on the screen.

No matter how fast or far I ran, somehow, the weeds of my childhood kept tripping me at the ankles.

I swiped to open the message.

Cora: I won't be at the house for another week.

That was it. No hello, no goodbye. No explanation or apology. No, *I love you, I miss you, I can't wait to see you.*

But when had there ever been? I scrolled up to my mother's earlier messages—the reason I was here in the first place.

Cora: Your father and I are making some changes, and I need to speak with you. I'll be at the house in Valentine Bay next week.

Me: I can be there on Wednesday.

Cora: Fine. I'll see you then.

Her attitude wasn't surprising, and anyway, I was immune to her indifference. It was my body that responded to the rejection, a physical reaction that had been programmed into my system as a kid, and I hadn't yet worked out how to shake it. The twinge in the chest, the involuntary intake of breath, the hot, tingling palms. I hated all of it, and I hated feeling out of control, but she was the last challenge I had to conquer, the final chink in the armour I'd banged together over the years.

I switched off the phone and left it on the dusty bedside table. My mother was in no rush to see me, and the feeling was mutual, except for the fact that the sooner she got here, the sooner she could tell me if she was finally divorcing my dad. My twisted curiosity was the only reason I was back in Valentine Bay, and hopefully, it wouldn't take long to satisfy because I had something to take care of elsewhere that just couldn't wait.

3

ISAAC

BIRDIE MAXWELL WAS back, and if someone had tried to tell a teenaged me that one day, she'd show up again out of nowhere and throw herself at me buck naked, I'd have died on the spot. Died or demanded to hear the catch. And, of course, there was one. Birdie wasn't trying to have sex with me. The hug was innocent, the nakedness was circumstantial, and there was no evidence to suggest otherwise. Birdie and I were friends.

But… *Birdie Maxwell was back.*

Her hair had been damp, so maybe that was why it was a little darker than the startling red I remembered, but her smile was just as wide and warm as it had been when we were kids. Her electric blue eyes were just as intelligent. Her small, soft shape—inked here and there with tiny, bright tattoos—had rounded into well-proportioned and generous curves, and I could still feel them pressed against my body.

I tugged at my crotch to give my dick a bit more room, then headed to the kitchen. Birdie Back Then might have put hearts in my eyes, but Birdie Right Now did things south of my belt.

As I waited for her to follow, I let my memories of her float to the surface. Birdie and I had spent every summer together for ten years, the two of us plus a bunch of kids from the Bay who, like me, behaved as though Birdie was a city-made brand of adventure we couldn't get anywhere else. She was two years older than me—the clever, confident older woman who never made a big deal about our age difference—and that was never clearer than in that final summer. She'd just graduated high school and was about to start a degree in applied mathematics. The girl was a bona-fide genius, though she never let on to anyone but me—unless you counted the way she taught half the kids in the Bay how to play poker then gambled us out of our pocket money.

We spent a lot of time alone together, too, exchanging secrets neither of us had shared with another soul. I told her about my terrible first kiss, my humiliating second kiss, and the way kids at school made fun of my height. She told me how much she'd hated being sent away to boarding school and how her parents didn't really love her.

I'd wanted to tell her *I* loved her but never had the guts.

I'm not sure why she gave me so much of her time that year. I felt lucky, and I think she felt lonely.

After Birdie's last summer in the Bay, we kept in touch for a while, exchanging emails every week, then every month, then only at Christmas, until she went radio silent three years ago. I'd tried not to let that bother me, and on some level, I hadn't been surprised. She'd always been fun and impulsive, with an independent streak a mile wide. On paper, our friendship didn't make a lot of sense. In practice, there'd never been anyone in my life who knew me the way she did.

Jesus. Walking in here tonight, Birdie was the last person I expected to find. I wasn't expecting a dildo to the face either, that was for sure.

Switching on the kitchen light and absently pacing the floor, I pressed my fingertips over my left cheekbone and winced.

"Sorry about the sneak attack," Birdie announced from the doorway, and I risked a glance in her direction. As promised, she was dressed. The decent man in me was relieved, but the horny guy who'd fantasised about this woman more than once *and* hadn't had sex in a year was disappointed. She set a half-filled wine glass on the kitchen table and turned to the refrigerator. "Let me see if there's something in here for you to put on your eye."

"It's fine," I said, ignoring a twinge of pain. "Don't worry about it."

She paused and flung out her arms, lips twitching. "Look at me, Greene, all covered up again. Can I get a real hug this time?"

"Hell, yeah," I replied with a grin, scooping her up inside my arms and lifting her off the floor, spinning as she clung to me and laughed. Her hair smelled like apples.

"I can't believe you kept getting bigger," she commented as I set her down. She immediately stretched up on her toes to compare our heights. "You must have grown another few inches after I left."

I patted the top of her head, teasing her compact frame. "Yeah, just a few."

She rolled her eyes as she reached into a cupboard for a second wine glass, and when her fingers couldn't quite get to it, I stood behind her and got one for myself, stepping back quickly when my hips brushed against her back. After she'd poured me a drink, Birdie led the way into the living room, where she settled onto the sofa, tucking her fuzzy-socked feet up underneath her. I sat across from her and took a sip of the wine.

"So, spill," she said. "What's new?"

"You want the long or the short version?"

Birdie shrugged. "Eh, the highlights will do."

"All right. I'm a cop, but you knew that. I bought the house next door, but you know that now, too." I squinted at the ceiling, realising I'd already reached the end of my list of notable achievements. "And there you have it: Isaac Greene—the highlights reel."

"Oh, no," she argued, shaking her head. "There must be more than that. Is your family still in the Bay, and is everyone well? Is there a dog in your life? A cat? A body in the basement? Are you dating? Married? Divorced?"

"Yeah, Mum and Dad are still here, and so are my sisters—all three of them, all married, and they've got at least a hundred kids between them. No dog, no cat, no body in the basement. No basement, for that matter." I took a sip to wet my throat. "And no significant other, past, present, or otherwise."

"Uh-oh, I've hit a nerve," she observed, watching me over the rim of her glass as she took a long gulp of her wine. "What is it?"

I rubbed my eyes with a forefinger and thumb. "I forgot how well you could read me—and how did this conversation become all about me anyway?" I looked up and mirrored her cocked eyebrow. "I'm a cop now. I'm better at asking questions and listening to the answers."

"You were always a good listener," she murmured.

"You weren't always a good talker," I countered. "Why'd you stop returning my emails, and what are you doing here after all this time? We haven't seen your parents in town since your last summer here, so this house has been empty for a long time."

"I never meant to ghost you," she mumbled, and there was a hint of chagrin around the corners of her mouth. "Life just got in the way, and as for why I'm here... Cora—my mother—asked me to meet her to take care of some family business. She'll arrive sometime next week."

I nodded slowly. Birdie's relationship with her parents had always been a sensitive topic. I knew I had to ask, just like I knew she might not give me any answers. "Does that mean the two of you are on better terms these days?"

"Nope."

"And is your dad coming too, or did they finally get that divorce?"

"Hope not, and I don't know."

"Does that mean you never told her—"

"I know what you're going to ask, and I don't want to talk about it."

"Fair enough." Reading between the lines, I figured Birdie had no plans to stay in the Bay longer than it took her to sort out her family business. Disappointment swirled in my gut, and I took another swig of wine to dilute it. "So," I ventured, "you won't be staying long?"

Birdie shrugged and shifted her legs out from underneath her, crossing them like a kindergartener. "I haven't decided yet, but I have somewhere to be in six weeks."

I poked her in the arm, and she widened her eyes at me with faux innocence. "What?"

"This is like pulling teeth! Come on, Red. What's going on in your life? Last I knew, you were working overseas. Though, come to think of it, you were vague about the details, even in your emails. Let me guess. You sailed through some sort of mathematical PhD program, then got snapped up by a top-tier tech company in Silicon Valley, and you've been over there making millions ever since. Am I right?"

She snorted. "You're so far off the mark, it's not funny." She hesitated, then said, "Okay, since you really want to know, I dropped out of university a semester before I graduated and took up professional gambling before joining the pro poker circuit. *That's* how I've been making my millions."

I blinked at her serious expression. "I can't tell if you're telling the truth or lying through your teeth."

She smirked and sipped her drink. "That's because I'm good at my job."

I shook my head, shifting uncomfortably. "And it's all… legal?"

Birdie rolled her eyes, but her chuckle was amused. "Yes, officer. It's all above board. I'm between tournaments right now. I flew into Sydney yesterday from the World Poker Tour Australia tournament up north, and I'm due in Las Vegas at the end of next month for a big game. I play online, too, mostly the super high roller events, but I prefer the energy of casinos, and it's easier to read people when they're in the same room."

I was starting to believe she was serious.

"And you win these games? You're really making millions?"

Her smile grew smug. "I win more than I lose, and yes, I'm *really* making millions."

"Wow," I breathed, then I laughed. "Wish I'd known that before I confessed how pathetic my life is."

She leaned towards me and dropped her chin, waiting until I met her eyes. "It's not pathetic. It sounds like you've got a nice routine going here. A home, a job, nieces and nephews, family. Lots of people want that much and never have it."

Birdie's scarily accurate laundry list of my life sounded sadder out loud than it did in my head, and after the day I'd had with Amanda dumping me and wondering if a bunch of octogenarians held the secrets to a better sex life, it was like saltwater in an open wound. I groaned and dropped my head onto the back of the sofa. "Never have I felt more like a loser than I do right now."

"What the hell? Why?"

I turned my head and narrowed my eyes. "Are we talking about me again?"

"Yes, and resistance is futile. What's the matter?"

And just like that, she was inviting me to lean on her. Insisting that she help me. Making it too easy to be myself. Just like old times.

I stared into the last mouthful of white wine in my glass. "This feels a lot like the last summer you spent in the Bay. The one after you graduated high school. Remember?"

"The one where we stayed up most nights playing cards. You just couldn't get the hang of poker, could you? Don't think I could have made it simpler for you to understand."

I huffed out a humourless chuckle. "Yeah, also known as the summer I played spin the bottle at a friend's sixteenth birthday party, and all the girls refused to kiss me."

Birdie stretched to place her empty glass on the coffee table, then set an elbow on the back of the sofa and propped her cheek in her hand. "Bet those little witches hate themselves for it now. A lot has changed since then."

I glanced at Birdie from the corner of my eye to see her watching me like she knew I had something to tell her. I rubbed the heel of my palm over my forehead.

"And a lot has stayed the same," I said.

"Is that what's bothering you?"

Sinking back into the cushions of the couch, I met Birdie's gaze and tried to mirror the unflappable attitude she wore like a uniform, but her blue eyes were too smart.

"Don't lie to me, mister," she ordered.

I thought about it. I thought about spinning a story about all the women I'd dated, the relationships I'd had, the hearts I'd broken. If there was one woman in the world I wanted to think well of me, it was Birdie. But I couldn't lie, not to her, and fuck it—I had nothing to lose.

So, I told her about Amanda. I told her almost everything.

4

BIRDIE

ISAAC HAD NO game. He didn't know how to flirt. He thought his relationships were tracking fine until every woman he'd dated had either walked away or punted him to the friend zone.

It began back in his teen years—probably when those girls at the party let him believe he wasn't good enough to kiss. Had Isaac made that connection? I didn't think so, and I wasn't going to be the one to point it out.

I'd wager I recalled the night Isaac was talking about better than he did. I'd been eighteen at the time, loitering on Main Street with ice cream for company and avoiding going home for as long as I could. When I spotted Isaac's tall, lanky frame moping along the beach at sunset, I went over to ask him what was wrong. There were only two years between us, and it had never been an issue, but he seemed so young that night.

He didn't want to tell me anything at first, so we went back to his place and played cards in his living room until the sun came up the next morning.

He lost almost every hand at poker and didn't seem to care, but it made me furious. Not that I minded the winning streak, but anyone being okay with losing over and over left me mad at the world, so we switched to Go Fish before I flipped the table.

The cards were just a cover for all the talking, anyway, and it had worked. He told me all about it in the end—that he'd been publicly rejected and humiliated in front of his mates, all because of a stupid schoolyard rumour that he was a bad kisser started by the girl who'd given him his first kiss a week before.

Man, kids were arseholes.

Now, I was left with a puzzle. Isaac was a beautiful man. He looked carved from marble, some sort of modern-day Adonis, but now that I was forced to think about it, I had to admit he didn't have that *something extra*, the heat that made panties drop with just a look. I could appreciate that he was get-me-a-glass-of-water gorgeous, but facts were facts: he was missing the sex factor. It was almost like he went out of his way to mute his sexual energy. Isaac was friendly. Platonic. Safe.

"Are you a virgin?" I hadn't meant to whisper it like it was a shameful secret, but that's how it came out.

"What? No!" he snapped, a pink flush burning in his cheeks. "God, Red. Way to kick a man when he's down."

"I'm sorry." When he spared me a withering look,

I choked back my chuckle and tried again. "Give me a minute. I wasn't expecting to have this conversation on my first night back in the Bay."

He glanced around at the shadowy house as if seeing it for the first time. "I've totally crashed your night. You've been travelling, and you're probably exhausted. I'll get out of your hair and let you settle in. Maybe we can catch up properly in a few days."

I frowned as he got to his feet, then tugged on his hand to pull him back down again. He landed on the sofa with a grunt.

"You can't hand me a problem then walk away before giving me a chance to solve it."

"I'm not a maths equation," he grumbled.

"I know, and this is nowhere near as complicated."

He snorted. "Thanks, Red."

I was good at reading people. No. *Good* wasn't an accurate enough description. I read people for a living, interpreting even the smallest signs of confidence or concern among competitors who, like me, did their best to never let anything show. I was *fantastic* at reading people. Right now, Isaac was in all sorts of pain—and I couldn't stand it.

"All right, Romeo. Show me what you got."

Isaac frowned, and his eyes narrowed warily, but I didn't miss the twitch on his top lip that betrayed his interest. "What do you mean?"

"Oh, I think you know. Try something on me. Show me how you make a move."

He shook his head. "Red. No."

"Why not? This is a safe space. We're friends. You've seen me naked, so you know I'm not easily embarrassed."

"You might not be, but *I* am."

If Isaac didn't want to play my game, he'd get up and leave—but he didn't, so I pressed the advantage.

"That's the point. You've got nothing to be embarrassed about. Let me be the judge of whether your routine is that bad. If you've created this all in your head, then I can put your mind at ease, and it'll be happy days from here. If it's *not* all in your head..."

One of Isaac's eyebrows quirked, and he tilted his head expectantly. His eyes were narrowed slightly, guarded but intrigued. "If it's not...then what?"

I bit back a grin. "If there really is something wrong, I can teach you how—"

He groaned and dropped his head into his hands. "Just when I thought this day couldn't get any worse."

I allowed five seconds for him to get up and go, and when he stayed put, I shifted my position on the sofa, setting my feet on the floor and crossing my legs at the knee. "I'll set the scene," I said, picking up my empty wine glass. "We've just been on a second date. You offered to cook me dinner, and you blitzed it in the kitchen. The night went well, and now we're having one more drink before it's time to call it a night—or not, if you get my drift."

"I get your drift," he muttered, raising his head and shooting me a pained look.

I rolled my lips to stop a smile, then leaned into the cushions and put a soft, second-date kind of look in my eyes. "I had a really nice time tonight, Isaac."

He tugged once at his earlobe—a nervous tell I tucked away for later—and took a deep breath before mumbling something unintelligible. Finally, he turned to me and said, "Me, too."

I waited, giving him a chance to say more, but when nothing followed, I purred, "You're a really great cook."

His smile was small and tight. "Thank you."

For an unexpected second, I was uncertain. Was he being deliberately difficult because he didn't want to play along, or was this how he behaved on dates? Perhaps I needed to make it easier for him.

I set a hand on his knee, and he glanced at it before slowly setting his large fingers over mine. I thought for a moment we were getting somewhere, but then nothing else happened.

"So," he said, "Thank you for a good night."

"No," I replied, adding a little more pressure to my hand on his leg, letting my eyes briefly drop to his mouth. "Thank *you.*"

A moment passed while I waited for him to lean in, brush my cheek, or draw circles on the back of my hand with his thumb. A moment turned into a minute, and the longer the silence lingered, the more awkward it felt.

"Right," Isaac announced, getting to his feet again. "It's late, and I should be going."

I frowned up at him, not sure if we were still in character or if he was putting an end to the charade. I decided to stay with it in case it was part of his plan. If this were a real second date, then a kiss at the door might be more appropriate. I supposed not everyone wanted to be mauled on the couch so soon in a relationship.

He led the way to the front door and opened it, and I wiped all evidence of confusion from my face as I gazed up at him with a reasonable level of invitation in my expression.

"Goodnight, Isaac."

"Goodnight, Birdie."

I saw the hesitation in his rapid blinking, his stilted movements, but then he pulled me close. My cheek pressed against his broad chest, and my nose was filled with the scent of him—clean soap and something sweet and earthy, like leather. Proud of him for taking the risk, I snaked my arms around his waist and breathed him in, trying to put a name to the scent that was just him. The seconds ticked over, and before I knew it, my pulse had slowed, my eyes had closed, and I'd relaxed against him. I almost forgot the reason I was wrapped up in his arms in the first place until the intimacy of the moment stunned me back to reality. It took an effort to keep my muscles loose.

I was good with one-night stands. I was up for holiday flings. I was more than okay having sex with no names, no numbers, and no strings attached. I was *not* available for lingering embraces that triggered feelings of safety and tenderness and warmth. Isaac's hug was all those things, but it was nowhere near sexy…

Until he lowered his head to mine. I felt the heat of his mouth against my temple, and I swear, the man buried his nose in my hair, inhaling a little too deeply for it to be a regular breath. The move was over so fast I might have imagined it, but it sent warm, welcome tingles rushing to all the right places.

Isaac dropped his arms and stepped away, watching me with wary eyes. "How was that?"

"That's it?" I blurted, feeling cheated as well as a little off-balance. He couldn't give me more of those safe sexy feels to erase all memory of the dangerous warm-and-fuzzy ones?

"What? I hugged you. I touched you."

"Did you want to kiss me?"

He frowned as if unsure how to answer the question. "I mean... Does that matter? If a woman wants to kiss me, she will. You had plenty of chances. I waited as long as I could."

Oh, God. The boy was worse off than I realised, but... Good. This was good. This totally worked in my favour. It gave me something defined to focus on—a problem that needed to be solved. That was easier to face than the bitter aftertaste of unwanted *emotions*.

Shaking my head, I set my hands on his hard chest—to comfort him, not to cop a feel—and stared up at him. "I hate to say it, Romeo, but you need my help."

He closed his eyes as if he couldn't bear to look at me. "Tell me this isn't happening."

"I told you this is a safe space, and I meant it. We can fix this."

"Am I really that bad?"

"Not bad," I hedged, "just…"

"Not good," Isaac finished.

"You've got potential," I assured him.

He groaned and launched himself off the porch, his long legs carrying him more than halfway back to his place before I could catch up with him.

"What's wrong with potential?" I called out.

He spun around and faced me, arms flung wide, and I stumbled a little as I pulled up short. "Look at me, Red," he demanded, eyes blazing and jaw feathering with frustration. "Do you know what women think when they set eyes on me? Do you?"

I blinked once at the command in his voice. The growl. The *heat*. I knew what *I* thought when I looked at him in that moment—and fuck me, officer, now we were talking.

"Is this a trick question?"

He exhaled loudly and dropped his arms, and that brief flare of fire blew out. "I know what women think about me—what they assume when they take in my size and find out what I do for a living—and so far, I've failed to live up to expectations."

He took off again, and I had to take two steps for each of his to keep up. "That hug right now?" I practically shouted. "It made me warm."

That stopped him. He froze, and I halted alongside him, watching the play of his thoughts as they flickered across his silvery moonlit profile. "What do you mean?"

"Just that. It was a good hug, and it made me warm."

I crossed my arms over my chest, annoyed at the flutter of vulnerability in my pulse, and kept my face poker straight.

Isaac couldn't completely hide the way his mouth twitched. "Warm like you wanted to kiss me?"

"Warm like you have potential," I clarified.

Isaac cocked a dark eyebrow. "Right."

"Look, there's only one way to be the best at something, and that's with training and practice. I know you're nervous about putting yourself out there again, but all you really need is a few wins under your belt, and I can give them to you. Theoretical ones, of course." I had to make this part perfectly clear. "There's nothing real here, so the stakes are low."

"Yeah," he agreed, barking out a short, humourless laugh. "The only thing I have to lose is my pride, and what's that worth?"

I was getting tired of the *poor me* routine. Patience was something I had to work at, and nothing riled me more than when people conceded defeat before they'd even been dealt their hand. Isaac was a winner, and it was time he behaved like one. I planted my fists on my hips. "Do you want my help or not?"

His green eyes studied me for a long, quiet moment, and I met him stare for stare. I wasn't going to be the first to look away.

"I appreciate the offer," he said, squeezing my shoulder. His eyes darted away and back, and I wondered what he was trying to hide. "But you've been witness to my humiliation one too many times tonight. I've got my limits, and I need to draw the line somewhere."

"Your call," I replied with a false, exaggerated shrug. "You know where to find me when you change your mind."

"Not going to happen."

"Want to bet?" I quipped.

He grinned but shook his head, then slid a large, warm hand around my neck. He pressed his lips against my forehead, the heat of his mouth an echo of the hot buzz in my own body, and I both loved and hated the way it made me wonder if it meant anything. If *I* meant anything. "Welcome back, Red."

5

ISAAC

MY SHIFT ON Friday was a late one, and when I went home afterwards to shower and change before heading to The Stop for drinks with the crew, I tried not to look too hard at the Maxwell place. It was dark and quiet but for a dull yellow light peeking through the curtains in a room on the second storey, so I took that as confirmation that Birdie was settled in for the night.

I'd tried and failed to knock on her door a dozen times in the last forty-eight hours, and there were a couple of reasons for that. The first: I'd been thinking about her in ways that were really fucking wrong.

I kept recalling the shape of her mouth when she grinned and the confidence in her quirked eyebrow, and how those simple things made me want to keep her close. I relived over and over the moment in her hallway, the press of her bare breasts against me and the way she'd felt warm and soft against the hardness of my body.

I couldn't get the vision of her naked form, damp and pink from the shower, out of my head, nor the picture of her writhing in the sheets as she used that vibrator on herself. I put it all down to the fact that I needed to get laid, but that wasn't new, and I hadn't spent the last year fantasising about any other women in my life. Just Birdie.

Pausing on my front porch, key in the lock, I glanced up at the lit window again. Was she in her bed at that moment? Was she touching herself right now?

I scowled into the darkness and let myself into my house. The second reason I couldn't talk to Birdie was that my woeful performance in her little skit kept coming back to haunt me, and her offer to *teach* me things kept replaying in my mind. She was inviting me to touch her, but every time I convinced myself I'd be an idiot not to take her up on it, I also knew I'd live to regret it.

I hadn't been joking about my pride being at stake, but it was more than that. Birdie's heart wasn't in it, and mine, for better or worse, was.

And the icing on my shit-for-batter cake? The more I thought of Birdie's offer, the more I was reminded of Dot's invitation to her book club and what had compelled her to give it to me. There was a capital "L" for *loser* stamped on my forehead, and the only thing that could make that permanent was admitting I needed...*love coaching*.

Christ, I was a mess.

Rinsing off the day and shrugging into dark blue jeans and a clean white T-shirt, I snatched up my keys and wallet and walked down to Main Street.

It was as busy as it ever got for a Friday night in a town the size of Valentine Bay, which was to say, the gelato shop was buzzing with teenagers and young families, a bonfire blazed on the beach, and classic rock music from the cover band inside The Salty Stop floated into the street at regular intervals as the front door swung open and closed to let sober patrons in and drunk patrons out.

One of the latter stumbled onto the footpath just as I arrived, and I shot out an arm to steady him. It was twenty-two-year-old Burt the Fifth, the latest in a long line of Burts who owned the Spies and Sons' local hardware store. He stared at me with blurry, bloodshot eyes before recognition lit his features, and a happy grin stretched across his mouth.

"Sergeant Greene!" he practically shouted as he clapped me on the shoulder. "Fancy seeing you here."

"Evening, Burt." I grunted, righting him as he tripped on his own feet. "Big night, I take it?"

"Heck, yeah." He locked his knobbly knees to stop the wobble in his legs, but it did nothing to help the way he listed to one side. "It's my bucks' night, you know. I'm gettin' married next week."

"To Chloe," I added, recalling how the gossip mill had spun into overdrive at the news of their engagement.

It was as close to star-crossed lovers as this town hoped to get—the heirs to the region's largest two hardware stores falling in love and tying the knot against their parents' wishes.

Say what you wanted about the good people of the Bay, but there was nothing they loved more than something to whisper about over their back fences. The Spies and Sullivan Scandal had kept their chatter tanks fuelled for years, and there'd be a good handful of folks disappointed the story was coming to a happy ending. Delighted at the outcome but disappointed in the dissolution of good gossip all the same.

"Yeah," he said with a sigh. "*Chloe.*"

Burt closed his eyes, his face taking on an expression so dreamy I wondered if he'd fallen asleep on his feet. Just as I was about to call a patrol car to collect him and see him home safely, Chloe herself slipped through The Stop's door and into the street beside us, looping her arm through Burt's protectively.

"I've got him, Sergeant," she said. "I'll take him home."

I ran an open palm over my beard to hide a smile. "Not his bucks' night, then?"

Chloe chuckled as she braced her drunk fiancé against her side. "No, it is, if you can call it that. He wanted me here, silly man, so I dragged my girlfriends down for dinner and cocktails, and we made a party of it."

"You've got yourself a good guy, present condition notwithstanding," I replied with a grin. "You sure you're okay to get home?"

She pointed at a silver station wagon parked a few steps down the street. "We're right there, and I haven't been drinking myself." She set a delicate hand on her stomach, which I noticed was slightly rounded. "It doesn't agree with me these days."

"Congratulations on the wedding and the—"

"Ah! Shh." She pressed a finger against her lips. "Not common knowledge yet."

"Got it." I winked at her. "Here, let me give you a hand."

I helped Chloe pour Burt into the car, fastening his seatbelt as she scooted around the other side and slid behind the wheel. Then I watched her drive away until her rear brake lights disappeared around the end of Main Street.

Shaking my head, I entered the bar. There was someone for everyone, apparently. Everyone but me.

Inside The Stop, the air was thick and warm, and there was a decent-sized crowd celebrating the end of the working week. It was late enough that there was a good number of people gyrating on the dance floor, and I wound my way through the throng to the dark booth at the back unofficially reserved for the crew—the mates I went to school with and still called my best friends. I was the last to arrive tonight, so I snatched up a chair on my way over and set it down at the open end of the table, taking a seat without any fanfare.

"Didn't think you'd make it," Logan said, raising his glass of water at me in greeting. Jess was snuggled under his arm, pressed against his side. The two had been inseparable since they got together a couple of months ago, and though I was happy for them, I felt the sting of their happiness a little more keenly tonight.

"Late shift," I explained, standing and raising a hand to get Will's attention over at the bar. He nodded at me to say he'd bring another round.

On Jess's other side, her best friend Abigail Ellison licked at the salty rim of a margarita glass before reaching for the chilled jug in the centre of the table. "Where's Amanda?" she asked, topping up both her glass and the two others like it on the table. "You promised we'd meet her this weekend." When I opened my mouth to answer, her face folded in a pretty scowl. "You can't hide her forever, Greene. Not that I understand why you want to. I'm excellent with newbies, aren't I, Jones? Tell everyone how I single-handedly made you feel at home in the Bay."

Emily Jones, a tiny, dark-haired thing currently perched on my mate Joshua Ford's lap, smiled and collected her glass of white wine from the table. She'd moved here a little more than six months ago, healing Josh's broken heart at a time when we thought it might never happen. Theirs was a love story with an unlikely start and an even unlikelier ending. Who'd believe a fake relationship could turn into something real?

"Absolutely, Ellison," Emily agreed. "You're a one-woman welcome wagon."

"See?" Abbie raised her brows at me expectantly, then glanced over my shoulder towards the front door. "So, where is she? I'm too nosey to be kept in suspense like this and too drunk to pretend to be patient."

I tugged at my earlobe, then splayed my hands on the damp table. "She's not coming. She just wants to be friends."

"Oh no!" Jess exclaimed, looking at me with so much disappointment that I was disproportionately grateful when Will appeared at my shoulder with a chilled schooner of IPA. I downed half the glass in a single swallow, and when I returned my eyes to the faces around the table, everyone was staring at me with various expressions of sympathy.

"It's fine!" I set my beer down and leaned back in the chair, crossing my arms over my chest and my legs at the ankles, anything to demonstrate how *not* bothered by this I was. I even managed a passable chuckle. "It's not that big a deal."

The silence stretched on a heartbeat too long before Will smacked me on the back and pulled up a chair of his own. One glance at the bar told me he'd left service in the hands of his new hire—the brunette he'd been flirting with the day Amanda dumped me.

"Can't say I'm too cut up about it," Will said. "It's nice not to be the last bachelor standing."

"Or the last bachelorette," Abbie added. "I'm glad you're still one of us too, Greene. Plenty of time for settling down and all that rubbish"—her gaze skipped over the two happy couples cosied up in the booth—"if that's what you're into. But for now? Have fun, I say."

"Abbie's right," Jess said. "Forget Mandy or Amy or whatever her name is. She's obviously not the one."

"Best part?" Abbie added, dragging two of the full cocktail glasses across the table towards her. "More margaritas for me."

The conversation stalled awkwardly, and I cleared my throat, righting myself in the chair and taking another sip of my drink. "Guess who's back in town? Birdie Maxwell."

I might have been trying to jump-start the party before I died of humiliation, but I still had no idea why I said what I did. Five chins jerked up, and five pairs of eyes bored into me like I'd just announced a million dollars was hidden under one of the high tops, and it was finders-keepers at the sound of the starting gun.

"Birdie Maxwell?" Emily asked, looking around the booth warily. "Is she someone…special?"

"Not exactly," I replied, and my answer didn't feel like a lie until the words were off my tongue. I shifted uneasily at the feeling I'd betrayed Birdie with that description and tried to explain. "Her parents own the Old Maxwell Place next door to mine, but they were only ever holiday-makers, and they haven't been back in more than ten years."

"She was so much fun," Jess murmured right as Abbie exclaimed, "That bitch gambled me out of three years' worth of Christmas money. God, I loved her."

"Okay," Emily said with a stunned laugh. "You're going to have to spell this out for me."

We did our best to paint a picture of our long summers and too-short winters with Birdie. She'd show up for dinner at someone's house every night and refuse to eat her peas. Her name miraculously appeared on the bonfire sign-up sheet every date it wasn't already taken, and then she'd drag us all down to the beach with enthusiasm so enormous you'd think she'd never before danced under the stars. We'd tried to teach her to surf, but she never quite got the hang of it. She'd hosted notorious card games at least three times a week in my old tree house and fleeced us all out of every cent we had, and we'd always go back for more.

Emily expelled a breath as if she'd been holding it the entire time we talked. "Well, Birdie Maxwell sounds special. I'd love to meet her. Is she staying long?"

"About six weeks," I said. "She's a professional poker player now—"

"Oh, God, that's perfect," Abbie interrupted.

"And there's some big tournament in Las Vegas she needs to go to at the end of next month."

"Six weeks," Josh commented. "Just like old times."

"Did you get her number?" Abbie fished her phone out of her bag, ready to punch in Birdie's digits. "I'll text her so we can catch up. Oh!" She speared Jess, then Emily, with wide and excited honey-brown eyes. "Girls' night tomorrow?" A grimace passed across her mouth so quickly I might have imagined it before she rolled her eyes and popped her lips with pretended peevishness. "My place is too small, so we'll have to go out since you two lovebirds have boys living at yours."

"I'm in," Jess said, brushing the tip of her nose against Logan's in apology.

"Me, too," Emily agreed. "Josh will be sleeping before his night shift anyway."

"Excellent," Abbie replied as she swiped open her phone and busied herself opening her contacts list. Then she glanced at me, her fingers poised over the screen. "Number?"

"I didn't ask for it," I said, reflexively pulling out my own phone as if to prove it had no details about

Birdie hidden behind the passcode.

"Hm. Maybe she's on social media."

Abbie bent her head over her phone, and the murmur of conversation picked up. Curious now about the question of Birdie and social media, I opened one of my apps. A quick search of her name turned up nothing, so I tapped on my notifications icon and scrolled through updates. I had an unread message, and I opened it without thinking.

The name attached to the message was one I hadn't thought of in years, another ghost from my past, but this time, there was no confusion about the way it made me feel. My heart pounded painfully hard before it lurched upwards and lodged in my throat. It kept beating a mile a minute, and a surprised, strangled sound escaped my throat—something between a gasp and a cough to choke it back.

Again, everyone looked at me. This time, heat prickled my neck as I stared at the screen, tried and failed to swallow, and pretended not to notice their demanding stares.

Will peeked over my shoulder to look at the screen, and he whistled at what he saw. "I didn't know you were still in touch with Lisa."

"Lisa?" Abbie craned her neck to get a look at my messages. "Who's Lisa?"

"Nobody," I answered too quickly.

Josh and Logan exchanged knowing smirks, which I ignored.

"A girl from the police academy," Will said over me, drawing everyone's focus like moths to an irritating flame.

"Do we...*like* Lisa?" Jess asked, her cautious glance sliding my way.

"No, love," Will said with a grin. "We *love* Lisa."

"She was just a friend," I said, glaring at Will so he'd get the hint to shut up, but it was obvious from the expectant silence I wasn't getting out of things that easily. I rolled my eyes. "We were friends at the academy, and okay, I had a bit of a crush, but nothing ever came of it. We stayed in touch for a while after graduation, but she was stationed four hours' north, so contact slowed down, then eventually stopped."

"And she's messaged you out of nowhere after all this time?" Josh wondered, running a hand through his blond curls. "That's weird."

"Not out of nowhere," I mumbled, twisting to put my back to Will and block his view of my screen, but that only made him curious enough to stand to get a better view. I hunched and read the message Lisa sent. "There's a reunion event happening next weekend, and she wants to know if I'll be there."

Jess and Emily swapped excited glances before Jess asked, "And will you?"

"Yeah, sure," I mumbled, re-reading the text. "I'd already sent in my RSVP."

"Does her message sound...interested?" Logan asked.

"It, uh—" I looked around at my friends, every one of them more invested in what was on my phone than the drinks in their glasses. The expectation on their faces felt a lot like pressure, so I sighed and shrugged. "I have no idea."

"Oh, give it here," Abbie huffed, extending her hand, palm up. Once she had my phone, she read the message with a crease between her brows, the fingers on her other hand tugging at her bottom lip.

"It says," she began, rolling her shoulders as though she were delivering a proclamation. "'Hi, Isaac. It's been a long time, but it looks like you're doing well. Just wondering if you'll be at the reunion next week? I've decided last minute to make the date work, and it'd be great to see you there. I probably owe you a drink after all the trouble we got into at the academy! Let me know, and we maybe can catch up before the event.'" Abbie put down the phone and dipped her chin, her voice dropping to something low and breathy. "Signed, 'Lisa. Ex-oh. Ex-oh. *Kiss emoji.*'"

"Two exes *and* two ohs *and* a kiss," Emily said with a wise nod. "She's fishing."

"'It looks like you're doing well'?" Logan added. "Code for, 'I've pulled up every photo I can find of you on the internet—'"

"'And I like what I see,'" Abbie finished.

"Do you think so?" I took my phone back from Abbie, but I didn't open the message again. Nobody here needed to know how excited I was at the idea of Lisa wanting to see me or how terrified I was at the same time.

"I think it's reasonable to assume she might be interested," Jess replied. "Flirt a little when you text her back and see how she responds."

"Okay," I replied, but suddenly my palms were clammy.

"And if you get a good vibe, pick things up at the reunion," Abbie suggested. "Keep the flirt going, you know?"

"Exactly," Will agreed. "Don't lose the momentum."

"Find out where she lives," Logan said. "That'll help you work out if she's looking for a hook-up or something more serious."

"Where she lives," I repeated, nodding along as if none of it freaked me out. "Something serious."

"But don't go in too strong," Abbie amended. "Feel her out if you get what I'm saying."

The way she wiggled her eyebrows suggestively was enough to send me spiralling.

Because it wasn't a crush. Lisa had been the first woman I'd felt anything serious about after Birdie left, and I'd made all the same mistakes. I spent six months at the academy and another twelve months in training, hoping Lisa would look up one day and see Isaac, the man, and not Isaac, the friend. It hadn't happened. We'd been given permanent stations on different parts of the coast, and time eventually wore away at my feelings. It wasn't a clean break, though—not for me. It was a long, languid and, frankly, lacklustre one. But judging by my reaction now, maybe I never really let her go. Her name reignited some sort of chemical memory in my blood and set it to racing.

Could ten years have changed me enough that I might stand a chance with her? It had to be possible. All I needed to do was play my cards right.

6

BIRDIE

THUD, THUD, THUD.

The phantom sensation of my head hitting the headboard with a delectable rough and rhythmic thump faded and morphed into the sound of someone connecting their fist with my front door. Sunlight brightened the inside of my eyelids, so I rolled over and buried my face into my pillow, muffling a disappointed moan.

That was a freaking fantastic dream, and the last visions of it were already fading—Fantasy Man stretched out over me, railing me with the kind of possession I'd never experienced in real life. But *he* knows.

In my fantasies, his have-to-have-me is extreme as he takes charge of my body, does all the thinking, and demands that I sink into the experience. Of course, he's a figment of my imagination, so he knows without me having to tell him all the places I like to be touched.

He kisses me the way I want to be kissed and applies just the right pressure here, then there. Goes slow when I like it, moves fast when I need it. Always makes sure I finish… Unless I'm interrupted by a dickhead doorknocker at some God-forsaken hour on Saturday morning.

I waited a moment in case whoever it was gave up, and when a minute passed in blissful silence, I slipped a hand into my underwear. Lightly brushing my folds and finding them wet, I circled my throbbing clit and couldn't help the little whimper in my throat. Yes, that had been a *fantastic* dream—too good to let it go to waste—but as I pressed more firmly on that swollen bundle of nerves, I shied away from thinking too deeply about the face attached to last night's incarnation of Fantasy Man.

All I'll admit to is he had thick, muscular arms and midnight-dark hair. A beard, too. Fantasy Man had a beard, and the sensation of it grazing the insides of my thighs felt almost real enough to—

Thud, thud, thud.

Oh, for fuck's sake. This had better be important.

I threw on my silk robe and dragged my fingers through the knots in my hair as I ran down the stairs. The thumping grew louder.

"I'm coming!" I shouted, then mumbled, "Just not the way I want to."

I flung open the door and found Isaac standing on the other side. He looked all sorts of bothered and not in a let's-go-for-it-against-the-wall kind of way. His eyes were pinched, his T-shirt rumpled, and his hair stuck out at odd angles, like he'd run his hands through it one too many times. Jesus, he was adorable.

"What's wrong?" I demanded, tightening my robe around my waist.

He held up his phone, the screen lit up and facing out, but all I could make out was a series of random text messages.

"I think she's interested," he said.

"Who's interested in what?"

"Lisa. In me."

"Okay, you're going to have to give me a little more than that." I gently pushed his arm down to his side, then ushered him into the living room. "And I'm going to need coffee before I even begin to attempt to solve whatever problem you've got now." I eyed him up and down, considering the wisdom of offering this man caffeine. "You want a cup? I'd offer you breakfast to go with it, but I've got nothing in the kitchen except coffee grounds and an ancient tin of corn."

"Yeah, sure. Thanks." He dropped onto the sofa, elbows on knees, thumbs poised over his phone, eyes never leaving the screen.

He was in the same hunched-over position when I returned to the room with two steaming mugs. I set them on the coffee table and waited for him to look up. When it took a while, I cleared my throat to get his attention, and he finally raised his head.

"You were saying something about a woman named Lisa?" I prompted.

"Yeah. We were at the police academy together—"

"Oh, *Lisa*," I said, recalling what he'd told me in our emails. "I remember her."

"You do?" he asked, clearly surprised.

I tapped my temple. "Eidetic memory."

"Right, I forgot about that," he replied, some of the tension releasing in his shoulders. "So, you understand why I'm nervous, right?"

"Not yet. I think you've skipped the middle part of the story."

"Right. Sorry." He picked up his coffee but didn't drink it. "Our class has its ten-year reunion next week, and she sent me a message asking if I was going and to meet her for a drink. The crew all told me to flirt a little—you know, in my text messages—so I did. At least, I think I did, and she flirted back. Maybe. Here." He thrust his phone at me. "Tell me what you think."

I scanned the messages. There was banter about college. Reminiscing about old times. When I reached the part where Lisa asked if Isaac was seeing anybody, I squinted at the screen. He'd told her no, and they'd arranged a time and place to meet for drinks an hour before the reunion was due to start.

She was interested, and it did something funny to my stomach. Something I didn't like.

I wasn't jealous—I didn't believe in jealousy, or monogamy for that matter—and I wasn't getting all stupid and possessive either. I decided that the hard clench in my abdomen was a dormant protective streak come to life, and the only way to ease it was to give Isaac the help he needed. But how?

I had to tread carefully—walk the line between encouragement and setting realistic expectations. If I was going to promise him a win, I was determined to deliver. He would *not* crash and burn with this woman.

"Good chance she's available," I said, handing him the phone. "But it's hard to read people via text. There's nothing overtly sexual in there, but there's nothing I'd consider a stop sign, either. No harm in making a move and seeing where it goes."

"That's it?" he said. "That's your solution to my problem?"

"And what *problem* are we talking about, exactly?"

"You know..." When I only watched him with exaggerated patience, he rolled his eyes. "The flirting problem. The friend-zone problem."

"My solution to *that* is for you to let me teach you how to let a woman know you want her," I replied, blinking away the vivid frames of last night's X-rated mind-movie as they flashed in front of my eyes. "You know, review your moves and show you how to improve them."

"You say that like it's not the most embarrassing situation ever."

"Do you have another option?"

"Not today, I don't," he mumbled. "It'd be only a few basics, right?"

I didn't try to hide my self-satisfied smile. *I win.* "Never a better place to start than the basics."

Finally taking a sip of his coffee, he glanced once at his phone and shook his head, almost as if he couldn't believe what he was about to agree to. No, not agree to. Suggest we do. Isaac needed help, and he knew it.

"All right, Red. We've got six days until the reunion, and I want her to see me as a man she could *be* with, not just some guy she used to know and can live without."

It occurred to me then that Isaac had this all wrong. He didn't see what I saw, which was that the answer to his women woes was *confidence*. He went into relationships with a shield up—an intimacy wall he didn't know was there. He'd rather be set aside as a friend than rejected as a man, and he subconsciously believed rejection was always the probable outcome.

It didn't take a mathematically minded brain to know that with a heart as big as his, plus a body that turned heads and dropped jaws—if not panties—yet—the odds should have always been in Isaac's favour.

I stuck my hand out to make a deal, only not the one Isaac assumed. "You're on. Six days with me as your coach, and I guarantee you'll have a bag of tricks to let Lisa know exactly how you feel."

A bag of tricks—and the self-confidence he needed to pull them off.

I sent Isaac home so I could shower and dress, and he reappeared on my doorstep two hours later with a bag of groceries in one hand and a brown paper bag marked with the logo for Tony's Place—the local coffee shop—held aloft in the other. It smelled like heaven, and if that wasn't enough to get my tummy rumbling, the oily spots of bacon grease at the edges of the paper only made me hungrier.

"You are a legend," I declared, pushing away the rise of irritation I felt at someone looking out for me. I didn't like it, and I wouldn't get used to it, but this was Isaac, and I didn't want him to think I was ungrateful. Still, he needed to know I could take care of myself. "How much do I owe you?"

"I don't know," he said. "Only your first-born?"

"Joke's on you. I'm never having kids." Snatching the bag from his hands as he strode past me and made his way down the hall to the kitchen, I took an enormous bite of the bacon and egg sandwich as I followed. "What you got there?"

"Sustenance," he replied over his shoulder, but when he reached the open-plan kitchen and dining area, he pulled up fast enough that I ran into his back.

"What?" I asked, peeking around his arms. "Oh, don't mind the mess."

"What the hell happened in here?" he asked, moving forwards and hefting the groceries onto the kitchen island, his eyes scanning the debris littering my dining table: pens and highlighters, Post-its and notebooks, poker chips, index cards, two open laptops and a large-screen monitor, as well as a stack of theoretical physics textbooks I kept on-hand as palate cleansers and last but probably not least, an assortment of takeaway food containers and empty plastic water bottles.

I ripped a chunk of bread off with my teeth and started to chew. "It's work. There's more to poker than showing up on the day, you know. It's a full-time job. Study, practice, strategy, observation. Mindset. Next month's tournament's a big one, and I've got to avoid tilt. What do you think I've been doing holed up in here the last two days?"

A curious flush of red crept up the back of his neck as he replied, "I don't know. I hadn't thought about it. Meanwhile, didn't anyone ever tell you not to talk with your mouth full?" He spun away to stack milk and juice, butter, cheese, and eggs into the fridge. Bread went into the pantry, along with a jar of peanut butter.

"Mm-hm," I mumbled, tearing off another portion with my teeth. "The nuns."

Isaac straightened, a bag of apples in one hand and a bunch of bananas in the other, both forgotten. "The *nuns*? I didn't know your boarding school was Catholic."

I shrugged and pointed at my stuffed cheeks, and he turned back to the cupboards, hunting for a fruit bowl, while I hopped up to sit on the island and masticate my way through breakfast.

Swallowing, I said, "I was a real disappointment, even as a kid, but my parents gave them enough money that they had to take me back year after year. They were happy to see the back of me, but they still took credit for my perfect grades and university scholarships, so you know what I did?"

Isaac gave me a sidelong glance. "Do I want to know?"

I chuckled. "After my first big poker win, I sent them a photo of me standing outside a Las Vegas casino holding an enormous novelty cheque for half a million bucks." Isaac groaned, but I only laughed harder. "I wrote a letter to Sister Mary Antoinette explaining how I'd dropped out of my maths degree just shy of graduation to take up professional poker and how I never could have done it without her."

Isaac's eyes widened a little. "Oh, don't look so horrified," I said. "I also included a donation to the abbey for $100,000, and I have it on good authority that the sister framed that photo. She keeps it on her office desk to show other delinquent teenage girls how profitable gambling can be."

"She does not," Isaac disagreed, trying not to laugh as he stowed the last of the food in the pantry. "There. Now it's almost like you actually live here."

"You didn't have to do that," I replied, recoiling from the suggestion I might ever actually live anywhere. The concept made my skin feel three sizes too tight. "I was going to get to it eventually."

"You've been here three nights, Red. How have you not starved to death yet?"

"I ordered in and bought enough to last me a while."

I watched as a question he wanted to ask but didn't know how vibrated across his eyelids.

"Go ahead," I said. "Ask me."

"You've got millions in the bank." He looked around the room, then marched over to the dining table and started scooping up the scattered rubbish. "Why not live like it? Or at least, go shopping and buy yourself some decent food?"

"Money's bullshit, Isaac. It turns good people into arseholes and arseholes into cretins." I rolled the greasy paper bag into a ball between my palms, tossed it in the sink, and then jumped off the island. "It doesn't solve your problems, make you happy, or buy you the things you think are missing."

"No, but it does buy groceries."

"True fact." I swiped the small plastic bin from under the sink and offered it to Isaac. "You don't have to clean up after me, you know. I'm a big girl. I can do it myself."

He dumped the food wrappers into the bin, then took it from me. "All evidence to the contrary, Red."

As he shoved the bin back into the cupboard, I pulled out one of the tall stools lining the kitchen island, eager to shift the focus from me to him. I was always more comfortable calling the shots.

"All right, Romeo. Let's get on with it. Take a seat and buy me a drink. Show me what Lisa's got to look forward to."

Frowning against the protest that had to be behind the line of his lips, Isaac settled himself in the chair. I did the same before bouncing up again to retrieve two wine glasses, which I filled with orange juice.

"Props," I explained. "And I'm thirsty."

Once I was in position, Isaac angled his chest towards me slightly, and I nodded approvingly. "Nice body language," I said, and his grip on his glass relaxed.

"Do we need to act out an entire conversation?" he asked.

"Let's assume we've muddled through the awkward small talk, and we've hit a lull," I suggested. "There's music playing, people socialising around us, and you notice a little *tension* between us. What do you do?"

Isaac set down his glass, and his glance darted between me and the stone top until, finally, he slumped and dropped his head back, eyes closed.

"I've got performance anxiety." His chin dipped down, and he scowled before I could make the obvious joke. "Not the kind you're thinking of."

I lifted my hands, palms up. "I didn't say anything."

"You were thinking it. Admit it, Red. This isn't going to work."

"Like hell, it isn't." I yanked on his arm, and he straightened begrudgingly. "Let me direct you this first time, okay? Sort of like an icebreaker. Let me tell you what would turn me on if I wanted a man to show he was into it."

"Yeah, okay." Isaac's spine straightened even further. "That doesn't sound too bad."

"Good."

I mirrored his posture and turned my body towards him, crossing my legs in his direction and leaning one elbow on the bar. I tilted forwards at the waist to give him a peek down my shirt. His eyes dipped in that direction before darting up again, and I smiled.

"What are you sensing, Isaac?" I asked in a voice that was breathier than I intended. "What do you see?"

"You're facing me," he said, eyes lowering again to my chest. "Did you mean to sit in a way that shows off your, uh…cleavage?"

"I did. Bonus points for noticing. Now, do what I do. Set your elbow on the bar and lean in a little. Good. Now drop that arm and brush mine while you do it. No, don't look at your hand. Try to make it appear accidental. You didn't mean to touch me, but oops! You did."

The look of concentration on his face was oddly charming, but it was the touch of Isaac's fingers that had me schooling my face to stillness. They left a trail of static on my forearm, and I watched as his throat bobbed with a deep swallow. He felt it, too.

"Perfect," I murmured. "Now place your other arm on the back of my chair. That's it. Very good. See how you've almost got me caged, and see how I'm still leaning in—not pulling away? I'm into it."

He nodded and scanned the shape of his arms, noting where he'd placed his hands. I could see his mind ticking over, and that just wouldn't do.

"Don't think so much. Just do what I say when I say it. And look at me. Make eye contact." His gaze found mine, but there wasn't any heat in it. "Now, think about me naked."

Isaac jerked back, dropping his arms as I sat up straighter and folded mine. He'd ruined the moment.

"What's wrong?" I demanded.

"Why the fuck would I think about you naked?"

"Well, if the idea repulses you so much—"

"That's not—"

"Think of *Lisa* naked," I spoke over him, "or any other woman you'd like to have sex with. I want to see desire in your eyes. I want to see heat and lust. Give me the impression that you want me."

He pressed his thumb and forefinger against his eyelids and took two deep breaths through his nose. I waited, and when he was done, he set his arms in the previous position and leaned in. Closer this time, and we stared into each other's eyes.

"This is weird," he mumbled through closed lips.

"Shh," I admonished. "Sex, Romeo. Think about sex."

He wasn't wrong. It was weird for another moment or two, but the silence first grew comfortable, then loaded as I watched the story shift behind Isaac's exquisite green eyes. He was thinking about sex, and now, I was too. Sex and a certain dream I'd had last night.

When the energy was palpable, I gave another instruction. "Drop your gaze to my mouth," I whispered. "Like you want to kiss me."

He did, lingering there long enough that I licked my lips involuntarily before he met my eyes again, only this time, they burned with need. I noted his breath came a little faster, and for the purposes of this exercise, I gave in when my body wanted to inhale a little faster too.

"Ask me to dance," I whispered. "And when I say yes, let me stand first. When you do the same, brush against me just enough that we only touch in a few places. Fingertips. Chest. Hips. Okay?"

Isaac nodded imperceptibly, never dropping his gaze from my eyes, but he let another minute pass—and I had to give him props for prolonging the tension—before he said in a low voice, "Would you like to dance?"

The deep rumble in his chest stirred something primal between my thighs.

I stood, and Isaac waited until I was upright before he followed, leaving barely any room between us, leaning in just enough that I felt the heat emanating off his skin. His broad chest grazed against my nipples as he rose, and they always had been sensitive—even that light touch left them tight, budded, and aching underneath my T-shirt.

"Take my hand," I whispered, and he threaded his warm, calloused fingers through mine. "Set your other hand on the small of my back and guide me to the dancefloor."

He turned my body and did as I directed, but the pressure was too firm. "Lighter," I said. "A feather touch, almost like a tickle." The press of his hand lifted, and now it was a brush of warmth and a graze of fingertips, a combination that triggered a rush of goosebumps under my clothes. "Perfect."

We moved to a square of open space between the kitchen island and dining table and turned to face each other. He knew enough to take my right hand in his left and set the other on my back, but his muscles were too stiff, and the posture was too formal.

"Move a little closer. Slide your right hand down a little lower… A little more… Now pull your left hand in and curl my hand against your chest."

Isaac followed each direction and did it well, and then we were swaying gently in the silence.

Just like that, I was living a rom-com. And oh, the irony. I hated those things. Soppy and stupid with their happily-ever-after endings. Fucked up fairytales for girls too old to believe in fairy godmothers but still hoping that, magically, things would turn out in the end. Women who believed there was a man out there who could save them, complete them, love them just the way they were.

Idiots.

I chanced a look up at Isaac. He was staring down at me, and my irritation fell away so quickly that I practically heard it hit the floor at my feet.

The moment stretched until gradually—so gradually I couldn't tell if it was him or me or both of us moving—our faces drew together like slow-motion magnets, getting close enough that our noses brushed, and my lips parted in response to his breath on my mouth.

The mellow movements of our dance slowed then stilled, but Isaac's hands remained on my body, and I was suddenly certain he was about to kiss me.

I was less certain about my ability to *not* kiss him back, and I wasn't sure we were there yet.

"So, at about this time," I said, dropping his hands and taking a long step away from him, "you could lean in and touch your lips to hers. A *light* touch. Nothing porny."

"Yeah, right. Good idea." Isaac blinked a few times as he ran a hand over his chin and jaw. "So, uh, how did I do?"

"Pretty darn good, Romeo." Something lit up inside me as his grin brightened the room, a tender warmth that pulsed in counterpoint to the physical attraction I couldn't quite shake, and it made me anxious enough that my change in the subject was clumsier than usual. "Lisa's going to be weak in the knees when you pull out those moves."

"I hope so," he replied, but there was a hint of ego on his mouth that wasn't there before. On some men, that kind of thing looked arrogant. On Isaac, it was straight-up sexy.

I returned to my chair and took a sip of my juice. "So, we should probably do this a couple more times before Saturday. That way, you're properly prepared."

"Really? I thought—"

"Practice, remember? Training. You can't stop at your first win and call it a day. The world doesn't work like that. You have to keep showing up."

"I suppose so."

"And what if she kisses you? Would you know what to do next?"

"Uh, kiss her back?"

"And?"

"And…" Isaac frowned, then he crossed his arms over his chest, biceps flexing underneath the thin cotton, and tried to smooth out his grimace. "I guess you'll see for yourself at our next session."

"Atta boy," I replied with a wink, refusing to think about the way my body thrilled at the thought.

7

BIRDIE

"OKAY, LADIES. LET'S go." I set the dealer button on the green felt-topped table in front of me, then shuffled the cards in my hands. "This is standard home-play no-limit Texas hold 'em. Blinds. No antes. Em, you're up."

It was eight o'clock on Saturday night, and I'd been given four hours' notice via a flying visit from Isaac—in his police uniform no less, and *damn*, did that sight do magical things to my lady parts—plus a social media message from Abbie that I was invited to her girls' night out. Vague memories of treehouse poker were raised, not-so-vague challenges and wagers were thrown down—ambitious promises were made about margaritas and munchies—and somehow, I found myself hosting Abbie, Jessica, and Emily for a night of cards and cocktails in the game room of my parents' summer house.

And I wasn't mad at it.

Professional poker was predominantly a man's game, but that had never bothered me. I was what people called a social butterfly. I didn't shy away from strangers or feel uncomfortable in crowds, so if I ever needed human interaction, I went looking for it. I didn't dwell on the fact I had no lifelong friends or real family in my life—it had been that way for as long as I could remember—and I was adept at getting my emotional needs met via random conversations and occasional hook-ups. Only now, with Abbie, Jess, and the new girl, Emily, sitting around the table, did I remember something I'd forgotten about this town, this house, and these people. The kids from Valentine Bay had given me the closest thing I'd ever had to a real home.

Dark-haired, elfin Emily on my left hesitated with her slender fingers hovering over the multicoloured poker chips stacked in front of her. I was about to give her a nudge when she said, "No, don't tell me. I've got it." Then she picked up a white disc and set it in the centre of the table.

"Good," I approved. "Abs? Big blind."

Abbie, sitting one more place to the left, picked up two white chips and added them to the pot. I nodded, a small smile teasing my lips as she threw me a dramatically competitive glower.

"I'm winning my Christmas money back tonight, Birdie Maxwell, if it's the last thing I do."

"Looking forward to it," I replied, lifting my cocktail glass in her direction. "Mind topping me up while I file for bankruptcy?"

"Of course not, honey." Abbie swept her long blonde curls over one shoulder, then lifted the jug of pink margarita mix she'd made and poured me a generous serving.

I took an immediate and appreciative slurp, noting the ratio of tequila to grapefruit juice was way in favour of the liquor. "Mm, that's good." I downed the rest and brandished my empty glass. "Here, fill it again."

"You like?" Abbie asked, adding to my glass, then doing the same for Emily and Jess. "I stole the recipe from Will when he was distracted by a pretty face. Do *not* tell him, okay? It'll make him wonder why I go back to the bar if not for the bottomless margaritas."

"Why do you go back to the bar if not for the margaritas?" Emily asked, leaning her elbow on the table and propping her chin in her hand, coyly fluttering her lashes at Abbie.

"For the food," Abbie said, shooting Emily a scowl. "I think I liked it better when you were timid and shy. Old Emily never gave me this much shit about Will."

Emily raised her hands in surrender. "Fine. I apologise. I won't say another word about it."

I picked up the deck, burned the top card, then dealt to the table so we had two cards each, face down. "Jess? Your bet. Then, you can tell me what I'm missing here."

Jess pushed her dark-framed glasses higher onto her nose, lifted the corners of her cards to check the suits, and threw two of her chips onto the table. "Call," she announced before leaning towards me conspiratorially. "Will and Abbie have a pact to get married if they're both single by the time they're—"

"We do not have a pact to get married!" Abbie's nostrils flared as she sucked in a breath that I think was supposed to be soothing, and when she went on, her voice had come down an octave. "We have an *agreement* to grow old together while seeing as many people as we like. We make-believe the happy ever after, and it keeps my mother off my back. Will is my get-out-of-marriage-free card, not my fall-back guy. And that's the last time I'm going to say it."

"Sounds like a sweet deal to me," I said, ignoring my hole cards and setting two chips on the table. "Call."

Abbie swallowed her gulp of margarita with theatrical aplomb. "Thank you. Finally, a woman after my own heart."

"Really?" Jess asked, helping herself to a slice of cheese from the platter set in front of one of the table's empty seats. "So, you're not seeing anyone, Birdie?"

"God, no." I gestured at the table, then the cards in front of Emily. "You want to call, Em?"

"Yes. Sorry." She peeked at her cards, then added another chip to the pile.

"Abs?" I asked.

"I'm good," she replied, picking at the grapes.

I burned another card, then dealt the flop, and the betting went another round. At ten cents a chip, we were just having fun—playing for something to do with our hands while the conversation and cocktails flowed—but I enjoyed going through the motions as much as I did the company. And after nearly two of Abbie's margaritas on an empty stomach, I could already feel a warmth seeping into my skin from the inside out.

"No offence to the lovebirds in the room," I explained, "but I'm not a relationship type of woman. All those feelings and emotions, one man for the rest of your life... *Blergh*. You get less for murder. And it doesn't suit my lifestyle. I travel too much. I'm focussed on my career. I've got no time for anything that lasts longer than a weekend."

"Maybe I should become a travelling yoga instructor and take my studio on the road," Abbie mused. "I'm running out of men, and there's a whole world of peen out there."

"That there is," I agreed, setting out the turn card and prompting another round of bets. "But honestly, sometimes it's easier to do the job yourself, you know? It's been a long time since anyone really impressed me in the bedroom."

"There are definitely some duds out there," Emily agreed with a sage nod. "I almost married one of them."

"Really?" I waved my empty glass at Abbie, who topped it up. "My heart goes out to you."

"Josh is more than making up for it now," Emily quipped with a cheeky grin. "Don't you worry about me."

"Isaac said you're here for six weeks," Jess said, popping a slice of pear into her mouth. "Is that right?"

"Six weeks at most," I clarified. "I need to be in Vegas by then for my next big tournament."

"It'll be good to have you around for a while," she replied. "You've always fit in here. Hanging out with you tonight, it's almost like you never even left."

"You're right. It doesn't feel like twelve years since I was last here."

"Why *are* you here?" Abbie leaned back in her chair, cocktail glass balanced between her fingers, our half-done poker game forgotten for the moment. "This house has been empty since the last time you were here with your parents."

I thought of the text message I'd received that morning from Cora, delaying her arrival by another few days at least. No preamble, no explanation. Just, *"My schedule has changed. I'm unable to travel until the weekend."* That'd make this trip a ten-day brush-off so far, but who was counting?

"My mother's meeting me here next week to talk about the house," I replied, working to keep the shortness out of my tone.

"What about it?" Emily asked.

"I don't know exactly." My palms began to itch, and I rubbed them distractedly as I tried to keep the conversation from getting too serious. "Fingers crossed she's divorcing my father. Maybe she's thinking about moving here permanently."

For fuck's sake, Birdie. Shut up. No more tequila for you.

"Oh, I'm sorry to hear that." Emily gave me a lopsided smile that was too sympathetic for comfort.

"I'm not," I replied. "Divorce would be the best thing to happen to my parents."

It'd mean my mother had taken my side for a change. She'd be forced to acknowledge the secrets she'd made me keep, and maybe it'd thaw the ice in her veins. I drowned the flicker of longing I felt with another mouthful of margarita. My parents' marriage was another reason I would never commit to one person for the rest of my life. It had turned Cora into less than half a person, and I refused to give up that much of myself for any man.

"Ugh," I groaned, reaching for a bowl of chocolate buttons. "Let's talk about something else. Anything else." When nobody volunteered a new subject, I gave in to the tequila and threw caution to the wind. "Tell me, what's the deal with Isaac?"

"The deal?" Jess echoed, swapping suspicious looks with Abbie and Emily. "What do you mean?"

"He came around, we had a chat, and he explained a few things. He gave me the impression he's not exactly single by choice."

"He's a teddy bear. That's his problem," Abbie observed, tipping her head back to drain the last drops from her glass. "Too sweet for his own good."

"He picks the wrong women," Jess added.

"He doesn't know what a catch he is," Emily said.

I looked at them one by one. "This isn't news to you, obviously."

Abbie snorted. "Of course not. He's one of our best friends, and he's spent most of this year watching his mates fall in love or get married one by one. There's only him and Will left standing, and only one of them wants to be a bachelor. Spoiler alert: it's not Isaac."

I hefted the cocktail jug and poured for us all. "He was always a shy kid. Remember?"

Abbie and Jess nodded at the same time.

"He was so bloody tall," Jess said. "It took him years to grow into his height. He was always self-conscious about it—and the kids we went to school with weren't always kind."

"Most of them were downright dickheads," Abbie muttered, earning a reproving look from Jess. "What? They were."

"Maybe it stunted his emotional growth?" Emily offered.

"It stunted his *confidence*," I corrected. "He's too shy around women, and I'm going to do something about it."

Emily quirked an amused brow, and Abbie's eyes sparkled like she knew where this was going, but Jess appeared to be completely clueless.

"You're going to do something about his confidence?" she asked. "How?"

"Do you all know about this police academy reunion coming up—"

"Oh, we know." Abbie flung out a hand and gripped my forearms so tight it almost hurt. "Did he tell you about Lisa?"

That irritating knot of not-possessiveness—*protectiveness*—curled up tight inside my stomach. "Yep," I said with a smile I didn't quite feel, "and he's agreed to a little love coaching."

"*Love* coaching?" Emily repeated, setting down her glass.

"Yep. I'm going to teach that boy so many moves, Lisa will be putty in his big, broad hands."

Abbie clapped quickly in applause. "Oh, this is fantastic! I wish I'd thought of it." A heartbeat passed before she shuddered and added, "No. Better you than me. Flirting with Isaac would be like flirting with my brother."

"It doesn't sound like something Isaac would do," Jess said, sipping her cocktail and eyeing me with speculation. "I can't believe he agreed."

"He didn't—not at first—but then I persuaded him to show me his goodnight-kiss routine and…well, there's room for improvement."

"But there's potential, right?" Emily asked. "I haven't known Isaac for very long, so I don't see that boy you're all talking about. All I see is a very well-put-together man."

"I think that's part of the issue," I replied. "One look at Isaac, and you think: he must be a beast in the bedroom, right? The take-charge kind. He's a cop, so there'd be handcuffs, obviously. Maybe even a baton. Bondage? Totally up for it. A little praise and degradation, perhaps, and with hands that large, he's got to have an enormous—"

"You've given this some thought, huh?" Abbie smirked at me over the rim of her glass.

"The point is," I said, giving her a wink that sent her into a fit of giggles, "all that expectation has him spooked. That, and a series of rejections from women starting when he was sixteen. Now the guy's a little gun shy, so to speak."

"And so, you're going to rate his moves, show him some new tricks, pump him up before his big date with Lisa?" Jess wore a slight frown, and the tip of her nose twitched nervously.

"That's the plan," I confirmed. "But keep it to yourselves, okay? I don't want him to get cold feet and chicken out."

"It's really nice that you care so much about him," Emily murmured, picking up her cards again.

I scooped up the deck and settled into my poker face. "He's a good guy. We're friends. I can help him, so why shouldn't I? Isaac behaves like he's never had a win, and that kind of attitude drives me up the wall, especially coming from a guy as great as he is."

"So, Isaac's love life is some sort of game?" Jess asked, the tone of a mama bear edging her voice. "I don't know how I feel about that. He's sensitive, and I don't want him getting the wrong idea or getting hurt. Not that I'm accusing you of anything, but…"

"It's fine. I get it. But you can trust me with this. I've set the terms of the offer—purely philanthropic, no strings attached—and Isaac agrees. I promise you, Jess. I'm taking it seriously. I'm taking *Isaac* seriously."

The burning sting of needles across my palms was the sign I needed that the discussion had again grown too heavy for comfort. It was time to lighten the mood.

"But lucky for me, this here *is* a game." I burned a card and dealt the river, and with the five community cards face up on the table, I knew instantly I was about to take the pot. Just like I knew that before I left Valentine Bay in a few weeks, Isaac was going to think of himself as a winner, no matter what I had to do to make it happen. "All right, girls. Place your bets. Things are about to get interesting."

8

ISAAC

I OPENED THE door to the conference room located at the rear of the Valentine Bay Library and Community Centre and found Dot standing behind an ancient lectern, banging a tiny wooden gavel against its matching sound block. A dozen or so members of the VBFYRRRBC—only two of them men—stood around talking and ignoring the persistent *bang bang bang*. A circle of blue plastic chairs had been set up in the middle of the grey-carpeted space, and a trestle table topped with a coffee urn and paper plates of store-bought baked goods was set up against one wall.

Every person there had to be at least sixty years old, and I seriously thought about making a run for it before anyone noticed me hovering in the doorway with a plastic container of homemade orange and poppyseed friands still warm from the oven clutched in my hands. What the hell was I doing here?

"Order. *Order!*" Dot shouted. "This meeting of the VBFYRRRBC is now in session!" Her eyes lit on me, one foot still out in the hallway. "Ah! Sergeant Greene. Welcome! I'm so glad you could make it."

There went my last shot to bail. I tugged my ear and ducked my head, moving all the way into the room and letting the door swing closed behind me. "Good afternoon, Mrs March." I nodded around the room, recognising each and every one of the wrinkled faces that had turned to me with mixed expressions of surprise and horror. Fuck, this was mortifying. "Hello, everyone."

Burt the Third pushed himself to the front of the crowd and planted his fists on his hips, blue coveralls straining around his middle, tufts of white hair sticking out from under his worn baseball cap. His cheeks were redder than usual, his expression darker than a thundercloud.

"Dorothy March, have you lost your mind?"

Dot rolled her eyes and stepped out from behind the lectern, settling a soothing arm on Burt's shoulders and ushering him into a chair. "Calm down, Burt. Let me explain."

Oh, fuck no. Please don't *let her explain*.

Agatha Braverman sidled up on one side of me, and I turned away from the argument about to kick off in the middle of the room. Agatha must have been one of the younger people in the club, barely into her mid-sixties, with unnaturally dark hair that she wore in a neat knot at the back of her head and a wardrobe that featured animal prints more than anything else. She passed a manicured hand over my bicep and set the other on the box of cakes, which made no sense to me until she pressed her enormous bosom against me. Her cloud of perfume was cloying.

"How lovely to see you here, Officer," she said. "I've been lobbying for young blood in our ranks for years now. Couldn't get it past a club vote." The woman's sharp glance slid over to where Dot was fending off a clutch of angry retirees, and then she turned her false-eyelashed gaze on me. "I've never been so pleased to see Dot go rogue."

I cleared my throat and gently extracted my arm from her grip. "Nice to see you too, Mrs Braverman. I didn't know you were a member of the, uh, the group."

"A *founding* member," she corrected, dragging a red-coated fingernail over my left pec. "Oh, my, Sergeant Greene. Have you been working out?"

"Agatha! Please!" Dot shuffled over, inserting herself between me and my admirer, and took hold of my arm protectively. "Give him a moment to find his feet before you sweep them out from under him."

Agatha laughed throatily, then winked at me. "I'll give you a fifteen-minute head start, Officer."

"Come on, dear," Dot said, guiding me over to the last empty seat as everyone watched. I was dying inside, but as Dot took her place in another of the chairs, I smiled tightly at the faces that weren't too hostile and nodded at the ones that looked ready to commit bloody murder.

"What you got there?" Bill Christakos, seated on my left, tilted towards me and jerked his chin at the box in my hands. "Cake? New members got to bring cake."

"Yeah." I thrust the container at him, practically begging him to take it. "I baked them this morning. They're still warm. Maz gave me the recipe."

Bill cracked open the lid, and as a warm waft of sweet, citrussy air escaped, Irena Kowalski, seated on Bill's other side, raised her grey-topped head. Her eyes brightened at the sight of the little sugar-dusted cakes. "Are those Maz's orange and poppyseed friands?"

On my right, Lorraine Langley leaned over my lap to get a better look. "Oh, those are delightful if done right," she declared, waving an open palm at Bill. "Here, give me one, and I'll tell you if they're any good."

Stretching out to take a cake, Mrs Langley rested her forearm precariously close to my crotch, but her attention was so focused on the cakes that I don't think she realised how awkward it was. I shifted, hoping she'd get the message and get off me, but I only made things worse, and now my old history teacher's bony elbow was wedged in my groin. Jesus, kill me now.

"Hey!" Burt's rumbly shout sounded from the opposite of the circle. He sat with his arms crossed over his chest and a sour look on his face. "There are no private parties here. Share 'em 'round."

The plastic box made its way around the circle, each member of the club plucking out a cake and then passing the container along. The pleased murmurs and relative silence as people dug in gave me the impression that I hadn't screwed the cake part up, at least, but it was times like this I wished I cared less about doing the right thing and making sure people like me. If they hated the cake, maybe they'd have kicked me out, and I wouldn't be sitting here wondering what the actual fuck I'd got myself in for.

Directly opposite me, sitting on the chair next to Burt, Agatha leisurely wrapped her red-coated lips around a friand and shot me another wink.

That's it. I was out of here.

Dot chose that moment to clap her hands together—once, twice. Loudly. "All right, everyone. Now he's proved himself with a batch of something tasty, perhaps we can try again to welcome the newest member of the VBFYRRRBC?" She glared at Burt, who returned the look with indignation, his cheeks filled with cake. "Isaac Greene, it's a pleasure to have you here."

A smattering of applause rang around the room, and I carefully avoided meeting Agatha's eyes. "Thanks for inviting me."

"Now, I know it's an anomaly to have members join the club before they're old enough for the pension, but as I explained to Burt just now, Isaac is a special case. The circumstances are extenuating."

The burn of humiliation raced up my neck as Burt nodded knowingly. "We've got ourselves a Dot-and-Thomas type situation."

A chorus of "ahs" and "ohs" swelled around me, and everyone nodded in understanding. Apparently, they were all familiar with Dot and her history with husband number five.

"I appreciate the, uh, sympathy," I said, wiping at the light sheen of sweat that had sprung up on my forehead.

"But I still don't know what I'm doing here. Mrs March, I'm grateful you want to help, but—"

"Call me Dot, dear. I know. I know. There's still a piece of the puzzle missing, but this is it. *We're* it. Thomas and I founded this book club after he kissed me on that sixth date. The secret to that kiss was too good to keep to ourselves, but not something he was comfortable shouting from the rooftops. He was a shy man, my Thomas."

"Oh, for Pete's sake, Dot," Burt grumbled. "The poor kid's dying over there. Look at him! About to sweat his way through that too-tight T-shirt he's got on. Get to the darn point."

Dot frowned at Burt but let the comment pass. "Very well." The old woman climbed to her feet, and everyone else did the same. They settled one hand over their hearts and raised the other palm up like they were about to swear to God or make some kind of pledge, and for a second, I was convinced I'd accidentally joined a cult.

"Welcome, new member, to the VBFYRRRBC," they intoned together, watching me in a way that made me feel like their next meal. "Do you solemnly swear never to share what we discuss between these walls, including the true name of the VBFYRRRBC, which, when disclosed, will bond you to us until the end of time?"

Jesus Christ, it *was* a cult.

That didn't stop me from getting to my feet, though, as a snarky voice in my head reminded me if I didn't see this through, there was a good chance I'd keep embarrassing myself trying to prove myself in Birdie's kitchen, not to mention strike out with Lisa at the reunion. It didn't stop me from covering my chest with one hand and raising the other, letting Dot's little nods encourage me as I replied, "I do solemnly swear."

"Wonderful!" Dot exclaimed as she fished a hot-pink satin sash out of her pocket. I stared around the room with something bordering on horror as everyone, even Burt, slung matching sashes across their bodies, each one marked with black lettering that spelled out in excruciating detail the top-secret name of this top-secret book club. Realisation dawned, but it was too late to back out now.

"Welcome, Isaac," Dot proclaimed, "to the Valentine Bay Forever Young Randy Romance Readers Book Club."

On the other side of the room, Agatha let out a growl.

9

ISAAC

I MUST HAVE briefly blacked out in some sort of shock-denial response because when I came to a few seconds later, Dot had settled herself back into her chair, and everyone was pulling e-readers out of their pockets or bags. Three or four people had pens and notebooks balanced on their laps.

"This week's book was hit and miss for me," Mrs Langley began. "I'm generally a fool for the forced proximity trope, but I don't know... Something about the story just missed the mark."

"I agree," Burt said, sitting there with his pink sash across his portly stomach, his glasses perched on the end of his nose, and not a hint of irony about him. "I like a slow burn, and this moved too fast. I think that was the problem."

"Was there anything we *liked* about the book?" Dot asked the group.

Agatha cleared her throat. "That scene in the hot tub was quite—"

"Hold on!" I practically shouted, *really* not wanting to hear Agatha Braverman give me a blow-by-blow of a hot tub scene in a book being read by a club that called itself "forever young" and "randy" in the same breath. "Can we back up a little here? What kind of books do you read exactly?"

Mrs Langley looked at me over the top of her wire-framed reading glasses. "Smut, Mr Greene."

"Oh, Lord," I groaned, dropping my head back and rubbing my hands over my face.

"What?" Burt barked. "You think just because we're old, we don't have sex?"

"Yes. That's exactly what I think."

"It's not about the sex, dear," Dot said, and I raised my head, though it felt heavy enough that the lifting required effort. "It's about the romance. We all share a passion for passion, and we enjoy *love* stories. Okay, most of them include a level of detail that some would consider pornographic, but to those people, we say, lighten up."

"I skip the rude bits," Bill mumbled beside me. "Don't like 'em. I'm just here for the happy ever afters."

I suddenly remembered that Mrs Christakis had died before I was born, leaving Bill a widower in his late forties. They'd never had kids, and he never married again.

Fuck. I was behaving like a judgemental prick, and that wasn't the way I wanted to live my life. It wasn't who I was. So, all right, fine. I'd keep an open mind.

"Okay, can we rewind for a minute?" I rubbed my palms over the tops of my thighs. "You obviously all know what it means that I'm in a *Dot-and-Thomas type situation*"—Burt met my eyes and nodded once, and I tried to be magnanimous as I returned the gesture—"but I'm not sure I know why I'm here, or how you can help me."

"Thomas and I knew each other for years before he asked me out," Dot began, setting her device on her knees and clasping her hands on top of it, "and we went on six dates before he kissed me."

"I remember that part of the story," I replied.

"And you wondered what it was that gave him the courage to make a move."

"I did…" Realisation dawned on me as I studied the wrinkled, spectacled faces around me, each one illuminated from below by the glow of a dozen e-readers. "Thomas got the idea for that kiss from a *romance* novel?"

"The kiss was only the beginning, wasn't it, Dot?" Agatha asked, elbowing the pink-haired woman in the ribs and chuckling slyly.

"Oh, absolutely." Dot pretended to neaten her tightly coiled curls, patting them modestly. "The things these books can teach a man… You wouldn't believe it, Sergeant Greene."

"Is that—" I cleared my throat. "Is that why you're here, Burt?"

"Better believe it." The sash seemed to have mellowed Burt a little, and he considered me without a hint of the hostility he'd been flashing around before. "Mrs Spies is insatiable, Sergeant. *Insatiable.*"

"Right," I mumbled. That was more information than I'd ever wanted to know about anyone's sex life, let alone Burt's. "And does she know you're here? That this is where you get your, uh, inspiration?"

"Holy heck, no. She thinks I'm the eighth natural wonder of the world, and I plan to keep it that way."

"It's why the club is so exclusive, you see," Dot explained. "The stories we read are always great entertainment, but that's not all they are. Each of us is here for different reasons, and they're not always reasons we feel comfortable sharing with anyone else. For me, it makes me feel close to Thomas. It was his idea to start this club, and it meant a lot to him. It's why I kept it going after he died."

"I'm secretly writing a novel of my own," Irena offered. "All the reading and talking we do together help me with that."

"The books make it easier to manage the pain in this darn dodgy hip," said Romana Camillo, one of the younger people in the room, who walked with a cane on good days and used a motorised scooter on the bad. "They're fun too, you know? A distraction that makes you feel good, that's what they are."

Mrs Langley reached for my hand and caught my eyes with a determination that surprised me. "They always have a happy ending. That cheers me up when I'm sad, and some days I'm sad a lot."

"These books make me feel young," Agatha added at a volume barely above a whisper, all evidence of her flirty bravado gone for the moment. All but one person around the circle nodded in silent agreement.

My gaze slid to Bill, who stared into nothing, his dark eyes blank and his head somewhere far away.

"Well," I said, swallowing the lump that had inconveniently sprung up in my throat. If the people in this room could be honest and vulnerable with me, I'd try to do the same. They deserved nothing less. It wasn't easy, but I forced the words out anyway. "Looks like I got lucky with this invitation because here's the truth. I could use your help. I've had nothing but bad luck with women, and I've got a date coming up with someone special. I need to turn things around."

"A date, eh?" Burt waggled his bushy eyebrows. "Anyone we know?"

My lips quirked as everyone leaned forwards to listen. "Her name's Lisa. I had a thing for her at the police academy but never made my move. I'm having a drink with her on Saturday night when we'll both be in the city for our class reunion."

"Right," Dot said, fishing a pair of glasses out of the pocket of her voluminous blue windbreaker and settling them on her nose. She began to tap and swipe at her e-reader. "We need slow burns. Friends to lovers—or a second chance, perhaps? Law enforcement is a given, of course."

"Unrequited love?" Burt suggested, triggering a murmur of agreement around the room.

Mrs Langley looked up from scrolling. "Workplace romance, at a stretch."

"Alpha hero," Agatha purred, back to her old self again, and everyone looked at me, nodding slowly like doctors who'd finally diagnosed the patient with an unknown infectious disease.

I sat there, totally confused, for sixty long minutes while the VBFYRRRBC exchanged comments and suggestions about the books they wanted me to read. The terms and concepts and subtext flew right over my head, but by the end of the meeting, I had a stack of half a dozen paperback romance novels to read—a selection from the club's own private library—plus a no-excuses expectation that I'd come back for next Sunday's meeting to tell them not only how I liked the books, but how things went with Lisa.

As much as that prospect made me want to cancel everything and pretend like that afternoon had never happened, I couldn't bring myself to let these people down. There was an energy about them that hadn't been there before, an excitement that was palpable, and I didn't want to be the reason it evaporated into nothing.

"It's a shame you don't have someone in your life you can practice with," Agatha said at the end of the meeting, popping out from the crowd and cornering me as I was trying to say my goodbyes. "You're going to learn a lot from these stories, but you'd do better on your date if you gave them a trial run first. I could—"

"Actually, I already have someone for that."

"Oh?" Dot shuffled over, elbowing Agatha out of the way. "Who might that be? Anyone we know?"

I rubbed the back of my neck, wishing I'd kept my big mouth shut or at least found a smarter way to stop Agatha from making an offer I'd have to awkwardly refuse. I checked the faces around us, but nobody else seemed to have overheard our exchange, so I jerked my head, and the two ladies followed me to the door. Even separated from the rest of the group, I dropped my voice.

"Birdie Maxwell's back in town."

"Oh!" Dot clapped her hands together. "The summer girl. How nice. I recall the two of you being thick as thieves when she was in town. Such a pretty little thing and so clever. Do you know she used to spend almost every morning she was in town in this very library? I don't know how it happened, but by chance, one year, she offered to help the Cheever boy who was struggling with his maths homework, and word got around that she was an excellent tutor. Soon enough, she was running unofficial summer study sessions a few times a week, and she refused to take a single cent for any of it."

My eyebrows climbed higher at each word. How did I not know this about Birdie? I was more surprised by the fact she never mentioned it than I was by the idea itself. It made sense and totally fit her character. She'd always looked for any excuse to not be in her house with her parents. She loved numbers. And she'd always gone out of her way to help people, me included. Some things never changed.

"That sounds like Birdie, all right," I said. "She was the intruder at the Maxwell place the other night, and when I got there to check it out, we had lots to catch up on."

"Including your love lives?" Dot surmised.

I pressed my forefinger to the side of my nose. "Spot on."

"And how is she these days?" Dot brushed at her jacket as though the most important task in the world right then was sweeping away invisible lint. "Happy? Settled?"

"Happy, I think. Yeah."

"Still pretty?"

"Oh, yeah." A vision of Birdie's smiling face floated before my eyes. "Very pretty."

Agatha dropped her head to one side. "And this woman is going to be your test subject?"

"Sort of. When she heard about my, uh, predicament, she offered to rate my moves and teach me a few things. I'm an idiot, so I took her up on it, and I've already struck out twice. I have to redeem myself. It's one of the reasons I'm here today. I need to get my act together for this date with Lisa, sure, but Birdie will be gone again in a few weeks, and I can't keep embarrassing myself in front of her. I can't live the rest of my life knowing she thinks I'm a dud."

"You're not a dud, Isaac," Dot said, but she was distracted. "Birdie Maxwell, you say?"

I frowned at the emphasis she put on Birdie's name. "Yes. Why?"

Dot shook herself, then smiled and looped her arm through Agatha's. "No reason. It sounds like an excellent idea to me. Doesn't it sound like an excellent idea to you, Aggie?"

"I suppose," she grumbled.

"Wonderful!" Dot set a hand on my arm and turned me towards the door, gently pushing me out into the hallway. "Now make sure you're back here at the same time next week, all right? Bring those books back with you, and we'll find new ones to replace them. And good luck on your date with Lisa. We can't wait to hear all about it."

Dot unceremoniously dragged Agatha back into the room and slammed the door in my face, leaving me standing in the hall with a bag of books in one hand and an empty Tupperware container in the other.

I hefted the first and tucked the second under my arm, turned on my heel, and began the short walk to my car.

Well, that didn't go the way I'd expected.

Better, I decided in the end.

Could I really improve my game by taking advice from a romance novel? I had to believe the answer was yes, and as much as I tried to think about Lisa on the drive home—the pages of the books on my back seat practically catcalling me the entire way—I couldn't stop worrying about the next time I'd have to prove myself to Birdie. That made sense, right?

The more I thought about it, the more confident I was that it was completely reasonable to be thinking so much about Birdie and not Lisa. I had to get *through* one to get to the other. Birdie was my ticket to happiness because, without my love coach's tick of approval, I'd freeze on my date next week, and that was the stuff of my nightmares.

No. I was doing the right thing. Birdie wanted me to

be better at this—she said so herself—and I wanted to impress her for all the right reasons.

By the time I pulled into my driveway, I'd decided there was nothing dishonourable or dishonest about using the ideas in these books to sweep Birdie off her feet. Absolutely nothing at all.

10

BIRDIE

AFTER THE GIRLS' night in, I hibernated for three days. The first of those I spent nursing the hangover from hell, so it was entirely possible Isaac tried to call me, and I threw my phone at the wall, or I mistook his pounding on my front door for the pounding in my head. Nothing—not even a bearded boy with pretty green eyes and pledges of coffee in an IV—could have dragged me from my bed after the night I'd had with Abbie, Jess, and Emily. Cards were played, snacks were eaten, laughs were had, and copious amounts of tequila were consumed—so much that it took a solid thirty-six hours to recover enough and decide that the pain and nausea afterwards were absolutely worth it.

I spent the following two days working. I signed up for some low-stakes online tournaments, downloaded a new-release poker strategy textbook, and analysed the video recordings of two recent games that had landed in the headlines due to their controversy. Both featured ballsy bluffs that upset the big-name players and had rookies taking home massive wins.

After I cleaned up in the tournaments, I stepped through the familiar routine of assessing my performances and tallying my takes. It was repetitive, comforting work that I loved. Time had no meaning when I had cards in my hands, virtual or otherwise, and when I slipped into gaming mode, hours and hours could pass while I forgot to eat or drink or go to the bathroom. I'd long learned to set reminders to stay alive. Drink a glass of water every hour. Have dinner at seven. Walk around the room at nine. Go to bed before sunrise.

Yes, sunrise was my standard bedtime. I'd never been an early riser, and I did my best work in the dark. I rarely—no, *never*—made commitments that began before midday, so when my phone chimed just before midnight on Tuesday, I swiped open the text message from Abbie and groaned at whatever madness I'd agreed to do when I was drunk.

Abbie: Don't forget tomorrow morning's yoga class. Seven o'clock sharp. I'll have a mat, blocks, and blankets for you. Just wear something comfortable.

I set aside my notebook, scribbling my thoughts on a Post-it and using it to mark my page, then tapped out a reply.

Me: New phone. Who dis?

Abbie: You warned me you'd try to get out of this, and I promised to drag you there kicking and screaming if I had to. You're coming!

Me: Don't think a verbal contract made while under the influence of bottomless margaritas will hold up in court. Better luck next time. Make it a midnight class, and I'm all yours.

Abbie: I do those, too. At the beach under the full moon, but you need to be nude. I'll sign you up, but you still have to be there tomorrow. You told me to tell you, "This next tournament's too important to screw up. Do yoga. Avoid tilt." You wrote it down and everything.

Abbie's message was followed by a photo of a crumpled-up Post-it note, my lopsided handwriting all over it, an exact mirror of Abbie's message. Fuck. It was rare that my own smart-arsedness came back to bite me, but there it was.

Next month's tournament *was* too important. It was going to be the game of my life—a huge prize, an international audience, and a sponsor who didn't want me to win, which of course meant I *had* to accept the winning cheque right from his hand as cameras captured the excruciating discomfort on his face. The closer I came to the big day, the more nervous I was going to be. More tense. More emotional. More likely to get frustrated and make bad decisions at the table. Yoga probably wasn't a bad idea.

Bloody hell. Only I could find a way to piss myself off this much.

Me: Fine. I'll be there but let the record show that Drunk Birdie is a danger to reasonable women everywhere, and if she ever shows her face again, I'm going to have to take her down.

Abbie: Cool, cool. See you in the morning!

Setting down my phone and gazing at the half-finished strategy I was sketching out in my notebook, I scooped up a textbook instead, along with grid paper and a pencil, then switched off my computers and the overhead dining room lights. After a quick shower, I made my way around my bedroom, pulling closed the curtains at all four windows. At the last one, I paused, taking my time with the drapes as I surreptitiously scoped out Isaac's property. The house was dark, but his car was in the driveway, which meant he must have arrived home from work within the last hour or so. He'd been gone all day—not that I was keeping tabs.

I crawled into bed and set a reminder on my phone that would limit my time to an hour of wind-down theoretical physics before I tried to fall asleep. At this time of night, I was going to toss and turn for hours. What was I thinking by agreeing to leave the house almost before the sun was even up?

Setting the textbook at my side and propping my notebook on my knees, I'd only scrawled out a half-dozen lines of algebra before my gaze drifted over to the window.

Was there a reason Isaac hadn't been to see me in the last three days? Had he heard from Lisa? Did I want to know the answer to that? Did I care?

An hour passed too fast, and although I wasn't tired, I turned off the lamp and resigned myself to a long night of restlessness. I never expected to fall asleep almost as soon as my head hit the pillow—but I thoroughly enjoyed the dreams that followed soon after.

The obnoxious buzz of my alarm set off a reflex in my body usually associated with airports and luggage and the rush to get somewhere fast because, predictably, I always ran late. I hit the stop button on my phone and rolled my face into the pillow, allowing myself a moment to calibrate the idea that I wasn't due on a flight in the next two hours. Instead, I was expected to show up at a yoga studio down the road because, apparently, I was a drunkard with a big mouth and a penchant for self-improvement.

The house was dark and a little cool, which made me madder about throwing off the covers. By the time I wrapped myself in my too-thin silk robe and added a second pair of socks to my feet, I was scowling. Stupid tequila and stupid yoga and stupid Drunk Birdie who did stupid things like get attached to people and try to be Zen.

I zombied down to the kitchen because first, coffee, then dragged my feet up the stairs again, fingers wrapped around the steaming mug and feeling only slightly mollified by the pep of caffeine sliding down my throat.

My eyes were more closed than open as I dressed. Socks off. *Wah.* Tights on. Sports bra and tank top. Deodorant. Hoodie. Socks back on. If anyone wanted to comment on the socks-and-sandals combo I was about to rock, they were welcome to it.

I flipped my head over and scraped my fingers through my hair, righting myself and twisting my locks into a knot at the top of my head. By the time I was presentable, the first glimmers of daylight had begun to tease the edges of the bedroom curtains.

I pulled them open as the finished cup of coffee finally pressed my better-mood buttons. The prospect of strolling down to Main Street and seeing the beach at sunrise didn't feel so painful anymore. Maybe Drunk Birdie had been onto something.

But as I yanked open the final drape, all thoughts about the wonders of nature, of the beach and the sun, and of the stretch of tight muscles as I got my yoga on were wiped from my head. None of it mattered. No sunlight on the waves or releasing that knot in my neck could top the six o'clock sight from my bedroom window.

Isaac was in his backyard. *Working out.*

Any evidence to the contrary, I hadn't given much notice to the view of his property from the second storey of mine other than to check—in passing, of course—if he was home. There really wasn't much to hold my attention. It was a house. He kept it neat. Fences. Lawns. Garden beds.

There were three sets of complicated wooden climbing equipment set up at intervals across the backyard, and I'd assumed they were to keep his hordes of nieces and nephews busy when they visited. I'd missed that those timber frames were sized for adults, not kids, but my misunderstanding was being thoroughly corrected now.

Isaac was shirtless in the pearling dawn light, a yellow glow from inside his house spilling out through the back windows and giving the scene a warm illumination that slowly faded as the sun's light grew stronger.

I leaned against the frame of the window, mesmerised, as Isaac leaped and gripped onto a metal bar over his head before hoisting his bulk over it in a set of pull-ups that rippled the lines of every muscle in his shoulders, arms, and back.

Holy hell, his *back*.

I may or may not have whimpered a little as he demonstrated his strength, his head clearing the bar over and over as he pulled his weight north, his power jumping in thigh-tightening undulations under his smooth, lightly tan skin. His legs were crossed easily at the ankles, his knees bent, until he landed on the lawn with a silent thud.

He turned, and I saw his charcoal hair was matted, his cheeks flushed. Even from here, I could see the droplets of sweat crawling down his neck, over his collarbone, and onto his carved chest. They drew my eye down… down… Over pecs that needed a licence. Across abs that should have been illegal. Along V-lines that had my teeth biting my lip and my lady parts panting. Straight to…

Oh, good God, the man was in cut-off grey sweats slung low enough on his hips that I just knew, with a quick tug of my teeth, I could have those babies down around his ankles. And right then, I wouldn't have needed tequila to make *that* bad decision.

Making a mental estimate that I could stand to ogle for at least another ten minutes before I risked running late for Abbie's class, I crossed my arms and settled in for the show. And I was not disappointed. Isaac was methodical and determined as he worked his way around what I now could see was a type of resistance course that had him working every muscle in his body in ways that worked certain muscles in mine.

The pull-ups were followed by reverse sit-ups that had me imagining the hardness of his stomach. He swung himself on monkey bars proportioned for his enormous frame, and the muscles in his arms danced. He ran up and down the length of his long yard, calves flexing and thighs powering, only to reach a wall that was at least two feet above his head. Over he went, his legs and arms launching his bulk so easily that it looked almost as though he weighed nothing.

Isaac was strong and graceful as he manoeuvred his criminally hot body around the yard, but I must have missed the majority of the performance because, well before my ten-minute limit expired, Isaac stepped away from the final frame. He swiped a towel from where it hung over one of his outdoor dining chairs, used it to wipe the sweat from his face, and disappeared inside. It took me a full minute and a half, staring into his empty yard, to accept that was all I was going to get.

When I caught myself considering getting up early again the next day just to witness an encore, I deliberately shook my head and shut the curtains. I was not a brainless ninny, and I refused to accept that the sight of a half-naked man was the kind of thing I'd lose my head over.

I took a towel from the linen closet on my way down the hall, grabbed a bottle of water from the fridge, and slipped my sock-covered feet into the pair of slides I kept by the front door. Locking up behind me, I didn't realise Isaac was doing the exact same thing at his house until we met each other on the footpath at the end of my drive.

"Hey, Red," he said with a grin. "You're up early." His gaze dropped to my feet, and his smile stretched wider. "Nice outfit."

"My feet were cold," I replied, giving his arm a playful shove as I scanned the navy T-shirt covering his broad chest and the board shorts that had replaced the grey sweats. I decided I wasn't disappointed with the wardrobe change. Not in the slightest. "Abbie conned me into a yoga class while I was drunk. Otherwise, I'd still be in bed. Trust me."

"Yeah. You need to be on your guard around that woman. Are you on the hook for today only, or did she sting you with an annual membership?"

"I—" A rogue memory of the poker night floated up through a margarita-fuelled fog. Price negotiations. Money transfers. Some sort of four-way handshake... Oh my God, I *did* buy a year's pass to Abbie's studio—

something I never would have done while sober. Ever. I never stayed in any place long enough to need a twelve-month discount on anything. I was pretty sure I'd also bought memberships for Jess and Emily, which I felt much better about. Maybe I could transfer my subscription to someone in town who needed it.

Isaac burst out laughing at the look on my face. The sound was so generous and honest, I had to concentrate on scowling. "You *did* get a year's worth of classes," he crowed, wiping at his eyes. "Ellison's an evil genius."

"She plied me with bottomless margaritas. I was compromised." I elbowed him in the ribs and got no indication that he felt it, then started in the direction of Main Street. Isaac walked with me.

"Where are you off to this early in the morning?" I asked.

"Down to the beach. Now that Logan's back in the Bay for good, the boys and I decided to resuscitate our old surf rowing crew. We've been training a few mornings a week but haven't competed in years. The next event is going to be a bloodbath. We're old, we're out of practice, and we're out of shape."

I couldn't stop the snort that greeted Isaac's statement, and I rolled my eyes at his curiously quirked eyebrow. "You fishing for compliments, Romeo? You're not old or out of shape, and you know it."

Though it was early, there was a surprising amount of traffic on the roads the closer we drew to the main thoroughfare of Valentine Bay. It was a weekday, I supposed, and I remembered that people started their days early here. As we stalled at a curb to check for cars before crossing a moderately busy street, Isaac brushed the small of my back with his open hand to indicate when it was a good time to step out, and he kept it there as we crossed. When we safely reached the other side, he silently set a hand on my shoulder and guided me to the inside of the footpath so he could walk closest to the cars zipping along beside us.

And the gestures, both thoughtful and done without thinking, made me hold my breath.

Isaac's old-fashioned chivalry should have made me bristle. His casual assumption I needed to be taken care of should have had me fuming. Instead, I could only be mad that these small tokens came as naturally to Isaac as walking or smiling, and I didn't hate it. The guy was a cop. The instinct to be protective was as much a part of his DNA as his soaring height or careful hands.

I could only be angry with myself that a part of me appreciated it. Liked it, even. What was *wrong* with me?

"So," he said, and I could tell by the way he tugged on an earlobe that he was anxious about whatever he planned to say next. "The date with Lisa is only three days away, and, uh…"

"You want to get in a little more practice?"

His shoulders loosened, and he nodded. "Yeah. Are you free tomorrow night?"

"Sure."

"And just so we're clear, we're picking things up where they left off last time, right?"

I cast my mind back to the slow dance in my dining room, the almost-kiss, and his promise to show me what he'd do if things progressed to actual tonsil hockey.

A vision of Isaac shirtless and sweating came to mind, setting off a flare that flashed hot and fast in my stomach before swirling its way south, leaving a coil of damp need between my legs.

"You going to kiss me, Romeo?" I teased, determined to keep things between us flippant. Friendly. Low stakes.

"Nope." A pink flush started creeping up the back of his neck, and the subtle tightness around his eyes told me he wasn't feeling as cool on the inside as he tried to behave on the outside. His gaze remained ahead as we walked. "*You're* going to kiss *me*."

It was impossible not to respond to his burgeoning confidence, and I couldn't stop the grin on my face. Still, old habits died hard. "Want to bet?"

Before he could worm his way out of a wager, which I knew he was about to do, a woman stepped out onto the footpath in front of us. With long blonde hair braided around her hairline, fine lines around her mouth and eyes, and an ensemble that looked like she'd draped herself in layer upon layer of light, worn linen, Dawn Linley was another figure of my childhood summers.

She'd tried—and failed—to befriend my mother many times, and no matter how harsh Cora's rejections had been, Dawn always tried again. My mother had called the woman a small-town snoop only interested in gossip, but I used to tutor her daughter when I ran my impromptu summer maths clinics at the local library, and when I was eleven, Dawn picked me up when I fell and scraped my knee, then patched me up before walking me home. I'd liked her a lot after that.

"Dawn!" I wrapped my arms around her and gave her slight frame a quick hug. "It's good to see you. How are you?"

"Birdie Maxwell! I heard you were back in the Bay. How are you, sweetheart?"

"I'm good, thanks."

"And where are you two off to this morning?" Dawn's eyes sparkled, and I intuitively knew what she must have been thinking. Assuming. "It's quite a sight to see you two side by side after all these years. You make such a good-looking pair."

"Birdie has a yoga class," Isaac replied in a brisk voice that sounded all official and policeman-like. A bit take-charge. It was hot. "And I'm meeting the boys on the beach for a training session. We bumped into each other on the way over, and we're not a couple, Dawn. You know that."

Dawn flapped a hand. "I didn't say you were a *couple*, Sergeant. Just that you're a good-looking pair. Those are two very different things if you think about it. But now that you mention it, I was just saying to Maz last week that it was almost time for me to help things along for you in the dating stakes. Just a nudge. Look how well things turned out with Josh and Emily! And wasn't that all my doing? I must know at least a dozen women who would be perfect for you, Isaac, if you'd give them a chance. But then Maz told me you have a date this weekend—"

Isaac made a choking sound. "How on Earth do you know about that?"

I glanced up at Isaac and resisted the impulse to put a soothing hand on his arm or slip my hand into his, but he looked so harried that before I knew what I was doing, I went and did just that.

Perhaps my mother had been right about Dawn, but I didn't believe that made me wrong. A woman could be kind to a kid who needed it *and* like to gossip on the side, and though it didn't change the fact I liked Dawn, I hated the idea of Isaac feeling like fodder.

I slid my arm through his, locked my slender fingers around his broad ones, and leaned against him.

Putting on a face I hoped came across as adoring in a slightly over-the-top way, I gazed up at him, biting my lip to stop from laughing at his astonishment.

"You've got nothing to worry about, Dawn," I said with a sigh, turning my beatific smile on her. She seemed delighted at my display of affection, and I was delighted in return. This would give her something new—and ridiculous—to talk about. "Isaac's going to be primed and ready for his date this weekend. Prepared for *anything*." I allowed myself the selfish pleasure of giving Isaac a smack on the bum. The muscle was as firm as this morning's workout suggested, and for as long as I lived, I'd never regret taking that opportunity to cop a cheeky feel. I had to give a hundred points to the man—he barely batted an eyelid—and I winked at Dawn. "I'll make sure of that."

The other woman blinked, quickly and beadily like a bird, and her smile faltered, then faded, as she tried to work out what I meant. For once, she seemed at a loss for words.

"Come on, Romeo," I said, pulling on Isaac's arm. It was like trying to budge a tree before he shook off his stupor and let me lead him a few steps. "I've got a delinquent yogi waiting for me, and you've got a boat to row."

I tried not to laugh at the bewilderment on Isaac's face, but when I choked on a snort, he swung an arm around my neck before dragging me against his side in a gentle headlock, and I tripped over my own feet as we kept on walking.

"You don't know what you've done, Red," he muttered. "That little exchange will be all over the Bay in an hour."

"If it takes an hour, I'll be very disappointed in Dawn." I shoved against his abs—and yes, they were hard enough to be illegal. "Now, let me go—"

"Isaac! Birdie! Wait a moment!"

We were a dozen steps down the road when Dawn called out to stop us. Isaac grimaced at my grin before we turned and watched her close the distance, digging around in her oversized canvas bag for a brightly coloured flyer she finally waved at us. Isaac took it and frowned.

"The boat. The rowing," she said before shaking her head and starting again. "You just reminded me. The surf life saving club confirmed the date for the local qualifying surf rowing event. It's in a little more than a month, so hopefully, that gives you and the boys enough time to prepare. And Birdie, you need to be there. I'm sure Isaac would appreciate the support. Plus, it's so much fun. You don't want to miss it."

"Sounds like a party," I agreed, not objecting to the thought of watching Isaac man an oar. I scanned the information printed on the sheet in Isaac's hands, and a hard, sour lump crawled up my throat. The competition date fell the week after my big tournament in Las Vegas.

I'd have left the Bay behind by then, and I had no plans to return. Ever. Good riddance, right? That was the way it had to be. I always moved on. I always said goodbye. I always dodged commitments and never expected other people to keep theirs. That was the best way to avoid disappointment. That was the only way to stay safe.

I stepped back from our little circle and hitched my towel and water bottle between my arms. "I'll be gone by then. Work commitments."

"Oh." Dawn's expression was disappointed, and her gaze bounced between Isaac and me, all shrewd curiosity again. "Are you sure you can't— No? Well, it can't be helped, I suppose."

Beside me, Isaac cleared his throat and stuffed the flyer into his back pocket. "Thanks for that, Dawn. I'll let the boys know. I doubt we have any chance of qualifying, but hopefully, we won't embarrass ourselves too badly."

"I'm sure you're underestimating yourself, Sergeant, and we'll all be there cheering for you," Dawn offered before saying her goodbyes.

Isaac and I silently strolled the last block to Main Street, and I wondered if he was quiet because I wasn't talking or if it was the other way around. His introspection made me twitchy, but before I could think of something to say, we reached the boardwalk and drew to a stop.

"Abbie's studio is another few minutes that way," he said, pointing towards Surf Parade, then he stuck his thumb over his shoulder. "The crew will be waiting for me down there."

"Right." I smiled and punched him playfully on the shoulder. "Well, thanks for the police escort."

He huffed out a laugh. "Yeah, right. Anytime."

"And I'll see you tomorrow night?"

"Uh, yeah. Tomorrow night."

"About eight o'clock sound all right to you?"

"Sure. Sounds good."

I shoved away the last of my unease and attempted to jump-start the conversation at its last known point of life. "And you really think I'm going to kiss you, Romeo?"

The question ignited a light in his eyes, and it set off butterflies in my stomach.

"Yeah, Red. I really think you will."

11

ISAAC

BIRDIE WAS DUE at my place any minute, and I was ready. I'd never been more ready. I'd powered through four of the six books Dot had given me at the VBFYRRRBC meeting, and the experience had been… enlightening.

Two of the stories were tame enough that they could have been made into PG-rated movies. The others were practically porn. Five had a police officer as the hero. All of them had taught me something. I'd defaced them with sticky tabs marking moves I thought might impress Birdie, which in turn would give them the stamp of approval for my drink with Lisa. Still more notes were stuck to scenes I was saving for another time if—when—things progressed to the next level. With Lisa, of course.

But Jesus Christ. I'd had no idea women wanted this kind of stuff. A near-impossible combination of possessiveness, power, and play mixed with respect, consent, care, and humility—and that applied in the bedroom just as much as out of it. The last four, I understood in my bones. The others… Well, I was starting to get the idea, and the hottest tip I'd picked up so far was that no matter who the hero was, nothing was ever more important to him than his woman and her pleasure.

And that right there was a big fucking turn-on.

What I wasn't expecting was that all this research would make me think more about the things *I* wanted to do and say in bed—talk dirty, take control—but for all the scenes that had my palms itching and dick twitching, there were those that came with a hard pass. It was oddly reassuring. This experiment wasn't about to turn me into someone I wasn't. I'd be the same Isaac Greene, just with a little more confidence and a few less inhibitions.

I picked up my phone and checked for notifications, and when none popped up, I re-read the messages Lisa had sent. I hadn't heard from her in four days, and I kept finding reasons not to text her first. Too busy. Too tired. Too distracted. Too bloody nervous.

At a tap on my front door, I took a deep breath before slipping my books into my dresser and covering them with a stack of T-shirts. Stepping into the bathroom to give my beard a once-over and check my breath, I bounded down the stairs and opened the front door before Birdie had to knock again.

"Hey, Red." I attempted my best sexy smirk and prayed she wouldn't be able to tell I'd spent twenty minutes practicing it in front of a mirror. "Come on in."

She offered me an amused quirk of her eyebrow as she silently strolled through the door and right past me, looking cute and casual as usual but no less sexy for it. Her loose, cropped tee revealed the smooth, fair skin of her stomach and hinted at the roundness of her tits. Her black denim skirt skimmed her legs to the mid-thighs, and her hair was twisted in a loose braid that swung temptingly across the small of her back. Like a lightning bolt, the image of Birdie's copper hair wound around my fist flashed through my head and went straight to my dick, and I shifted to make room in my pants. It didn't help.

After she'd shucked the slides off her sock-covered feet and given the entry hall a silent once-over, Birdie wandered first into the living room, then the kitchen. I watched, entertained, as she completed a circuit of the ground floor, one finger dragging over my dust-free furniture, before she returned to where I waited by the door.

"You're a neat freak," she accused, arms crossed over her chest. "I should have known."

I shrugged, then set my hands on her shoulders to turn her around and guide her to the back porch. She felt so small and soft under my palms, her skin warm through the thin fabric of her shirt. "My house only seems freakishly neat because yours is freakishly untidy. Now, are you hungry?"

"Starving. What's for dinner?"

Ushering her through the back screen door, I paused behind her when her steps stalled, then held my breath as I waited for her verdict.

On the compact timber porch, a two-seat table was set with a linen tablecloth, a small vase of roses, and dinnerware. The sun had just fallen below the horizon, but I'd strung metres and metres of fairy lights over the exposed-beamed roof, and the glitter of them became more obvious by the minute. Set at intervals along the timber balustrade were flickering white candles—those little ones in tiny glass pots—and quiet music from a small wireless speaker floated in the air. I'd chosen a playlist of songs perfect for slow dancing.

"Okay, Romeo," Birdie murmured. "I'm moderately impressed on a theoretical level—I'm not really a dinner-by-candlelight kind of woman—but if you think this is enough to make me pucker up, you're going to be very disappointed when we say goodbye in about an hour and all you get is a handshake."

A pit of disappointment opened in my stomach before I reminded myself that I hadn't gone to all this effort for Birdie. Not really. "But do you think Lisa would like it? I was trying to recreate the atmosphere of a restaurant or bar. You know, to set up what it'll feel like on Saturday night."

Birdie was unnaturally still for a moment, then she patted the hand I still rested on her shoulder and slipped out from under my grip. "Don't listen to me. This is beautiful. Should I sit?"

I darted over to pull out her chair. "Can I get you a drink? I've got wine—red and white—as well as water and juice."

"You don't have to do that," Birdie said, resting a hand on the back of the seat. "I can pull out my own chair."

Her expression was so well composed that, not for the first time, I wished she'd let more of her thoughts show on her face. "I know you can."

"And you don't need to waste all your gentlemanly moves on me. Save them for Saturday."

I frowned in confusion. The convince-Birdie-to-kiss-me part of the evening wasn't due to start until after we'd had dinner. "I'm not wasting anything," I replied. "These aren't my moves. Do you think these are my moves?"

She closed her eyes briefly and shook her head. "No. Forget I said anything."

"Because I've got moves tonight," I insisted. "Real ones. Good ones."

"I'm sure you do."

"You'll know them when you see them."

"I'm sure I will." Birdie's smile didn't sparkle in her eyes the way it always did, and she scrunched up her shoulders before dropping them with a small huff. "So, what's on the menu? If it's chicken, I'll take a white wine. If it's steak, I'll have the red. And please tell me you've got dessert. I have a ton of work to do later tonight, and truckloads of sugar are required."

Although Birdie was difficult to read—always had been—I could tell something was off, and it had to be my fault. This woman never lost her footing in any situation. Hell, she'd even put Dawn in her place on the street yesterday—and though the slap on my arse had seemed a little unnecessary, I loved the way Birdie always did what she wanted without worrying about what might happen next. Why couldn't I be more like that? Fuck my life. Fifteen minutes into a promise to make this woman kiss me, and I'd already screwed it up.

No. Birdie wanted a winner, and that was what she was going to get. And why was I overthinking this anyway? What was a fake seduction scenario with a friend compared to the real, life-or-death challenges I faced as a cop?

Before I could second-guess myself any further, and before all the confidence I'd had an hour ago deserted me completely, I took one of Birdie's hands and pulled her out into the small square of open space. Lifting my arm and directing her under it in a slow spin, she silently followed my lead, even when I pulled her body closer to mine. I looped her left arm around my neck and tucked her other hand against my chest the way she'd told me to do in her dining room, then I pressed my right palm against her lower back.

"I think this is where we left things last time?" I asked.

"Mm. Give or take a sway or two."

Underneath my palm, the hem of her T-shirt rode up a little, so I slipped my hand inside it. Touch was important. Birdie's skin was hot and as smooth as satin, and I began to draw small, tight circles with my fingertips along the base of her spine. When goosebumps erupted over her arms, I couldn't stop my smile. It was working.

Words were important too, so I leaned in and murmured against her ear. "You like that?"

"I don't hate it," she whispered.

"I'll take it," I replied, turning my face into her hair and inhaling its sweet apple scent.

Ah, fuck. I tried to tell myself it was all part of the plan, that revelling in the smell of her was Romance 101, but I hadn't intended to do it, and with that small deviation, things veered off script.

My hand underneath her shirt travelled north, exploring the dip of her spine past the point I should have encountered the straps of her bra, but I found nothing and that one little discovery had me breathing a whole lot harder. I forced myself to keep my hands where they were, but I couldn't help imagining what it would be like to brush my fingers across her ribcage, perhaps caress the smooth underside of her bare breast, and an involuntary growl sounded in my chest. Birdie must have felt it because her next intake of breath was sharper, almost a gasp in response.

I let go of the hand I held against my chest, pressing her palm against my pec as I let go, and drew my head back a little so I could see her face. She kept her eyes carefully on the floor, so, setting my fingers to her chin, I turned her eyes my way. They were so blue, even in the candlelight, flickering with specks of gold and shards of shadow.

As the fingertips of my right hand tickled up and down the length of her back, I used the left to sweep a rogue tendril of red hair back from her face. Her pupils dilated. After that, the way I curved my fingers around the back of her neck and brushed my thumb along her cheek was instinctive. My body knew exactly what it had to do next.

I leaned in and nudged the tip of her nose with the tip of mine, hovering there over her upturned mouth. My thumb moved lower until I could drag it over her bottom lip, and it dropped open in reply.

Slowly, she drew closer, so slowly, until the soft warmth of her lips landed on mine.

I didn't think before I cradled her head more firmly or before I pressed her hips against me. My mouth had a mind of its own, tenderly tugging at her willing lips. They were open and pliant, and I braved a gentle brush with the tip of my tongue. She reciprocated, and the jolt I felt at the wet warmth of her went straight to my crotch. My dick stiffened, and with Birdie's stomach pressed against me as it was, there was no way I could hide it.

"Okay," she breathed, breaking away from the kiss and my grasp by taking a long step back. "Good to know everything works, Romeo."

"Everything works," I mumbled, feeling strangely bereft without the feel of her in my arms. I resisted the urge to pull at my pants.

"Functioning penis? Check. Pre-approved first-date moves? Check. Awkward moment involving an unexpected erection and the girl next door? Check, check, check."

Birdie's cheeks were a little flushed, her lips pink and parted, her breath slightly unsteady, and the sight of her like that was fuel on a fire. I'd never seen her undone, even to this minor degree, and it was sexy as hell. I ran an open hand over my face and tried to ignore the boner raging in my pants.

Holy shit. My moves—or at least, this last-minute version of them—had freaking *worked*. And they'd worked on *Birdie*. Satisfaction pulled my shoulders back and tugged at the corner of my mouth. Even the tent between my legs felt like something I should be proud of.

"Yeah, Red," I said. "I wish I'd taken you up on that wager now. Must be awkward to have to admit you can't resist me."

"I'm sorry. What?" Those pretty blue eyes practically bugged out of her head as she planted her fists on her hips, and I grinned at her indignation. She pointed a finger my way. "*You*"—she poked the same fingers against her chest—"kissed *me*."

"Ah, no. That's not what happened."

Opening the back door and striding into the kitchen to serve up the dinner I'd prepared earlier that afternoon, I tried not to smirk at the sounds of her stomping after me.

Birdie Maxwell had kissed me. I'd kissed *Birdie Maxwell*. Turning so I could run my tongue over my lips, hoping I'd still taste her on me, I busied myself with the food, all too aware of her eyes burning into my back.

When dinner was all plated, and my dick had finally given up his fight for freedom, I glanced at Birdie sitting on the other side of my small kitchen island, arms folded over her chest and her expression again the picture of perfect composure. No, only almost perfect. There was some of that unravelling still evident around her eyes.

I took a bottle of white wine from the fridge and tucked it under one arm, then nodded to the basket of bread. "Grab those rolls, will you?" I asked with a grin as

I walked around her to get to the back porch, a plate in either hand.

She snatched up the rolls and followed me, saying nothing until we were both seated, then she set her napkin on her lap with a flourish and picked up her cutlery. "Let's clear this up right now, bucko," she said, stabbing the knife in my direction. "You get full marks for effort. You get an A-plus for results. Whatever you're doing, you're doing right, but let's get one thing straight. I didn't kiss you. You kissed me, and you should own it."

"Let's go to the action replay, folks," I announced to the non-existent crowd before shovelling a forkful of dinner into my mouth. It was delicious, if I did say so myself. I was on a freaking roll tonight.

"Oh, what I wouldn't give for video of the last twenty minutes," she muttered, poking at her meal. "You'd be eating your words as a side dish to… What is this?"

"Baked tahini salmon with toasted almonds and fattoush," I replied as if it were nothing special.

"Maz?" she asked hopefully.

"Who else?"

She took a cautious, curious bite, then quickly went back for more. "Oh, it's good."

A few minutes passed in silence as we ate a little and drank wine until Birdie began to glare at me from across the table.

"What now?" I asked.

"Are you really not going to admit that you kissed me?"

"No, because I didn't. Are you really not going to admit

that you kissed me?"

"No, because I didn't."

I scooped a mound of salad into my mouth so she wouldn't see my grin. "Agree to disagree then."

"No way," she retorted. "I want a rematch."

I almost choked as toasted bread stuck in my throat. I swallowed and chased it with a gulp of pinot grigio. "This isn't a poker game, Red. There are no winners or losers here. Does it matter who kissed who? Like you said, whatever I'm doing, I'm doing right—and it worked." I threw a wink her way as I offered up a silent prayer of gratitude to Dot and the dirty books hidden in my dresser drawer.

Birdie's nostrils flared a little as she reined in her temper. Her tantrums as a kid had been few and far between, but when she snapped, the results were legendary—she'd flipped the little gaming table in my old treehouse more than once. I wondered why a kiss, of all things, had set her off tonight.

"It's not about winning or losing," she said tightly. "It's about facts and truth and *reality*, and while the confidence works in your favour, I can't—"

"You like my confidence?" Birdie wanted to talk about truth? The truth was, I was digging the confidence, too.

"I do," she admitted. "However, I can't say I'm wrong when I'm not—it's just not the way I'm made—and the idea that you won't admit I'm right makes me itchy all over. So, rematch."

Hang on. It sounded like Birdie wanted to kiss me again. Why the fuck was I arguing?

"So…you want to do tonight over?" I asked, my gaze dropping to her mouth.

"Yes," she said, snatching up her wine and taking a long swallow. "I mean, no. I mean, let's call tonight a wash and start over."

"When?"

"Oh, no. I'm not falling into that trap again. No prearrangements this time. No expectations that only tip the odds in your favour. That's not how the real world works. Kisses are supposed to be spontaneous. I can't say with any certainty that your moves tonight would have had the same effect in an environment that wasn't so controlled."

I frowned as I thought about what she was saying. Huh. Maybe tonight wasn't fair play. She came over here knowing a kiss was at stake and had probably been on her guard. In that light, it seemed unlikely that what I'd picked up from a few books in a few days would be enough to seduce her so easily. There was no way I was *that* good. Maybe I did kiss her after all, and not the other way around.

Dammit.

The gentlemanly thing to do would have been to admit defeat. Concede that maybe she was right, and the kiss was my doing, which would effectively cancel out the need to go ahead with her rematch. Why did I care so much about how it happened? The kiss was a success, and for the purposes of our deal, that was all that counted. I felt fairly certain I could do it all again with Lisa on Saturday night… though maybe with less finesse.

But before I could say the words that would let Birdie off the hook, I recalled the way her mouth felt on mine, the willing touch of her tongue, and all thoughts of my date that weekend dissipated like sea mist in the sun.

"You're on," I said, sticking out my hand. "Sometime in the next forty-eight hours, when you least expect it, you're going to kiss me, Red."

She placed her palm against mine, and we shook on it. "Oh, no. You've got that backwards. If there's going to be a kiss, Romeo, *you* are going to have to kiss *me*."

12

BIRDIE

NINETEEN HOURS. THAT'S how long it had been since Isaac kissed me, not that I was watching the clock. It was just a random fact that popped into my head when I checked the time and realised I was due to meet the girls on the beach in fifteen minutes.

But now that I thought about it, I told myself again that I was right about this—Isaac had kissed *me*, not the other way around.

It might have been kinder if I'd let him think I gave in to him, and it definitely would have been better for his ego, but his ego seemed to be doing well enough that it could handle a gentle knock. Whatever worries Isaac might have had ten years ago about his skills, there was zero need for them now. The man knew what he was doing, and though I didn't like to admit it, the kiss had interfered with my faculties just enough that I went on the defensive without taking a moment to think about strategy.

He kissed *me*, and that had to be true. There was no way I'd been the one to lean in. Isaac was my friend. This arrangement was philanthropic. Flirting with him was supposed to be clinical. Strategic. Charitable, even. And last night's kiss was none of those things. It was warm. Impulsive. Self-indulgent. Bloody hell. Candles and music and dancing, and I'd gone and lost my mind. I'd behaved like a freaking cliché—and I refused to be a cliché.

That explained the rematch. I needed one more chance to prove to myself that I still held the cards in this game. I reassured myself this last challenge made the perfect test run for Isaac's date the following night, but at the thought of him with *Lisa*, that pesky coil of protectiveness pulled tight in my gut again. What if things went badly on his date?

What if they went well?

Contemplating the answer to either question made me tense. As his love coach, I was obligated to root for outcome number two: things going well. As his friend, I should have wanted the same thing, but a little voice I didn't much like kept yammering at me about what it might mean for me if things fell over. Would Isaac need more practice if he bombed out on his date? And why did the idea of that set off tingly explosions across every inch of my body?

I'd never wish for Isaac to fail, but I couldn't help fantasising about what would happen if he did.

Ugh. I hated feeling like a shitty friend, so I forced myself to focus instead on what Isaac's next move on me might be. What would he do—and when?

I didn't know if it was genius thinking or plain stupid to take away the element of control, mostly because when I recalled the way my mouth had run on ahead of my head last night—I'd fucking *babbled*—I also had to think about why I'd been so unhinged.

I collected a towel and a wide-brimmed hat before letting myself out the front door and setting off on foot in the direction of the ocean. The air was warm and salty, and breathing deeply helped me evaluate the situation with a clearer head. By the time my toes hit the sand, I had a satisfactory explanation for the predicament I'd put myself in.

Isaac was hot. I was attracted to him. Given the hard length in his pants the night before—and Jesus, how that memory made my nipples ache—it was safe to assume he was attracted to me, too. This whole thing between us was simple biology, and you couldn't argue with science any more than you could argue with mathematics.

The reason for my behaviour last night was obvious, and though I felt stupid that it hadn't occurred to me earlier, my relief was palpable. Hormones, people! This buzzy, fevered tension under my skin was all about sex, and I was completely comfortable with sex. Sex, I could handle. Sex, I enjoyed. Sex, I could solve with a generous glass of wine and a date night with Mr Big Boy.

I slipped off my slides and scooped them up, then started the short trek across the sand to where Abbie stood, waving me over with big, enthusiastic sweeps of her bronzed arms. Emily, Jess, and another woman I didn't recognise sat around Abbie's feet on towels spread out under a wide, navy-striped canvas canopy.

"You made it!" Abbie gave me a tight squeeze, leaving the faint scent of coconut and sunscreen lingering on my skin. "There's a spot for you here," she said, pointing at an empty patch of sand between the other women, "and it's a good one. We've got a clear view of the water, and believe me, you'll be thanking me profusely in about twenty minutes."

I shook out my towel and took a seat, folding my legs underneath me. "Hi," I said to the dark-haired girl I didn't know. "I'm Birdie."

"Sorry! I forgot you two don't know each other yet." Abbie settled onto the last available towel and reached into the large blue cooler beside it. "Tash, this is Birdie. Birdie, this is Tash. Tash married Luca Rossetti a couple of months ago."

Ah, so this was the infamous Natasha. Isaac had filled me in on the recent drama between Luca and his new wife, Tash, and his ex-girlfriend Jess, who was now dating his best friend, Logan. It was all very television soap opera-ish, albeit with a happy ending.

"Nice to meet you, Tash."

Tash put down her bag of crackers, dusted the crumbs from her palms, and took the hand I offered. "Nice to meet you, too. I've heard a lot about you."

"Only some of it bad," Abbie promised, handing me a bottle of water dripping with the icy water from the cooler.

"I promise I'll get over the Christmas money one day, but in the meantime, you can't blame a girl for venting. It's unhealthy to keep these things bottled up."

"Vent away," I said, cracking the lid on the water and taking a sip before I squinted down the length of the beach. The swell was reasonable, the breaking waves were loud and foamy, and the sand was dotted with umbrellas and sunshades—the people underneath set up for an extended stay with low chairs, food, and drinks. "Explain again what I'm doing here and why real estate on the beach is at such a premium today?"

Emily's shoulders vibrated with an excited shimmy. "The boys are competing in a friendly today."

"Friendly?" I echoed, leaning back on my elbows and stretching out my legs to wiggle my toes in the sun. "For the surf rowing competition?"

Jess hummed. "Once the date was set for the main race, the club at Scarborough Cove challenged our Valentine Bay crew to a demonstration event. But we all know what this really is."

"They're sizing us up," Tash confirmed.

The natural competitor in me was instantly invested, but I recalled what Isaac had said on the street with Dawn a couple of days earlier. Our side was short on practice. "Are we worried? Isaac mentioned they haven't been doing this for very long, and they're a little out of shape."

All four of my companions exchanged knowing looks over small, secretive smiles. "We're not worried." Abbie patted my arm, then jerked her head towards the ocean. "Check it out."

A little way down the beach, where a corridor of sand had been left free between the Valentine Bay spectators and those who had travelled down from Scarborough Cove, two surf rowing crews carried their bulky surf boats closer to the water's edge.

Each long, wide watercraft was held up on both sides by the five-man teams, and they moved like it weighed next to nothing, their footsteps confident and quick on the sand. Still, their exposed shoulders, backs, and biceps showed the strain of the load, muscles slick with sunscreen and sweat rippling and glistening in the sun.

All around us, people—mostly women—sat up straighter, and heads popped up from the crowd in a way that reminded me of a meerkat documentary. Shamefully, I was one of them.

Our boys were beautiful. All five of them ripped, tanned gods of sun and surf, with lines and ridges of solid, well-defined muscle over every inch of their bare upper bodies. I recognised Isaac right away; he had the broadest shoulders, the darkest hair and was the only one with not only a beard but a light covering of hair across his hard, wide chest.

The sun suddenly grew hotter, even under our canopy, and I tugged at the neck of my sundress to get a little air moving across my skin. I watched the boys mill around in preparation for the race, and when I was confident that I'd matched the other faces with my memories of the kids I'd known as a teenager, I turned to the girls for confirmation.

"Let me guess," I said, pointing at each of the guys in turn. "The Italian stallion there is Luca, correct?"

Tash nodded distractedly, unable to tear her hungry gaze away from her husband. I couldn't blame her. The guy looked plucked from a European catwalk, and at the same time, totally at home on this sunny Australian beach.

"The blond at the front has to be Josh," I continued, noting that the size of his arms was impressive enough to give Isaac a run for his money. "Am I right, Em?"

"Huh?" she replied, her chin turning my way, but her eyes glued to her guy. "Oh, yeah. The blond. Josh. Right."

"The darker blond with the sexy scruff and serious ink has to be Logan," I observed.

"That's my man," Jess confirmed, watching the show while biting her lip.

"So, Mr Dimples on the right there must be—"

"Will." Abbie rolled her eyes, but her attention returned immediately to the men getting ready to enter the water. "Yes, he's gorgeous, but he knows it. No need to belabour the point."

I turned my head so she wouldn't notice my grin. "Oh, your babies are going to be so beautiful, Abs."

"My… My what?" I watched her from the corner of my eye as her delayed reaction finally landed, and she twisted around to scowl at me. "Not. Funny. Maxwell."

"Come on. It was a little funny."

"Shh!" Jess interrupted, flapping her hand at us.

"They're about to start," Emily added, sitting up on her heels.

"Oh, this is the best part," Tash squeaked, eyes wide as she stuffed another cracker in her mouth as though it were popcorn. Even Abbie dropped the glower and returned her attention to the guys.

"What's the best part?" I strained my neck to get a better view, then finally got to my knees for a clear shot. "What happens now?"

Nobody answered me, but nobody needed to.

Around the boat, the boys peeled off their board shorts. Isaac's pants dropped to his ankles, then he kicked them to the side before standing tall in a tight, black speedo that hugged his arse and left nothing to the imagination. *Nothing.* My fingers involuntarily twitched with the desire to touch, and my mouth was suddenly as dry as the sand beneath my feet.

The five men arranged themselves around the boat and pushed it into the surf. As smaller waves lapped over their ankles and up the sides of the craft, each and every one of them wedged their swimmers between their bum cheeks and splashed ocean water onto the exposed pale, bare skin.

"What on Earth…?" I mumbled as my stomach performed a somersault. Oh, God, his arse was perfect. Round and muscular and smooth and… Oh, God. *Perfect.*

"It's for grip," Abbie muttered without looking my way. "Stops them slipping inside the boat."

Tash giggled. "Luca's the sweep, so he could wear shorts if he wanted to, but we made a deal, and he promised to flash me whenever I'm around to watch."

"The way I hear it, you're on the beach for almost every training session," Emily said with a chuckle, and Tash threw her a wink.

Both teams guided their boats into the water, fighting against the rough push of the waves. When they'd reached a certain depth, they waited for the signal to start, then everyone but the sweeps jumped inside, settling themselves quickly with an oar in both hands.

At this distance, I could just make out the power of each pull against the water, the strength in every arm on that boat as the ocean crashed against it. A few more metres, and Luca, as well as his counterpart on the Scarborough Cove crew, leaped into the stern, and the boys began to row.

Within moments, I was peripherally aware that everyone on the beach—me included—was on their feet, watching and cheering as the crews beat their oars against the breaking waves.

The boats bounced over and through every crest of the water, each swell drenching the crews as it attempted to throw them back towards the shore. The oarsmen rowed, chests straining as the waves rolled higher and higher, smashing their boats roughly into the face of the heaving water until, finally, they rode up a wave so steep the boat almost pitched over. I held my breath as they violently sailed over the top and finally moved past the breakers to cleaner water in the back.

Coming up to their gate cans, Scarborough Cove looked slightly in the lead, and when they spun their craft around the buoy first, I screamed like a maniac, waving my arms and cheering our team forwards. Beside me, Abbie, Jess, Emily, and Tash did the same. The Valentine Bay boys rounded the gate can, and by the time they were righted and rowing again, there were less than two boat lengths between crews.

The oars on our boat powered rhythmically through the ocean, the tension showing in the undulations of muscles rolling across the boys' backs and shoulders as we waited for the water to build behind them. Within seconds, a wave picked them up, and the boys stilled their oars, riding the momentum and gaining on Scarborough Cove, who were unlucky enough to be positioned on the soft edge of the crest. Our boat slid down the face of the wave like magic, gaining half a length on the competition. When the push slowed, the boys picked up their oars and continued their slog to shore.

Both crews hit the whitewater at the same time, but Scarborough Cove collected the slingshot and were practically thrown to the shallows. Our boys put their last reserves of grit and strength into paddling, and they slid up onto the sand seconds shy of first place.

"Oh! We lost." Emily frowned a little as she scooped up a towel. "Josh was so tense about this, and I know he'll be disappointed. I'm going to check on him."

"Logan was the same," Jess said, grabbing an extra bottle of water. "I'll come with you."

"Me, too," Tash agreed, tucking her crackers into the pocket of her loose dress.

"We may as well join," Abbie said with a put-upon sigh. "Coming, Birdie?"

I glanced over to where the guys were jumping out of their boat, dragging it onto dry sand with bums flashing and heads hung low. Losing was the worst. I knew that better than anyone.

I collected a bottle of water for Isaac. "Yes. Let's go."

By the time we reached the boat, we weren't the only ones trying to console the guys. Emily wound her way through the small crowd and tucked herself under Josh's wet arm as he shook hands with an older man who looked so much like him that even if I hadn't remembered him from a decade earlier, it could only be Josh's father, Jack. Next to Jack was Maryanne Diaz, an attractive, dark-haired woman who everyone called Maz and the Bay's answer to Ina Garten.

A few steps away, Jess ran a hand over Logan's sopping hair, and Tash wrapped her arms around Luca's waist as the man conversed with enough dark-haired, olive-skinned relatives that I had to assume his entire extended family had come down to watch the race.

Abbie and Will leaned side by side on the boat as he gratefully took the bottle of water she offered him, and I threaded my way towards Isaac.

He had his open hands over his face as he sloughed sand and sea from his skin and beard, and by the time he dropped his arms, I was waiting in front of him with a cold beverage held up between us. His eyes widened at the sight of me.

"You did well," I said. "It was close."

Isaac slowly took the water bottle from me, his brows drawn in a little. "I didn't know you were going to be here."

"Abbie invited me. Is that a problem?"

"What? No, I just… Sorry. I didn't mean I don't *want* you here. I just wasn't sure how today was going to go, and I'd much rather you watch us win, not lose."

He cracked the cap on the water and took a long draw while I watched, hypnotised by the sight of sweat and saltwater rolling over his neck as his throat bobbed with his swallows. My stomach did that inconvenient clench and spin number it was getting so good at, twirling its way south in a way that set off a throb between my legs.

"Next time," I mumbled.

"Oh, Isaac! Honey!" An older woman with short dark hair and a flowing white caftan threw herself at Isaac, wrapping her arms around his shoulders as he folded his much larger arms around her middle. "I thought you had it there. I really did. You'll get them next time."

"There's always a chance." Isaac cleared his throat and tugged on his ear as the woman dropped her embrace. "Mum, you remember Birdie Maxwell, don't you? She used to—"

Isaac's mother spun, and as soon as the recognition lit in her deep brown eyes, she enveloped me in an embrace no less enthusiastic than the one she'd given her son. I returned it with genuine warmth and not a small pang of nostalgia. I'd spent a lot of time as a kid wishing Kristin Greene could be my mother.

She straightened and held me with both hands at arm's length. "Birdie, sweetheart. It's so good to see you! Oh, you haven't changed a bit. What are you doing in town?"

"Hey, Kris. It's good to see you too. I'm only here for a couple of weeks while I sort out some family business."

On the topic of family business—and, more specifically, mothers—I spared a brief thought for Cora, who was due to arrive in the Bay within the next day or two. I hadn't heard from her to cancel or confirm, and I had no idea what that meant, but I did know better than to get my hopes up and assume she'd make good on her word. I wouldn't believe she was really coming to the Bay until I saw her on the doorstep with my very own eyes.

"Are you staying at your old house?" Kris asked, and at my nod, she narrowed her eyes at Isaac. "Right next door! And you never said anything."

"I was going to," Isaac muttered, thumbing his ear again.

"It seems like only yesterday you were the fifth little face around my dinner table. I've missed those sweet freckles. Oh! We're having a birthday party at the house tomorrow for Meghan's little boy. He's turning four, and it's very casual. Backyard barbecue. Cake. A few sneaky cocktails. Please join us."

"How is Meghan? And Sarah? And Jasmine?" I asked, recalling the faces of all three of Isaac's older sisters, as well as the way I used to daydream about having siblings of my own exactly like them.

"They're fantastic, and they'll all be there tomorrow. They'd be thrilled to see you. Please say you can make it."

The yes was halfway out of my mouth when I glanced at Isaac hovering over his mother's shoulder. He looked panicked, and it only took a split second to work out why. The clock was ticking. He had a little more than twenty-four hours to seduce me into another kiss, and if a good number of those hours were spent at a preschooler's birthday party in his parents' backyard, it reduced his chances of convincing me to give in.

Reflexively, my eyes dropped to Isaac's mouth, and I took a careful breath in through my nose to soothe the little skip in my chest. I *wanted* to kiss him. I wanted him to touch me like he had the night before. I wanted to feel his growl of desire as it reverberated in his chest and shiver at the touch of his fingertips on my skin. I wanted his mouth on mine so freaking badly.

A kids' party was exactly the thing to help keep my head on straight.

Cora came to mind again, but I dismissed the thought before it made me hope. My mother had a key to the house. She could let herself in. Let her wait for me for a change.

I grinned at Isaac, who looked properly distraught, and accepted Kris's invitation.

Sorry to make things so hard on you, Romeo, but this girl's got a lot to lose, and she's going to keep her cards close to her chest.

13

ISAAC

THERE WAS NO way this kiss was going to happen. The party had lasted longer than I expected, the day was slipping away, and I was almost positive Birdie was avoiding me. We'd barely said hello before she took off around the yard, making conversation with anyone who wasn't me.

And that felt a little like cheating.

I'd thought a lot about how to win Birdie's rematch, and I was pleased with the plan I'd finally come up with. Unfortunately, it meant I couldn't be too hard on Birdie for stacking the odds in her favour because I'd intended to do the same.

I'd known the morning would be a wash because Birdie liked to sleep in, plus I'd promised to help my sister set up for Mason's birthday party. The reunion started at eight o'clock that night, but I was due in the city an hour before—the time I'd agreed to meet Lisa for a drink at the hotel bar. In between morning and night, I'd planned to spend a couple of hours with my family before heading home, cleaning up, and knocking on Birdie's door with two shirts in my hand and none on my back and a plea to help me choose between them. That was where the cheating part came in. I'd noticed the way Birdie stared at my chest after the surf boat rowing race, and if half a dozen romance novels had taught me anything, it was that I didn't need to be shy about the fact I looked the way I did. The opposite, in fact. I could use it to my advantage.

But now, all my careful plotting was shot to shit because Birdie was sitting on a lawn chair in a circle with all my sisters, an Aperol spritz held aloft in one hand, hooting with laughter as they exchanged stories about God knew what. Work. Kids. Men. Sex. Me?

I kept an eye on them through the kitchen window as I scrubbed at a pile of ceramic platters, noticing the moment Birdie lifted her head and looked my way. Too casual to be genuine, she examined the watch on her wrist, then waved at me, the grin on her face no less heart-stopping because it was smug.

Damn. I couldn't believe I wasn't going to kiss her today, and if I didn't kiss her today, I'd never kiss her again. Our love coaching agreement expired the second my date with Lisa began. This was my last chance to have the taste of Birdie on my tongue, and I was going to miss it.

It shouldn't have bothered me. I should have been focussed solely on setting eyes on Lisa in a few hours, but that part of my night barely registered. All I felt was disappointment.

"Oh, Isaac. I'm glad I found you." Mum bustled through the swinging back door and set a stack of dirty glasses next to the sink. There was silver glitter in her hair, damp black and yellow streamers draped around her shoulders, and a joyful flush to her cheeks. "We need more ice, as well as candles for the cake. Can you believe I forgot the birthday candles? What a nightmare because the kids are so hopped up on sugar that we're going to need to wrap things up sooner rather than later."

"The party's already gone longer than it was supposed to," I muttered, dutifully transferring the sticky glassware to the suds in the sink.

A high-pitched squeal floated in through the open door, followed by the splash of someone—one of my nine nieces or nephews, most likely—being hurled into the pool.

"I know, but everyone's having such a good time. Who would have thought we'd get so lucky with the weather?" Mum leaned a hip against the kitchen top, and soapy water soaked straight through her neon yellow caftan. She didn't seem to notice. "Darling, would you mind running out to get what we need?"

I glanced up at the clock on the wall. "Any chance Dad could slip out instead?"

"He's having too much fun in the pool with the kids, and I don't want to be a party pooper. Come on, sweetheart. It won't take long, then you'll get back, we'll cut the cake, and you can leave. I know you have that reunion to get to."

I grimaced as I tallied up the time I had left. Barely an hour to run Mum's errands, then go home to shower and dress before I took off for Sydney. With a resigned sigh, I said goodbye to any lingering hope that I might still find a way to kiss Birdie.

"Yeah, sure. No problem." I dried my hands on a towel before stuffing my wallet and phone in the back pockets of my shorts. "But I'm going to have to run as soon as I get back. Everyone will be singing to Mason and serving the cake. Nobody will notice if I sneak away."

At that moment, the birthday boy himself came barrelling through the back door, wearing Batman swimmers and a hooded towel designed to replicate Batman's black cape, complete with little ears on top. "Uncle Isaac!" he shouted. "Have you seen my birthday cake? Does it look like the Bammobile? I asked for a Bammobile."

I lifted the little guy up into my arms and settled him on my hip. "You know what? I haven't seen your cake, but I did notice an enormous white box from the bakery hidden in Grandma's fridge. Do you want to peek inside it? Maybe we'll find your birthday cake."

I set a hand on the fridge door, but Mum pressed her palm against it. "Don't you dare go snooping in my fridge, you two. The cake is meant to be a surprise, remember?" Then she leaned in and whispered in Mason's ear. "I've seen it, Batman, and it looked like a Batmobile to me."

"Yay!" Mason squirmed in my arms, and I set him on the floor. "Will you stand next to me when I blow out the candles, Uncle Isaac? It's a dangerous job, so I think I'll make you my Robin in case something goes wrong."

My glance darted to the clock again, then back to the bright green eyes beaming at me from Mason's small, excited face. "Absolutely, Batman," I promised, giving him a high five. "I won't let you down."

"Woohoo!" he shrieked before bolting to the backyard.

I rubbed the back of my neck as Mum patted my arm. "There's still plenty of time before you need to leave. Why don't you pick up your clothes for the reunion on your way back here with the ice and candles? We'll cut the cake straightaway, then you can shower upstairs and go straight to the reunion."

I picked up my keys and planted a quick kiss on her cheek. "Good idea. I'll see you soon."

Half an hour later, I was wiping buttercream out of my eyes and beard while the party hooted with laughter. Apparently, Batman shared a body with the Joker because once all the singing and cake-cutting was finished and I was getting ready to dig into a weird-looking lump of black icing-covered chocolate cake, I received a tiny fist of soft, sugary Batmobile to the face.

"Oh, no. Isaac, I'm so sorry!" Meghan rushed around the table with a handful of paper napkins and began wiping my cheeks, but she couldn't contain her laughter. "Mason has been watching our wedding video on repeat for weeks. He loves the part with the cake."

Meghan's wife, Hannah, scooped Mason up into her arms and arranged his legs around her heavily pregnant stomach. "I got a pile of mashed potato to the nose three nights ago, so I know how you feel."

"Were there two dozen people standing around your dining table laughing at the time?" I asked, pretending to scowl at Mason. He ducked his head into the crook of Hannah's neck, and I tickled his tummy until he squealed with giggles. "Funny guy, aren't you, Batman?"

"Ah, no," Hannah said with an apologetic smile. "The mashed potato was a more exclusive event."

"Thought so." I reached out and picked up a chunk of cake from the closest plate. "Hey, Mason? What's that on your head?"

The little boy lifted his chin just as I squashed the cake into his mop of dark, shiny hair, and he screamed with laughter.

"Oh, Isaac!" Meghan admonished, abandoning the mess on my face and starting on Mason. "Really?"

"He started it," I replied with a grin. "I'm going upstairs to get cleaned up. Use the downstairs bathroom for Mason, okay?"

Meghan waved me away, and I navigated my way around the people milling between me and the house. Among them was Birdie, who watched me with a tilt to her head and an unreadable look in her eyes. As I passed her, I swiped a finger through the slice of cake she held on a plate and transferred the inky buttercream to the tip of her nose.

That was it. Game over. Like it or not, tomorrow would be a new day, and Birdie's lips would no longer be mine for the taking.

Lisa, I reminded myself. *Think of Lisa*.

I ran inside and took the stairs two at a time, pulling my sticky T-shirt over my head as I moved. I'd hung my clothes for the party on the back of my old bedroom door, so I detoured to get them and a clean towel on the way to the main bathroom, then thought better of it and headed to my parents' ensuite. If the downstairs bathroom was occupied with Meghan and Hannah trying to get Mason all cleaned up, the guests would need to use the upstairs main bathroom instead.

Stripping off and folding my clothes on the end of the bed, I turned on the shower and quickly rinsed off. Soaping up and taking a little extra care with my beard to make sure I wasn't walking around with cake on my face all night, I stepped out into the steamy bathroom and dried myself, rubbing the towel over my torso and legs, then throwing it over my head to dry my hair.

The entire time, I did my best to daydream about Lisa, to conjure some sort of excitement and enthusiasm for what tonight might mean for us, but all I could think about was Birdie and the opportunity I'd missed to kiss her.

"Holy fu—"

I yanked the towel off my head and used it to cover my junk, then goggled at Birdie standing in the bathroom doorway. Truth be told, she looked just as shocked as I was, her round blue eyes stuck on my crotch.

"Um, can I help you?" I asked, my heart flying.

She dragged her eyes away from my dick, and her gaze drifted north to my face. A pretty shade of pink bloomed on the roses of her cheeks, and her lashes fluttered with rapid blinks. "Your mum told me to use her bathroom. There's a line for the one downstairs, and we thought you were in the main bath."

I nodded, dazed, as my chest heaved and a little voice in my head shouted that this situation, ripped from the pages of a good romance novel, was fate giving me one last shot at that kiss.

But I wasn't a character in a fucking book. I couldn't just drop my towel and show her my hard-on, which was the first idea that came to mind. Yet I had to find out if, given the chance, Birdie would kiss me. I had three seconds to improvise.

"No, I'm here," I replied, trying to be cool as I shifted the towel and wrapped it around my waist in a way that gave her another look at the goods. Just as I'd hoped, her focus fell below my waist as if drawn by gravity.

"Well, Romeo," she said, clearing her throat. "This is certainly an unconventional way to get a girl to kiss you." Her glance rose and dropped below my hips again just as her teeth caught on her bottom lip.

"I didn't plan this," I said, need making my voice rougher than I'd intended, "but by the look on your face, maybe I should have."

I took a slow step towards her, then another, and when she took a step back, I followed until her shoulders hit the frame of the open bathroom door. Giving her a moment to slip away if that's what she wanted to do—and she didn't; she stayed exactly like that, watching me and running her tongue over her lips as the rise and fall of her chest grew faster and deeper—I inched closer still, and when I was close enough that her tits were pressed up against me, I rolled my hips against her, letting her feel what she did to me. My reward was a stifled whimper.

I waited until she met my eyes, then ran a finger over the outline of her plump mouth.

"Do you want to kiss me, Red?" I murmured.

She parted her lips, her eyes dropping to my mouth, but she didn't answer.

"Do you want *me* to kiss *you*?" I whispered because, at that moment, I didn't care about the rematch, about winning or losing, or about who was right and who was wrong. All I cared about was kissing her before the chance was lost to me forever.

And fuck, was today my lucky day because as Birdie's lids grew heavy, she nodded.

Groaning, I curled my hands around her head, falling hungrily on her mouth. This kiss was nothing like our first, which had been careful and tender and sweet. This one was all heat and need and desperation, and when she opened her mouth, I plundered her with my tongue, stroking and savouring the taste of sugar and wine.

Her fingernails dug into my arms and I pressed my hips harder against her, this time pressing my throbbing cock into the soft flesh of her stomach. Her hands dropped to the towel on my hips, and she latched onto the fabric as if sheer will alone was all that kept her from tearing it off.

Oh, Jesus. I wanted it gone. I wanted her hands on my dick so fucking much. Her hands and her mouth and her...

I dragged my lips away from her and took a step back, running one hand down my face and gripping the towel with the other to be sure it didn't fall. Birdie was plastered against the bathroom wall, breathing heavily, staring through the mosaic-tiled bathroom floor.

"Holy shit," she breathed. "That was... I wasn't prepared for that."

"Me neither."

"But it was good. It was great. It was... You know. Well done."

I frowned as a flash of irritation burned me up. Birdie could pretend all she wanted, but what we'd just done wasn't because of a fucking wager, and she'd been into it as much as I had been. There was no way that kiss was anything but real.

"So, good luck on your date," she said, pushing away from the doorframe and patting my bicep as though she was about to send me out of a locker room and onto a playing field. She wouldn't meet my eyes. "Not that you'll need it. Can't wait to hear how it goes."

And before I could reply, she was out the door. Just... gone.

I stood staring through the open door for a good few minutes before I dressed in a stupor, snuck out of the house without telling anyone I was leaving, and drove the almost two hours to Sydney without recalling a single minute of the journey. When I arrived at the hotel car park, I pulled into a space and shut off the engine, then sat gazing into nothing until five minutes before seven.

I didn't want to go in. *I didn't want to go in.* And that told me everything I needed to know.

I wasn't the type of man who'd ever leave a woman waiting for me at a bar, so I stepped out of the car, straightened my jacket, and resolved to have one drink with Lisa before I excused myself. And all those tricks I had up my sleeve? I didn't need any of them. Not tonight, anyway.

Half an hour and one soda water later, I was back on the freeway heading north.

I didn't want to be with Lisa. She'd been perched on a stool and sipping a martini when I walked in, legs flashing and eyes flirting, but the entire time all I'd wanted was to be somewhere else. I had no impulse to kiss her, and I was never going to spend the night pretending I wasn't thinking about someone else.

As a kid, I thought I'd loved Birdie, and I could no longer deny there was something still there. I didn't want to deny it. There was only one woman I wanted to kiss—tonight, tomorrow, and maybe always—and I was going to make damn sure she knew it.

14

ISAAC

THE DRIVE HOME took close to ninety minutes, so by the time I pulled into my driveway and saw the lights on next door, I'd talked myself out of a passionate declaration of love. Birdie was attracted to me—I was more certain of that than anything else—but what if that's all this was to her? A physical connection. The novelty of "love coaching." A game.

The more I thought about it, the more certain I became that Birdie would not be receptive to grand romantic gestures or suggestions of commitment. She'd baulked at candles, music, and a homemade meal, for Christ's sake. She'd turned green at the idea of a year's membership at Abbie's yoga studio. She'd never lived in any place long enough to make it her home. God only knew what an honest confession of affection would do to the woman.

If all my extra reading had taught me anything, it was that Birdie wasn't ready for that. Not yet.

By the next morning, I'd twisted myself into and out of so many circles that I did the only thing I could think to do. I stowed my romance novels in a discrete black gym bag and made my way over to the library.

"So, how did it go?"

Dot asked the question, but every member of the VBFYRRRBC leaned towards me, a circle of beady-eyed senior citizens literally on the edges of their seats. I dropped my head and rubbed the back of my neck before looking up again warily.

"Not according to plan."

A wave of groans sounded around the room.

"Didn't you read the books?" Burt demanded with a scowl. The man looked affronted, of all things, as if my answer was a personal insult.

"We all know you've been practicing, so that can't be your problem," Agatha purred before she laughed at my bafflement. "Dawn told everyone about her conversation with you and Birdie on the street. She led me to believe that girl was all over you."

"Of course she did," I muttered, refusing to acknowledge the way everyone nodded their agreement as I raised my voice to an audible level. "Yes, I read the books—thanks for your concern, Burt—and yes, I practiced. A lot. That's why I'm in this predicament."

I was hit with a wave of questions, too many at once to pick out a single one to answer, but Dot came to my rescue, hushing everyone with her hands flapping as she shot the loudest offenders stern looks.

When silence fell, she turned to me with a sympathetic smile. "Do you want to tell us what happened?"

Playing with the neon-pink sash looped around my chest, I nodded. "Actually, I do because I could use your advice. I, uh, didn't go to the reunion last night. I drove all the way to the city, had a single *platonic* drink with Lisa, then got back in my car and drove straight back home again."

A few people exchanged puzzled glances, but Dot's eyes narrowed as she studied me. "And you did this because…?"

I drew in a deep breath. "I'm attracted to someone else."

Dot rolled her lips, giving me the impression that she was trying not to laugh. "Someone like Birdie Maxwell?"

I shifted my head so I could squint at her from the corner of my eye. "You don't seem surprised."

"Well, I am a little." Dot clasped her hands together and set them on her knees, then raised an eyebrow at me. "I rather suspected you had feelings for the girl, above and beyond any physical attraction."

"I— You suspected *what*?" How could anyone have known I had feelings for Birdie, let alone Dorothy March? I'd only figured it out for myself twelve hours ago.

Dot chuckled. "I've been doing this a lot longer than you have, Sergeant, and I've been married six times. I know things."

"Right. Well, since the cat's well and truly out of the bag"—a quick glance around the circle told me nobody was surprised at this little plot twist—"maybe you can tell me what the hell I do now."

"Language, Mr Greene," Lorraine said to my right, giving me her best disapproving-history-teacher stare.

"Sorry, Mrs Langley," I mumbled.

"I don't see what the issue is." Romana shifted, hitching at her sash when it caught on the corner of her chair. "This is a classic friends-to-lovers situation. You've fallen for the girl next door. Tale as old as time."

"That's right," Irena agreed. "And law enforcement still applies."

Agatha winked at me. "Birdie's a professional poker player, isn't she, Sergeant? Perhaps we need to consider brought-together-by-a-bet?"

Dot watched the conversation with shrewd eyes. "I think there's more to this than we know," she declared. "Isaac, if you want our advice, we're going to need all the details. So, go on. Out with it."

"You're right. There's more." I rubbed my palms over the tops of my thighs. "I…like…Birdie, and while I'm certain there's chemistry between us, I wonder if that's all it is for her. There's every chance she doesn't feel for me what I feel for her, not to mention that she doesn't live in the Bay. She was only ever doing me a favour by stepping in as a sort of short-term love coach, and it was all supposed to be over last night. But then…the kiss happened." The memory of her mouth on mine burned across my lips. "We're friends who thought we could play with matches and accidentally started a fire."

"A fire, you say?" Agatha set her elbows on her knees and leaned over, flashing a wide expanse of cleavage—deliberately, I thought, if the curve on her lips was anything to go by. "Now you have our attention."

I threw up my hands and dropped my head back. "Yes, a fire caused by a freaking fantastic kiss, and now I don't know what the hell to do." I straightened, ignoring the reproachful look coming at me from Mrs Langley. "The woman is completely against commitment—she won't even sign up for a gym membership—and she's leaving town in a month, if not sooner. What could I possibly expect from her?"

"Are we talking a friends-with-benefits type of scenario?" Romana wanted to know, pulling out her e-reader as she waited for my answer.

The idea made me feel a little nauseated. "I don't know. I don't think so. Wouldn't that make Birdie feel cheap?"

"Oh, I don't know about that," Dot replied, "but it would be dishonest, don't you think? Friends with benefits implies the absence of certain emotions."

"Yeah, that's how it feels. Dishonest. At first, I was going to tell her the truth, you know? Just explain to her how I feel. Admit that I bailed on my date and all the reasons why. Miscommunication and lies are always what screw things up for the characters in these books, so the lesson has to be to always tell it like it is, right?"

Burt looked at me askance. "Sounds stupid, if you ask me."

"I know, Burt. That's madness, and I can't do it, right? It *would* be plain stupid—too much, too soon, and it'd only make Birdie run a mile in the opposite direction. But what am I even saying? She doesn't live here. She doesn't live anywhere, and she doesn't want to. I'm falling for a woman who won't commit to so much as a library card, let alone a relationship, and I don't think I can stay away from her. Even if Birdie and I only have another week together, I want to spend every minute of that time with her making memories neither one of us will forget. If I do this any other way, I'll live to regret it. I know I will."

A hush settled over the room.

"Do you think you might be able to convince her to stay?" Bill asked quietly, but in the silence, almost everyone heard the question.

Fuck, I hope so, I thought, but that was a dream I wanted to keep to myself for now, so what I said was, "I suppose you never know."

Bill nodded thoughtfully.

"But Isaac," Dot said, compassion in her smile. "Things might not work out the way you want them to. Are you willing to risk the chance of a broken heart at the end of this?"

I cleared my throat and nodded slowly. "Yeah. I think I am."

"Well, then." Dot nodded once, then rolled her shoulders back, set her glasses on her nose, and gestured at the group. "Come on. Pull out your e-readers. Let's start researching. We need friends-to-lovers, neighbours-to-lovers, and law enforcement to start."

"Opposites attract?" Burt suggested.

"Friends with benefits," Irena added.

"Dating coach," I offered, garnering proud looks from the club. I rolled my eyes, more at myself than anything else. I don't know why it felt so good to be embraced by this group, but it did, and my budding plan to pursue Birdie for real felt a little more thrilling and a lot less terrifying.

"And brought together by a bet. You were right, Mrs Braverman. Well played."

If I'd been aware of the days passing too quickly while Birdie and I were engaged in our temporary teacher-student arrangement, I was a million times more conscious of the fact that now that our deal was done, she could disappear at any moment. The only thing keeping her in the Bay was the unfinished family business we never spoke about, which made every minute with her living in the house next door too precious to take for granted. So, while I would have preferred to take another few hours to prepare myself for what I was about to do—including re-read a couple of particular scenes I'd marked up in my books—I couldn't bring myself to delay it longer than it took me to escape the book club meeting. I excused myself after forty-five minutes with another half a dozen novels under my arm, plus Dot's shrill admonishment to invest in an e-reader ringing in my ears.

On the drive home, I detoured past Tony's Place to pick up Birdie's favourite coffee and breakfast—no doubt she'd been up all night and forgotten to eat again—and after pulling into my driveway and parking the car, I went straight from the driver's seat to her front door, knocking before nerves got the better of me.

I waited impatiently, checking my watch again for the time. Almost midday. She had to be awake by now, right? I lifted my fist to knock again but then heard the quiet sounds of movement inside.

The heavy timber door opened, and Birdie glared at me through the closed screen. She looked like she'd just rolled out of bed, which was probably exactly what she'd done—her vibrant copper hair was loose and wavy around her shoulders, her face was folded into a murderous frown, and she'd teamed her thin silk robe with a pair of mismatched fuzzy socks.

Was it possible for a woman to be this cute and this sexy at the same time? Yes. The answer was a solid yes.

"Can I help you?" she grumbled, eyes darting to the coffee in my hand and away again.

"I didn't think you'd still be asleep at noon," I replied, proffering the takeaway cup. "But I brought the good stuff."

She jerked her chin. "What's in the bag?"

"Tony's double-stacked BLT." I waved it in front of her face. "You know you want it."

She deliberated for a moment before huffing, pushing open the screen door, and snatching at the coffee. "This better be good. I pulled an all-nighter playing an online tournament. Don't let my open eyes fool you. I'm still asleep here."

"Did you remember to have dinner?"

She took a long sip of coffee. "This is good. Thank you. Um… Dinner… Dinner… I'm almost certain I ate a bag of pretzels. Might have been dip involved."

"Did you at least win?"

She covered her mouth with one hand as she yawned. "You bet."

I handed over her breakfast, and Birdie's stomach rumbled as I followed her into the living room. She set the coffee on the table, fell onto the sofa, and took a bite out of her sandwich. I waited as she grumpily made herself comfortable, increasingly amused by her bad humour. Nerves swirled in my stomach, but I was oddly relaxed now that we were in the same room again. As long as Birdie was within arm's reach, she was still a possibility. *We* were still a possibility.

After another pull on her coffee cup and two more bites of her breakfast, she rolled her head along the back of the sofa and looked at me with hooded eyes. "Okay, I'm a little more human now."

"Glad to hear it."

"So," she began, inspecting her food like it was the most enthralling thing about our conversation. "How'd it go last night?"

I tugged on my ear and met her curious eyes. *Just say it fast, like ripping off a Band-Aid.* "It didn't."

Suddenly, the sandwich wasn't so interesting, and Birdie jerked upright. "What do you mean, *it didn't*? What happened? What went wrong? Whatever it was, it was her fault and not yours. We've been practicing for a week, and you've come so far. You're good, Romeo. Like, really good." Birdie snapped her mouth closed and slouched back against the sofa, chomping violently at her sandwich. "I don't like to lose," she said between chewing. "You know that."

I watched her with curiosity and a small sense of gratification. It counteracted some of my anxiety. She was unravelling again like she had the night on my porch.

I could reach those buttons she usually kept under lock and key. *Me*. And fuck, I loved this side of Birdie—the side without so many defences.

"I went in, had one drink, and came home," I explained, regaining some of last night's confidence.

"What do you mean you had one drink and *came home*?" Birdie set the greasy brown paper bag aside and crossed her arms. "You were looking forward to this. It's what we've been working towards this entire time. Why on Earth would you only have one drink? Oh, no. Did you…? Did you choke?"

"What? No!"

She grimaced. "Sorry."

I shook my head and took a breath, then held her gaze so tightly she couldn't look away. "I drove all the way down there, bought Lisa a martini, then shook her hand and came straight back home."

"But *why*?" Birdie's expression wasn't confused anymore. It was expectant and maybe even a little anxious. Hopeful, maybe? I'd never been able to read so much on her face, and I fucking loved it.

"I think you know why," I murmured, waiting for her to confirm what I wanted to be true.

She gently shook her head, but she closed her eyes. Yes. She felt it too.

"The kiss," I said, leaving it there until her lids opened again. "Yours and mine."

"Isaac. No. That kiss was—"

"Really fucking hot?"

Her mouth quirked up in a smile she couldn't hide. "Yes, it was really fucking hot, but it was not a good reason to bail on your date. It wasn't real."

I blinked against the twinge between my ribs. "It felt real to me," I disagreed.

Her gaze dropped to my crotch and back, and I knew we were both recalling the press of my hard cock against her soft curves. "We're friends, Romeo, and I don't have many of those. I never want to jeopardise what we've got."

"Neither do I."

"Sex and friendship do not mix."

I didn't want to hear the f-word anymore. *Friends.* "Says who?"

"And you're not interested in just sex," she said, ignoring my question. "You're looking for something serious."

"Yes," I agreed slowly, walking that fine line between honesty and self-preservation. "But I don't need anything serious today or even tomorrow. Serious will happen when the time is right."

"I don't belong here. I'll be gone in less than a month, and I'm not coming back."

I growled with frustration and ignored the things I didn't want to hear. "I'd rather have a month, a week, a *day* with you now than spend the rest of my life wondering what it would have been like."

She dragged her bottom lip between her teeth. "Wondering what *what* would have been like?"

"This."

I wrapped a hand around her neck and pulled her to me, taking her mouth in the way I'd dreamed about—like she was mine to take. Like she belonged to me.

Birdie met my tongue with hers, moaning against my mouth as our lips tugged and teased, and I dragged her over my lap. She straddled my thighs, her silk robe sliding up her legs and off her shoulders to reveal a white cotton cami-and-shorts combo. She wound her fingers through my hair and pushed me back into the sofa, leaning towards me and grinding her hips against my throbbing cock.

"Oh, fuck. This is a bad idea," she panted, dropping her head back and exposing the long, pale stretch of her throat as her hips writhed. My dick swelled painfully as I trailed my mouth over her jaw, down the side of her neck and across her collarbone, moving north again to nibble on her earlobe while my hands teased the hem of her top, tickling the dimples in the base of her back, moving high enough to graze the bottom of her rib cage, then the shape of her shoulder blades, then almost-but-not-quite the swell of her breasts.

"It doesn't feel like a bad idea," I whispered against her ear. "Does it?"

"No. It feels so freaking good." Birdie wrapped her arms around my neck and circled her pelvis, riding me with her clothes on. I growled at the friction, at the way I could already feel the wet heat of her pussy seeping through her underwear and at the sight of the sexy flush creeping over her chest and burning in her cheeks. "But—"

"No." I gripped her hips and yanked her harder against my dick, lifting my arse to give her what she needed. "No buts."

"I just want to— Oh, Jesus. I want to establish the rules first, before… Before…"

I slipped a hand up her shirt and brushed my thumb over the hard peak of one nipple, smiling at the gasp she gave me before I ran my tongue along the side of her neck and up to her earlobe. "Before I make you come so hard you forget your own name?"

"Yes. No." Her grinding grew more intense, and I pulled her mouth to mine, cupping one breast and holding her against my chest as she melted against my body. She kissed me fiercely before pulling away enough to say, "Before things go too far."

"Okay, Red." I took my hand out from under her top and tugged at the ties on her robe instead, waiting for her to stop me. When she didn't, I loosened them and pushed the robe onto the floor before briefly pressing my lips to the dip in her throat. "What are the rules?"

"An extension of our original arrangement," she replied breathlessly, watching as I skated my palms over her arms, sending an eruption of goosebumps across her body.

"I'll tell you what I like in bed, you'll show me what you've got, then we'll compare notes afterwards and always do better the next time. Coaching between friends, like we planned all along. No long-term commitment. No strings and no stakes. No regrets when I go—from either one of us. Deal? You'll— You'll thank me when this is over."

It was impossible not to hear the warning in her words. *Don't get attached, Romeo. Don't expect too much.* I heard it, but I distracted myself from the meaning by planting a row of kisses over her shoulder, inhaling the apple scent of her and slipping the strap of her cami down in the process.

"Are we talking friends with benefits?" I murmured against her skin, hating the way that sounded—hating the thought of her leaving—but knowing I could only take whatever she was willing to give me for now.

"Friends…who find each other physically attractive… and who both need something only the other person can give."

I drew back a little in surprise. "What do you need from me, Red?"

Whatever it was, she was going to have it.

She slipped her warm hand into my underwear, and I moaned as she wrapped her fingers around my dick, then set her lips to the shell of my ear. "Satisfaction."

15

BIRDIE

I'D HAVE SAID I had no idea what got into me, but that would be bullshit. I knew *exactly* what had got into me: a week of wet dreams starring the man underneath me, that kiss in the bathroom which was, as Isaac put it, really fucking hot, and hard—*hard*—evidence that my theory about Isaac's cock was correct: the man was big everywhere. *Everywhere.*

So, while I wished I could have said I was a stronger, smarter, better person than a woman at the mercy of her hormones, it simply wasn't true. I had less self-control than a horny teenager, and I wanted nothing more than to give in, lose my head and let my libido take the lead.

I wanted Isaac more than I'd ever wanted any man, and I wasn't afraid to admit it, not now that we'd agreed on the rules. We knew what this was about, and we were free to take full advantage.

And not a minute too soon.

"Now, Red," he said, need tightening his voice. "As much as I love the feel of your pretty little hand on my dick right now, that's not how this is going to go."

I ran my hand along his throbbing length in one light, teasing stroke. "It's not?"

"No," he replied, sounding strangled as he folded his fingers around my wrist and removed my hand from his pants. "Lesson one is mine, and I'm not done kissing you."

Then he slid his hands underneath my arse, and I gasped as he lifted me up and flipped me onto my back along the sofa.

Isaac stretched his brawny frame over me and captured my mouth with his. The way his lips and tongue moved mirrored the greed I felt in my core—I was hungry for him, starving for a taste, and as he lowered his body over mine, he opened my legs with his hips and settled between them.

His hard cock pressed against my centre as the fabric of both my shorts and his made a flimsy but frustrating barrier between us. I moaned—a little petulantly, I'll admit—as I circled my pelvis against him, and he grinned against my lips.

"We're kissing, Red," he murmured.

I moaned again and lifted my chin as he ran his mouth over my jaw, circling one earlobe with the tip of his tongue, leaving a trail of hot kisses down the side of my neck. All the while, my hips ground against him, searching for friction, but when I grabbed onto his arse and pulled him in tighter against me, he drew back a little, and the kisses paused.

"I'm running this session, remember?" he asked, taking my arms and positioning them over my head, trapping my wrists in one of his much larger hands with a grip that felt like iron.

Hot. Hot. Hot.

Where the hell was this coming from? It wasn't the time to question it, but I was surprised Isaac had this in him. I'd dreamed about him taking control, doing what he wanted, taking what he needed, treating me like his plaything, but my fantasies were different from what was happening between us now. The Isaac in my dreams was cocky and strong, a little rough and kind of an arsehole. Real Isaac was cocky and strong, and he knew what he wanted, but there was nothing rough about him.

Not yet, anyway. Now that I knew what he was capable of, we could work on that later. Until then, I was completely on board with whatever he had in mind because Jesus, Mary, and Joseph—the man had skills.

I closed my eyes and concentrated on not hyperventilating as the longing between my legs tugged heavier and heavier. I wrapped my legs around Isaac's and tried to pull him nearer, searching out the hard promise in his shorts, and he allowed it—or perhaps he didn't notice—because he kept kissing me, sweeping his lips across my collarbone, following with decadent swirls of his tongue over the upper slopes of my breasts. Each press of his lips sent shivers cascading through me over and over, and as my nipples budded into firm, tingling peaks, the wet pulse between my legs grew heavier and more insistent.

I fought against the grip he had on my wrists, trying to twist free so I could touch myself, but the more I struggled, the tighter he held on. Pathetic whimpers fell from my mouth, and Isaac growled.

"Jesus," he muttered in a voice that was all gravel. "Make that noise again, Red. It's the hottest thing I've ever fucking heard."

I happily became more vocal about the way my body was sparking, and Isaac's lips grew more insistent. He ran his mouth over the fabric of my cami, kissing me through the thin cotton until he reached the bottom hem. He pushed it up to reveal my stomach, which he covered in open-mouthed kisses, and I squirmed as he circled my navel with tickling touches of the tip of his tongue.

I inhaled the sweet, clean fragrance of him mixed with the earthy undertones of leather, and with every sweeping touch of his mouth, the soft scratch of his beard was one layer of stimulation too many. I may have whispered a plea for more as he moved upwards, pushing at my top to free my straining breasts and aching nipples.

"Oh, Christ," he moaned. "Your tits are fucking incredible. *Fuck.*"

He set his lips to the valley of my chest, planting a line of hot adoration along my sternum. The rough brush of his beard complemented the soft press of his tongue, and my desire spun tighter as he circled my tits, inching closer to my stiff nipples, his actions slow and deliberately teasing.

Just when I thought I might scream with frustration, I cried out in relief as the warm wetness of his mouth folded over one stiff peak. He propped himself up on his elbow to tweak the other breast with his free hand, and oh, God. I almost came right then and there.

As Isaac used his tongue to flick and lick one nipple, I inhaled sharply as he grazed his teeth over the tip while lightly pinching the other between his fingers. As his enormous hand cupped my breast, stroking and kneading with torturous pressure, his mouth worked the other, pulling it stiffer and tighter and sending jolts of heat straight to my clit.

"Oh, Jesus," I moaned. "I'm in pain here, Romeo. I need more."

"You know what they say," he murmured between kisses. "There's a fine line…"

But he dragged his hand from my breast, down over my stomach, and tilted his hips so he could slip under the waist of my shorts and slide his fingers into my underwear. He grazed my folds with a light touch, and the kisses did stop then, long enough for him to groan and drop his forehead onto my shoulder.

"You're soaked, Red. Is this all for me?"

"Mm," I moaned, thrusting my hips against his hand as he stroked me, but too lightly to provide any relief.

"I want to hear it," he said, dipping the tip of a finger into my core, then out again, returning to the teasing brush along my lower lips. "Tell me I'm the reason my hand is fucking drenched."

"It's you. You did this to me," I replied, widening my knees as he groaned and explored my entrance again with a fingertip. When his thumb hit my clit, my hips lifted, and I let out a strangled sigh.

"I want you inside me," I demanded, thrusting against him.

"I'm still not done kissing you," he whispered roughly, and even in my desperation, I gave myself a point for the frustration in his voice. He wanted me as badly as I wanted him.

"Please," I begged with an exhale of breath. "I need it."

He groaned and released my wrists, shifted lower on the sofa, and dropped a kiss on one hip bone, then the other, grazing the tip of his nose across my abdomen in a move that kicked my heart rate up a notch. Then he sat back on his knees and hooked his fingers into the waist of my shorts and knickers.

He was wild about the eyes, heaving in laboured breaths, a trail of perspiration beading on his temple. "And *I* said I'm not done kissing you, so if you've got anything against coming on my tongue, Red, now's the time to say so."

"Holy hell." I lifted my hips and let him drag off my clothes. "No. Nothing against— Oh!"

Isaac moved like lightning, hooking my knees over his thick arms, spreading me wide and diving between my legs. After a single, generous drag of his tongue, he lifted his head just high enough to murmur, "Jesus, Red. You taste like fucking heaven."

I arched back and tossed my head as the flat of his tongue swept a hard, greedy line up my centre, swirling once, twice, around my clit before he did it again. He kissed either side of my entrance, licked my folds and lapped at my wetness, wrapped his lips around my throbbing clit and sucked until I was practically sobbing with need.

When he thrust his tongue into my core and added his fingers to the mix, circling my sensitive, swollen bundle of nerves, my breathing sped up, and I began to see stars.

"Oh, fuck. I'm going to come," I panted, threading my fingers through his hair and grinding down against his face. His tongue stroked and plunged, working me into a knot of sexual frenzy that I just couldn't satiate. Isaac seemed to sense the line I was walking, and he began tonguing my clit just as he pushed two thick fingers into me.

"Yes," I gasped, untangling one hand from his hair so I could claw at the sofa instead. He curled his fingers inside me, crooking them against the spot that sent forks of light and heat shooting through my abdomen. "God, yes!"

Isaac moaned as my core fluttered around his fingers, and my juices began to really flow. On his next thrust, he added a third finger and pressed his tongue hard against my clit. It sent me careening over the edge into an orgasm so magnificent I held his face so hard against my pussy that had he been a weaker man, I may have murdered him.

My hips jerked, riding the pulses of my climax as I came so hard even the aftershocks sent bursts of hedonistic pleasure through my trembling body. Again and again, it washed over me, and I kind of floated away as I gave in to it all.

A lifetime later, I remembered where I was. Oh, Jesus. What the hell was that…? And who was I again?

Birdie, I reminded myself. *Birdie Maxwell.*

I languished there in darkness until I realised my eyes were closed, and Isaac was gliding his fingers through my wet folds as he waited for me to surface. His touch set off tiny tremors in my thighs, and when I cracked open an eyelid, he was sitting up on his knees between my legs again, his cock tenting his shorts with the world's largest—and probably most painful—erection, gazing down at me like I was some sort of deity.

It was gratifying… And too much. I had to level the playing field.

"I wish you could watch yourself come," he murmured, moving his hands away from the main attraction and caressing my thighs instead. "You're a fucking goddess."

"No, thanks," I replied, wriggling away and disentangling our limbs so I could reach for his cock. "Sounds like the kind of thing that'd give a girl nightmares, and I'd much rather get a look at *your* sex face first. Come on, Romeo. You're up. Literally."

He chuckled but circled my wrist with his large fingers before I could get my hand between his legs. "I didn't kiss you to get something in return, Red. I kissed you because I wanted to."

"Oh, no. That's not how this is going to work." I tried for his shorts again but couldn't shake his hold on me.

"You don't owe me—"

"It's not about owing. It's about *reciprocating*." I strained for him again, but he only smirked. "I'm a woman. I know what it's like to walk away from sex unsatisfied."

Isaac's gaze roamed over my half-naked and dishevelled body. "I'm satisfied. Trust me."

I nodded at his erection. "Something tells me you're lying. You're a pornographic Pinocchio."

He laughed louder this time and let go of my wrist to run his palm up my arm and over my shoulder, where he cupped my neck. "What's the rush, Red? Next time—"

I cut him off with an impatient groan. "This isn't a relationship, okay? It's an arrangement—and a transactional one at that."

Isaac dropped his hand and shifted his gaze to somewhere over my shoulder, and I regretted my words immediately—or at least, the way they came out—but it needed to be said. Isaac couldn't forget for even a second that sex didn't equal real intimacy. And I couldn't either.

"Well, as much as I'd love to hang around and *transact* with you," he said with a self-mocking smile, "I actually need to get to work."

"What about"—I waved a hand at his shorts—"that?"

He stood up and adjusted himself, then scooped up my robe from where it had puddled on the floor and handed it to me. "It'll be there tomorrow. Trust me." A hint of genuine mirth played on his mouth, and I breathed more easily. "I don't know, Red. After what we did today, lesson two had better be pretty darn good."

I cupped his balls and smirked when he closed his eyes and moaned. "Lucky for you, I perform well under pressure." I released him and took my robe, and when he opened his eyes again, *that look* had returned.

Assuring myself it was because the sight of me signalled an impending orgasm and not actual feelings, I stuck out my other hand. "Panties, please?"

"What? Oh." He swiped my shorts and underwear from where he'd dropped them on the floor and passed them to me, then jerked his chin towards my feet. "Cute socks."

I rolled my eyes as I shimmied into my clothes and wrapped myself up in the robe. It was a weird time to come down with a case of self-consciousness—the man had just had me for breakfast, for crying out loud—but the way Isaac's gaze followed my every move set off a burn in my cheeks that had nothing to do with desire.

"So, I'm going to take a quick shower," I announced, surging to my feet. "Do you have to leave straightaway? Feel free to, uh, use the downstairs bathroom. I think there's tea in the kitchen. Water in the tap. No food, but—

"I already ate."

"Seriously?"

Isaac's green eyes sparkled. He speared me with that cocky smirk he'd grown so fond of, and I shoved at his shoulder—the guy didn't move—which only made him laugh. I was more at ease with his playful nature, and it was hard not to smile.

"So, what time do you want to get together tomorrow?" I asked.

"Why don't you come over to my place around seven so we can have dinner first?"

I lifted one eyebrow. "Is that code for—"

"No, Red. Get your mind out of the gutter."

I chuckled and led him to the front door. "Seven for dinner *first*," I agreed. "Sounds like a plan."

I held the door open, and he stepped through, pausing on the porch before turning back to me. "So, what's your verdict on lesson one? Can we check kissing off the list?"

"You call what you just did between my thighs kissing, Romeo?" I grinned wider at his blush. "Full marks for effort. A-plus for results. Whatever you're doing, you're doing right, but let's get one thing straight."

He raised an eyebrow, but I noticed the anxiety that tightened the corners of his eyes and pulled awkwardly at the curve of his mouth. His confidence wasn't watertight yet, and it gave me a reason to believe I belonged in the Bay—at least for as long as I had to wait for my mother to show.

"There's still so much I can teach you, Romeo. So very, very much."

Then without a word, he slipped a warm hand around the back of my head and dropped a gentle kiss on my mouth. It was soft and sensual, like sinking into a warm bath, and I closed my eyes and kissed him back, stumbling forwards when he pulled away before I'd had enough.

"Can't wait," he said quietly before stepping off the porch, crossing the lawn, and disappearing into his house next door.

I locked my knees tight, but the moment he was out of sight, I backed into the hallway, set a hand against the wall, and took a moment to breathe.

Yes, we could check kissing off the list. Isaac had all the moves he'd ever need in that department. Holy shit, did he have moves.

This love coaching thing might just be the best idea I'd ever had. I refused to think about *that look* that came and went in his eyes—the one that threatened to melt more than just my panties. Both were temporary and transactional, just like this arrangement.

After closing the front door, I headed to the upstairs bathroom, feeling keyed up all over again. Perhaps a session with Mr Big Boy was in order. Detouring past my bedroom to collect my electronic lover, I absently checked my phone charging on the bedside table, and my heart stopped as the screen lit up with a notification.

Missed call from Cora.

Trying to swallow even though my mouth was suddenly dry, I dropped onto the edge of the bed and quickly swiped at the screen. Holding the phone to my ear, I listened to the tone of an outgoing call. It rang once. Twice. Again. Then again. After the sixth ring, it defaulted to her voicemail, but I reflexively punched the end-call button at the sound of her recorded message.

She'd called, and I hadn't answered. She'd been available to talk, and I'd missed my opportunity. Was she in town or calling to say she was on her way to the house? I felt like a kid who'd been given an ice cream cone only for the giant scoop to fall onto the ground before the first taste. She'd been *right there*, and now she was gone.

I didn't leave a voice message—not when she hadn't left one for me first—but I spent the next twenty-four hours with my phone glued to my hand and one ear listening for a knock on the door. If what Cora needed to tell me was important enough for her to call me in the first place, it had to be important enough for her to try again, right? I let myself believe that for longer than I cared to admit.

An hour before I was supposed to knock on Isaac's door for dinner, I still hadn't heard from her, and a familiar sense of abandonment had me breaking all my usual rules. I pulled up Google and punched her name into the search bar.

I never let myself do this. Stalking my parents on the internet only ever made me feel like crap. But what if my mother really had divorced my father, and she'd tried calling to tell me? Maybe the news had already broken, and she'd wanted to make sure I knew before I found out in the tabloids.

My parents were only minor celebrities—famous because my father was the mega-rich owner of a commercial investment firm—but Mum was a regular on the social circuit, and she needed her name in the press the way she needed her sauvignon blanc chilled to exactly twelve degrees and her bedroom drapes opened every morning at seven-oh-seven. The problem was that every time I let myself look at a picture or headline with her face or name in it, it added a fracture to the armour I'd been working to build most of my life. Every window into her world was a reminder that I wasn't part of it, and she'd never wanted me to be. I was happier—more stable, safer—when she wasn't on my radar and when I didn't dare to hope.

I was so angry at myself for thinking it, and yet I couldn't help but wonder…

Maybe this time would be different.

Google generated a list of news items with "Cora Maxwell" as the keywords, and I hit on the most recent. Attached was a photograph of my mother on the red carpet at a charity benefit, in an emerald-green dress, primped to within an inch of her life, beaming at the camera. My father, in an expensive navy suit and auburn hair, slicked back, was on her arm.

And the caption: *Cora and Seymour Maxwell were honoured last night at the annual wildlife fund gala after donating $250,000 in honour of their thirty-fifth wedding anniversary.*

I'd barely eaten all day, but I was about to throw up. Then I was going to punch something.

There was no divorce. Nothing had changed. Whatever "family business" my mother wanted to talk to me about, it had nothing to do with making my dad accountable for all the times he'd lied and cheated on both of us. Cora wasn't going to turn up on my doorstep and tell me I was right. She wasn't even going to return my call.

My life had always been a competition. From the moment I was old enough to understand the stakes, I'd played hard to win my parents' affection. Their approval. Their attention. And as smart as I was—as dedicated and disciplined and downright stubborn—I was still waiting for the day they'd tell me I was a winner. *Their* winner.

Today was not that day, but I could only be disappointed in myself for letting myself believe it might have been. There were no such things as happy endings for the players in this game—least of all for Birdie Maxwell.

16

ISAAC

I DECIDED NOT to cook for Birdie again. I wanted to take her on a proper date—even if it only looked like dinner with a friend to the rest of the world—so I made a reservation at a local restaurant called Coconut Joe's. The quirky bistro was a little more expensive than the dozens of family-friendly eateries in the Bay but not so fancy that it should bother Birdie. Certainly not romantic enough that it would freak her out—fingers crossed.

Ten minutes before seven o'clock, I was dressed in snug dark jeans and a white button-down with the sleeves cuffed to expose my forearms—according to my research, wearing it that way did *things* to women.

My beard and hair were neat, I wore the lightest splash of cologne, and I was six chapters into one of my new books. Agatha had recommended this one, and it was easy to see why. I stood up from the bed and attempted to adjust my pants, but there was no room in them to give. Jesus, this was going to be a long night.

I tucked the book into my dresser drawer and went downstairs to wait for Birdie and calm my dick by thinking unsexy thoughts. No surprise that those two goals were incompatible.

I'd been a confused mess following what happened at her house the day before. On the one hand, I was pretty bloody pleased with myself after the orgasm I'd managed to deliver, not to mention the superhuman strength it took to walk away afterwards, but that had been a solid non-negotiable. Birdie needed to know I wasn't a horny arsehole playing her love-coach game for selfish reasons—and honestly, there'd been too high a chance I'd humiliate myself and come all over her hand the moment she touched me. I'd had to jerk off twice last night and again that morning to take the edge off.

On the flip side of feeling like a freaking hero was frustration, and I didn't know what to do with it. Maybe I'd read too many romance novels and my expectations were too high, but even when she'd been laying down the rules that meant we could extend our agreement, part of me believed Birdie was only moments—and an orgasm—away from opening up to the idea of something real. That was before she'd called what we had *transactional*, which was when things got real for me. Birdie Maxwell wasn't going to forget who she was and fall into my arms because we were good together in bed. The only way to win her was to prove we were good together, full stop—in the sheets and out of them.

And while I'd agreed to sex with no strings attached, and I still believed I could survive the possibility that one day Birdie would leave and never come back, I couldn't accept that all she'd take away from our time together were multiple orgasms. I had to teach her something in return.

We'd known each other too long to pretend we weren't connected in more ways than sex. We shared a history and a childhood. She'd told me enough about her relationship with her parents for me to understand why she made it so hard for anyone to get close to her. And yet, over the last two weeks, I'd seen glimpses of her vulnerability, and it gave me hope. I was going to prove to Birdie that it was safe to be vulnerable with *me*. Safe and maybe even life changing.

I was pacing the living room when Birdie knocked on my front door. I smoothed my hair, brushed at my shirt, and opened the door. "Hi—"

The woman cut me off by planting both palms on my chest with a smack and storming inside, shoving me deeper into the house.

"Okay, Romeo," she said, fumbling at the fly on my jeans. "Take off your pants and give me that gorgeous cock. Lesson two starts right now."

It happened so fast I was responding to her hands before my head caught up, blood surging right past the feeble alarm bells sounding between my ears on its way to my dick.

When the pants wouldn't drop fast enough, Birdie forgot my fly and launched herself at me, flinging her arms around my neck and wrapping her legs around my waist as she sucked greedily at my lips.

I stumbled back a little before gripping her hips, spinning us around, and pinning her against the wall, capturing her mouth with mine as my *gorgeous cock*—fuck, yeah—strained painfully against the zip on my jeans.

Birdie clawed at my shoulders through the thin cotton of my shirt as I rolled my hips between her legs. Her thighs gripped me tighter, her kisses grew wet and messy, and it took me another minute of sloppy grinding and groping to get a hold on enough sense to realise something was very wrong with this picture. Something was wrong with Birdie.

"Wait," I grunted, pulling away from her mouth and carefully setting her on her feet. "Wait. What's going on with you? Why all the aggression?"

Her cheeks were pink, her lips were swollen, and her chest rose and fell with quick, frenzied breaths as she glared up at me with fire in her blue eyes. "Can't a woman just take what she wants? That might happen one day in real life, you know? You might date someone who's the take-charge kind."

She reached for my fly again, but I gently brushed her hands away and took another small step back. Her brows drew down in a glower. "Isn't this what you asked for, Romeo? Lesson two: I show you what I want, and you learn a few new tricks."

I rubbed the back of my neck, catching my own breath and fighting against the daze of Birdie's almost violent enthusiasm. I wanted to sink inside this woman so badly, but not like this.

I'd spent enough years as a cop to know impairment when I saw it, and it wasn't always alcohol or drugs that put people out of their right minds. Depression did it. Shock. Rage. I wasn't sure yet what was going on with Birdie, but I was certain this was not about sex. It wasn't about her wanting me, either, as much as I wanted it to be. And I'd never sleep with anyone, least of all Birdie, when they were behaving like this.

"Uh, sure," I said, trying to get the night back on track. We could talk over dinner, in a public place where she couldn't maul me, and when I had more information, I'd be able to make better decisions. "But I thought we might head out for dinner first."

"I don't need dinner," she retorted. "I just need your dick."

I blinked in surprise as Birdie tore open my shirt, pressed her hot lips to my chest and swirled her wet tongue over one nipple. I closed my eyes and dug deep for that super-human strength I'd had the day before. It was in there somewhere because the next moment, I was gripping her shoulders and pushing her away. I held her at arm's length and stared down at her until she reluctantly met my eyes.

"You're acting strange, and I don't believe for a second that this is about sex lessons or love coaching. You're upset, and I don't understand why, so if you think we're sleeping together while you're acting this way and refusing to explain, you better think again."

"Don't you try to tell me—"

"I'm not your scratching post, Red, but I am your friend." My fingers flexed against the soft muscles of her upper arms. "Something isn't right. Talk to me."

"I don't need a fucking scratching post, and I don't need a friend," she snapped. "What I need is a freaking punching bag."

Finally. Something I could understand.

Relieved that maybe there was something I could do to get through to her, I wordlessly let go of her arms, took her hand, and led her through the house to the backyard.

"What are you doing?" she muttered, trying to yank free of me, but I held on tight and kept moving. "Why are you taking me outside?"

At the back door, I flicked on the porch light before guiding Birdie into the twilit yard, weaving my way through my DIY resistance course to the furthest frame, where a heavy leather punching bag swung from a short silver chain. Dropping Birdie's hand, I stood behind her and set my hands on her shoulders, then squared her up to the bag.

"There you go," I said. "Have at it."

"You can't be serious," she scoffed.

"You said you needed a punching bag, and here's a punching bag. What are you waiting for? Lay into it."

I moved back a few paces to give her room, then crossed my arms over my chest and waited as her little fists clenched and loosened and shadows of emotion flittered across her face. Her brow creased. Her mouth turned down. Her nose crinkled. And she landed the knuckles of her right hand into the bag with a dull smack. A shadow of pain crossed her brow, and as she flexed her fingers, I resisted the urge to check her hand for injury.

When Birdie was ready to be soothed, I'd be the first in line, but right now, she needed to expel whatever emotions were raging so close to the surface. Maybe then, she'd be ready to talk.

"Feel better?" I asked.

"Not yet," she muttered before jabbing her left hand into the bag, following with a right hook. And then there was no stopping her.

Birdie unleashed on that bag, punching and kicking and grunting as she expelled whatever stress and rage simmered under the surface. On the one hand, I was impressed at how much strength she had, but as the hits became more frenzied and her breathing more laboured, I had to harden every muscle in my body to stop me from dragging her back and into my arms, because Birdie was not okay.

She was angry, yes, but when she'd worked out that first burst of rage, I heard what I suspected was a broken sob, and it very nearly broke me. She thumped that bag over and over, and as the impacts grew weaker, the emotion choking her became more obvious until she finally screamed, attacking the bag in a flurry of tiny, hard blows.

I waited, my heart in my throat and a sting behind my eyes, until her punches slowed, then finally stopped, and she clung onto the leather as if it were the only thing keeping her up. And maybe it was because when I approached her and set a hand on her back, she curled towards me and let me pick her up, burying her face against my neck and locking her legs around my waist. Her breath hitched as she did her best not to sob, but I could feel the dampness of tears on my shoulder.

Fuck.

As I made my way back into the house, I wrapped my arms tighter around her body and pressed a kiss against her apple-scented hair. I'd never felt more helpless in my life nor so determined to figure out what was wrong—and fix it. I was going to make sure Birdie never had a reason to fall apart like this again.

17

ISAAC

I CARRIED HER inside, up the stairs, and to my bedroom. Gently setting her down in the centre of the bed, she unwrapped her legs from my waist and looked around with reddened eyes. She looked so small and so vulnerable, the steel that normally straightened her spine bowing with the defeated curl of her shoulders, that I couldn't stop myself from reaching out and brushing a soothing thumb across the flushed skin of her cheekbone, but she only cocked a mocking eyebrow at me.

"What are we doing here, Romeo?" she asked, her voice thick.

"Don't jump to any conclusions," I replied. "I thought you might be tired, and my sofa's not comfortable enough to stretch out on."

"Then you need a better sofa," she said, but she settled herself back against the pillows, then curled up on her side, tucked her hands under her cheek, and closed her eyes. "I'm embarrassed."

"Nothing to be embarrassed about. You must be hungry." At her small shrug, I added, "Thirsty?" When she nodded, I headed straight for the door. "Don't move, and don't fall asleep yet. I'll be back in ten minutes, okay?"

She opened her eyes again, and I had trouble swallowing when I saw the openness in them. No walls. No defences. No armour. "Okay."

I hurried downstairs to the kitchen, where I first called the restaurant to cancel our reservation, then made us both sandwiches, trying to work fast while talking myself out of jumping to any conclusions.

The problem wasn't me, right? Things had been going well between us, and tonight she'd come to me for, well, support of sorts. There was only one—obvious—reason why Birdie would be this distressed. Her parents. And it was such a sensitive topic that I knew better than to broach it. I just had to be there for her, like I was all those years ago, and hope that Birdie still trusted me enough to tell me the truth.

Locating an oversized plate large enough to double as a tray, I set the sandwiches on it, along with two bowls and spoons and the carton of strawberry ice cream I had in the freezer. I tucked two bottles of water under my arm, at the last minute remembered to grab the chocolate sauce and a stack of napkins, then returned to the bedroom, half-convinced I'd walk in to find Birdie snoring.

When I rounded the door frame and discovered her waiting with her big blue eyes glued to the door, that hitch in my throat tightened right up again.

"All right," I said, clearing away the croak. "Dinner is served. Nothing fancy, but—"

"It's perfect," she said, sitting upright and tucking her legs underneath her. Her hair, pulled loose from its braid, curled around her face in tendrils that tickled her freckled cheeks. I had to hold myself back from leaning over and sweeping them away. "But if you don't mind, I'm going to start with the ice cream."

"It's all yours." I thrust a bowl and spoon her way, eager to do anything that might make her a little happier, but she ignored the first, took the latter, and dug straight into the tub.

"So," she said around a mouthful of ice cream, "I suppose I owe you an explanation."

I sat on the bed and reclined against the pillows, crossing my legs at the ankles and picking up a sandwich. Totally cool, and not like I was hanging on her every word. "You don't owe me anything," I said, and I meant it. I wasn't interested in keeping a tally board. No matter what Birdie tried to tell me, nothing about our relationship was *transactional.* Not the sex, not the emotional intimacy. Not one thing. Still, I was desperate to help fix what had caused tonight's meltdown. "But if you want to talk, I've been told I'm a good listener."

"Oh, yeah? Who told you that?"

Memories pulled at the corner of my mouth as I shrugged one shoulder. "Just a girl I used to know."

Birdie smiled sadly into her ice cream tub, poking at the dessert with her spoon. Nearly a full minute passed before she sighed and shovelled another spoonful into her mouth. "It's my parents."

I nodded, unsurprised by her answer. "I'm sorry."

Birdie breathed out a sigh. "I told you that's why I came back to the Bay in the first place, right? Cora asked me to meet her at the house, but she didn't show up when she was supposed to—shocking, I know. She delayed her arrival more than once and then stopped texting me altogether. But yesterday, while you and I were…in session…she called. I saw the notification on my phone, and I'm an idiot. I let myself believe it meant something."

I swallowed my bite of sandwich. "Something like what?"

Birdie glanced up at me with an ironic half-smile. "Like maybe my parents were finally getting divorced, and she wanted to tell me before I found out in the tabloids? That she needed to meet me at the house to… God, I don't even know! Support her? Console her? Make a fresh start together?" Birdie chuckled without any humour. "For someone so smart, I can be so, so stupid."

I set my dinner aside and turned to give Birdie my full attention. "You are not stupid, but maybe I am because I'm not following. What makes you think none of those things might be true?"

She stabbed her spoon in and out of the melting ice cream. "She didn't leave me a voice message, didn't pick up when I called her back, and didn't bother to try reaching me again, so I… Ugh! I Googled her."

Those alarm bells sounded in my head—easier to hear this time without Birdie's mouth on my skin, her hands between my legs, and the blood pounding in my ears. Birdie's face darkened, and her jabs into the ice cream grew savage, so I gently extracted the tub from her grip. She gave it up, then dropped her head into her hands.

"And what did you find?" I murmured.

"They're still married. Still pretending everything's perfect in their world. Still behaving as though I don't exist."

I clenched my jaw, tamping down the rage I felt as Birdie so casually and defeatedly confessed that her parents behaved as though she didn't exist. How could anyone who had ever been lucky enough to cross paths with this woman want to create a make-believe reality where she didn't live and breathe and light up every room she entered? These people didn't deserve a daughter as magical as Birdie. Birdie didn't deserve to have parents as abhorrent as the ones she got.

Now *I* wanted to punch something. I also wanted to scoop up Birdie, settle her on my lap, and hold her forever. Instead, I crossed my arms over my chest and tucked my clenched fists away where she couldn't see them, then weighed what to say next. There was something I needed to know before I could make sense of Birdie's situation, but if I made the wrong move, she might shut down the whole conversation. Then again, she was the one to bring up the topic of her parents, and given the information she'd already willingly given me, I decided a gamble now was worth the risk.

"Red, I have to ask," I said quietly. "Did you ever tell her?"

Birdie kept her face hidden behind her palms, but when she didn't end the discussion right away, I held my breath and waited.

The final summer Birdie came to the Bay as a kid, we grew exceptionally close. I was suffering through the humiliation of being branded that freakishly tall, goofy young guy who slobbered when he kissed you—about the worst life could get when you're an insecure sixteen-year-old trying to make a good impression on the limited girls in your social circle—and Birdie was always there to talk. But our friendship went both ways. I was there to listen, too, and she'd had plenty to share at the time. Birdie had been grappling with a family secret, and she had zero idea how to handle it.

Her father, the billionaire businessman Seymour Maxwell, had a second life—a whole other family that nobody knew about. There was another woman he lived with when he wasn't at home with Birdie's mother, and together they had a daughter only a year or two younger than Birdie. Mr Maxwell doted on that little girl in ways he never had with Birdie.

Birdie had uncovered the truth after stumbling upon a series of odd coincidences and clues—the girl had never met a problem she couldn't solve—and the revelation that her father could love a daughter who wasn't Birdie sent her spinning in all sorts of directions. Shock. Rage. Depression. Hope—because what if she told her mother the truth? Would this betrayal somehow bring the two of them closer together? Would making her father a common enemy forge a bond between mother and daughter that, so far, she'd never been able to have?

I didn't know the answers to any of those questions because, by the end of the summer, Birdie had made me swear not to mention it to anyone ever and never bring it up with her again. Now, I suspected we were about to reopen old wounds.

"I did," she said eventually, scrubbing her hands down her cheeks. "It took me two years to find the right time, but I did it. I told her everything. I had pictures by then. Solid evidence. I sat her down in her fancy formal living room and laid it all out on the table. Literally."

I could tell by the sardonic twist to Birdie's mouth that whatever happened next wasn't good.

"And?" I prompted.

Birdie chortled. "She already knew."

"She *what*?"

"Yep. Cora knew everything. All about the other house, the other woman, the other girl. Anastasia is her name. Blonde hair, brown eyes, uncommonly pretty. Smart, too, not that she ever did anything with it. Never had to. My father set her up for life. She got married three years ago to an up-and-coming executive at my father's firm, and she's already had a baby. My dad's a granddad—and loving it, apparently. Helps that nobody knows about it, I suppose. Can't imagine he'd be too thrilled about being branded an old man in public when he can enjoy the perks behind closed doors."

Birdie tilted her head, and her eyes narrowed. "Calm down, Romeo. I'm not used to seeing you so fired up. You'd think these were your parents treating you like garbage, not mine and me."

Nostrils flaring, I dropped my head back, closed my eyes, and gently tapped my skull over and over against the wall. This kind of thing had always been an open wound of mine—parents who didn't deserve the title. In my line of work, I saw things I'd never be able to un-see. Kids in horrendous environments, and not a damn thing I could do about it.

Birdie was an adult now, and her father had more money than God, but that didn't change the fact that her family life had been—still was—emotionally abusive.

For Birdie's benefit, I adopted a mask of calm. "So, your mother knew? What did she say when she realised you'd figured it all out on your own?" Again, I knew the answer was going to hurt, but my stomach twisted as Birdie recounted exactly how diabolical her mother could be.

"She was furious." Birdie closed her eyes briefly as the memory played across her face, then opened them again and pushed those little strands of hair back from her face. "She said I'd always been a thorn in her side, and if I knew what was good for me, I'd keep my mouth shut and get on with my life. But I demanded an explanation. How could she stay in an unhappy marriage knowing her husband was leading a double life? I couldn't understand it, and I didn't want to believe it."

Birdie scoffed under her breath and shook her head. "Cora explained that my father met his other woman—Lauren—long before he became involved with her. But Lauren wasn't the *right kind* of person for my father's family. They encouraged him to pursue Cora instead and all but forced them into their socially acceptable marriage. Still, my father was never happy, and he never stopped seeing Lauren. Cora knew it, but she turned a blind eye and hoped that feigning ignorance would be enough to keep him in their marriage."

Again, Birdie paused, but I was too dumbstruck to interrupt.

"She was terrified he'd leave her, then and now. Still, to this day, I don't know if she loves him, but she definitely loves his money." Birdie looked up at me then, the pain obvious in her eyes. "So, what plan do you think she concocted to keep her cheating husband bonded to her forever?"

"She had you to trap your father in their marriage?" I whispered in horror, and Birdie nodded as understanding lit my face.

"Oh, yeah. She tried to tell me she believed that a child would make him happy, but who knows if that's true? Regardless, it didn't work out that way. Once I came along, there was no way his family would let him leave us—nobody could know that the CEO of one of the world's most respected investment conglomerates was a liar and philanderer; the optics would be bad for business—and my existence only made him resentful."

Birdie snorted with derision. "Soon after, he set Lauren up in her own house on the other side of the city and built a secret life with her. One that included a daughter he actually wanted. Back in the real world, his wife was spending his cash and living it up while the inconvenience of being a mother was managed by handing her little girl over to nannies and the nuns at the state's most prestigious boarding school." Birdie tapped the side of her nose. "Only the best for the Maxwell heir. Had to keep up appearances, you see."

"Fuck, Red." I dragged a hand down my jaw, outraged and devastated for her, yet knowing I needed to keep my reactions muted in case it all got to be too much and she closed up again. But as I stared at her, searching for a clue about what to do next, she gave me a watery smile, and I let my instincts take the lead.

I leaned over and picked her up, then snuggled her in my lap. Her muscles tensed for a brief moment before she leaned her head against my chest, and I wrapped one arm around her slight frame. The weight and warmth of her soothed the edges of my anger, and maybe it was the wrong time to think it, but Jesus, how I wished this was my reality—that I could hold Birdie like this all the time, no emotional crisis required.

"I'm so sorry," I murmured.

I felt her shrug underneath me. "That conversation happened ten years ago, right before I dropped out of university. I've had time to get used to it."

"Something must have happened tonight to unleash all

this rage in you. I mean, aside from the Google results, although I know that must have hurt."

She sighed. "I'm mad at myself more than anything. No matter how hard I've worked on letting go of all my family baggage, the possibility of a relationship with Cora has always been my kryptonite. I need to grow up and get over it. I've always known that, but what I realise now more than ever is that I need closure."

Something about the way she said the words raised the hackles on my neck. "What do you mean, closure?"

"She finally sent me a message just before I got here tonight. Apparently, her schedule changed unexpectedly, and she'll be overseas for the next three weeks. She said when she gets back, she'll meet me at the house to talk about her plans for it."

"What kind of plans?"

"She didn't say, but if it's not to be sold as part of a divorce settlement, I can only imagine she wants to tidy the place up a little. Maybe start using it as a holiday residence again."

"And where do you fit into that?"

"Maybe she thinks she can convince me to stick around and manage the renovations? I'm not sure. It'd be just like her to treat me like an employee."

I breathed steadily against the hope that set my pulse leaping like the ocean in a storm. Could it be that easy? Birdie might stay in the Bay because her mother needed her to oversee her construction project? It might not be forever, but it would take longer than the few weeks I had left with her. Much longer, and a lot could change in that amount of time. Happily-ever-afters could be created in a matter of months.

"I hope she does ask me for a favour or support," Birdie continued. "It'll make it that much more satisfying when I tell her to stick her house and her money and her text messages in her designer luggage and up her arse because I don't want a part in any of it anymore. Not her life or her unreliable communication, or her twisted interpretation of family. I've got my own money, I've got my own world, and I don't need anything from her. I can't wait to see the look on her face when I tell her so. I won't keep wondering if one day she's going to change. She never will, and it's a little girl's dream to wish otherwise."

The hope I had of holding on to her for a little ebbed away. "You mean, she'll arrive in the Bay, and you'll up and leave? Just like that?"

"I have to," she replied. "I have the tournament in Las Vegas, remember? And I haven't told you the best part about that."

An instinctive turn in my stomach told me I didn't want to know, but still, I said, "Oh, yeah? And what's the best part?"

"The competition is happening at the opening week of my father's sparkly new casino, and when I win the whole thing, he's going to have to hand me the seven-figure cheque with the entire world watching. There'll be live streams and cameras and reporters, and he'll have to smile, shake my hand, and congratulate me on taking a million dollars of his own money. They're going to ask him if he's proud of me and if he taught me everything I know, and what's he going to say? He can't admit that he barely knows who I am—that he'd walk straight past me if he saw me in the street. I'm a winner, and Seymour Maxwell is going to finally acknowledge it—to my face."

I could hear the bravado returning to Birdie's tone and almost see the way she was reconstructing the walls she kept built high around her heart. But she'd let me in now, and I wasn't about to say her plan was a problematic one and risk being on the wrong side of those defences. She needed unconditional love and support, not judgement or negativity. But as she laid out her intentions, one possibility occurred to me, and I knew no matter how hard I might try to deny it, I wouldn't be able to let it go.

If Birdie's scheme worked and she could finally resolve her strained relationship with her parents, perhaps she'd stop running from commitment. She could return to the Bay after all this was done, move into the house next door, and make a life here. She might need to go away for a little while—I didn't need her brains to know how important it was for her to break free from the toxic bonds she had with her parents, and maybe, in a twisted way, this poker tournament could do that for her—but she didn't need to be gone forever. Birdie could come back. I just needed to create something worth coming back for—and make sure the possibility of a life here with me was clear enough for her to see it.

I rubbed her arm, then dropped a kiss on the crown of

her head. "Sounds like you've got it all worked out, Red."

"Yeah, I think I do." Then she grinned up at me, and I smiled at the sparkle that had reappeared in her eyes. "Now that we've talked that out, I'm feeling more like myself again, and I've had a fantastic idea. What do you say to playing a little game I like to call strip poker?"

18

BIRDIE

"THIS REALLY ISN'T fair, you know."

"You knew what you were getting into when you agreed to play." I laughed and nodded at Isaac's waist. "Lose the underwear."

He shook one broad hand, drawing my eye to the solid silver watch circling his left wrist. "Why can't I take this off first?"

The concept of an aroused woman biting her lip is so overdone, but there really was nothing else I could do as I ran my gaze over Isaac's near-naked body.

Every line was cut to perfection. The light dusting of dark hair over his chest was just the right kind of masculine. The shadows in his lamp-lit bedroom played across the planes of his beautiful face and darkened his green eyes to a heart-stopping mossy tone. His legs were thick and strong, the skin a little paler on his thighs, and his arms were beyond incredible, with shoulders and biceps that made my mouth *actually* water. Yet, for some reason I couldn't articulate, I was distracted by his forearms and the way his silver watch looked against the tanned muscles roping their way up to his biceps.

The watch was classic, almost old-school—just like Isaac—and it did *things* to me. The sight of his hands holding his cards fanned in front of his eyes practically hypnotised me. The way he dropped them on the covers between us, then set his elbows on his knees just so he could stare at me, sent tingles dancing across my skin. Every move he made was competent and confident and sexy, and I wanted that watch to stay *on*.

"It doesn't count, so it stays where it is," I declared. "Underwear, Romeo. Now."

Isaac glanced around the room, where his jeans, shirt, and both socks were tossed on the floor. He really hadn't been wearing very much—five hands of very easy poker, and the guy was going to be in his birthday suit. Me, on the other hand…

"You're still fully dressed," he grumbled, then set his feet on the floor before standing and looming over me. He hooked his thumbs into the waistband of his briefs and narrowed his eyes. "So, if I take these off next, and the watch doesn't count, where does that leave us exactly? Game over, right?"

My lips curved upwards in an anticipatory grin. "Game over," I agreed. "And our next lesson begins."

Isaac closed his eyes like he was searching for strength.

"Oh, come on," I said, twisting my legs to cross my ankles underneath me, bouncing on the bed like a kid excited to finally be getting her birthday gifts. "I've seen it all before, remember? There was that sneak peek in your parents' bathroom. You've got nothing to be embarrassed about. Believe me."

"I'm not embarrassed…exactly," he mumbled before squinting down at me. "Your clothes will come off eventually, right?"

"Oh, you can bet on that."

"Fine."

In one quick move, he pushed his underwear down to his ankles, then kicked them to the side. Standing tall, Isaac crossed his arms over his chest and waited while I devoured the sight of him—shadows caressing his skin, his towering cock teasing me with its girth, and the silver watch glinting in the glow of the nearest lamp.

My heart thundered so hard that I was surprised he didn't call the whole thing off and call for an ambulance. I was *sweating* because, holy fuck, Isaac Greene was fantasy made flesh.

"Okay, Romeo," I whispered in a voice that was unintentionally husky. Licking my lips and swallowing to return a little moisture to my mouth, I went on. "Here's what we're going to do next." I climbed to my feet and stood in front of him, keeping my eyes only on his face—though I deserved a freaking medal for managing it. "You're going to undress me. Slowly. The aim of this game is to wind me up so tight that you should be able to finish things with not much more than a well-positioned touch."

Isaac skated his fingertips up my arms, over my shoulders, and to my face, where he brushed a few loose strands of hair away from my face. "Sounds like torture, Red."

"The best kind."

I wore fewer items of clothing than Isaac had been when our night began—once he removed my tee, shorts, and panties, I'd be as naked as the day I was born—and still, he managed to draw the process out.

He skimmed his warm palms over my hip bones, then slipped his hands under my shirt to graze the sensitive skin beneath my navel. He unbuttoned my shorts and opened the front, then pushed them down a few inches before abandoning them and running his hands up under the back of my tee, dragging a featherlight touch down the dip of my spine, the bottom of my ribcage, the curve of each breast. Waves of desire collected in a wet mess between my legs.

I raised my arms in the air to show I was ready to be naked. Isaac took the hint and pulled up my shirt, peeling it off as though he wasn't in a rush, but the groan he made as soon as the fabric cleared my breasts told me this process was going to push him to his limits as well.

Good.

"Is kissing allowed?" he murmured in a low voice.

"Encouraged," I replied, tilting my head to the side to indicate he should begin at the slope of my neck.

Like the star student he was, Isaac fell on me with hot swirls of his tongue and decadent presses of his mouth.

The relative roughness of his beard heightened every soft slide of his lips. The kissing went on as his hands explored my body, cupping my breasts and tweaking my nipples with sharp pinches and gentle circles that had me gasping and moaning in turns.

He deliberately ignored my mouth, skimming past my lips every time I leaned in to capture his. I enjoyed it all, but when I began to wonder if he was going to take the torture part of the lesson just a little too far—my shorts were still on, and I really needed them not to be—I dug my fingernails into his forearms hard enough to make him pause.

"Kneel," I whispered.

And God help me, he dropped to his knees.

I twined my fingers through his hair as Isaac sucked on one nipple, then the other. He licked a line between my breasts, then pressed kisses over my ribcage and down my stomach as he tugged my shorts and underwear over my hips and down my legs. Stepping out of them as they hit the floor, I didn't stop Isaac when he smoothed his palms up my thighs, pressing to open them wider.

I shifted my legs a little and heaved in breath after heavy breath as he used his thumbs on my lower lips to spread me open, then flicked the tip of his tongue to tickle my clit.

My knees shook as Isaac snaked one strong arm around my waist to not only keep me upright but brace my pussy harder to his face and stroke his tongue even deeper.

"I think… I think…" I gasped, but I couldn't think. Not with his mouth on me like that.

"Mm?" he replied, the deep reverberation against my clit setting off sparks in my abdomen.

"I think I have to lie down," I panted. "Throw me on the bed."

Isaac looked up, a question in his eyes. I twisted my fingers in his hair and tugged—hard—to show him I was serious. "Throw. Me. Down. Show me how much you want me."

His fingers pressed hard into my hips before the muscles in his arms corded, and he lifted me off the floor, tossing me onto the mattress. I cried out as I landed sprawled on my back, and before I had a moment to get used to the new position, Isaac was kneeling at the edge of the bed, gripping onto my ankles and yanking me towards him.

"Oh!" I widened my eyes at the greed on Isaac's face, and when he hooked my knees over his shoulders and dropped his head between my thighs, I didn't fight it. I gripped his hair and hung on tight, moaning and panting as he worked his goddamn magic.

As the throbbing in my core worked its way up to the grand finale, I came to my senses long enough to squirm a little. I'd waited long enough and dreamed too often about the sensation of this man filling me up, and after the night we'd just had, I'd never wanted it more. "Wait. Wait. I want… I need you inside me."

He groaned against me but pulled back, and I took one of his hands and set it over my pussy. Covering his fingers with mine, I squeezed my sex, feeling the slippery wetness dripping over his hands as well as my own. I pushed his finger inside me, then added one of mine, and he swore at the sensation of my snug muscles wrapped tightly around us both.

"I want you in here, Romeo. Tell me you want that, too."

"Jesus, Red." Isaac ground his palm against me, and I dropped my head back with a groan. "I want it."

"Tell me. How do you want me? How much? Talk to me."

I wasn't prepared for the way he pulled out of my pussy and slipped his hands under my arse, lifted me up and roughly tossed me towards the centre of the bed. I wasn't prepared, but fuck, I loved every second of it.

He climbed up after me, used a thigh to roughly spread my knees, then hovered over me in a way that tightened every muscle in his shoulders, arms, and chest. I scraped my teeth over my top lip, cataloguing the lines of his body as they danced and twitched with restraint.

"I want to fucking *wreck* you," he growled, and the sound of his voice had me arching my back, clinging to his arms, and searching for his cock with my twisting hips. "My dick is so hard it hurts, Red, and as much as I wish I could sink into you slow enough to torture you the way you asked, all I really want to do is slam into this tight, wet pussy over and over, hard enough and fast enough to make you fucking scream my name."

"Do it." I reached between us and wrapped my hand around his dick. Isaac choked back a curse, and maybe I imagined it, but his cock felt hotter and harder and more desperate than I'd have believed possible. "I like it rough."

Isaac groaned as he straightened and retrieved a condom from his bedside table. I watched as he ripped open the packet and rolled on the rubber, feeling like I'd won some sort of penis lottery and desperate to know how it would feel to be that full.

As the moment teetered on its edge, Isaac paused and pressed his hands to my inner thighs, massaging his way up to where I was damp.

"Just for tonight, let me be what you need," he said suddenly. "Whatever it is, I want you to have it."

"Romeo, I—" His words broke open something inside me and I simply…let go. Of what, I had no idea, but that's the only way I could describe it. I let something inside me go. "I don't want to think anymore," I admitted. "I don't want to be in control. I don't want to be the one always looking for solutions to a million and one problems. What I need you to do is take charge. Take over. Just…do what you want with me."

His eyes widened a little, but I was only telling the truth. In my dreams, I never had to make the rules. I never even needed to know what they were. When the gamble was imaginary, I could let go and let someone else call the shots. That was the factor that made sex in my head so freaking fantastic, a factor I'd never let happen in life. Now, I wanted to know what it would feel like, and there was only one man I felt safe enough with to try.

Still, he hesitated.

I set a hand on his forearm and gave it a squeeze. "I trust you."

Isaac's nostrils flared as he lunged for my mouth, kissing me hard enough to border on violently. I flung my arms around his neck and kissed him back, stroking his tongue with mine, opening my mouth wider to invite him in.

I protested a little when he pulled away, but my nonsensical whimpers transformed into a sharp inhalation of anticipation as he lined himself up to my entrance and pushed the tip of his cock into my throbbing centre. I held my breath until, an interminable time later, he gave me another inch before pausing again.

"I know I told you to do what you want," I panted, clawing at his arse as I tried and failed to drive him inside me, "but please let what you want be to wreck me *now.*"

With a strangled grunt, Isaac entered me with a hard, almost brutal thrust. I gasped at the sudden feel of it—intense pleasure and overwhelming satisfaction underscored by a twinge of hedonistic pain. Isaac shifted his hips and pushed deeper, sweat beading on his forehead as my pussy stretched to accommodate his size. The resistance began to soften, and he groaned as his pelvis began to rock. I was a goner after that.

Isaac pistoned into me, sliding in and out of my wetness with slick, urgent pulses that had me carving scratch marks in his back.

"Fuck, Red. I need more—"

Isaac cut off with a moan and threw my legs over his shoulders. The angles shifted, and I gasped as he ground against me, stimulating my clit and setting off little explosions of pleasure deep within my core.

He leaned further forwards until I was folded in half, and in that position, I finally felt him bottom out.

"Oh, Jesus." Isaac rolled into me in tight, exquisite circles. "You're so tight and so wet, and I fit so fucking—"

"Perfect," I moaned.

He grunted in agreement and lowered my legs, pressing against my knees to open me wider and applying the pad of his thumb to my clit. I inhaled sharply at the pressure and jerked my hips for more. He kneaded one breast with his other hand, at once reverent and rough, his fingers circling the hard bud of my nipple. I loved the way he treated my body like he owned it—like I was his—though somewhere in the deep, irritating recesses of my mind, a tiny voice shouted that I belonged to nobody—needed nobody—least of all a man. I stuck a sock in her mouth and promised myself I'd deal with it later.

I fisted handfuls of my own hair as Isaac pumped into me, and I moaned in nonsensical monosyllables as he sucked my nipples, nipped my lips, and ran his tongue along my collarbone. Then, in one strong, smooth movement, he slid an arm under my waist and flipped us both over, leaving him on his back and me riding his cock.

The sudden switch took my breath away, the size of him reaching places deeper and more primed than they'd ever been, and as I bucked my hips, I knew I was about fifteen seconds away from a fucking glorious orgasm.

"You've done it now, Romeo," I said breathlessly. "I'm about to come all over your gorgeous cock. Is that what you wanted?"

"With you taking my dick like you were made for it? Fuck, yes."

He gripped my hips and guided my movements, making them rougher, more carnal. His words, his hands, his voice, landed like they were tailor made for Birdie Maxwell, and it was the beginning of a wonderful, wonderful end.

My climax took hold, and I fell forwards on Isaac's chest, grinding and rubbing as every cell of my body caught fire. I screamed, loud and long and hard, just like my orgasm, and distantly registered Isaac rolling his hips up into me, his fingers gripping painfully hard into my thighs, a string of raspy curse words spilling from his mouth and echoing against my ear as he poured himself into me, giving himself over to his release just as I gave myself to mine.

Collapsing, I rested my forehead in the crook of Isaac's neck, fighting my way back to the surface. His chest heaved as erratically as mine, and our bodies were soaked with mingled sweat. I'd never fucked anyone so hard. Never been fucked that hard either. Never thought it was possible.

That was my cue. Too serious, too intimate. It was time to get up and run.

Except this time, I didn't want to run. I didn't want to walk the twenty paces from Isaac's front door to mine. I didn't want to sleep alone in my bed, knowing this man was so close, sleeping alone in his. And yet, I didn't know how to—or even if I should—say so out loud.

I stayed there on Isaac's chest long after our breathing had slowed. I didn't want to move, but eventually, I risked a look up at him through my eyelashes, and he was already staring down at me. We locked eyes for a moment before he dropped a soft kiss on my forehead.

"One moment, Red. I'll be back."

I eased off him and rolled onto my side, watching his beautiful bare back as he headed to the bathroom. The seconds ticked by as I tried to figure out a way to broach the subject of my staying a little longer… I didn't have to use the words *sleeping over*, did I? Maybe I didn't need to use words at all. Maybe if I closed my eyes, he'd assume I was already asleep, and an overnighter would happen by accident. Yes, that could work.

But my stupid, traitorous eyelids fluttered open at the sound of him returning, some primitive pocket of my brain unwilling to pass up the chance to get another look at Isaac in all his wondrous, naked glory.

Primitive Birdie was one hundred percent right. Open eyes for the win.

Isaac pulled back the covers and slipped underneath them, resting on his side facing me. "So, do you have work to do tonight, or could you stay a little longer?"

"Oh, Romeo," I said, disguising my pathetic schoolgirl longing with a dependable veneer of snark. "If you think I've got another round in me, think again. It's been a big night, and I'm spent, and after a performance like that, I'm going to be sore for days."

The corner of his mouth twitched. "I'd say I'm sorry, but I'm not, and I'm willing to raincheck round two for at least twelve hours, so long as you're here in the morning when it's time to collect."

Rolling away from him and off the bed, I held my tongue until after I'd visited the bathroom. In the mirror, my hair was wild and matted, my cheeks were flushed, and my lips looked bitten and swollen. I looked younger, I thought. Prettier, and I rarely gave much thought to things like that. I didn't think too much about why these observations occurred to me now.

I stepped back into the bedroom, noting that Isaac had opened a window, and a cool breeze now drifted into the room. Isaac lay on the bed looking up at me, one hand underneath his head, the covers on my side pulled back. There was no way I could walk away from him, even if I wanted to.

"Okay, Romeo," I murmured. "I'll stay a little longer."

I slid in beside Isaac, and he immediately wrapped an arm around my waist and pulled me against his chest. I'd never snuggled before, and the experience was strange but…nice.

I wriggled against his warm, hard body until I was comfortable, but as the night air tickled my bare arms and my toes rubbed against the cool cotton sheets, I curled my legs tighter against my stomach, seeking to soothe the agitation with my own body warmth.

Maybe this sleepover idea was a bad one. I was totally unprepared. I didn't have a toothbrush, and I couldn't sleep if my feet were cold.

"What's with all the twitching?" Isaac mumbled against my hair, his voice low and lazy with the promise of sleep.

"Nothing. Don't worry about it." I twisted my legs together and tried to tuck my toes in somewhere warm, but it didn't help. I never slept without socks.

Isaac lifted the sheets and peeked underneath, where he frowned at the picture of me tangled up like a pretzel. "Seriously, Red. That doesn't look comfortable."

I sighed, unravelling my legs and flopping onto my back. "My feet get cold real quick, so I always sleep with socks. It feels weird going to bed with bare feet."

"What if I did this?" he asked as he readjusted his position, shifting me over and to the side, then captured my toes between his calves. "Warm enough now?"

The heat of his skin soaked into me, and I practically purred with contentment. "It'll do, I suppose."

He barked out a short laugh. "Good."

Half a minute passed before I jiggled my toes and whispered, "Can you really sleep like this all night?"

Isaac took a deep breath of my hair. "I've never come so hard in my entire life, and I'm about ready to pass out. Nothing's keeping me awake for much longer than the next five minutes, and nothing's going to stop me from keeping you warm. So, settle in, Red." He flexed his leg muscles and squeezed my feet. At the same time, he wrapped an arm around my waist and scooped me closer. "You're not going anywhere."

A knot loosened in my chest, and I breathed deeper than I had in a long time. Another expansive inhalation followed, and another after that, but that's all I remembered before I opened my eyes the next morning, sunlight streaming in the open window, Isaac's heavy arm around my middle, and my toes still safe and warm where he held them.

19

ISAAC

I WOKE UP with Birdie tucked in against me, her knees drawn up tight between us, her warm breath tickling the hair on my chest, and her feet wedged between my calves. I took care not to disturb her as my breathing shallowed and my dick grew hard, replaying the night we'd just had. The way she'd given up control and let me do what I wanted with her, the way I wanted. Talk the way I wanted. I'd swear under oath she liked the way I used her body as my plaything and loved the filthy things I whispered in her ear. More than loved it. She craved it.

Part of me wondered if it weren't for Birdie reappearing when she did, if I'd have ever found someone perfect enough for me to do half the stuff I'd already done with her or try a fraction of the things I still dreamed of doing. I couldn't imagine letting down my walls like this with anyone but her.

I inhaled the smell of her—warm with sleep and with a hint of apples—and committed it to memory.

Fuck, what a night. I wanted to do it over and over for the rest of my life, starting with the part where she told me she trusted me. That meant just as much, if not more, than everything that came after.

I watched her sleep as long as I could, drinking in the sight of her wrapped up in my grey sheets, dark lashes resting on her pale, freckled cheeks, and her long copper hair spilling across the pillows. Her lips were pink and relaxed in a plump little pout, and the whole combination gave her the appearance of a nymph.

I had a sex goddess in my bed, and I never wanted to let her go.

Eventually, because I couldn't help myself, I danced my fingers over the bare skin of her arm, leaving trails of goosebumps in my wake. The first flickers of awareness lit across her eyelids and tugged at the corners of her mouth, and my touch grew firmer as I slid one hand under the covers and smoothed a palm over her firm backside.

"Mm," she moaned sleepily, eyes still closed. "Good morning, Romeo."

"Morning, Red. How'd you sleep?"

"Pretty good, thanks to your nuclear levels of body heat."

"Available for your personal use at any time."

Her mouth twitched in a small smile. "Thanks. And how about you? Did you sleep all right, even with me stuck to you like a barnacle?"

I clenched my legs around her feet and gave her arse a squeeze. "Never slept better in my life."

"Explosive orgasms will do that to a man."

Birdie extracted her feet from between my legs and flipped over onto her back, pointing her toes and raising her arms over her head in a feminine, almost feline full-body stretch. I pulled back the covers and watched with rapture as her muscles tensed and released until, unable to keep my hands to myself, I ran one over her nakedness, starting at the hip, brushing past her smooth pussy with a teasing touch that had her opening her thighs, then travelling up, around her navel and over her ribcage, skimming past the multicoloured dragonflies, flowers, and birds she had needled into her skin.

I cupped one breast while I closed my mouth around the opposite nipple in a brief, hot suck before I chased one palm up along her arm, where she held them both over her head, and finally enclosed her wrists in my grip. It took no effort at all to restrain her with one hand, but that's not what I was aiming to do.

Almost immediately, I drew her arms down and turned her hands palm up, exposing the ink she had scrawled into the insides of her wrists. It was only this close, in a proper light, that I could make out what was permanently written there.

"Hold," I read aloud, running the pad of my thumb over the black lines and blue veins in her left wrist. Doing the same to the right, I said, "Fold."

"Yep," she said, looking at them with me.

"Like in poker?"

"In poker. In life." Birdie pulled away, and I let her go. She twisted to mirror my posture, propping up on one elbow and setting her head in her hand to face me.

"Years ago," she explained, "around the time I bailed on my mathematics degree months before I finished it, I went out and got them to celebrate giving up one dream so I could chase a new one. I wanted those words there, forever on my skin, to remind me there are always two ways to face a challenge—two ways to handle a problem. One: back your hand no matter the cards and no matter the cost. Bluff if you have to but see it through. And two: duck your head, cut your losses, and give the hand away. Do better the next time around."

"There's no middle ground?" I wondered. "It's all or nothing? Win or lose?"

"Always. I don't live in the grey areas. Everything's either black, white, or technicolour."

Something about Birdie's rigid approach to life didn't sit right with me, but it wasn't the time to say so. And it wasn't surprising that this woman, who'd never in her life known a day of unconditional love, looked at things through such an arbitrary lens.

I really understood then, for the first time, that Birdie existed with this gaping void in her life. To distract myself from a pang of sadness, I traced the little butterflies etched into the skin between her ribs. They were no bigger than the tip of my forefinger, and there were only two of them—one fiery red, the other a striking green.

"What about the butterflies?" I asked. "When did you get these?"

Birdie dragged her fingers through her hair, rearranging the strands so they no longer twisted around her neck and shoulders. "Um, about three years ago. At a hole-in-the-wall studio in Brooklyn, New York."

Before I could ask about any of the other patterns etched into her skin, Birdie flipped back the covers. "Don't go anywhere," she said with a cheeky wink as she glanced down at my swollen cock with a suggestive grin. "I'll be right back."

I wasn't an idiot. Unwilling to take the risk of monster morning breath, I waited until Birdie had closed the ensuite door before I snuck away to use the bathroom down the hall. I was back in bed and under the covers before Birdie reappeared.

Jesus, she was beautiful. My heart forgot its even rhythm at the sight of her, and the confidence in her naked strut went straight to my cock. When she wriggled in beside me, pressing the length of her body against mine, I squeezed my eyes closed and dropped my head back as she trapped my engorged dick between us. The warmth of her skin was a torturous echo of the wet heat I knew waited for me inside her body.

Birdie ran her open hands over my arms, starting at my fingers and finishing at my shoulders, which she kneaded while pressing her mouth to my throat in a line of licks and kisses that skated my collarbone. As my groan vibrated against her lips, I felt her smile as her hands slid down my pecs and over my stomach before latching onto my arse. With a hard, almost painful grip, she yanked my pelvis closer to her body.

"Aren't you sore, Red?" I murmured, capturing her mouth with mine and parting her lips with a gentle probe of my tongue. She opened her mouth and let me in, and I stroked her there while slipping my hand between us, seeking her pussy. She widened her knees, and I gently grazed her velvet-soft folds before circling my palm against her sex and letting her wetness slick my hand. Fuck, I'd never get over how drenched she was for me.

"A little," she replied before chuckling and squirming away from me as she tried to shimmy down the mattress. "Okay, a lot. You're seriously packing, Sergeant Greene, but while we wait for me to recover from the railing you gave me last night, there are plenty of other things we can do."

I watched as her copper head moved further south, my heart thundering at the way she'd purred my name and my dick jumping at the picture of Birdie Maxwell descending into my lap. I squeezed my eyes shut and sucked a breath in through my nose as she slipped a hand under my balls and ran a fingertip along the sensitive spot behind them. Then she wrapped her cool fingers around the base of my cock, and I twisted my fists into the sheets as her tongue brushed the tip, gently exploring the slit with hot, teasing strokes.

My eyes were closed. Why the fuck wasn't I watching this? I'd never see anything better than the picture of Birdie sucking my cock, and it was an image I wanted burned deep within my brain just as permanently as the tattoos on her skin, but when I opened my eyes, I was immediately distracted by the sight of her legs tucked up beneath her and her bare, ivory arse bouncing temptingly in the air.

With a primal growl, I looped an arm around her waist and spun her around. Her squeal provoked the caveman in me, and I threw her legs on either side of my shoulders, repositioning her so she straddled my face.

She squeaked again when I nipped her thigh with my teeth, and after that, I couldn't wait another second.

I stiffened my tongue and plunged into Birdie's dripping pussy. She cried out and then moaned her pleasure before falling on my cock, and as I ran the flat of my tongue along her centre, lapping at the irresistible flavour of her, I was struck by the sensation of her hot mouth slipping down my dick, and I almost lost my goddamn mind—my mind and my load, straight down her hot, hard throat.

Things got wet and messy fast. I ate her with no finesse, burying my lips into every fold I could find, circling and sucking her clit in turns, twisting my tongue in her core, anything that would elicit a gasp or a groan to tell me I was doing this right. But the more intense things became at my end, the more ferociously Birdie worked my cock—every moan in her chest reverberating through my dick and into my body, her hands slipping on the wetness of her mouth as she bobbed up and down on as much length as she could take. Her fist took the rest, gripping and twisting with a desperation I reciprocated until her thighs began to tremble, and I felt the flutter of her impending orgasm on my tongue.

Tilting her hips a little higher in the air, I latched onto her clit, sucking and flicking it with the tip of my tongue just as I slid my thumb into her core and set a wet finger against the tight ring of muscle a little higher, circling first and then pressing firmly enough to slip the tip inside.

She released my cock with a wet pop, her hand still working me with slippery, sloppy strokes. "Holy fuck, that feels… Where the fuck did you learn to do that? Oh, God. I'm going to come."

I pressed the length of my thumb deep inside her and played her with my tongue and fingers as everything grew wetter. I growled as she came, her grip on my dick contracting at the same time her core tightened around my fingers. Every muscle in my body seized up, and even as tremors of her orgasm rippled through her, she sank over me and pressed my cock between her tits, rubbing and stroking me until I painted her chest. Over and over, I coated her with wet ropes of release, sinking into the feel of me captured between her soft curves, wishing I could see the way Birdie looked covered in my cum.

"Jesus," she muttered, collapsing beside me on her back, eyes closed and her breath coming in quick, laboured pants. "That was… Fuck. What was that?"

"I think it's called a sixty-niner," I mumbled, trying to catch my breath as I skimmed my eyes over Birdie's body—flushed, damp, and, yes, dripping with my load. It was sexy as hell, and my dick started to harden again. "And you're fucking gorgeous."

She twisted her head to look at me, the unexpected softness in her eyes fading fast as she smirked. "I'm a fucking mess, and so are you, Romeo. You should see your beard."

I ran a hand over my jaw. She was right, and it gave me an idea.

Jumping to my feet, I grabbed her ankles, dragged her to the edge of the bed, then picked her up and flipped her face down over my shoulder. As I headed towards the bathroom, I set a gentle kiss on her hip, and at the same time, she gave my arse cheek a hard pinch.

"Hey! What did I do to deserve that?"

"You're treating me like a piece of meat. What's with the 'me Tarzan, you Jane' routine?"

You're the only one who makes me feel safe enough to be me, I thought, *and you told me you trust me. I'm going to make sure you never regret saying it—or feeling it.*

But I wasn't stupid. Saying that shit out loud was asking for trouble—trouble and a shower all by myself. So, what I said was, "You like it rough. You like it when I take charge. And you need a shower. So, I'm taking care of business and soaping up my girl."

We reached the bathroom, and I set her down on the cool tiles. I clocked the "fight me" look on her face—eyebrows drawn, mouth open, blue eyes glinting with gold fire—and I glowered right back. "Shut up, Red. Let me do this. Let me take care of you."

I saw the argument gather behind her eyes and prepared myself to leave her in my ensuite while I pictured her slippery and wet as I jerked off in the guest bathroom.

Then, without warning, her frown faded, and she stretched up on her toes, looping her arms around my neck and pressing her cheek to mine. "All right, Romeo," she whispered, her voice warm against my ear and submissive in a way that had me struggling to swallow. "You can take care of me, but just this once."

20

BIRDIE

FOUR DAYS AND fourteen—count 'em, *fourteen*—orgasms later, I stood at my bedroom window in the twilight before dawn, a hot mug of coffee steaming between my hands, and the curtains tweaked just enough that I could peek out into Isaac's backyard. His house was still dark, though his bedroom light had flickered on three minutes ago, so I knew he was awake.

I justified the change in my routine by reminding myself that I had to get up early anyway. Isaac's parents had invited me to a family breakfast, and it started at nine. Isaac had gone to work the night before, so I'd crammed eight hours of tournaments and study and bookkeeping in before midnight, then I was ready for an early night. All the sex had exhausted my body. I hadn't worked so many solid hours in days, and my brain was full to bursting. It had been time to go to bed, simple as that. I didn't plan to be awake in time to watch the boy next door work out. It just happened that way. Total coincidence.

I slurped down a scalding mouthful of coffee and grimaced. I was an idiot. A sexually gratified idiot, sure, but still an idiot, and a short-sighted one at that. I was leaving in less than a month, and the better the sex got, the harder it was going to be to say goodbye. For Isaac, that is. Not for me. Goodbyes were my thing. I lived for a solid goodbye. Nobody did goodbyes better than Birdie Maxwell. But Isaac wasn't built for them, and even though we both knew our arrangement had an end date, I worried that he was starting to forget that I couldn't hang around forever and no good could come of that.

I chewed on my lip and stared into the shadows. Isaac and I had been close as kids, and while we'd sort of picked up from where we left off twelve years ago, we'd only truly revived that old intimacy when he'd set me in front of his punching bag, and I'd told him the truth about my parents.

If I was ever going to lose it with a witness nearby taking notes, it could only have been Isaac. I'd never had good friends, let alone a best one, and Isaac was as close as I'd ever come—then and now. I didn't regret opening up to him the way I had as much as I cringed at the memory of all the blubbering, but I didn't want him to read anything into my sudden openness. My complicated relationship with my parents changed nothing about my plans to leave the Bay. If anything, it was more essential now than before that I disappeared.

I glanced at my phone charging on my bedside table. I'd received another message from Cora. She'd wanted to know how long I'd be in Valentine Bay, and I'd told her I'd be at the house for another three weeks—and that was it. She hadn't given me a date or a plan for her arrival, and I refused to ask. Her behaviour only reinforced the fact that I had to put an end to the way I let my parents torture me. They had to know I didn't need them. I didn't need anybody.

As I watched and impatiently waited for Isaac to appear, I went over my plan for us again. The new plan I'd come up with to replace the original one that lay balled up on the floor like a pair of my sodden underwear.

With all the sex and all the sharing, the student-coach segment of Isaac's study program was well and truly over, and phase two had begun. It was my job now to use the time I had left in the Bay to build up Isaac's confidence, though there really wasn't much left for me to do in that department either. The thought had me smirking over the rim of my cup. Who the hell would have bet on the fact that by teaching Isaac a handful of new moves, I'd create the cocky monster he'd become?

Not me, but if I had known, I'd have jumped his bones *much* sooner.

The guy could be a freaking animal, and when we were together, he didn't play down those parts of himself.

I loved every minute of it, and Isaac knew it. He'd thrown me down, held me up, flipped and folded me every which way, murmured deliciously dirty things in my ear, taken what he wanted and given me what I needed every time. The hottest part was I never had to ask for it. Anyone would think having a blank cheque to tell a man what you want in bed would be a fantasy come true—and I won't lie to myself, the sight of Isaac kneeling because I told him to will never not get me wet—but I was more turned on by the thrill of *not* having to ask for anything.

The last four days had proved to me that once Isaac had his hands on me, I couldn't predict what would come next—aside from me. Many, many times.

A shiver ran up my spine. Sex with Isaac was *that* good.

So, it wasn't a hardship for either of us to make sure that when I was gone, he'd have a firm handle on his hot new skill set. It was my job to make sure his confidence didn't desert him the moment he tried something with another woman.

I squinted into my coffee, then sniffed at it. Ugh. Was the milk off? I set the mug aside as I swallowed to settle my sudden queasiness, then scowled at Isaac's shadowy back door. It wasn't sour milk. It was that protective streak rearing its inconvenient head again.

Should I worry about him? I mean, *could* Isaac do the things he did to me to another woman? Would he want to?

Yes, Birdie. He could, and he would. That's what this is all about. There's no special reason you're the first girl he's teased and pleased for six hours straight, and you won't be the last. You got lucky. Right time, right place, blah, blah, blah…

I stood straighter as Isaac's porch light came to life, and the man himself stepped out the back door.

What the actual fuck, Romeo? Why are you wearing a shirt?

Isaac crossed the timber-decked porch, shoulders straining and biceps bulging underneath the dark, long-sleeved Henley he wore with his faded blue jeans as he concentrated on something he held in one palm—an open book. He had a cup of coffee in the other hand, and without lifting his eyes from whatever he was reading, he set the mug on a little side table then lowered himself into the single armchair next to it. And that was it.

Great. I'd woken up early, and there was no show? I picked up my cup and took a sip, grumbling internally about missing out on a private performance.

Was he just going to sit there all morning? *Reading*? I was unreasonably pissed off, but I couldn't take my eyes off him—off his inky hair and perfectly trimmed beard, his strong jaw and wide shoulders, his thick thighs stretching the denim of his jeans. The longer I stared, the less irritated I became. Very quickly, I grew warm, starting with a flush in my cheeks and a burn across my skin, and ending with a nice hot pulse between my thighs, because what's a greater turn-on that a hot man at the gym?

Hot. Man. Reading.

I squeezed my thighs together as Isaac leaned forwards, set his spectacular arms on his knees, and frowned at the book in his hands—those magical, miraculous hands that had greased me up and flipped me over like a pancake before he had me for breakfast just twenty-four hours earlier, were now turning pages with smooth, sexy movements that tortured me like three hours of foreplay.

He ran a hand over his beard and took a swallow of coffee before flicking backwards a few pages to re-read the same passage again. His brows drew down, and his lips moved like he was reading aloud or trying to memorise the words on the paper, and I whimpered at how adorable and downright seductive he was. And all he was doing was reading.

Never mind that he wasn't working *his* muscles that morning. I needed to work mine, and after a quick glance at the toiletries bag perching precariously on the clothes still spilling out of my open suitcase, I dismissed Mr Big Boy and decided to ride the real thing.

Three minutes later, I was knocking on Isaac's door and climbing that man like a fucking tree.

Three hours later, Isaac opened the unlocked front door to his parents' house and let us both in. I sighed as a wave of air-conditioned air caressed my face and checked that all my clothes were in order. Happy voices, children's squeals, and peals of laughter floated down the hall towards us, and as Isaac shut the door, he cast his eyes towards me, and his face broke into a grin.

"Do something about that flush in your cheeks, Red. You look like you just came hard all over my fingers in the front seat of my car."

I checked my reflection in the smudged mirror above the hallway table and discovered he was right. I smacked him hard across one shoulder, which only made him laugh. I loved the dirty talk. I loved the confidence. But I also loved his family, and I wasn't about to sit across the table from Isaac's dad looking so much like sex they'd cast me as the bad girl in their son's good cop routine.

"Shh! Don't say shit like that where your mother can hear."

He only chuckled harder, then threw a bulky arm around my neck and dragged me against his side so he could mess up my braid. "There. Now they'll never suspect a thing."

I faked a grumble and tried to neaten my hair, but the possibility that Isaac wanted his family to know we were balls-deep in a four-week fling made me feel all kinds of weird. Giddy? No, that wasn't it. Uncomfortable? Not that, either. Suffocated. Terrified. Irritated. None of those fit.

Proud? Satisfied? Smug? No. No. No. That was just plain weird.

We slipped through the doorway that led to the dining room, where the long family dining table had been extended with a shorter, round table at one end and a wobbly trestle table at the other, all covered with a patchwork of brightly coloured tablecloths. It was kind of nice that every face in the room was familiar to me now—Isaac had done all the introductions and re-introductions at Mason's birthday party—and I grinned at the picture of everyone diving at platters overflowing with eggs and pastries, fresh fruit and fried bacon, spooning mounds of each onto plates.

We arrived just as Mason knocked over a water glass, spilling the entire contents across the table into the lap of one of his cousins, which triggered a nice, strong, ear-piercing screech. Isaac's sister, Meghan, jumped to her feet while Dan, one of Isaac's brothers-in-law—with a newborn strapped to his chest—rushed straight past us and into the kitchen. It was rowdy. It was mayhem. It was a family.

Isaac lifted my hand and slowly guided me a step backwards. "I don't think they've noticed us yet," Isaac muttered from the corner of his mouth. "It's not too late to bail."

I elbowed him in the ribs, eliciting a subtle *oomph* that I took great pleasure in hearing. "It's your sister's birthday. Do your brotherly duty and smile like you love her."

Isaac grunted noncommittally as Kris spotted us hovering at the edge of the room. Her face brightened as she sprung up, arms extended towards me. I stepped into them so I could return her hard hug, but she collected Isaac with her other arm, and I was squished between them as Isaac gave his mother a squeeze.

"Oh, honey," she said, letting me go and setting a cool palm on my cheek. "Is it hot out there already? The weather report did say it'd be a scorcher. You look like you could use a cold drink. Mimosa sound good?"

She pulled me to the table, and Isaac followed, swiping a strawberry from a fruit platter on the way. He wrapped his mouth around the tip of it and winked.

Was it *totally* inappropriate to be thinking about dragging him upstairs and blowing him in the bathroom?

Yes, Birdie. Yes, it was. Understandable? Sure. But totally—*totally*—inappropriate.

"A mimosa sounds perfect," I said, and as Kris filled a champagne flute with a respectable ratio of sparkling white wine to orange juice, Isaac's father, Rusty—a retired police officer with greying auburn hair, a thick goatee, and shoulders almost as wide as Isaac's—pulled out a chair for me.

"It's good to see you again, sweetheart," he said as I scooted in beside him. "We want to see your face at this table at least a dozen more times before we have to say goodbye again." He smacked Isaac affectionately on the backside of his head. "You hear that? Bring this girl around more often. Your sisters miss her."

Sarah, Jas, and Meghan grinned and sent their distracted hellos across the table and over the noise of Meghan trying to wrangle a wriggly Mason and Jas attempting to soothe her drenched little girl. Olivia, I remembered her name was. Six years old. I mouthed a quiet *happy birthday* to Jas, and she mouthed an equally silent *thank you* my way.

"Let's get through breakfast first," Isaac quipped as he took his father's hand and pulled the older man into a one-armed embrace. "One meal with this lot might scare Birdie away forever."

I sat down just as Kris handed me the cocktail, and Rusty pressed a fatherly kiss to the top of my head. Taking a sip, I pretended that his gesture didn't trigger a bloom of warmth inside my chest, the same way I ignored how the reminder that I was leaving soon tightened the muscles in my throat.

As he took a seat across from me, Isaac shot me a small smile, but it was tighter than the grin he'd given me in the hallway, and it didn't quite reach his pretty green eyes.

21

BIRDIE

BEFORE I KNEW it, an hour had passed in a cacophony of noise and mess and laughs, everyone playing a covert game of musical chairs as the conversation ebbed and flowed between different members of the family. There were nine adults in the Greene family—Isaac's parents plus Isaac and his sisters and their partners—and between them, they had eight kids and another one on the way. All they needed was for Isaac to catch the procreation bug, and the Greenes on the senior side of eighteen would be seriously outnumbered.

That constricted feeling in my stomach balled up into something heavy, hollowing out a gaping void where my vital organs should have been. Isaac was going to make a fantastic father someday. His babies would be adorable… And he'd have them with someone else.

I'd never be a mother—or a wife. Cora's twisted legacy ended with me, and I'd never be any good at family life anyway. What the hell did I know about raising children or being a good parent? As if I needed any of that. But this was a solid, insurmountable reason Isaac and I were only ever meant to be friends.

I blinked rapidly. Of course, we were only ever supposed to be friends. Good friends. Friends who happened to have great sex. Why had thoughts about babies even occurred to me? I wished I could rewind the last thirty seconds and scrub *that* image from my brain. But try as I might, I couldn't manage it, and I was relieved when Sarah slid into the empty seat beside me.

"Hey, you," I greeted her with a smile.

Like Isaac and both her sisters, Sarah had ebony hair, but she wore hers to her shoulders, and under the light, I noticed glittery hints of silver glinting through in places. Her eyes were as dark brown as their mother's—only Isaac and Meghan had inherited their father's startling green colour. Sarah scooted her chair a little closer and helped herself to half a croissant as she leaned her head towards me and dropped her voice a little.

"I need to ask a favour," she murmured.

"Oh?" I glanced around the table, but nobody seemed to notice the clandestine nature of Sarah's posture. Nobody but Isaac, of course.

After his glance skated across the two of us huddled around our plates, he averted his eyes and returned to Josephine—Sarah's youngest at nine years old. They were fifteen minutes into an intense discussion about the summer soccer season—tactics, teammates, strategy. Isaac had coached Jo's team for the past two years, as well as Sarah's eldest girl, Imogen's team, the two years before that. By the looks on the girls' faces—both bouncing in their chairs with wide eyes and words that ran over each other—and the way Isaac responded—all amused mouth and sensible instruction—he enjoyed acting in that role as much as his nieces loved having him in it.

"It's about Liam," Sarah said, and at the mention of her teenage son's name, I scanned the table and realised that, at some point in the morning, he'd slipped away.

"Is he okay?" I wondered.

"Oh, he's fine. He's just..." Sarah set her pastry down and brushed the crumbs from her hands. "I don't know if Isaac mentioned this to you, but Liam's been placed in an accelerated mathematics program at school. He's only fifteen, but at the rate he's learning, he'll be able to complete his high school maths requisites two years early."

It was a story I'd heard—no, lived—before. Sarah had my attention, even though I wasn't sure yet why she shared this information with me. I tilted my head to one side. "No, I didn't know. That's incredible. You must be proud."

"Oh, I am—we are—but I'm worried as well. Put it this way, when a fifteen-year-old boy sneaks away from a family birthday breakfast and hides himself away, what's the first thing that comes to mind?"

"He's off playing video games somewhere?" I offered, but Sarah shook her head, so I tried again. "Texting his friends? Calling a girl?" More head shaking, and I wondered for a moment if it was something more serious. "Oh, no, Sarah. Is it…? Is it drugs?"

She chuckled under her breath. "No. He's upstairs studying."

"He's—" I frowned. "Studying?"

Sarah nodded, then plucked a grape from a near-empty platter and stuffed it in her mouth. "All he ever does is study, and I worry about the pressure he puts on himself. The kid is smarter than I can ever hope to be—and he doesn't get it from his father, that's for sure." Sarah waved at her husband, Robert, across the table. He returned the gesture suspiciously, and I covered my smile with the leftover corner of my toast. "I love my husband to the ends of the Earth," Sarah sighed, "but the origins of Liam's genius are lost to history, I'm afraid."

"I suppose these things can crop up when you least expect it," I agreed. "But really, I don't know how I can help."

Nobody at this table knew about my own experience with academia—nobody but Isaac, and I'd sworn him to secrecy years ago. Even with Sarah broaching the topic now, in this way, I didn't believe for a second that Isaac would have betrayed a confidence of mine, even one so small and apparently insignificant. This had to be about something else, and it was.

"I was talking to a couple of other parents about it last week—Dawn among them. Her neighbour's cousin's daughter, Willow Winterbourne, is in her late twenties now, but Dawn told me how she struggled with her homework as a teen and that you used to tutor her during the summer. Most mornings in the library. Do you remember?"

"I do," I replied, marvelling at the reach of the Valentine Bay grapevine—and its infallible collective memory. I used to hang out in the library a lot back then, reading and studying—anything to get me out from under my parents' feet. The tutoring happened by accident, and the group of kids I worked with wasn't always that large, but I loved helping out. It made me feel like I had some use in the world. "Willow had loads of potential but not a lot of interest in numbers. Still, Mr Winterbourne kept me updated on Willow's test results throughout the year, and she got there in the end."

"She did, and in no small part, thanks to you. You studied mathematics at university, didn't you?"

"I did," I replied slowly, trying to get a step ahead of whatever was coming next.

"I can only assume that the high school curriculum would be simple stuff for you, so...would you mind?"

I cocked a puzzled eyebrow. "Would I mind...what? Tutoring Liam? It doesn't sound like—"

"Oh, no. No, no. You're right. He doesn't need a tutor. If anything, I think the suggestion that he needs help would make things worse. It's the opposite. Could you look at his work and reassure him that he has nothing to worry about? I love that he's so dedicated, but his studies have become all-consuming, and I'm not even certain he'll sign up for soccer again this year. I can count on one hand the days he's gone out surfing this month. And he won't listen to me or his dad. We don't understand, apparently." She grimaced and shrugged, but I could see the glimmer of hurt in her eyes. "He's growing up, and I thought I was prepared for this phase, but I never could have predicted I'd be dealing with a kid as bright as he is. How many mothers need to tell their fifteen-year-old boys to study less and play more? I want him to have a childhood, you know?"

"I do." Boy, did I know, maybe better than anyone. Certainly better than Sarah realised. I wiped my fingers on the napkin in my lap, then dropped it onto my plate. "I'll go talk to him. Where is he?"

"Meg's old room. It's the only one with a desk."

I gave Sarah's hand a quick squeeze, then pushed my chair back and left the room, only too aware of Isaac's curious eyes following my every step.

I knew to go left at the top of the stairs, and when I found Meghan's room, the door was only partway closed. I paused a moment to get a look at Liam—a long, lanky boy who reminded me a little of Isaac when he was young, only with sandy blond hair on his head—sitting hunched over his homework, a lamp lighting his textbooks, and his back to me. I tapped my knuckles against the door frame, and Liam's head jerked up.

"Oh, hey," he said. "Bathroom is further down the hall, on the right. Can't miss it."

"Thanks," I said, taking two steps into the room.

Liam sat up straighter, recognised something in my expression, then groaned and rolled his eyes. "My mother sent you up here, didn't she?"

"Yeah, she did." I wandered over to the desk and looked over his shoulder, running my eyes over the scratches he'd made on his grid paper and the equations he'd been poring over. It was complex stuff, much more suited to a first-year university student than a kid in the tenth grade. There was one question he'd obviously been stuck on. Line after line struck through and started again. I tapped my finger against the error that had sent him on a tangent—ha! "Check this cosine again."

Liam narrowed his brown eyes at me before his focus darted back to the paper, his gaze running like water over his workings before understanding lit his features. Quickly, he redid the equation, and I watched his pencil fly across the paper as he calculated his way to the correct answer.

"Good job," I commented as I lowered myself onto the bed.

Liam spun around in the desk chair, wonder on his spotty face. "How'd you do that?"

"Honestly? I'm a genius."

I don't know why I said it—why I so casually confessed something I'd always kept on a need-to-know basis, but I felt an immediate kinship with this kid, and he needed to hear it more than I needed it to stay a secret.

Liam chuckled, then stopped when I sat there, staring at him with a straight face. "Like, a real-live genius?"

I lifted one shoulder. "That's what the doctors told me." Liam laughed again, and I smiled. "Put it this way, I could give Stephen Hawking a run for his money—if he were still alive, of course."

"Wow." Liam glanced at his homework, then back at me. "You know, I think I might be a genius, too."

"By the look of the equations you're doing there, I'd say that's entirely possible."

A small smile pulled at the corners of his mouth, but it was all too brief, and soon he was frowning again. "But I don't think I'm a natural genius, you know? I'm the kind that has to work for it."

"Nothing worth doing should be easy. Otherwise, how would we know what makes a person special? But I'm curious. Why do you say that?"

He started doodling on his papers, giving him an excuse to avoid my eyes. "Because just when I get a handle on something, I go on to the next thing, and it's like starting all over again. If I was really, truly smart, wouldn't this stuff just click in my head without all the effort?"

I could tell there was more at stake here than Liam's confidence or an unhealthy attachment to his studies. In fact, I already had the impression that he knew he was intelligent, but he was worried about that intelligence failing him one day. Afraid there was a limit to what he could do. He thought most days about not being enough or being defined by what he produced on paper and letting people down if he reached a limit to his abilities. He dreaded his parents discovering he wasn't a winner after all.

Or maybe I was just projecting.

"Well, in my experience," I said, "that's just the burden people like you and me have to bear. We master a concept, and our brains itch to learn something new, so we seek out the next challenge and keep chipping away at it until we master that one as well."

"Yeah, that's it. It's like, it's never enough, right? I always want to know more. Do more. Be more."

"You want to know the scary part?" At his nod, I grinned. "It's never going to feel different. I still study every day, try something new every week, and push my limits over and over. If the maths was easy, why would I bother? The hard is what makes it fun, right?"

Liam nodded slowly, looking at his papers again as if seeing them for the first time. "Yeah, I suppose that's true."

"And if all this is starting to bore you, I have some great theoretical physics texts you can borrow. The kind of numbers that'll blow your mind."

"Really?" I immediately warmed at the look of excitement on his face. Only another numbers junkie could mirror the thrill I felt at talking about physics. "Hey, maybe we could study together? Nobody ever understands anything I say—not even my teachers half the time—and you could show me loads of new stuff."

Too late, I realised I'd unintentionally given Liam the impression I was sticking around the Bay, and I was shot through with a pang of guilt. Truthfully, I'd forgotten myself for a minute and been carried away in a fantasy of connecting with this kid, building a friendship on a common ground I didn't have with many people.

"Liam, that's a great idea, but—"

"I'm sure my parents would pay you," he added, a flush to his cheeks. "I didn't think you'd do it for free. I'm sure you've got a million better things to do than be in a study group with me."

"Would you believe I don't? Studying with you is almost the best offer I've had since I came back to the Bay, but the problem is, I'm not staying. I'm only here for a few more weeks."

"Oh. That sucks."

"Yeah, it does suck." I chewed on my bottom lip as I searched for a way to wipe the disappointment on his face. I knew better than to let my own show on mine. "But you know what? It's not all bad. I have a fantastic life thanks to mathematics. I've got a great job—"

"Really? What do you do?"

"I'm a professional poker player."

"Holy shit! You're what?"

His enthusiasm for my occupation brutally eclipsed his response to my genius, and I grinned harder. Perhaps the two of us had more in common than either of us originally thought.

"A professional poker player," I repeated.

"Bullshit! I thought I was going to end up a maths teacher or something boring like that."

"Hell, no. Maths can take you anywhere."

"Can you teach me to play?"

Oh, crap. "Uh, well, that's not really what your mother asked me to talk to you about."

Liam rolled his eyes the way only teenagers could, and I had to stop myself from laughing. "She wanted you to tell me that I didn't need to study so hard, right?"

"Well, she's not wrong. You're going to burn yourself out and grow to hate the thing you love unless you balance it out with other activities you enjoy. Your mum mentioned soccer and maybe surfing?"

"Yeah, yeah," he muttered before his expression brightened. "But poker could be that something else, couldn't it? What if I talk to my mum and dad and make a deal? Like, I'll sign up for soccer and go surfing once a week, as long as you can teach me poker?"

Oh, fuck. "I don't know—"

"Just leave it to me, Birdie. I know how to take care of my parents."

Liam's grin was so wide it broke his face in two, and I had to bite back a groan. *Way to put your foot in it, idiot.*

"If Sarah and Robert say yes," I said, holding up a finger to stop him from interrupting, "*and* you sign up for soccer, *and* you show me how well you surf, *and* we squeeze a little physics somewhere in there, then fine, I'll teach you the *mathematical theories* of poker."

"Just like the pros use," he added, thrusting out his hand.

"Yes, fine, just like the pros use," I amended, shaking on our deal and wondering if the Greenes might not be happy to see the back of me after all.

22

ISAAC

"LAST NIGHT, I woke up with a weird stabbing pain in my elbow," Birdie announced from her seat at my dining room table. The thing was covered in stacks of textbooks, notepads, pens and pencils, balled-up pieces of paper, and half-empty takeaway containers—and with her hair in a messy knot on the top of her head, pyjamas still on, and thick fuzzy socks on her feet, Birdie reigned like a delinquent queen over her mess. "Sarah's got a voodoo doll. I'm sure of it."

"She does not," I said with a chuckle. I gulped down the last mouthful of my breakfast smoothie, then rinsed the cup before adding it to the dishwasher. "It's been a week since the family breakfast, and in the last seven days, Liam's not only signed up for the summer soccer season, but I've convinced him to volunteer as a referee for the junior games as well, and he woke up early this morning to go surfing with his buddies. You worked a miracle, and Sarah's about ready to kiss your feet. So yeah, if your toes start to tickle, maybe we can file a complaint about your voodoo doll theory."

Birdie grimaced, then started doodling on a blank sheet of grid paper. "But the poker thing—"

"You spoke to her *and* Robert about this, and they both agreed that teaching Liam about the mathematical theories of a card game is not the end of the world you seem to think it is."

Still focused on her nonsensical swirls, Birdie said, "I've never much cared about being called a bad influence, but when it comes to your family… I don't know. It's different. They're maybe the only people in the world I want to like me."

"Too bad for you that they already love you," I replied, hiding my grin by pacing over to her and dropping a kiss on her head, burying my face in her sweet apple hair. It was the smile of a winner—of a man who was trying to convince his girl she belonged with him, here in this town, and doing a damn good job of it.

"Yeah, yeah," she grumbled, but I heard her pleasure in the uptick of her tone, and I claimed it as another point for me. "You're just saying that to make me feel better."

"I'm not. It's the simple truth. My family thinks you're amazing." I checked my watch. "Look, I hate to cut this conversation short, but I'm late for an appointment. Liam will be here in an hour, right?"

"Yep." She glanced around at the table, then down at herself. "Thanks for the reminder. I should probably go home and shower."

"I threw some of your clothes into the washer when I did a load yesterday," I said as casually as I could, scooping up my keys as if my announcement was no big deal. And it wasn't—to me. "So, if you want to shower here, you've got something clean to change into. I left it all hanging in my wardrobe."

"You didn't have to do that," Birdie murmured, climbing to her feet and tugging irritably at the oversized tee she liked to wear to bed. That bed had been mine the last four out of seven nights, not that I was counting. "I can wash my own clothes."

"I know you can, but you had some things here and I was doing laundry anyway." I plucked an apple from the fruit bowl and changed the subject. "Will you be home later?"

"What time? I have an online tournament later this afternoon, so I'll be at my place."

I took a bite of fruit to hide another smile. Whether or not she realised it, Birdie instinctively felt the need to point out which "home" we were talking about—hers or mine. "I'm on shift this evening, so I can meet you there around ten?"

"Perfect." Birdie's blue eyes lit up, widening enough to show the whites all around. "Can you bring doughnuts? The cinnamon kind. They're my favourite."

I scowled suspiciously. "Is this a cop-and-doughnuts joke? You making fun of my gut, Red?"

Birdie laughed as she sidled over to me, and I groaned as she slipped her hand up the front of my T-shirt and ran her fingertips over the ridges of my abs. "Maybe, maybe not." I dropped my head back as Birdie's fingers skated their way down my V-lines, then danced along the waistband of my shorts. My cock stiffened, and she ran her palm over my shorts, tracing my length. "But I still want them."

"Fine," I said with a strangled moan as I closed my eyes, "but you're going to eat a real dinner before the doughnuts, right?"

I jerked my head up as Birdie abruptly disappeared, the warmth of her hand just a memory. "Sorry!" she said, stepping away while poking at one ear, then the other. "I can't hear you. It's all the sex. It short-circuited my sense and—oh! Would you look at the time? Don't you have somewhere to be?"

"Very funny." I landed my hand on her soft, supple arse and yanked her towards me, trapping my hard dick between us. "Eat something, Red. You're going to need your energy later. Understand?"

Her gaze dropped to my mouth and back to my eyes, a pretty pink colour blooming in her cheeks as I held her gaze. I leaned in, hovering over her upturned face, a hairsbreadth between her lips and mine.

"I understand," she agreed breathlessly, and only then did I capture her mouth with my own.

Her lips were eager and warm, her tongue curious, and as our connection deepened, I wrapped my arms around her waist and moulded her body against my own. I could have kissed that woman every morning just like this, for hours at a time and never get enough, but my phone sounded with a reminder notification, and I had to pull away.

"I really do have to go," I said, grunting my disappointment as Birdie stepped back to give me room to adjust my shorts.

"It's okay. I'll see you tonight. My place, right?"

"I'll be there."

Ten minutes later, I pulled into a parking spot on the street outside the Valentine Bay Library and Community Centre and turned off the car engine. I quickly opened my phone to scan all the texts I'd been ignoring that morning. As anticipated, I had a stream of unread messages on my group chat with the boys.

6:00 a.m. Logan: Where are you, Greene? Surf's cranking this morning, and we're heading out.

7:15 a.m. Josh: We're about to file a missing person's report, but we need the number for the cop shop. Return your messages, man. Will's worried.

8:00 a.m. Will: Seriously, bro. We only ever see you at training, and you skipped the last session. You're dodging us. Is this about the non-date with Lisa? As we said, it's her loss. Plenty more girls out there. Trust me.

8:30 a.m. Luca: Just ran into Dawn at Tony's Place. Is it true? Have you got a thing going with Birdie?

8:34 a.m. Will: It's true. Sort of. I cornered Ellison, and she held her tongue for about six seconds. Greene, what the hell? Love coaching, dude?

8:38 a.m. Josh: Jones confirmed. Boys... the teacher is in.

8:41 a.m. Luca: Tash doesn't know anything, but she overheard a conversation between Dawn and Maz sometime last week about Birdie pinching Greene's arse on the street. She assumed it was a mistake and forgot all about it.

8:47 a.m. Logan: Jess says Birdie was showing him enough to get to second base with Lisa. So, what the fuck happened, man?

8:53 a.m. Will: Don't listen to these dickheads. Meet us for a beer later at The Stop. You can tell us all about it then.

Fuck. They found out about the deal with Birdie.

Yeah, I'd been avoiding the boys. Love coaching wasn't something I was about to brag about—though apparently, Birdie didn't have the same reservations, given that the girls had known what was going on the whole time. Maybe it should have bothered me, but the idea that Birdie had bonded with the crew was a pleasant surprise, and her friendship with them only worked in my favour. It didn't matter what they did or didn't know now anyway. I wanted to tell the boys about Birdie because if I had my way, everything about our arrangement—no, scratch that, *relationship*—was about to change. But I really was running late, so I'd deal with the guys later.

I tucked my phone in my pocket, then thought better of it. Sighing, I pulled it out again. Swiping open to the chat, I tapped out a response.

8:58 a.m. Me: Can't tonight. Got plans. I'll fill you in at training on Wednesday.

The phone pinged again immediately.

8:59 a.m. Will: Plans with Birdie?

9:00 a.m. Me: Running late. Can't talk.

9:00 a.m. Will: Fine. Wednesday. But we're getting the full story.

9:01 a.m. Me: Bring beer. It's a long one.

I stepped out of my car and stowed my phone and keys, then collected my gym bag—overburdened with paperbacks—from the back seat. Ducking my head, I made my way to the conference room where the Sunday meeting of the VBFYRRRBC had probably already begun.

When I opened the door, I found everyone milling around and talking loudly enough that they didn't notice me slipping in, but when the door closed behind me with a loud click, all heads swivelled around, and I was pinned to the wall by their accusing eyes.

"I know. I'm sorry," I said, holding up my free hand, palm out. "I missed the last three meetings."

"This isn't the gym, you know," Burt barked. "You can't just drop in when you feel like it. The club is a *commitment*—"

"Oh, hush, Burt," Dot admonished, flapping her hands until the red, round man dropped himself into a plastic chair, still grumbling under his breath. "Isaac's young enough to be our grandson, and he has a lot more responsibilities than a group of retirees with nothing better to do than tend their roses and read their stories. We can make an exception to the attendance policy." My breathy sigh of relief cut off as Dot shot me an unforgiving look. "Just this once."

"Noted," I replied. "I've been, uh, busy, but to make it up to you, I've got a couple dozen novels to add to our private collection." I set the heavy gym bag on an empty square of trestle table next to the store-bought baked goods. Unzipping the bag, I pulled out my final peace offering. "And a double batch of Maz's orange and poppyseed friands."

"You're forgiven, Sergeant," Irena said, pushing her way to the front of the crowd that had collected around the books. "Now, hand over the cake before I change my mind."

I bit back a smile and extracted myself from the frenzy that new books and warm sugar had set off, stepping away from the group and watching with amusement as the oldies elbowed each other out of the way. Dot shook her head in the way preschool teachers do when the class gets a little rowdy, then shuffled over and stood alongside me.

"You look well, Isaac," she commented.

"I feel well," I agreed.

Dot glanced up at me, a knowing curve on her wrinkled mouth. "Things developing nicely with Birdie, are they?"

"Maybe," I replied evasively, but Dot's eyes sparkled too brightly, and I sighed. "Why? What do you know?"

"I know *the look* when I see it, and if I'm not mistaken, you've got *it* written all over your face."

Opening my mouth to ask what she meant by *it*, then spotting Agatha throwing me a speculative look over her pursed lips, I snapped my jaw closed. I didn't want to know what either woman could read in my expression. Given the amount of sex I'd had in the last week, this conversation had the potential to be awkward as fuck.

"I really am sorry it's been weeks since my last meeting, but I've been busy with work and—"

"Birdie."

I rubbed the back of my neck self-consciously. "Yeah, and Birdie. Actually, I was hoping to talk to the group about it again today. All the advice you gave me last time really helped, and I think I'm at a bit of a crossroads."

"Oh? You've got my attention, young man. Let me corral these sugar fiends into something that resembles socially acceptable behaviour, and the floor is yours."

Dot shuffled over to her lectern and picked up her gavel, smacking it against the sound block with a firm *bang, bang,*

bang. "Order. Order! This meeting of the VBFYRRRBC is now in session! Order! Or I'll confiscate the cakes and dole them out when the meeting is over."

"Whoever thought it was a good idea to give that woman a gavel?" Romana muttered.

"I heard that, Romana," Dot deadpanned, lifting one eyebrow in the other woman's direction.

"I meant you to," Romana replied sweetly.

Once everybody found a chair in the circle, donned their sashes, and recited the club pledge, we all took a seat.

"Before we talk about this week's book," Dot announced, "Isaac would like to share an update on his…situation… and ask for a little more help."

"What happened with the last advice we gave you?" Burt demanded. "You didn't screw it up, did you?"

"Ah, no," I replied, using my soothe-the-suspect voice. "Your advice has been so spot-on that things with Birdie are going great. Really great. I think it's time to take things to the next level."

"You haven't seduced her yet?" Agatha asked, her heavily made-up face aghast.

I smirked a little. "No, that part's well and truly taken care of." At the sound of their quiet, approving murmurs, I ran a hand over my beard to hide my smile and guided the conversation to the real issue I needed to discuss. "I'm talking about emotional intimacy. Commitment. You all know Birdie's not that kind of girl, but we've spent the last month getting to know each other again, and things have shifted between us. She's opened up to me. Told me things she wouldn't tell anyone else, and it was kind of a breakthrough moment. She's spending time with my family, and they adore her almost as much as I do. I took her to my sister's birthday breakfast last week, and you wouldn't believe how well she fits in."

Glancing around the group, I saw approving nods and went on. "Sarah asked Birdie to talk to Liam about his studies, and next thing you know, the two of them have set up some kind of mathematics workshop at my dining room table. There are books and papers and pizza boxes everywhere, and you know what? I don't even care about the mess. I just love seeing her there in my kitchen every day. And I think… I think she likes being in my kitchen every day."

"We're happy for you, Isaac," Dot replied, "but I'll admit I'm a little concerned." Her wrinkles deepened as she looked around the room, exchanging worried glances with everyone there. "What exactly do you need from us? What's the next level you want to reach?"

I didn't love that their looks of concern mirrored the anxiety burrowing away in my gut because if they saw my problem as easily as that, it meant I wasn't making things up in my head.

Taking things to the "next level" wouldn't be easy. I pressed a fist to my mouth and cleared my throat, then rubbed my clammy palms across the top of my thighs. "I think I've reached that part in the story where it's time for me to make my grand gesture."

"Your grand gesture?" Bill echoed. "What do you mean? Like, the big move at the end of the book?"

"Yeah, exactly like that."

Their murmurs increased in volume, and I shot a frustrated look towards Dot, who correctly read my expression and smacked her gavel again. The noise died down, and I tried again.

"Birdie has a one-way plane ticket out of here in less than three weeks, and I want—no, I *need*—to ask her if she'll come back after she's fulfilled her commitments in Vegas. Come back to me and stay. Maybe forever."

"You want to propose *marriage*?" Burt exclaimed. The incredulity in his tone was borderline offensive.

"Ah, no. I'm not that stupid—but thanks for the vote of confidence, Burt. All I'm saying is that Birdie needs to know how important she is. I want her to understand that she has a home here with me and with my family—with all of us. She doesn't need to live on the road anymore. There's no reason for her to keep moving all the time, not when I'm here to create a home."

"So, do you want our opinions, Mr Greene?" Lorraine asked. "Some ideas on how to go about this grand plan of yours?"

"Well, not exactly. I was hoping to get your moral support. I probably wouldn't even be in a position to contemplate this without the help you've already given me." I gestured to the e-readers in everyone's hands and the stack of books on the table behind me. "It's not dramatic to say this club and these books changed my life, and I'm about to take the biggest risk I've ever taken with any woman. I've always been the best friend and never the leading man, and I'm about to ask the woman I love if she'll love me back the same way."

I didn't quite realise what I'd confessed to until silence greeted me, broken only when Bill asked quietly beside me, "You love her?"

I'd never said it out loud before or even in so many words to myself, but that didn't make it any less true. I'd been circling it for weeks. I loved Birdie. I'd loved her when we were kids, and I loved her now that we were grown. I didn't want to go back to a life without her in it because I would love her always.

"I do."

"And do you believe she feels the same way about you?" Bill wondered, scratching one dark grizzled cheek and watching me over the top of his wire-frame glasses.

I licked my lips, my throat feeling suddenly dry. All I had to go on was a hunch and hope and a few dozen romance novels that had shown me more than how to make my girl scream in bed. They'd taught me that when two people loved each other, someone had to be the one who said it first—no matter if they knew for sure yet if the other person was ready to say it back.

"I know she trusts me. I know she feels safe with me. I think if she allowed herself to really consider it, she'd realise she has strong feelings for me too."

"Enough to stay?" Burt added.

I'd known from the beginning Birdie intended to pack up and go, but the closer we came to the day she was supposed to get on that plane and the more time we spent together in bed as well as out of it, the harder it was for me to accept that I might have to let her go. It made me sick to think about her leaving and even sicker to imagine letting her walk away without some sort of fight.

"I sure as hell hope so," I replied, trying—and failing—to keep my tone light. "But I guess we're about to find out."

"She doesn't live a conventional life, dear," Lorraine said gently. "Do you expect her to give up her career? Stop travelling and settle down so the two of you can make a home here together?"

"You said she doesn't want marriage or children," Irena added, a thoughtful turn to her mouth. "And we know you come from a large family. These things are important to the Greenes. Are you willing to compromise?"

"No," I said. "I mean, yes. I mean… Look, I'm not ever going to stand in the way of Birdie's career or her doing what she loves. I know I—we—will need to think about all these things eventually, but we can do it together once she knows exactly how I feel about her. Isn't that what it's all about? Love wins in the end. It always does." I stuck my fidgeting hands in my armpits and stilled my bouncing knee. All the questions made me want to climb the walls. "We'll figure it out."

There was something a little more cautious in the looks everyone shared this time around, but I refused to let it bother me. I knew what I was doing. Or perhaps, I knew what I had to do. I knew myself well enough to know the regrets I could live with and the ones that would eat me alive for the rest of my life.

I nodded once at Dot, and she returned the gesture.

"All right, then." Dot smacked her hands together and rubbed her palms industriously. "Grand gestures. Declarations of love. Fighting for our happy-ever-afters. Come on. Out with your e-readers. What do we know, and what do we suggest?"

23

BIRDIE

I STARTLED AT the sound of someone thumping a fist on my front door. Squinting at the clock on my computer and realising it was already a couple minutes past ten o'clock, I blinked away the daze of six straight hours in front of the screen as my stomach grumbled. Thank God for doughnuts. I was starving because, of course, I'd forgotten to eat dinner.

Stretching as I got to my feet, I congratulated myself for having the foresight to wash and braid my hair that morning—in my own home and my own bathroom, changing into clothes I'd washed and folded myself, thank you very much—because as I checked myself in the oversized hall mirror, I didn't quite resemble the troll I feared I would. Still, there *was* a chocolate sauce stain on my shirt. I whipped it off and stuffed it into the umbrella stand, then approached the door in nothing but the sheer blue lace bra I had on underneath and a pair of black linen shorts.

I unlocked the door and swung it open. "Hey, there— Oh my God."

There on my doorstep was porn made flesh. Lit overhead by the golden porch light was Sergeant Isaac Greene in all his police officer glory. Rocking his fitted navy uniform and fucking *aviators*, for Christ's sake, he was all muscled shoulders and chiselled jaw, dark beard and heavy boots, attitude and authority. And sex. So. Much. Sex. I swept my eyes over him, taking particular note of the corded muscles roping up his crossed forearms, then the baton and handcuffs attached to his belt, and my knickers incinerated on the spot.

"Can I help you, officer?" I asked, my voice low and husky where it caught in my throat.

"Do you always answer the door in your underwear?" he replied, a note of irritation in his deep voice.

"It's been known to happen." I opened the door all the way, then stuck my thumbs into the waistband of my shorts and shimmied them off, kicking them deeper into the hallway. Straightening, I gave him a minute to appreciate that the only thing protecting my modesty now was the flimsy lace covering my nipples and the skimpy matching G-string between my legs. I leaned against the edge of the door and gave him a rebellious, come-and-get-me look. "Why? What are you ~~going to do~~ about it?"

It was the absolute right thing to say because he flashed me the tiniest smile before he whipped off his glasses and gave me the sexiest smoulder I've seen in my life.

"Miss Maxwell, I'm afraid I'm going to have to ask you to move inside."

Isaac took a step towards me, his boots thudding on the floorboards, and I took a slow step back. When he cleared the doorframe, he swung the door closed with a slam, and before I had a chance to catch my breath, he closed in on me, latching onto my wrist and spinning me around, flattening me against the hallway mirror. With one cheek pressed to the glass, I panted as Isaac set a hot, firm hand between my shoulder blades. Adrenaline coursed through me, racing the desire that sped through my veins.

He pressed the length of his body against mine, teasing me with the hard length of his cock still inside his pants. "Is this all right, Red?" he asked before setting his mouth to my neck in a line of soft, sensual kisses. The fingers of his other hand brushed across my skin, barely touching the swell of my breast, the shape of my ribs, the curve of my hip. "Tell me to stop, and I will."

"Don't stop," I begged, breathing in the reassuring scent of him—clean soap with a salty hint of leather. He was a paradox, and it drove me wild. The very fragrance of him triggered feelings of safety and trust, but in that moment, I was living for the flicker of apprehension whipping at my pulse. "Don't you dare fucking stop."

"I was hoping you'd say that."

In a move that surprised me in the best possible way, Isaac wrapped the tail of my braid around his fist and pulled my head back. I hissed at the sting in my scalp, then moaned as he set his lips to my ear.

"You have the right to remain silent." A shiver of anticipation ran up my spine at the sound of Isaac unclasping something from his belt, and my knees almost gave way as the tip of his baton skated its way up the inside of one leg. When he reached my pussy, he pressed the top of it against the damp fabric of my underwear. "You also have the right to scream my fucking name."

In a whip-quick cop move that made me squeak in surprise, Isaac kicked out my heels, widening my stance, and yanked my waist back against his body before he pushed my shoulders down so I was leaning forwards, my hands splayed against the mirror.

"That's right," he whispered. "Spread your legs for me, Red. Let me look at you." Watching his expression in the mirror above me, my underwear was drenched all over again as an arrogant smirk curled his lips. Pressing his palm against the small of my back and tilting my hips up, he murmured, "There you are, pretty girl."

It was hot enough to make my knees buckle, and it wasn't an overstatement to say the only reason I could still stand was that Isaac held me in position, especially when he began rubbing the length of his baton along my slick folds. "You like that?" he growled, restraint obvious in the rough edge of his voice.

I whimpered and nodded, my nipples hard enough to ache, the throb between my legs growing wetter and heavier, and my body getting more frustrated as Isaac ran his baton over and over my pussy, playing me like a fucking violin without any promise of reaching the crescendo.

Meeting my eyes in the mirror, Isaac's jaw feathered as he jerked his chin. "Pull down your bra. I want to see those tits bounce when I fuck you."

Groaning as every word he said sent fresh pulses of desire to my clit, I tugged on the lace, freeing my breasts one at a time.

"Hand back on the mirror," he ordered, strumming me with the baton over and over.

"No," I panted. "I need more." Making a brief stopover at my chest to give my nipple a much-needed tweak, I snaked my fingers down over my stomach. Destination: clitoris.

"Did I say you could touch yourself?" Isaac growled, pulling me upright by my braid and using the tip of his baton to press my body hard against the mirror. Then he dropped the weapon on the floor and unwound his fist from my hair before crossing my wrists in an X above my head and handcuffing me.

Holy fucking hell. Jesus fucking Christ. This was the hottest thing to ever happen to me, and we'd barely even begun.

He wrapped an arm around my waist and lifted me off the floor, setting me down further away from the wall. He folded me over, and I braced myself against the mirror, the cold, heavy metal of the cuffs keeping my hands close together. With one hand kneading my arse cheek, Isaac undressed. I closed my eyes and concentrated on not hyperventilating as I listened to him remove his belt, unzip his fly, kick off his boots, and drop his pants to the floor. Again, he kicked my heels out, softer this time and not so wide, then ran his thumb along the edge of my G-string, massaging my wet pussy, dipping in and out of my entrance as he slicked my arousal up and down my arse. I moaned quietly as he slipped one finger inside me, then two, all the while teasing that tight ring of muscle with the pad of his thumb.

I rocked my hips over his hand, biting my lip as I rode microbursts of pleasure in my core and waited impatiently for the telltale tear of a condom wrapper being opened. When it didn't happen, I opened my eyes to find out what was taking so long. I exhaled a moan at the sight of Isaac behind me in the mirror, pants off and shirt unbuttoned, fisting his cock while he watched himself finger me.

As another breathy sigh of longing escaped my throat, his hooded green eyes flickered up to meet mine in the reflection and held me there. His fingers pumped in and out of me, the hard flesh of his dick slid through his closed fist over and over, and his eyes burned hotter and hotter into mine. I groaned as I leaned into it, tipping my pussy up higher and higher, inviting him to finally take hold of my hips and drive into me, please, God, *now*.

"You want me inside you, Red?" he asked, sounding strangled. His fist around his cock pumped faster. "You want my dick deep inside this tight, wet pussy?"

"Yes," I replied, my voice barely audible above my fast, hard breaths.

"Louder." Isaac withdrew his fingers from my core and let go of his dick, leaving me bereft of both the delicious friction on my sex and the delectable sight of this god of a man fucking his hand while he finger-fucked me. I whimpered at the loss, and he smirked as he plucked a condom from the pocket of his shirt, opened it, and rolled the rubber over his impressive girth. The entire time, he watched me as I watched him, that smug look of self-satisfaction pushing every erotic button I'd ever had and some I didn't even know existed.

"Yes!" I shouted, jerking at the cuffs around my wrists. Not that I thought I could escape them, but I wanted to touch this man, and I wanted him to know it. By the way his lips twitched, he saw it, he knew it, and he loved it. "I need you inside me." Isaac notched the tip of his cock against my entrance, took hold of my hip bones with two confident hands, and I breathed to relax my muscles. "I need it deep and hard and— Oh!"

Isaac slammed into me, and I hissed as the sudden fullness of him sent a twinge of pain through my core, quickly chased by a thrill of pure pleasure. Anchoring me to him with one firm hand, fingertips digging into my skin, Isaac looped his other arm around to meet my pussy, slipping his fingers through my wetness before stroking firm circles over my clit. As the dual points of gratification twisted my arousal higher and higher, my core relaxed enough to take him even deeper, and he rocked into me with increasingly harder, faster thrusts.

"Your pussy was made for me, wasn't it, Red?" I nodded wordlessly as my eyes rolled back into my head with euphoric bliss, and I cried out as he moved his hand north to cup one breast, plucking hard at the stiffened peak with his fingertips. "That's right. Nobody else could take my dick like you do, and don't you ever fucking forget it."

I knew he'd bottomed out when he dropped his head forwards and grunted, and his hips picked up the pace, his cock firing into me roughly enough that I had to tense the muscles in my legs and push back against the mirror to steady myself.

He abandoned my breast to wrap a thick forearm around my pelvis to grip me closer against him, fucking me with abandon—like I was his to fuck any way he chose.

And I was.

I embarrassed myself with all the moaning, the helpless whimpers, and wordless cries of pleasure. My entire body vibrated with stimulation: the wet mess of our connection, the erotic smack of his skin hitting mine, the filthy things he murmured in my ear, the otherworldly sensation of being so thoroughly filled by this man and still wishing I had space to take more.

The coil of my climax started building between my legs and deep in my core, and I rocked my hips against him, chasing that final push over the edge. "I'm going to come. Fuck, I'm about to come so hard."

"Look up," he commanded through clenched teeth. I barely registered it, and he wrapped my braid around his fist again, tugging back on it enough to lift my face to the mirror. "Look. Up."

I opened my eyes and found his in the reflection. Sweat beaded over his glorious face and down his magnificent chest. Every muscle in his athletic legs was corded with tension. One hand dug hard enough into my hip that I was going to have bruises the next day, and the other clung so tightly to my hair that even the slightest stretch against it sent prickles dancing across my scalp.

"Watch yourself come," he ordered.

I dropped my eyelids, unable to think of anything I wanted to do less than see my own sex face, but as I shied away from the picture in the mirror, Isaac growled and gave my hair a quick tug, and the frantic thrusts of his cock inside me slowed to a pace that I was certain only tortured us both.

"You're fucking magic, Birdie," he breathed, and my stubbornness wilted at the softness in his tone. "We're magic together. Open your eyes and *look*."

I didn't want to, but Isaac's words landed strangely, like the way he said my name really was the magic word that broke the spell. I opened my eyes and gazed up at him, and when he was confident I wasn't going to look away again, he returned to the punishing pace I so desperately craved. I watched him for a moment longer, and then, because I couldn't help it, I watched me.

If I ever thought this scenario couldn't possibly get hotter, I was about to be freaking re-educated.

I'd always liked my body, but right then, I hardly recognised myself. My cheeks were flushed, and my freckles were dark, my eyes blue and wide and glassy. My lips were swollen and pink from where I'd been biting them. My hair had come loose around the edges, leaving wispy curls wild around my face. All the tattoos I didn't see anymore because I'd grown so used to them seemed to jump out at me. Bursts of colour and stitches of ink that marked milestones or heartaches in my life—they told a different story now, one of triumph.

Legs spread, tits bursting out over the lace of my bra—and yes, bouncing obscenely with every thrust of Isaac's cock. Thong hitched to one side, and my thighs glistening as a gorgeous man railed me from behind. I straightened a little, wanting to see this picture with my hands cuffed in front of me.

Isaac obliged, grunting as he dragged me against his body and lifted me up on my toes before shifting his stance and the rhythm of his hips to better fit the shape of me.

And then he let go of my hair and snaked his hand up and around my neck, just as he hooked the other into the thin elastic of my underwear and fucking tore the thing off me.

My head went hazy with lust as I watched him own me with a hand around my throat and rough, frenzied fingers massaging my clit, my wrists shackled in silver, and his cock rocking into me in a way that hit hidden, never-been-touched nerve-endings deep inside.

How had this become my life? Where in the journey from where I'd started to where I'd ended up did I do anything worthy enough to deserve this man? I loved the way his sexual confidence had exploded this last month we'd spent together. I loved the way he manhandled me and the way he took what he wanted. I loved the way he trusted me to speak up if any of this wasn't what I wanted.

I loved that even as he held me against him in a position that from the outside looked almost violent, he brushed the soft pad of his thumb over the delicate thread of the pulse in my neck to let me know he was thinking of me, taking care of me, protecting me, always.

I loved all of it. I loved…*him.*

Holy fuck, no.

With divine timing, Isaac shifted his hand from my pussy to my breast, circling the pebbled nipple with the rough centre of his palm in a way he knew drove me wild. It wiped all rational—and irrational—thoughts from my mind. My eyes rolled back in my head, and I was totally unprepared for the orgasm that tore through me. It twisted tighter and tighter, so fucking fast, and was so intense it pulled a scream from my core that, ironically, was probably going to bring the cops down on my doorstep. It burst outwards from somewhere deep inside, and I drowned. I drowned in ecstasy as wave after wave of release dragged me under, turning my muscles to water and pulling both Isaac and me to our knees.

I felt the throbbing pulse of his climax as I fell forwards on my hands and knees, and he thrust against the last pulses of his orgasm.

Thinking was a trial, let alone talking, so all I could do was breathe as the vision of what we'd just done inked itself indelibly on my brain, as permanent and irrevocable as any of the markings on my skin.

24

BIRDIE

I WAS STILL gathering the shattered pieces of me together when Isaac gently pulled out and got to his feet, scooped me up, and carried me upstairs. He deposited me in the middle of my crumpled-up bedcovers, and I fell to the side and closed my eyes.

There was more than one reason I didn't want to look Isaac in the face just yet. That had been the best, most raw and most vulnerable sex I'd ever had in my life. I also knew now that I loved this man. And I wasn't sure what to do with either of those pieces of information or if I wanted to share them. Now or ever.

"Pardon me while I sleep for three days," I muttered, waving my wrists in his direction. When he didn't take my hands right away, I added, "Don't tell me you lost the key." I cracked one eyelid open. "And where are my doughnuts?"

He laughed lightly as he dipped his fingers into his shirt pocket, then knelt beside the bed, a key in his hand. He picked up my hands and unlocked the cuffs, then dropped a kiss on the inside of each wrist, over the top of my *hold* and *fold* tattoos.

"The doughnuts are in the car. I'll go get them."

Leaning towards me, elbows on the bed, I couldn't avoid his eyes, and he stared into them too intensely for my comfort. "So, Romeo," I said with a quirked eyebrow and my best impression of a devil-may-care attitude, "for a guy who told me he had no game, you're really pulling out some unexpected bedroom moves. I'm starting to wonder if this whole 'help me, Red, girls don't like me' routine was all one evil genius plot to get me into bed."

My gaze dropped to his mouth as it curled up in one corner. Where did he get off being so freaking sexy after I'd just come hard enough to last me a month? Okay, fine—a day, at least. I rolled onto my back to put some much-needed distance between my weird-arse feelings and his kiss-me-'cause-you-love-me look. Staring up at the ceiling helped a little because the validity of my observation hit home.

"Well?" I demanded, turning my head a little, just not enough to meet his green gaze. He bopped me silently on the nose and got to his feet, and I watched his tight bare arse as he disappeared into my bathroom and shut the door.

I chewed my lip and rubbed my wrists together where the memory of hard steel still clung to them. Isaac was obviously hiding something, but from the sparkle in his eye and the arrogant smirk on his face, I instinctively knew he wanted to spill. So, of course, I was going to push the subject. My question was a good one, and I wanted an answer.

Isaac exited the bathroom, switching off the light behind him. I opened my mouth, but he quieted me with one lifted finger. "Doughnuts," he said. "Be right back."

"Put on pants!" I called after him.

I slipped into the bathroom myself while he was gone but was back in bed when three minutes later, he returned with a white bakery box. I reached out with grabby hands, and he passed it over as he shucked off his navy trousers and scooted into bed beside me.

I let him spoon me while I nibbled on a doughnut that was to die for, lulling him into a false sense of comfort before I asked him again. "Seriously. You're keeping a secret, and now that I've picked up the scent, I'm not letting you wriggle out of it so easily. Where'd you get the moves?"

I wriggled into the warm curve of his body, and he reflexively captured my feet between his calves as he rearranged the covers, then looped an arm around my waist and scooped me closer to him. His thoughtfulness was on-brand, and I'd stopped trying to fight it. The silence, however, was new. And maddening.

"Tell me now, or you and me? We'll have problems."

I felt a large sigh escape his lungs, and he buried his nose in my hair. The scent of apples was fresh from my shower that morning, and he spent a little longer than normal breathing it in. Sensing that a confession was moments away, I waited.

"I've been…reading," he mumbled against my head.

The picture of Isaac in the early hours of the morning on the back porch with a coffee and a book sprung to mind, but I needed more information. That picture didn't vibe with the man who just rubbed me up with his baton and screwed me from behind against a mirror. "Reading…what?"

"Texts recommended to me by parties interested in my romantic welfare," he said evasively.

I smiled to myself, having figured it out. "Well, if that isn't the driest, unsexiest way to say your mates gave you porn, I don't know what is."

"It wasn't the boys, and it wasn't po—" He cut off with a contemplative hum, and I could almost feel him thinking, then he kissed the crown of my head. "It's literature with spicy parts. When we started this whole love coach thing, I embarrassed myself more than once with my ineptitude. I had to do something about it so you didn't think I was a total loser."

I spun around under his arm, temporarily extracting my feet before tucking them back in as soon as I was comfortable again. I set one hand to his bearded cheek, cupping my fingers around his jaw, and met his eyes for a quiet moment until I was sure I had his undivided attention.

"You are *not* a loser," I whispered fiercely. "You've never been a loser. The only reason I suggested coaching you in the first place is because I've always known how incredible you are, and the fact you couldn't see it—well, frankly, it pissed me off. A man as magnificent as you needs to know his worth. That's all this was ever about. It wasn't my job to improve you. You were always a winner, and I only ever wanted you to embrace it."

His throat bobbed as he swallowed, and I read the contemplation on his face. It wasn't like me to be so transparent with my feelings, but I wasn't going to let him talk himself down, even in the sideways way he'd gone about it. I could be honest about my high regard for him. Confessing high regard was a far cry from declaring love.

"Birdie," he said for the second time that night, and I hated myself for the girlie thrill that swept along my spine at the sound of my name on his lips. He dragged his thumb along my bottom lip, wiping away a line of cinnamon sugar, then lifted it to his mouth. I watched, mesmerised by the sight of him sucking his finger clean. "I've never felt more like myself than I have this last month with you in my life. No. Scratch that. I haven't felt this *relaxed* since we were kids, playing cards in the dark on my parents' living room floor."

He brushed his knuckles across my cheekbone and along my jaw. "I love it here. I love the Bay and the people who live here. I have the best mates and a great family, and a job I actually want to go to in the mornings. But this time with you… I wasn't lying before. It's been magical."

I didn't mean to do it, but my poker face settled in place, and my brain looked a hundred steps ahead of this conversation to the possibility of Isaac asking me to stay. A hard-wired part of me wanted to bolt—just run far and fast in any direction that wasn't Isaac. A softer, newer part wondered what it would be like to stop moving.

I definitely wasn't ready to tell him what tonight had done to me. The smart thing to do would be to wait until the sexual hangover passed before I gave any weight to an emotional epiphany triggered by mind-blowing sex—but I owed him at least as much honesty as he was giving me.

"I admit, I wasn't expecting any of this when I came back to the Bay," I said. "It's been fun reconnecting with the girls and your family. Even this house." I looked around at the old-fashioned, floral-print papered walls of my bedroom, which might have looked plain to most, but represented a childhood of summers for me. "I wasn't expecting to feel so…"

"At home?" he suggested—hopefully, if I was reading him right. And given my skills in that department, I was. It set my heart twirling in a tiny pirouette of panic. I wasn't ready for this—the conversation or what he implied.

"Happy," I replied. "Happy that I could have this time with you. Happy I could revisit my childhood. Happy that people here remember who I am, and most of them still want to be friends."

"As long as you don't count me among those friends anymore," Isaac grumbled, drawing me tighter against his chest and tucking my head under his chin.

"Oh? And what am I supposed to call you?" I asked lightly, feeling the discussion turn in a way I didn't want it to go yet. "Friends with benefits. Wasn't that the deal, Romeo? Don't go changing the game on me now."

"Maybe it's time to raise the stakes, Red," he mumbled, and the tension in his broad arms grew tighter. "Maybe it's time to break the rules."

"You're not a rule-breaker," I reminded him, the spin and twirl of anxiety beneath my ribs picking up pace. Was I afraid of what he was going to ask me? Or terrified of the answer my heart wanted to give him? "And you're not a gambler. You wouldn't even play poker for matchsticks when we were young. It was only ever for fun."

He huffed out a laugh. "I was the only kid in town smart enough to not get swindled out of his pocket money every year, wasn't I?"

I released a relieved breath. Thank God for the easy change in subject. "That's right, Officer. You're a man of the law and a man of his word. And me? I'm a rebel. A wild card. Never know whether I'm coming or going."

"That's what I like about you, Red," he mumbled, fatigue creeping into his tone. "My life could never be boring with you in it. Promise me you'll never change."

Isaac's jaw cracked with a yawn, and I echoed it in solidarity. "That's the plan," I replied, snuggling in close against the light cover of hair on his broad, hard chest. With the immediate danger of a deep and meaningful conversation passed us for the moment, I closed my eyes.

I don't remember a time, even as a kid, when I'd fallen asleep feeling so watched over or so safe.

25

ISAAC

THE BOYS AND I dragged our surf rowing boat up and out of the water, running it higher onto the beach. It had been a great training session. Our strength was growing, our technique improving, and best of all, it felt like old times to focus on a task—just the five of us. With Logan having lived overseas for most of the last decade and Luca spending three years in the city, we hadn't been this close since we were in high school.

This little fact had its upsides as well as its downs.

"I think we're in with a real chance to win this competition," Luca commented, grabbing his towel and rubbing the salt water from his face. "We ran our best time yet today."

"We're not there yet," Josh grunted, scooping up a bottle of water from where he'd dropped it in the sand. He cracked the lid and poured a stream into his open mouth, then ran the rest of it over his upturned face to rinse away some of the salt. "Sanctuary Cove still has a shot at whipping our arses."

"Let those arrogant dipshits think they've got it in the bag," Logan muttered, shaking droplets of water from his hair as he dragged a pair of dry board shorts on over his speedo. "It'll make it that much sweeter when we take them out."

A cheeky "boo!" sounded from our unofficial fan club set up under Abbie's blue and white beach canopy further up the sand, and Logan sent a wave and a wink over to Jess. She responded by lobbing a balled-up scrap of something our way, but it fell short. Abbie, ever the best friend, jumped to her feet and cupped her hands around her mouth.

"Hey, Reeve! Frost says, take off your shorts!" she screeched.

Logan rolled his eyes, but the satisfied smirk on his face spoke volumes.

I dragged my fingers through my beard and over my hair, then spared a quick glance at the girls. Tash was here nine times out of ten—she and Luca were the definition of inseparable, and we'd grown used to seeing her little yellow umbrella at almost every training session—but on the occasions when the wider canopy was set up, it was usually because Abbie, Emily, and Jess came down as well.

Birdie had only ever been once to watch us row, and that had been the day we'd competed in a friendly with the

Sanctuary Cove team. I never even knew at the time she'd been there watching us—watching me. Today, however, I was viscerally aware that, for whatever reason, she was the fifth face under that sunshade.

I plucked my own shorts from where I'd dropped them on the sand. Straightening, a juvenile voice in my head wondered if Birdie was going to jeer me for getting dressed.

Just as I slipped them over my ankles and up my legs, Abbie's voice came careening down the beach. "Hey, Greene! Maxwell says, take off— Ow! Hey!"

I glanced up in time to see Birdie tackle Abbie to the ground. She waved at me and grinned. "As you were! Nothing to see here."

I watched, amused, as Birdie and Abbie wrestled for a moment before letting each other go. The girls all laughed, and I turned away before they could catch my grin.

It seemed like the truth about the two of us was well and truly out of the bag. Good. I had half a mind to "accidentally" mention something to Dawn and just be done with all the secrecy once and for all. I'd never been more certain that there was only one place my relationship with Birdie was heading, and that was full steam ahead towards our own happily ever after.

"So, Greene," Will said, running his hands over his drenched, salty hair as we caught our breaths beside the boat. "Session's done. I've got beer in the cooler. Time to tell us all about Birdie. Fuck, man. I'm almost offended you've kept this to yourself for as long as you have."

I tugged on an earlobe, then waved my hand at the cooler. Will crouched down to zip it open and extract bottles of beer for four of us—Logan stuck to his water—and when Josh flung his towel out onto the warm sand and lowered himself onto it, face up to the sun, we all did the same.

"I'm not sorry I kept quiet about it all this time," I began. "Fuck if I know if I'd be having this conversation if you losers had stuck your noses in before now."

"What conversation?" Will asked, passing me an open bottle. "What the hell is going on, Greene?"

I took a sip of Will's chilled IPA—man, he knew how to brew a good beer—and shook my head. "You know Birdie's been here a while now. She arrived in town about the same time I got that message from Lisa. I was in a fucking panic about that date. I didn't want to screw it up."

"Okay," Luca squinted at me, his arms looped around his knees, bottle dangling from one hand. "So, what? You asked Birdie to help you out?"

"I explained the situation, and she offered." I played with the condensation running down the outside of the glass in my hand. "You guys know I've had a bad run with women since…pretty much forever, right? I didn't want to mess up my shot."

"I remember how hung up you were on Lisa," Josh agreed, laying down and closing his eyes, propping one arm under his head. "That's nothing to be embarrassed about."

"Yeah, but after all the hype, I couldn't face the chance of striking out. That's where Birdie was supposed to come in."

Will cocked an eyebrow. "Supposed to?"

"Yeah." I smiled at the memories of our first couple of weeks of love coaching. "I showed her what I could do. She was less than impressed, so she insisted on teaching me a few things."

"Things that would improve your chances with Lisa," Logan clarified.

"Exactly. Except… By the night of the reunion, everything had changed. Birdie and I had kissed by then, and everything shifted. I drove all the way to Sydney thinking about nothing else, and by the time I got there, I didn't want to go in. I didn't even want to shoot my shot with Lisa. All I wanted was to turn around and find Birdie. Kiss her again."

Luca leaned forwards, beer forgotten. "So, what did you do?"

"I bought Lisa one platonic cocktail, got back in my car, and drove home."

Silence answered me until Logan splashed a spray of water from his bottle in my face. "He means, what did you do about Birdie?"

I wiped away the droplets of water and smiled at the memory. "I went over to her place the next morning, made her admit our kiss was really fucking hot, then, ah, proceeded to renegotiate the terms of our agreement."

Will's face was overtaken by a goofy, dimpled grin. "How'd that work out for you?"

"Pretty fucking amazing," I confessed.

The sounds of my mates' whoops drew the attention of the girls, and I groaned.

"For fuck's sake. Be cool, idiots."

"Sorry, man," Josh said.

Luca raised one palm in apology. "We're just stoked for you. So, what does this mean now? Are you guys official? Is she going to stay in town? Quit the travelling and settle down with the Bay's favourite cop?"

I rubbed the back of my neck, stealing a glance at Birdie, who looked like a burnished burst of copper sunshine among the blonde and dark-haired heads of the other women. "We haven't got that far yet. What started as a love-coach thing kind of evolved into a friends-with-benefits agreement, which has turned into her sleeping over more nights than not. Sharing meals. Hanging out with my family. Doing each other's laundry. I'm trying not to spook her because we all know how stubborn this woman can be, but seriously? We're practically living together."

Will snorted, and when silence followed, he looked around abashedly. "Sorry. I thought a little sympathy might go down well. How about a joke about the old ball and chain? No takers? Anyone?"

I landed a punch on his arm, which toppled him over into the sand. "Fuck, no. This is the best thing to ever happen to me. I just need to make it official."

"Like, you're going to *propose*?" Luca asked.

Josh and Logan exchanged wary glances, and I chuckled.

"I'm not that far gone. Birdie says she doesn't want to get married. Doesn't want to have kids. Doesn't want to live in one place or love one person for the rest of her life."

"Yeah, man. I can see why you want to rush her into a commitment," Will muttered. "She's giving you *all* the signs."

"You don't know her like I do. She says all these things, but you don't understand how happy we've been this last month. How perfect she is for me. How perfect we are for each other. I'm not asking her to marry me and have a million babies. I just want to ask her to stay. That's it. The rest will work itself out from there."

"Does that mean giving up her career?" Josh asked. "No offense, but that's some old-fashioned misogynistic bullshit, and I don't see Birdie putting up with that."

"Jesus, no way. Why can't she make a home here and travel for work? People do it all the time. I could go with her sometimes, and she plays a lot of virtual games as well. Birdie's never put down roots anywhere, and everyone in town knows her parents weren't the warm and fuzzy kind. Me—us—we're the closest to a family she's ever had. She loves the Bay."

There was a stretch of silence, but I refused to let their reservations undermine my confidence.

"So, it's Halloween in a few days," I continued. "It's also Birdie's birthday, though she doesn't know I know it. I'm going to suggest we host a Halloween party at her place. We'll invite everyone we can think of, then surprise her with a birthday celebration. It'll make her see just how much she belongs, and I'll ask her to come back and make a life with me after she competes in her tournament next month."

"That's it?" Logan raised his brows skeptically. "You're just asking her to stay? You promise you're not doing something rash with a ring or anything like that?"

"No ring, I swear," I said. "Trust me. I know what I'm doing."

"I hate to be the one to say it, but I think one of us has to." Luca grimaced. "Are you prepared for the possibility that she might say no? Just pack up her stuff and disappear all over again?"

"I've been prepared for that every second of every day since the night she threw a vibrator at my head." My mates swapped bewildered looks, and I shook my head. "But that chance has grown smaller and smaller the longer she's been here. I told you. I know what I'm doing." I rolled my lips and took a breath. "In any event, I don't really have a choice anymore. I… Fuck, I love her. If I say nothing, she's out of here in two weeks anyway. I can't let her go without at least giving this a shot."

Josh's eyebrows climbed his forehead, and Luca and Logan exchanged another, more knowing look. All three of them had locked down their happily ever afters this year, and I'd never seen any of them more alive.

"Magic words, mate," Will said, clapping me on the back. "We're on board for whatever it is you need us to do to help you win your girl."

"Thanks, Kidd. I appreciate that." I exhaled a thick breath. "I guess what I need help with first is throwing Birdie a surprise birthday party."

"Hey!" Birdie came running at us from the tent, where

the girls were packing up their towels and the remains of a picnic. She pulled up to a stop and dropped into the sand between me and Josh. "Abbie just told us she put her name down for the bonfire tonight. Just the ten of us." She was beaming like a kid at Christmas.

"Can't think of a single thing I'd rather do," Luca said. "Count us in."

"Wait a second," Will muttered, glancing over at Abbie suspiciously before narrowing his eyes at Birdie.

"What?" she asked, all wide, blue-eyed innocence.

"Where's the punchline?"

"No punchline," she replied, suddenly interested in the state of her cuticles. "Oh, but Abbie asked me to ask you if you could help with the booze and the food. She wants to kick off in a couple of hours."

"That woman will be the end of me, I swear," he mumbled, climbing to his feet and glaring at Abbie.

"Hey!" she shouted. "Babe! Did Birdie tell you the good news?"

"Hey!" he called back. "*Babe*. You want something from me? You're going to have to come here and ask me yourself."

The pretty blonde, bronzed yogi shook her head at the girls as if to say, "Why is life so hard?" She strode with long legs over the sand, sparing a wide smile for us all before sidling up beside Will and fluttering her lashes. "We're having a party. Can you whip us up a few bottles of margaritas? Oh! And ask Noa to make those yummy fried samosa things he served at The Stop last week. They were delish. Fresh and hot, please. Thanks!"

"Why do I put up with you?" Will grumbled under his breath, but he swung an arm around Abbie's neck, tucked her in against his body, and dragged her in the direction of his bar.

Abbie wrapped her arm around his waist as they closed the distance from our towels to Main Street. "I have no idea, Kidd. I really don't."

The rest of their conversation was lost as they made their way to The Stop, and we shrugged off this latest example of their weird dynamic. The what and why of Will and Abbie had a long, complicated history that nobody but those two knew anything about.

Logan, Josh, and Luca ran over to help the girls lug their gear to the far south end of the beach, where the bonfire stones were waiting, while Birdie hung back with me.

"So, a party, huh?"

"Yes!" she said. "I'm pumped. I always loved the beach parties when we were kids. I think I even convinced my parents to go to one."

"You did?" I took Birdie's bag from her and slung it over my shoulder. "I can't say I remember that."

"Oh, I think they stayed for about three minutes, but they did set foot on the sand. Back then, it felt like a win."

"I bet." Loaded up with bags and towels and Will's cooler, I added, "How about we drop this at home and find something warmer to bring back? The boys can take care of the boat, and once that sun sets, there'll be a chill in the air."

“Sounds good.” Birdie squeaked. “I didn’t think I’d get to a bonfire while I was here this time, and then Abbie does this! Gah! I’m so excited. I sound like an idiot, but that’s how much I love these parties. Don’t hold it against me.”

“Never.”

Because you know what, Birdie? Every time you admit to loving this place and these people and this life, you’re one step closer to admitting that maybe you love me too.

26

ISAAC

"SO, DID YOU have fun today?"

Birdie grinned up at me as we walked side by side along Main Street in the dark, mischief dancing in her bright blue eyes. "You know, I did." She reached around and pinched my arse. "Never a dull day when I get to look at these sweet cheeks in the sun, then drink tequila under the stars."

I pretended to scowl at her for groping me in public, but her light giggle turned into a laugh when I glanced around to check if anyone was around to see it. We were walking home from the beach late on a weeknight. All the stores closed hours ago. Most people were in their beds. We were as good as alone.

"Oh my God, Romeo. Are you really worried someone saw that?" She snaked her arm around me and did it again, then danced away before I could catch her.

"Quit it, Red," I said, finally collecting her hand in mine. To my relief, she didn't pull away from a PDA I considered pretty intimate, and we walked like a real couple at the end of a real date. It was awesome. "You know I don't mind the butt squeezes, but I'm a cop. I have to at least try to maintain appearances."

"The appearance of an officer of the law with a great big stick up his bum?"

"*No*," I drawled. "But how am I meant to knock on foggy car windows and send kids home where they belong if the night before they watched me get groped in the street?"

"Oh, Lord," Birdie groaned. "Please don't tell me you torture teenagers who are only trying to have a little fun before curfew."

My mouth turned down. "Of course I do. It's my job."

Birdie shook her head but swung our arms back and forth. "It's times like these I wonder how the two of us ever became friends in the first place. We are so different."

My frown deepened. There was that word again. *Friends*. I'd heard it a lot the last few days, ever since I cuffed her in her hallway and fucked her senseless against the mirror. Jesus, that was the best sex I'd ever had—and might ever have.

As good as it was, it hadn't stopped Birdie from trying to resurrect an agreement that, in my mind, had long expired, and I decided to call her out on it.

"I don't know why we make good friends and even better lovers, but haven't we covered this already? I thought we agreed that the game had changed, Red."

Her lips twisted to one side, and she shook her head. "I considered what you said, Romeo, and I'm afraid there's a gaping hole in that plan of yours to—what was it? Up the stakes? Break the rules?"

I tried to swallow, but my mouth was suddenly dry. "Oh, yeah? Tell me more about this gaping hole."

"All the rules you want to break are the ones *I* made. How's that fair? Why am I the one who has to change? Give a little, take a little. Isn't that the way?"

Okay, so this wasn't as bad as I'd feared. Actually, I wasn't sure what this was.

"You've lost me, Red." I tapped her temple. "Got to slow things down for those of us with half your IQ. Explain it to me like I'm in kindergarten."

She stopped in front of the shuttered-up bakery and turned to face me.

"When have you ever done something bad?" Birdie crossed her arms underneath her breasts and looked up at me, head tilted to one side. "When have you ever done something *naughty*?"

I glanced down the street the way we'd come. "I stepped over a sandwich wrapper a few blocks back. That's pretty irresponsible." I wasn't going to add I felt bad about it at the time, and now that I was thinking about it again, I kind of wanted to go back and pick it up.

Birdie clucked her tongue and shook her head. "Sergeant Greene: litterbug. How will you sleep tonight?" A smug smile curled her lips. "I bet you fifty dollars you can't think of a single deviant thing to do between this spot and my front door. Think of it—then do it."

I tugged on an earlobe. "You want me to do something illegal?"

She lifted one shoulder. "Not all misbehaviour is against the law."

"Come on, Red." I stepped in a little closer and gazed into her upturned face, unleashing my tried-and-tested smoulder. "Let's go home and be deviant there."

Birdie smiled as she sighed and reached up to pat my cheek. "So. Different."

She spun on her heel and kept walking, and I stared after her for a moment, her tempting copper braid swinging down her back.

Sure, we were different, but that's why we worked so well together. Birdie was impulsive and independent, ballsy and brilliant. I was responsible and reliable, steadfast and safe. Our differences were what made us perfect for each other. They were the reasons she trusted me, in the bedroom as well as out.

But that didn't mean I couldn't be spontaneous, did it? I could meet the girl I loved somewhere in the middle when that was what she needed. And the more I thought about it, the more I had to admit that what she'd said was true. I wanted her to redraw all the boundaries she'd put in place to protect herself, but what was I planning to do to prove to her that I was just as capable of change?

Birdie was all about adventure. She was born wild-hearted, flighty, and free. There really was no better namesake for her, and I didn't want her to think a life here with me meant she'd have to sacrifice any part of what made her who she was. And I had to show her that I could be vulnerable, too. I had to prove that I heard her, I understood her, and I trusted her.

My break-up with Amanda suddenly came to mind, and the piece of advice she'd given me right before she left me standing alone and confused in the street.

"Give the good-boy routine a break, okay? Find the bad boy hidden way, way down deep inside and let him out to play."

I took off down the street, lengthening my stride and catching Birdie in less than a dozen paces. Wrapping a hand around her upper arm, I dragged her into the adjacent darkened alley, moving deep enough that we disappeared in the black shadows, then guided her into an alcove I knew was there—an out-of-the-way nook between The Salty Stop and the empty warehouse next door that hid the back door to Will's bar. It toed the line between a public space and Will's private property, so I tucked us in behind a stack of empty crates before pinning her against the wall.

Leaning in, I nipped her earlobe, then whispered, "Whatever you do, don't scream."

Birdie's breath came shallow and fast as she bit her bottom lip and nodded silently.

I hitched her denim skirt up around her hips, dropped to my knees, and dragged her panties down. When they caught on her boots—soft brown leather with a pair of blue fuzzy socks peeking out the top—I gave up trying to manoeuvre her underwear over her ankles and tore the fabric. Birdie moaned.

"That's so freaking sexy, Romeo, but keep it up, and you'll send me broke buying replacements."

"I'll buy you an entire fucking lingerie store if it means I'm the only man who gets to do this."

Kneeling on the dusty ground, I kissed my way up the inside of one leg, my hands caressing their way along her silky-smooth calves and thighs until they reached her hips, which I held hard against the wall as I dragged my tongue over the hood of her pussy, flicking and teasing her clit.

"Lady's choice," I murmured before dragging the flat of my tongue along her rapidly dampening seam and revelling in the familiar, delicious taste of her. "Tongue. Fingers. Cock. What's it going to be?"

"T–tongue," she stammered.

"Then get ready to ride my face, Red."

Birdie squealed as I hoisted her up the wall and wrapped her legs around my shoulders. It was no effort to hold her aloft, pinned against the dirty brick wall with my face buried in her pussy and her fingers tugging at my hair.

I stiffened my tongue and plunged it deep inside, twisting and teasing as hard as I could before pulling out and attaching my lips to her clit. I sucked until she squirmed, the tension in her thighs like a vice around my ears, then shifted the position of my hands so I could spread her open with my thumbs.

I explored every fold and hidden crease of her, tossing my head and eating her with a rough hunger I knew drove her wild. Within minutes, Birdie was swearing up at the stars glittering over us in the small strip of black sky visible between the buildings overhead, and I was drinking in the evidence of her orgasm.

"Holy hell," she groaned, dropping one leg and catching her breath. I helped her set her feet on the ground, and she sank against the wall, eyes closed and one hand held against a flushed cheek. "Okay, you win. That was as unexpected as it was deviant. I owe you fifty bucks."

At the sound of my fly being unzipped, her eyes popped open and dropped straight to my crotch. I'd already pulled out my throbbing cock, and I gave it a long, slow stroke while she watched.

Fuck, if that wasn't the most erotic thing I'd tried from any of the books I'd read: Birdie's eyes on me as I fucked my hand.

Retrieving a condom from my back pocket, I rolled it on, then stepped closer and kissed her, long and slow and adoringly. She made sweet mewling noises as I cradled her head, tilting it back and shifting the angle to make sure I claimed this mouth as my own.

She clung to my arms, and when her hips rocked against me, shifting as she sought out friction against my cock, I hitched her knee around my hip, lined myself up, and sank the tip of my dick inside her.

The mewling noises turned to whimpers, and I gave her another inch.

The kissing grew more frenzied as I held us on the edge, the anticipation tormenting us both. Another inch, and she clawed at my shoulders hard enough to leave marks through the fabric of my shirt.

Another inch, and she writhed against me, trying to drive herself down on my rock-hard length.

Another inch, and she latched onto my arse, trying and failing to pull me deeper.

I groaned at the effort it took not to fuck her fast and hard until the wet, hot promise of her was too much to resist. Clasping her knee and making sure she was anchored there against my hip, I pulled away from her mouth at the same moment I slammed myself into her, sheathing myself to the hilt. She screamed, and I covered her open mouth with my free hand.

I met her wide, wild eyes as I pistoned into her with deep, desperate thrusts. My arse clenched with every rut, and her hot breath hit my palm as she breathed through her muffled moans.

"I told you not to scream," I growled, and her eyes rolled back in her head. "And you've been much too loud tonight. I should pull out now, but you coming in my mouth was your choice, and your orgasm on my cock is mine."

I removed my hand and palmed her breast through her tee while Birdie clamped her top teeth down on her plump bottom lip, biting her way through the jolts of pleasure I sent shooting through her body.

I railed her there in the alley, determined to prove with each reckless pulse that I could be the adventure Birdie wanted. I was as exciting as I was safe, but more than that, I was hers—and whatever was in my power to give her, I was going to deliver.

Birdie let out a strangled moan, and I clamped my mouth against the slope of her neck as her core tightened around my dick. Wave after wave of her climax bore down on me, sending me careening over the precipice.

Her pussy milked my dick as I unloaded everything I had inside her, and we came together, choking back our desperate moans, our orgasms lifting us both higher and higher, then dropping us down to Earth.

I set my forehead against hers, breathing as hard as she did, trying to find myself again in the haze of what we'd just done.

"Oh my God," Birdie sighed, returning her foot to the ground and collapsing against my chest. "What the hell was that, Romeo?"

I kissed her damp, salty temple and tried harder to breathe evenly. "That," I murmured against her skin, so quietly she couldn't have heard me, "was a promise."

27

BIRDIE

"THIS WAS A great idea," I said, loading the last of the grocery bags into the back of Isaac's car. They were filled with party food, drinks, and disposable dinnerware for the party I was hosting in less than three hours. "I haven't been to a Halloween party since I was a kid. Probably in this town, now that I think about it. We didn't get to celebrate at boarding school. You know, on account of Jesus and the—"

"The nuns," Isaac pre-emptively echoed with an amused eyebrow.

"That's right." I slid into the passenger seat as Isaac settled himself behind the wheel and pulled out from the kerb. "Witches—all of them. They never let us have any fun."

I reached into the shopping bag at my feet and pulled out the sexy kitten costume I'd found in Valentine Bay's one and only variety store. There weren't many options to buy fancy dress locally, and it was either this or a wizard's cloak. I went with the option more likely to get me laid because, you know—*Isaac*.

"What do you think?" I asked, setting the black ears on my head and holding the sleek black leotard up to my body. I wriggled the tip of my nose in a silly imitation of having whiskers.

Isaac spared me a quick glance before returning his eyes to the road, his fingers flexing on the wheel. "I think I'm going to have a hard time keeping my hands off you tonight."

I grinned. "Why wait? I'm sure there's a perfectly suitable public venue we could sneak away to right now." I pretended to examine the buildings, beach, and parks flying past my window, tapping my chin and frowning through the glass. "Oh, look! That park bench is almost concealed by a low-hanging branch. We could do it there, and nobody would ever know."

"Quit it, Red." Isaac cleared his throat and dropped his chin as a flush of pink began to mottle the back of his neck. "I lost my mind the other night, all right? And it was hardly a public place. It was the rear door to Kidd's—

"Kidd's bar," I said, squeezing my thighs together as I remembered it all. It had only been three days ago, but I'd replayed it so many times it felt like an hour. It was a night I'd never forget and never get over, and it was so unlike Isaac to do anything that risky. But he'd done it for me—and as much as I didn't want to lose my head like some loved-up nitwit, I was starting to think my fight against this man was a losing battle. In fact, I'd sort of forgotten why our relationship was something I needed to resist at all.

"Yeah, yeah." I placed my hand on his thigh and rubbed my way upwards and inwards, stopping short of the bulge that was rapidly expanding in his shorts. "What if I *bet* you, Romeo? It worked the last time. Ten bucks it'll work again."

Isaac shifted uncomfortably in his seat, then ran a hand over the back of mine, twining his fingers in a way that halted my stealth attack on his manhood. "Save the wagers for when you want it really bad, Red."

"Ah, so the daredevil has his limits." I nodded sagely. "Noted."

He lifted my hand to his lips so he could kiss the back of it and I deliberately ignored the implication of his comment, rolling my lips and gazing out the window while he drove us back to my place.

I'd been tallying the number of times Isaac made ambiguous remarks about our future—save this, wait for that, one day soon, let's do this again… He said something along those lines at least twice a day, and I let every one pass without comment. We'd both been avoiding the topic of my leaving the Bay, and neither of us had mentioned the fact I was due to fly out in five days' time. He hadn't come right out and said it, but his behaviour strongly implied that he was thinking about us beyond that date. Beyond my tournament.

I'd been thinking about it too.

My phone pinged in my pocket, and I twisted awkwardly in my seat so I could extract it without dropping Isaac's hand. Cora's name flashed up on the screen, and just like that, my good mood popped quicker than a balloon stuck with a pin.

"What?" Isaac demanded, looking back and forth between my face and the road. "What is it? What's wrong?"

I fixed my expression as I silently berated myself for letting my emotions show. "It's a message from Cora."

Ever since I quit school so I could create a new life for myself, I'd become an expert at compartmentalising the different pillars of my life. I was a poker player. A gambler. A nomad. A free spirit. In my new world, I was not a traumatised kid with dysfunctional parents and a broken home. But this last month in the Bay had worn at those boundaries. I loved spending time with the crew. I adored Isaac's family. I enjoyed studying with Liam—talking mathematics and watching him light up when I taught him something new were thrills I never knew I'd been missing.

I'd grown used to letting my guard down with Isaac, and I'd stopped worrying about keeping up appearances. But when it came to my parents—when it came to Cora—it was essential that I keep my complex parental baggage strictly to myself. I wasn't going to risk contaminating my time with Isaac with the negative energy that swamped me at the sight of her name.

I couldn't forget why I was here. I'd let myself get distracted, but I had to put an end to my family drama once and for all if I ever wanted to get on with my life. A life I never knew I wanted—one that might involve putting down roots right here in the Bay. All I needed was for my mother to get here so I could finally tell her how I really felt about her. And after I did the same with my father in Las Vegas—and took his money, of course—I'd finally be emotionally cut off from them both. Just like I'd always wanted.

Isaac's brows folded inwards as I sat there staring at Cora's name on the screen, but he waited with silent patience, brushing his thumb in soothing arcs across the back of my hand.

Like tearing off a bandage, I slipped my thumb over the screen and opened her text.

Cora: I'll be in Valentine Bay this afternoon, and I assume you'll be at the house. Let me know if that's not the case, and I'll make other arrangements.

A lump of thick, persistent hope appeared in my throat, and I swallowed it down. I should have been annoyed that she'd given me no notice. I should have been furious that she thought she could come and go whenever she pleased, and I'd be sitting on my hands waiting for her to show. And on some level, that was true, but all I could think was, could it be only a coincidence that Cora was finally coming to see me today—and today happened to be my birthday?

Nobody in the Bay knew it was my birthday, of course. Announcing your own birthday was obnoxious past the age of twelve, and I'd celebrated enough times over the years with single-serve takeout, solo cocktails at casino bars, and disappointing one-night stands to be less attached to my birthday than most people. But that little girl inside—the one I couldn't quite leave behind—lit up with expectation, and I'd never had enough strength to totally shut her down.

My palms tingled as I typed back my reply with one hand.

Me: I'll be there.

"She'll be here later today," I revealed, locking my phone and tucking it away. Saying it out loud didn't make it seem any more real.

"Right."

The energy in the car shifted. We pulled up to the corner of our street, and Isaac squinted as he checked for oncoming traffic before making the turn. He waited until we'd pulled into the driveway and were heaving the grocery bags out of the car before he asked, "Do you want to cancel the party?"

He was trying to be cool about it, but he was pulling at his earlobe so hard it should have been blue, and the tightness around his eyes was still there.

Dammit. So much for keeping my family shit separate from the rest of my life.

I plastered on a grin and snorted inelegantly as I led the way up the porch steps, grocery bags piled in my arms.

"No way. I am pumped for tonight." I wriggled my arse at him. "Pretty sure my costume includes a tail, and you know, there just aren't enough occasions in life when a girl can wear a tail."

He dipped his free hand into my back pocket and retrieved my keys, then slipped the correct one into the lock on the front door, turned it with a click, and paused. "I'm really glad you said that."

The door swung open, and a booming chorus of "surprise" flew out at me.

"What the—"

I stepped inside, wide-eyed and a little confused by the balloons and streamers swinging from the ceiling and the crowd of people crammed into my hallway, each one dressed in some sort of costume. Moving further in, I recognised more faces in the living room, and a sea of anonymous heads undulated back into the dining room and kitchen.

I choked out an unbelieving laugh. "What the hell is this?"

Looking back over my shoulder, I found Isaac hanging back, two bags of groceries in one hand, the other rubbing the back of his neck, a half-smile of abashed discomfort on his face.

"Happy birthday?" he said like it was a question.

"How did you know?" I asked, just as Abbie—dressed as a hippie from the 1960s with a margarita in her hand—launched herself at me, enveloping me in a tight one-armed hug.

"He's a cop," she replied. "He's been snooping where he shouldn't, obvs."

I lifted one eyebrow at Isaac, the implication clear that Mr Good Guy had been doing more than one thing he shouldn't. He rolled his eyes, but there was an adorable flush in his skin.

"I found your ID in your clothes when I did a load of your washing," he admitted. "I did *not* look at your personal records."

"Good thing, too," I muttered, stretching up on tiptoes to drop a kiss on his bearded cheek. "The things you'd read would blow your mind."

I was teasing him, but a look of speculation crossed his face, and I had to laugh.

"Okay," Abbie declared, taking the groceries I held and efficiently replacing them with the cocktail. She handed the bags over to Will, who was an explosion of fluoro colour in his '80s get-up, just as music started blaring from somewhere deeper in the house. "You boys sort out the food and booze while we get the birthday girl dressed for her party." She scanned the costume bag hanging over my other arm. "What you got there, honey? Ooh, a kitty cat." Latching onto my free hand, she dragged me up the stairs. "Come on, this won't take long."

Behind us, Jess—dressed as a bookish librarian with her hair slicked back, glasses on her nose, and a drink in either hand—and Emily—looking super cute in a Tinkerbell costume—followed up the stairs and into my bedroom. Once we were all inside, Abbie closed the door and collapsed back against it.

"Just stop," she ordered, her narrowed eyes flitting up and down my body. "The sex vibes are oozing off you, and all that bragging is unbecoming."

I opened my mouth, but Emily cut me off. "Don't try to deny it. Not only does Abbie have a sixth sense for sex, but your glow is so obvious even I can see it."

"Oh, yeah," Jess added, tilting her head as she considered me. "Big glow."

"And Greene's practically incandescent with satisfaction." Abbie strutted over and stood in front of me, arms crossed over her chest. "Orgasms a-plenty. Am I right?"

I kept my face impassive for all of three seconds before I broke. "Girls," I deadpanned. "You have no fucking idea."

Emily and Jess squealed like teenagers as Abbie threw herself face down on my bed, then lifted her head to glare at us. "I'm the only one in this room who still has to get her Os from an electronic device, and this fact does not make me happy."

Emily shot me a conspiratorial wink before she said, "Maybe you could talk to Will about—"

Abbie bolted upright. "Jones, I love you, but I will murder you without remorse if you finish that sentence."

"Sorry," Emily said, covering her mouth to stifle a chuckle.

"Frost," Abbie said, thrusting out a hand. "Margarita me."

Jess dutifully deposited her extra drink in Abbie's hand, and she threw half of it back in a single gulp.

I hid a grin as I stripped off my tee and shorts, then pulled the full-bodied black leotard of my cat costume on over my underwear.

Abbie *tsked.* "That won't do. You need a G-string under that thing or nothing at all."

"Right. Thanks."

I rummaged in my dresser for appropriate underwear as the three of them perched in a row on the end of my bed, and I couldn't tell if it was that image or the mouthful of tequila I'd just swallowed that warmed me from the inside out.

I slipped into the bathroom to change my underwear—Abbie was right; it helped with the smooth lines of the leotard, which clung to every curve—then returned to the bedroom to attach my tail.

"Can I ask you something that might make you uncomfortable?" Jess asked as I scraped my hair into a bouncy high ponytail.

"All right," I said cautiously, taking the headband with the cat ears from the costume bag and perching them on my head.

"Don't get me wrong. I'm happy about all the sex and everything, but when you told us about your arrangement with Isaac, I wasn't sure what to think. I was worried things would end badly, and now… I honestly don't know if I'm more concerned or less."

I paused, hunting around in my cosmetics case for the black eyeliner I planned to use to draw a nose and whiskers on my face, my focus darting to the girls on my bed. "What do you mean?"

"Do you remember what you called this thing when you first told us about it at our poker night? You said it was purely philanthropic. No strings attached." Jess exhaled heavily, and her mouth set in a flat line. "You might not want to hear this, but I think you need to know. When I look at Isaac, I see strings."

My heart stuttered for a moment and only picked up its regular rhythm when I remembered to breathe.

Abbie took a slurp of her cocktail, eying me over the rim of the glass, and even Emily had a contemplative look on her face.

I needed a moment to think, so I took a seat at my dresser and concentrated on my reflection in the mirror as I lined my face with black whiskers and dotted the tip of my nose with an inky blot. After adding a sleek cat's eye line to my eyelids, I set aside the pencil and picked up a gold tube of red lipstick. I painted my lips slowly and eyed the women in the room with me—three very different faces with identical expressions of cautious curiosity and a fierce protectiveness for Isaac that I shared deep in my bones.

The warmth wasn't the tequila after all, and by the time I was feline enough for the party, I'd made a decision.

I wanted to give this life a try, and whatever it took, I was all in.

"I think you're right about the strings," I agreed, spinning on the little dressing stool to face everyone. "But you don't need to worry. Those strings… They go both ways."

Emily's face broke into a pleased grin while Jess's eyebrows climbed to her hairline, and Abbie choked down her mouthful of margarita. "Say *what*?"

Jess flung out a hand and stopped Abbie's incredulity with a firm grip on her leg. "We're going to need more information."

"I can't believe I'm telling you this," I confessed. "I haven't even spoken to Isaac about it yet, but… I love Valentine Bay. Every holiday here when I was a kid felt more like coming home than returning to my own house ever did, and I was unprepared for how it would still feel that way. You girls… Well, I like hanging out with you. I like the crew. I adore Isaac's family. And as for Isaac, it's not just the sex because while there are no words for what that man can do with his hands, it's more than that. We are good friends, and I like that about us. I told him before things escalated that I never wanted to jeopardise what we had, and against all odds, it feels like intimacy has only made things better."

"So, the strings…?" Jess prodded.

"The strings are undeniable at this point. I have to fly out next week for an important tournament in Vegas, but when my commitments are settled, I want to come back and see what happens."

"You mean you'll move here?" Emily asked, inching forwards on the edge of the mattress. "As in permanently?"

"I don't know," I hedged. "I haven't thought that far ahead, and I haven't even talked to Isaac about it yet. My mother will be here any minute to talk about her plans for the house, and I have a hunch she's going to ask me to stick around to manage a renovation. Under normal circumstances, I'd say hell no. But who knows? It might work out well for all of us."

Jess grinned. "Isaac is going to be so happy."

My stomach flipped against my will, and I jumped to my feet, twisting in front of the mirror to do a final check of my costume.

"How do I look?" I asked.

Jess stood and wrapped her arms around my neck. "You're a knockout."

"Now, let's get downstairs." Abbie grabbed my hand as I swiped my near-empty cocktail glass from my dresser, tugging me towards the door. "Isaac's sex on legs these days. Not sure it's safe to leave him alone for too long."

"You don't have to ask me twice," I agreed. "Let's go."

We returned to the party, and as the girls disappeared into the crowd, I paused on the second-last step. Like a compass spinning to the north point, my eyes found Isaac right away. His head turned towards me as if he felt it too. He'd changed into snug, faded blue jeans and a plaid button-down, boots with spurs on his feet and a cowboy hat on his head. He tipped it at me and gave me a wink.

My blood burned hot enough that a light sheen of sweat sprung up on the back of my neck. *Yee-fucking-haw.*

"Hey, Greene!" Luca stuck his head into the living room from the kitchen and shouted over the music. "Can we get your help with the keg?"

Sparing me a quick, knowing wink before he turned away, Isaac dutifully disappeared into the other room. I was disappointed—until I got a good look at his arse in those Wranglers. Taking the last couple of steps and moving into the hallway, I was near the front door when someone rapped their knuckles on it. My stomach did that flip again, this time for an entirely different reason.

Anybody who was invited to this party would already be here or else knew enough about parties in the Bay to realise that when things got started, you walked right on in. That brisk, business-like knock had to be Cora.

It didn't occur to me that she should have let herself in. She owned the place. She had a key. Those facts dawned on me three seconds too late.

An older woman in a forest green skirt-and-blazer combo, her blonde hair blow-waved to within an inch of its life, stood on the porch, a glossy printed folder in her hand. She smiled at me brightly, white teeth sparkling, and stuck out her hand.

"Hello. I'm Rachael. Are you Birdie Maxwell?"

I hesitated a moment before I shook her hand, distracted by the man pulling a large signage board out of the back of a silver minivan parked in front of my house.

"Yes, I'm Birdie. Can I help you?"

Rachael swept her eyes over my body, cataloguing my cat costume, before she glanced past me into the house. She frowned for a brief moment before her smile returned with a vengeance. "I see I've come at a bad time, and I *am* sorry about that, but if I could borrow you for two minutes, I'll be out of your hair, and you can get back to your party."

With a sense of foreboding, I stepped out onto the porch and closed the door behind me, glancing again at the guy who was now setting the legs of the sign on the front lawn of my property. I took a few strides along the porch to try to get a view of the front of the sign, but it was no use at this angle. Rachael followed, and I turned to her, my arms crossed. Warning bells rang, and my stomach wasn't flipping so much as it was preparing for an all-in riot.

"What's this all about?" I asked, trying—and failing—to be polite.

Rachael's smile faltered, and she smoothed the front of her blazer before handing me the folder in her hand. I tucked it under one arm without looking at it, and Rachael wilted a little more.

The man with the sign pulled a rubber mallet from somewhere and began banging the board into the ground.

"I've just come from a meeting with your mother—"

"Cora?" I demanded, checking the street for a shiny Mercedes that wasn't there. "She's here?"

"She was." Rachael glanced once at the folder, then at her colleague on my lawn, and back to me. Her swallow was nervous, and her smile less certain. "She contacted me a month or so ago to discuss her plans for this property, and she was at my office earlier today to sign the contracts. Unfortunately, she had important business in the city and couldn't stay so—"

"She's *gone*?" It was my turn to swallow, choking back the bile that jumped into my throat. "She was here, and now she's gone?"

"Yes." Rachael's mouth turned down with discomfort. "Mrs Maxwell gave me instructions to inform you that she's selling this house." The woman gestured to the sign that was now embedded in the yard, and the guy who had hammered it in waved as if this was a social call.

My mother wasn't coming to see me on my birthday. She probably didn't even remember it. She didn't want my help with the house, and she wasn't going to give me a reason to stay. She couldn't care less about me.

But I already knew that.

Old instincts kicked in as I smoothed the hurt from my face. Something iced over inside—the numbness was welcome and familiar, cold and hard like steel buried in snow, and I clung to it as if my life depended on it. Right then, it did.

"I see," I said.

"I'm sure she would have preferred to talk to you about this herself, but as I said, she was unable to stay any longer than it took to review the paperwork. I offered to—"

"Is this it?" I said, waving the folder in front of her face.

"Uh, yes, that's—"

"Got it. Thanks for the message. Have a nice day."

I stalked past her and into the house, slamming the door behind me.

My own mother hadn't seen me in more than three years, and even with less than six blocks between us, she couldn't spare five minutes to see me. I *hated* her, but more than that, I hated myself for believing this time might be different.

Screw my mother. Screw my life. Screw everything I ever thought I wanted or needed or deserved because it was all fucking quicksand.

Around me, the crowd parted, and Isaac came into view. His grin melted as he met my eyes. If I were anyone else, I'd be blinking back tears right now, but in that moment, I finally remembered who I was, and I knew with painful clarity what I had to do.

I had to run.

28

ISAAC

I LOCKED EYES with Birdie across the crowded room, a beer in my hand and music thumping in my ears, and instantly knew something was wrong. Her freckled face was pale, her eyes unnaturally blank, and her hands curled as she rubbed her fingers against her palms. But the change was fleeting, and within seconds of meeting my gaze, there was a bright, wide smile on her face. Unfortunately for Birdie, I knew her too well, and though her grin plumped up her cheeks, it didn't quite reach her eyes.

I took a concerned step towards her, but she held up a finger to stop me. I hesitated, and she used that opportunity to slip around the knot of people between us and disappear.

Craning my neck, I spotted her pointed black cat ears and sexy ponytail bouncing into the kitchen and then watched as she swiped a plastic cup of beer from the row lined up on the island. Throwing her head back, she downed half the liquid in a single swallow.

Fuck, she looked edible in that costume. The sleek black Lycra clung to every curve of her soft body, and I'm not sure I'd seen her in heels before. They did things to her legs and arse that I was here for. But as much as I could have looked at her all night long and been the most satisfied man in that house, I couldn't enjoy it the way I wanted to. I couldn't shake a sense of unease.

Hours later, after Birdie had neatly spun and danced and dodged away from every attempt I'd made to get her alone, my concern had escalated from mildly troubled to the type of apprehension that made my stomach clench and my neck damp. She'd been dancing non-stop for more than an hour, pausing only to drink half her weight in Will's IPA. After watching her drain her third cup, I switched to water. I wanted to have my wits about me—now, so I could keep an eye on her, and later, when the party ended, and we'd finally be able to talk.

I didn't let myself think about what her behaviour might mean. I couldn't make myself believe it had anything to do with me—with us. This last month, I'd learned to read her almost as well as she read everyone else, and this shift in demeanour was only hours old. She'd seemed impressed by my cowboy costume earlier in the night. She'd been genuinely surprised and pleased by the party. Although a tickle of self-doubt continued to scratch at my throat, I forced myself to contemplate the situation logically and concluded that whatever bothered Birdie wasn't me.

I checked my watch and glanced at the front door before returning my attention to Birdie. She was occupied for the moment, dancing with Abbie and Emily in the kitchen, but the day was creeping into the evening, the sky outside darkening as night fell, and Cora still hadn't shown up. Some instinctive part of me knew the chances of her arriving now were slim and getting smaller by the minute. That fact couldn't have been lost on Birdie, either.

I watched as Birdie collected another filled cup from the island, then twirled her way to the square of space being used as a dance floor. To anyone looking at this picture from the outside, the birthday girl was just having a good time. Flushed cheeks and bursts of laughter as she swung her hips in time with the music—all signals that Birdie was celebrating and doing a damn good job of it. But she hadn't met my gaze in the last forty-five minutes, instead throwing me vague smiles and empty excuses as she weaved out of my arms and waved absently at me from across the room.

Fuck. My heart broke for her.

But I could fix it, I told myself from my perch on the kitchen stool, sipping iced water and keeping tabs on my girl like I was fucking hired security. I could make it better. I could tell her I loved her and wanted her to stay with me, and it would fill at least part of the hole those so-called parents had left in Birdie's heart.

My jaw clenched as I considered Birdie's mother and father. I didn't know them well, and as a cop, I always made an effort to consider a situation from all sides, but they belonged in a fucking prison. There was no way anybody could justify the hurt they'd caused this incredible woman or excuse the trauma they'd left her to manage all on her own.

Not anymore, I silently vowed as Birdie placed her hand in Will's and spun herself under his arm.

"Hey, Greene." Jess slung an arm around my shoulder and gave me a squeeze. She was dressed as if she were going to work in a pencil skirt and button-up blouse, dark-framed glasses on her nose, but her ash-brown hair, which had been neat when she'd arrived, was mussed now and loose around the edges. Her bright red lipstick was faded and a little smeared, all evidence of a good time. "Not drinking tonight?" she asked.

I tilted my near-empty cup at her to show her the ice chips in the bottom, then pointed it towards Birdie. "Thought one of us should have our heads on straight enough to kick you all out when the party's over."

"Smart," she agreed. "Birdie's having a great time, don't you think?" Jess leaned against my arm and sighed, the scent of lemon and tequila delicately floating on her breath. "It'll be fantastic when she moves back here."

I straightened as my heart stuttered, and my laser-sharp focus on Birdie temporarily shifted to Jess. "What are you talking about?"

Jess's hand flew to her mouth, and her dark brown eyes rounded like saucers. "Nothing. Forget I said anything."

"Oh, no. Not going to happen."

Jess glanced at Birdie, and I followed her line of sight, but Abbie and Emily—and Will—were enough of a distraction that she hadn't noticed Jess and me whispering a few paces away. I spun on my stool to put my back to our friends and pulled Jess to the left, blocking her view of them with my body. "Okay, Frost. What did Birdie tell you?"

Jess closed her eyes and groaned, shifting on her feet as she shook her head in self-recrimination. I waited with an outward show of patience that I didn't feel.

Did Birdie already have plans to move back here?

"I mean, she didn't say it was a secret *exactly*, but she did say she hadn't talked to you about it yet." Jess's nose wriggled the way it did when she was about to do something she thought was a bad choice, and she shot a quick look over my shoulder before she threw up her hands in defeat. "Fine. When we were upstairs helping Birdie get ready for the party, she might have mentioned how well things are working out for her here and that she's thinking about flying back after her tournament. Apparently, her parents want to renovate the place? Anyway, she wants to see how things go between the two of you. I think she— Oh, no. I can't tell you that."

My pulse was out of control. Birdie had already decided to come back? I knew it! I *knew* that by showing her what was possible, she'd see that what we had together was too perfect for her to ever walk away.

"You better bloody tell me, Frost." I grinned to let her know anything she was about to confide could only be a good thing. "Though I'm not sure what else you could say to top what you've already told me."

"She's into you, Isaac." Jess threw her arms around my neck, and, surprised, I enveloped her in a warm hug. She whispered her next words in my ear. "Hang on tight. This could be it."

I huffed out an ecstatic breath and held my friend tighter in a silent thank you. Jess said it, and I believed it because it felt like hearing something I already knew was true. "Thanks, Frost."

I dropped a chaste kiss on her cheek before she pulled back. "I think it's time for the cake," she declared. "What do you think?"

"I think the birthday girl could definitely use some carbs to soak up all the booze."

I helped Jess retrieve the enormous cake—a chocolate ganache-covered masterpiece from the local patisserie—and we dotted it with tall silver candles before lighting them and carrying the cake out to the kitchen.

The crowd parted to let us through, then closed around us again, and after setting the cake on the table in front of Birdie, I braved rejection by looping an arm around her waist. She allowed it, and as everyone busted out into an off-key chorus of *Happy Birthday*, she leaned against me. I took that as evidence that she liked me there beside her, not proof that her blood alcohol level made it difficult to stand upright.

Birdie accepted the fuss with glassy eyes and a smile that was too watery to be real, and the anxiety I'd forgotten following my conversation with Jess rolled through my system again.

On the upside, now that I had Birdie in my arms, I wasn't about to let go, and I didn't have to. Almost as if my physical touch had mended whatever bond Birdie had been shying away from all night, she let me lead her out into an open square of space and spin her into a close embrace.

Whoever managed the playlist switched things up with a slower beat to the next track, and someone dimmed the lights. Soon we weren't the only couple pressed together as we swayed in a slow dance. Some dances looked like inebriation, others exhaustion, and a few more like intimacy. Over the top of Birdie's head, half-hidden in the shadowed corner, Abbie and Will bowed their heads together until he held out his open hand. This was that part of the night where she rebuffed his offer—he'd been asking her to dance for more than ten years, and she refused every time. But to my surprise—and everyone else's apparently, as I exchanged stunned looks with Josh, Logan, and Luca—Abbie set her fingers on his palm and let him pull her against his body.

Caring less about their story right now than mine, I dropped my eyes to leave them to it. I pressed my nose against Birdie's hair and breathed in the fragrance of her shampoo.

"God, you smell so good," I mumbled.

"I smell like the floor of Will's bar," she replied, resting her forehead on my chest and closing her eyes.

Sensing that Birdie had moved past her urgent need for space, I set my hand on the small of her back and pressed her closer against me. "Is everything okay? You've been a little…off tonight."

The seconds ticked by, and Birdie said nothing. I ducked my head to see if she'd somehow fallen asleep standing up, but her lids flickered upwards to meet my eyes before they darted away again.

"She was here," Birdie whispered against my chest so quietly I almost didn't hear it.

"Who was where? At the party?"

She shook her head, snuggling closer against me and leaving black smudges of her cat's nose and whiskers on my shirt. "Cora. She was in Valentine Bay today, and she left without coming to see me."

Of their own volition, my arms tightened around Birdie, and my nostrils flared as I worked to keep my breathing even. "How do you know that?"

Birdie huffed out a sad laugh. "She sent a messenger. Cora met with a real estate agent this afternoon to discuss selling this place. She stayed long enough to sign the contracts—and not a minute longer. There's a sign on the lawn and everything. This house means nothing to her. I mean nothing to her."

"Fuck, Birdie." I kissed the top of her head, searching for words that would make her feel better and coming up empty. "I'm so sorry."

Her shoulders shifted in my embrace as she shrugged. "Shit happens, I guess." She craned her neck to look up at me, and I had to swallow at the resignation in her eyes. "I think I've had enough. Could you manage things down here while I disappear upstairs? I just… I need to shower and go to bed."

I tucked a strand of loose hair behind her ear. "Of course. I'll clear everyone out and come up as soon as I can."

"No, no. It's okay." She extricated herself from my arms and took a step back. Her absence felt significant. "I'm tired, and I really need to be alone tonight. I've had too much to drink and way too much sugar, and this thing with Cora… I need to sleep it all off. I'll see you tomorrow, okay?"

"If that's what you want…." I trailed off, hoping she'd change her mind, but she nodded her head woozily.

"It is. Thank you."

And before I could lean down and kiss her, Birdie slipped away, her gait surprisingly steady as she snaked through the dancing couples. I followed her as far as I could and then watched her climb the stairs.

What the fuck did I do now? I was furious with her mother, who thought it was acceptable to treat her only daughter with such neglect and contempt, but now wasn't the best time to tell Birdie I loved her. It wasn't supposed to happen like that.

I didn't know exactly where to start making things right, so I focussed on the most immediate things I could do.

I circulated the house and let Josh, Logan, Will, and Luca know that the party was over. It was still early enough that there was a little resistance, but together, we convinced the rowdiest partygoers to transfer their revelries to The Stop. Will and Abbie went with them, and within half an hour, the house had emptied of everyone but the rest of the crew. I assured them I could handle the clean-up myself—it'd take the best part of a day, but if it kept me close to Birdie, I was happy to do it. Within an hour of Birdie going to her bedroom, I was closing the front door behind Josh and Emily, then taking the stairs two at a time.

Something twisted behind my ribs when I tiptoed into Birdie's bedroom and found her curled up on top of the covers, still in her cat costume, her hands tucked under one cheek and her knees pulled tight against her body. Her pale feet were bare.

I went straight to her overflowing suitcase and dug around for a pair of the fuzzy socks she loved so much. She stirred without waking as I dragged them onto her feet, then I carefully pulled the covers out from underneath her before settling them over her shoulders.

I drew the curtains at all the windows, then for a moment, I stared down at her, a curious sense of apprehension and protectiveness tightening my fists.

Wherever things had gone wrong, they'd look better in the morning. Birdie would be sober, she'd be thinking more clearly about her mother, and we could talk about her plans to come back to the Bay.

I'd have to pretend I didn't know about her conversation with the girls, but now that I knew Birdie was already on board with the plan, I'd just tell her I wanted the same things she did. The grand gesture wouldn't be so grand after all, but the outcome would be the same, and that's what mattered.

Then again, if her parents wanted to sell this place, Birdie wouldn't have a house to live in… No, that wouldn't be a problem. She could live with me. I didn't think too hard about that solution, knowing that in other circumstances, it'd be the kind of suggestion that sent Birdie bolting for the nearest airport.

I left the room and pulled the door almost closed, then trudged downstairs to start the after-party clean-up. It could have waited until the next day, but there was little chance I was going to sleep tonight, and I didn't want to be far from Birdie in case she needed me. Tidying up took hours, longer than it would have if I'd not stopped every twenty minutes to look in on Birdie, setting my hand to her forehead to make sure she was all right.

When I was finally done, I stretched out on the sofa downstairs. Birdie wanted to be by herself, and I had to respect that, but when it came time for me to walk out that door, I couldn't stand the idea of leaving the woman I loved in this house alone.

29

BIRDIE

I WOKE UP with a groan that reverberated around my skull so loudly I might as well have stood in the middle of an empty chamber and screamed. A damp spot of drool stuck my cheek to the pillow, my mouth resembled the texture of cotton, and my leotard was wedged so uncomfortably high between my butt cheeks that it caused actual pain.

Plucking at the fabric, I rolled onto my back, flung one arm over my face to block the encroaching light, and lay there for a moment in ignorant, hungover hell. It lasted all of three seconds before the previous twenty-four hours came crashing in on me, and being the idiot that I was, I groaned again. Ouch.

The birthday party. The perky blonde real estate agent. The *For Sale* sign in the front yard. Isaac.

Cora.

I peeled open my eyes and squinted up at the water-stained ceiling before taking a deep breath. I never wanted to step foot from this bed. I also wanted to throw everything I owned in my suitcase, call a cab, and disappear.

I didn't know what I wanted other than a toothbrush and some painkillers.

I dragged my sorry self over to the bedside table so I could check the time on my phone and blinked at the glass of water and ibuprofen waiting for me. Glancing around the room for other hints that Isaac was nearby, I noted the way the curtains were closed tight, how the door hung slightly ajar, and the way the heels I'd worn last night were neatly tucked away near my suitcase. If I hadn't been capable of undressing last night, I doubted I'd positioned my shoes so neatly—hell, I kicked them off even when I was sober. And that's when I noticed the socks on my feet. I lifted the covers and looked down.

They were the warm and fuzzy ones I preferred for sleeping. I might have managed to put them on myself, but I knew I hadn't.

My stomach sank, an interesting sensation when coupled with the urge to throw up. How had I let things spiral so out of control?

Perhaps it was a blessing my head hurt too much to think.

I forced myself upright, then dropped the painkillers into my mouth before chasing them with the entire glass of water. When I was certain I wasn't going to bring them back up again, I went straight to the bathroom, where

I gratefully peeled off the skin-tight cat costume and stepped into a scalding shower.

Twenty minutes under the hot water loosened my muscles and gave the ibuprofen time to work its magic so that when I finally wrapped myself in a towel, I felt halfway human again. Still, a monster cup of coffee and a greasy bacon sandwich would have gone down well right about then.

After I'd dressed in baggy sweats and twisted my hair into a loose braid, I returned to my bed long enough to pull up a website that compared times and fares for flights to Las Vegas. I almost chewed a hole through my bottom lip as I clicked and unclicked the booking tab for flights due out that day, the next day, and the day after.

I didn't know why I hesitated. I was only supposed to stay in the Bay for another four days—it was essential that I arrive well in advance of the tournament to get over the jet lag—but cutting that time short even by twenty-four hours made my stomach turn in a way that had nothing to do with my hangover.

I was deliberately not looking too closely at the possibility it wasn't the leaving part that made me sick. It was toying with the intention of never coming back.

I was dangerously close to losing my balance. I couldn't afford tilt this close to the most important tournament of my life, and the realisation of what I was about to lose crashed over me with a suddenness that stole my breath.

I'd been working and waiting for an opportunity to best my parents my whole life. I'd failed with Cora, and this trip to Vegas was my last chance.

How could I let this happen? How did I allow myself to lose focus—lose half my head, half my *self*—over a man?

Still with no flight booked, I switched off my phone and made my way downstairs. There had to be something salty leftover from the party, and if I forced myself to down another half-dozen glasses of water on top of the vat of coffee calling my name, I'd be feeling more like my old self in no time. And I needed that. I needed to put solid ground under me again. Resurrect the Birdie Maxwell who existed three months ago. She never would have allowed herself to get tangled up in a mess that involved falling for someone and letting that person fall for her.

I rounded the corner to the kitchen, distracted enough to barely register that the party mess had all been taken care of or the smell of fried bacon lingering in the air, and staggered to a stop.

Isaac stood like a hulking vision in the kitchen, his black hair wet from his shower, plating up fresh breakfast sandwiches and pouring a tall glass of chilled orange juice. My heart surged with equal parts affection and terror, and it took an effort to swallow.

"Hey, Red," he said, turning towards me with a mug of steaming coffee. He pushed it into my hand before returning to the food. "Pull up a chair and dig in. You'll feel better after you eat."

"I'm not hungry," I lied as my stomach growled. I took a long gulp of coffee to appease it.

Isaac smirked and set his hands on my shoulders as he guided me to a seat in front of my breakfast. "Just take one bite and see how you feel." I let him press me gently into the seat before he returned to the opposite side of the kitchen island.

My mouth watered at the sight and smell of the meal in front of me, but I didn't make a move to eat anything, and I avoided looking directly at Isaac when I said, "We need to talk."

His movements stalled for a split second before he wiped his hands on a dish towel, then slung it over his shoulder. Dragging his breakfast towards him, he picked up half a sandwich so casually it could only be feigned.

"All right," he said, taking a slow bite.

I cleared my throat and locked my fingers around my mug. I had years of experience bluffing my way through games, keeping my emotions off my face and my impulses in check. It didn't come easily. I was impatient and irritable by nature. I liked to laugh and have fun and take the world by the balls. But the discipline required to succeed at the poker table gave me the tools I needed to get through life without letting anyone in. It had kept me moving and safe for as long as I could remember until I came back here and ruined it all.

I'd let Isaac in, and now I had to find a way to push him out because nothing good would ever come from me relying on another person. I was complete on my own. I didn't need anyone, and I didn't want to need anyone. I didn't like feeling so vulnerable and exposed. Believing in happily ever afters was for kids and fools, and if my own mother couldn't love me the way she was supposed to, I'd be damned if I gave anyone else a free shot at it.

"This has been fun," I said, squeezing my hands so tightly around my mug I was afraid it would shatter. "But we've been avoiding the fact that I'm leaving this week. Neither of us wants to suffer through a long and awkward goodbye, and I'm sorry I have to be the one to bring it up, but it's time."

Isaac eased his breakfast back onto his plate, then wiped his hands on the towel again. I could feel his eyes weighing on me, and he was quiet for so long that I was impressed. I was less impressed with the way I broke first, lifting my chin to meet his gaze.

"This doesn't have to be goodbye," he said quietly. He raised his palms as though he expected an argument. "I know this tournament is important to you, and I understand you have to go, but there's no reason for you to be gone forever and every reason for you to come back."

Emotion pricked the back of my throat and stung across the bridge of my nose as I shook my head. "I can't."

His brows furrowed in puzzlement. "You can."

"No," I snapped, latching onto the flare of annoyance that promised to keep me afloat while I sank. "I can't, and I don't want to."

"You don't..." Isaac cleared his throat, and his fingers wandered to his earlobe. "You don't want to?"

"I knew this arrangement between us was a bad idea," I muttered, feeling a stab of shame at the way Isaac's face fell, but I was determined to make him see all the reasons we couldn't pretend this was some sort of fairytale. We weren't actors in a rom-com, and we weren't characters in a book. We lived in the real world, and the real world sucked. "We're friends, Romeo, and I knew when we started this thing that sex was going to ruin everything. Ugh! What the hell was I thinking?"

"You were thinking the same things I was," he growled, and my head snapped up at the heat in his voice. "You were thinking how much you wanted me at the same time I was thinking how badly I wanted you. You were thinking that sex made everything better, just like I was. You were thinking that you belong here and that you could make a life here, and I was thinking those exact things too."

I set my mug on the stone with a smack. "You know what? I'm not even going to deny it. Yes, the sex is freaking unbelievable. Yes, I love it here. And for a brief, naïve minute, I considered coming back after I finish up in Vegas. But all the reasons you're going to give me to stay are the same ones I'm going to give you as the reasons I need to go."

Isaac mirrored my glower, but his voice stayed even. "That makes absolutely no sense."

"Doesn't it?" I crossed my arms over my chest as the sandwich grew cold. "I know what you're going to say, and yes, I *was* thinking about putting down roots and making this house my home. I was imagining what a day, a week, a month—longer—with you would look like without a deadline looming over our heads. I wondered what this"—I waved my hand back and forth between us—"might feel like without the pretence of love coaching in the way. And for a short moment, I believed it was possible."

A muscle feathered in his jaw. "What changed?"

I sighed and dropped my shoulders, wishing I was the kind of person who could lie and live with it. But I could only live with the truth, and if nothing else, Isaac already knew enough about me that he'd probably figured out the answer on his own anyway. "I was reminded of what happens when I let myself believe in love."

His nostrils flared. "Don't let what your mother did yesterday change what we are."

A frustrated, strangled chuckle bubbled up, and I scrubbed my open hands over my face. "It's not what she did yesterday, or not only that. It's what she—and my father—have done *my entire life*. You don't know what it's like to let yourself hope over and over *and over* that this time will be different and for your parents—the people who are supposed to love you the most in the world—to turn away from you every time. You have no clue what it feels like to grow up knowing that the only person you can depend on is yourself, but that's what I know. That's all I know. And that's what I'm good at."

Isaac paced around to my side of the island, and I drew back a little, anticipating an embrace. The last thing I could handle right then was his touch. He noticed but said nothing as he slipped onto the stool beside me. I stopped myself from anxiously rubbing my palms together and forced myself to stay seated.

"You're good at a lot of things," he said. "You're good

at us." He ducked his head to look into my downcast face. "Birdie, please don't do this. I love you."

"No," I mumbled as panic rose up in me. I tossed my head away, refusing to look at him. "Don't tell me that."

"I love you," he repeated, "and you love me too."

"But I don't want to, Isaac," I retorted. "I don't *want* to love you."

He reared back as if slapped, and my heart hurt as badly as if I'd actually struck him. No, worse.

"I'm sorry," I went on, wrapping dispassion around me like a cloak. It didn't fit as well as it used to. "But I don't ever want to love someone so much that it means losing the part of me that makes me who I am. I don't want to put my heart into anyone's hands. I hate the way this feels."

"You hate feeling vulnerable more than you love me?"

I breathed slowly as I thought about his question, but the answer wasn't going to satisfy either of us. "I don't know."

"Look." Isaac closed his eyes and pinched the bridge of his nose before rolling his shoulders and picking up my hands. I let him, knowing that this might be the last time I felt his skin on mine. "I know learning to trust other people is hard, but this is *me*. I'm not going anywhere, and I had no intention of pushing you past what you were comfortable with, but you've left me no choice." He squeezed my fingers. "You're it for me, Birdie. I love you, and I want forever with you."

"Please, stop," I whispered.

"No. You need to hear this. You trust me. I know you do. You're safe with me, and I know you feel that. I'm not asking you to believe in anything or anyone else. Just believe in me."

He made it sound so easy, and it would have been so easy to let myself get swept away in this moment. Let him pick me up and soothe my wounds and give me a reason to stop running. But I was just so darn scared, and it made me even more convinced that I had to walk away. How could I possibly live an entire lifetime terrified that I'd lose everything tomorrow?

There were other reasons, too—better, more practical reasons—why Isaac and I made a terrible match. And now was the time to remind him.

"I don't ever want to get married," I declared.

"I don't need a certificate to prove anything about us, Red."

"I don't want to have kids," I added, something catching in my throat.

His hand skimmed up and down my arm. "I've got plenty of nieces and nephews. That's enough for me."

"I'd be gone all the time," I said, my voice finally cracking. "Travelling and touring. It's all I know, and it's all I've ever wanted to know. I love my job too much to give it up."

"I'd never ask you to. I'll come with you when I can and wait for you here when I can't."

"I have no home." I let Isaac wipe away the tear that tracked down my cheek.

"Then you'll come back and live with me."

"No! Don't you see? You don't want me, Romeo. Not really. I'm not what you've been looking for."

"You know what, Red? That's bullshit, and you know it," he snapped, surprising us both. "You're exactly what I've been looking for. Someone who needs coffee in the morning before she can look at me straight. Someone who listens when a friend asks for help, then jumps into the mess without thinking twice. Someone who's smart and stubborn and so strong that whenever I'm with her, I feel completely safe and totally reckless all at the same time. I'm looking for someone who knows her own mind and isn't afraid to speak it. Someone who uses sex toys as weapons of self-defence and someone bold enough to hug a friend naked in a hallway and not even blush. Someone who isn't afraid to bet it all, no matter the odds, and who challenges me to step outside my comfort zone. Someone who looks at me the way you do and who turns me on so fucking much I can barely put one foot in front of the other!"

My eyes grew wider as his voice grew louder. Afterwards, the silence stretched, Isaac's declaration suspended in the air between us, waiting for me to cut it loose—or pick it up and hang on tight.

"I'm sorry, Isaac." I sniffed once and pulled away from his touch. I had to push him away for his own good. "I love you—I do—but for a million reasons, I think… I think we're better off as friends."

Isaac blinked, and his jaw tightened as he watched me, waiting for something, but I'd said it now and wouldn't take it back. My words echoed in the silence until, eventually, Isaac got to his feet and walked out the door without even once looking back.

30

ISAAC

I WAS WOKEN at around five o'clock the next morning by the sound of a car pulling up to the kerb on the street outside. Then again, *woken* isn't quite right as I wasn't asleep. How could I close my eyes after Birdie had told me she loved me right before she declared that she wanted to be just friends? No two statements could have been better crafted to raise my hopes higher than they'd ever been, then destroy them without mercy.

At the sound of a revving engine below my window, I was cautious enough to check for activity outside, so I climbed out of bed and shifted the curtains just enough to look down on the street. With the skyline pearling in the east and the closest streetlight casting a yellow glow across her front yard, Birdie lugged her oversized suitcase down the driveway towards a taxi idling on the street. The *For Sale* sign on the lawn mocked her the entire way.

Panic shot through me, and I'm not sure my feet hit the ground as I flew down the stairs and out my front door.

"Birdie!" I shouted as soon as I'd cleared the porch steps. She'd reached the car by then, her luggage already stowed in the back as she opened the rear passenger door. "Wait! What the hell is going on? Where are you going?"

I knew the answer, but my mouth had switched to auto mode, asking stupid questions with answers that were only going to get me hurt.

Birdie glanced into the car as if wishing she could fling herself into the back and flee, but then she looked at me, her gaze raking over my bare torso and loose grey sweats before meeting my eyes. The distance in her gaze hurt so badly that I wondered if I would have been better off pretending I never heard the taxi pull up. She was guarded like I wasn't me, and she wasn't Birdie. It was almost like we were strangers.

"What are you doing?" I demanded because we weren't strangers, and whatever game Birdie was playing, I refused to participate. "Were you just going to disappear without saying goodbye?"

"Actually…yes." She smiled tightly and with sympathy. "I wanted to avoid this whole conversation because we both know it's going to be awkward."

I clenched my jaw, reminding myself that her instinct to run was about her, not me, but then panic flared all over again. How could I overcome years of hurt in one conversation when six weeks together hadn't been enough?

All I knew was that I had to try.

"The tournament's not for five more days," I said. "I thought we'd have time to talk so we could figure this out. I can't believe—"

"I have things I need to do before play starts." Birdie crossed her arms over her chest and held my stare, not a flicker of emotion passing across her beautiful face. "I need to rest after the flight and get on top of the jet lag. I need to get my head back in the game and focus on what's important, which is winning this competition and confronting my father at the end of it. After what happened with Cora… Well, this tournament's all I've got left. I can't afford to turn my head right now, and this trip to the Bay has been one long distraction I can't afford."

I winced. Her words landed like physical blows, one after the other. *What was important.* Poker. *All she had left.* Retribution. *One long distraction.* Me.

But none of what she said felt true, and I didn't for a second imagine that Birdie believed what she was saying either. She was hurting, and I'd come too far and grown too much to let her push me away. What we had together wasn't an illusion. It was real, and it was love. She'd said as much last night, which meant that now, Birdie was bluffing.

"Look." Birdie dropped her arms and took a step closer, craning her neck to look up into my eyes. Then her hands were cupping my face, and she offered me a sad sort of smile. "You've graduated, okay? You're ready for the real thing. The woman you choose to spend your life with will be the luckiest bitch on this planet. I only hope she's smart enough to see what she has when she finds you."

"She's a fucking genius," I muttered with a lump in my throat. "I have faith she'll figure it out in the end."

I wrapped my hands around Birdie's wrists and brushed my thumbs over the tattoos inscribed there. *Hold* and *fold*.

"Hold for us, Red," I begged. "Please. I'm all in. I'm all in for you, and I'm betting absolutely everything I've got in me that we belong together. You can try to bullshit your way out of this, try to tell me this spark between us was temporary or transactional or whatever other story you think erases what we have, but we both know better."

She pulled her hands out of my grip, and though I didn't want to, I let her go.

Her throat bobbed in a swallow, and she dropped her eyes. "You're forgetting that there can only be one winner in a game of poker," she said. "Someone always loses their shirt."

"I—"

"And when it comes to love, someone always loses a lot more. There's no shame in folding when it means you'll survive to play another round." She tossed her head back and rolled her shoulders, hesitating a moment before rising on her tiptoes and pressing her warm lips to my cheek. "I'll call you."

"Come back." I grabbed her hand, and she let me hold it for too brief a moment. "When this is all over, and you've finished what you need to do in Vegas, come back, and we'll work this all out."

"I don't—"

"Don't say no," I interrupted. "Don't say anything. Just come back."

Birdie rolled her lips and blinked a thousand times. "Goodbye, Isaac."

I watched her slip into the taxi with a sick swirl in my stomach that only spun wilder as the car grew smaller and the brake lights disappeared at the end of the street. Although I'd known the risk I'd been taking when I put my love for Birdie on the table, no book could have ever prepared me for how painful it was to watch her drive away from me.

I stood there longer than I cared to admit, staring into nothing because, as well as I knew Birdie, I had no clue what to hope for next. I didn't know if she was going to come back or if this morning had been the last time I'd ever set eyes on the woman I loved.

31

BIRDIE

THE SATISFYING SNAP of poker chips being stacked was as soothing as white noise. The murmurs of curious spectators were a familiar kind of comfort. The cards under my palms and the rough ribbing of my competitors were as close to home as I'd ever be. And for the first time in months, my head was on straight.

I'd flown into Las Vegas with four days to prepare for this competition and hadn't wasted a single minute. From the moment I slid into that taxi and slammed the door on a life I didn't want to want, every boundary that had crumbled away in Valentine Bay had bounced back into being as if by muscle memory. And with my armour in place, I'd spent those four days at my hotel focussed on nothing but study, strategy, and sleep.

I was my old self again, which meant disciplined enough that I refused to think about Isaac. I'd been a winner for ten years and in love for only a month—and that month couldn't compete with a decade of stringent mental and emotional conditioning. I'd muted his messages and diverted his calls, stuffing him into a soundproof box indefinitely while making myself no promises about when—or even if—I'd open it again.

This was where I was meant to be—in casinos, on the move, never stopping for longer than it took to win the game. And while the stakes tonight were higher than ever, much more than the million-dollar pot on offer, I was professional enough not to let nerves beat me. I played the way I always played—to win.

Two years ago, my father's company bought its first casino in Las Vegas. Following extensive renovations and a multi-million-dollar advertising push, this three-day tournament was its grand opening. They'd scheduled five days of professional poker as part of a high-end marketing campaign to ensure his brand was splashed over every gaming network and social media channel in the world. If the size of the crowds this week were any indication of success, my father should have been somewhere stacking his gold bullion right about now.

I only knew as much as I did because the developments were frequently discussed in professional poker circles, and the tournament had been on my calendar for months. I hadn't had a direct line to my father since I dropped out of university—he'd never volunteered his personal phone number, and I was too proud to ask for it. So, for me, walking into his flashy building on day one of the tournament had been like entering a tunnel, not a playground. I saw nothing to the left or right of me, and the light at the end glowed around the silhouette of my father holding the winning cheque.

Now here I was, about to walk away from the final table, and there was no doubt in my mind I was going to reach him. I'd spent my life searching for a way to stand on a podium next to Seymour Maxwell, and he'd never miss a chance to stand in the spotlight—even if he had to share it with me. I was this close to proving all the hard days had been worth it.

My muscles were loose, and I had a practiced look of distracted confidence on my face. Three of the five players at this table had folded, and it was down to me and one other player—a guy who'd been on the circuit for less than five years, about my age, in a ratty old baseball cap he wore because he thought it was lucky. Well, I worshipped at the altar of numbers, and in my experience, that beat blind faith every time.

Baseball Cap Guy flared his nostrils—a tell I'd picked up early in the tournament—and my fingertips tingled. Every chip was in the pot, the writing was on the face of the gambler across the table, and the telltale fire of triumph blazed across my skin.

He flipped his cards face up, revealing mismatched spades that made up a flush. Given the maths, I'd been expecting it, and it could have been a winning hand in another game. There was an arrogance to his smirk that I really didn't like. Time to wipe it off his face the best way I knew how.

Silence fell as the room held its breath, the camera zoomed in, and I showed my hand.

Two tens gave me four of a kind.

Two tens gave me a million bucks.

Two tens gave me a ticket to my dad.

Cheers rose up, and I grinned as Baseball Cap Guy flung the hat off his head and onto the floor, blaming it, of all things, for the fact his million-dollar dream had just gone up in smoke.

Butterflies the size of seagulls took off in my stomach. I'd done it. I'd finally freaking *done* it. Did you see that, world? Birdie Maxwell was here, and she was a fucking winner.

"Okay, Miss Maxwell. Here's what happens next."

The Maxwell Group had sent its junior marketing assistant to escort me to the press room, where my father would present me with the tournament prize money. A gangly guy in an ill-fitting grey suit—what was his name again? James?—was giving me instructions on how the next few minutes would play out, and I did my best to listen, but even in the most important games of my career, I'd never been as nervous as I was right then. My palms tingled so badly they almost burned, my ribs were tight enough to hurt, and my mouth was uncomfortably dry. I was mere minutes and metres away from sharing air with my father for the first time in more than ten years. And I was going to confront him, right? In front of all those people?

Yes, that was the plan. I'd shake his hand, take his money, force him to act the part of a loving father and acknowledge me as his daughter. Birdie Maxwell wasn't just a name on a press release. I wasn't a mysterious, elusive heiress who chose gambling and rebellion over a secure rise to the top of the family business. I was an asset. A winner.

Would he put his arm around me? Would he tell the reporters how proud he was? Would anyone notice that we had the same nose?

I was tense and excited and so bloody scared. All the defences I'd reconstructed in the last week had crumbled again, and I simply didn't care. I'd waited for this moment for so long, and I wanted to feel every second of it.

James was talking, I realised. I'd been staring a hole through the closed door that led to the press room, lost in my thoughts, but something in his last sentence penetrated, and I set my hand on his arm to stop him mid-word.

"Could you say that again, please?"

He smiled tightly. "Of course, Miss Maxwell. I was just saying that when you step onto the stage, you'll be greeted by the casino's chief executive officer, Mr Jonathan Hough. Reporters have been instructed not to speak to you directly. Instead, Mr Hough will ask you one question about the tournament, which you are welcome to answer as briefly as you like before he presents you with the novelty cheque for one million dollars. He'll then ask you to stand with him in front of the casino-branded billboard we've made especially for these photo opportunities—please smile, shake his hand, that sort of thing, so the photographers can get what they need. Once the formalities are finished, you're free to leave. We have your information, and your prize money will be reconciled promptly."

"Do you know who I am?" I snapped, hating myself for sounding like a spoiled brat, but I was in shock. This idiot in a suit had implied not only that my father wasn't here but that he'd sent Jonathon Hough—the man married to my father's *other* daughter—to do the dirty work of dealing with me. Panic set in, and I flexed my tingling fingers.

James shifted his feet and glanced down at his clipboard. "I do, Miss Maxwell."

"So, where is my father?"

"It was decided that in the event of your win, the optics of Mr Maxwell's daughter being awarded money from the very company she will inherit would be…er, bad."

"Where is he?" I demanded, my escalating nerves whipping me into frantic urgency.

"Mr Maxwell—" James cleared his throat. "Mr Maxwell regrets that he can't be here today to congratulate you on your win in person. I'm sure he'd be happy to set up a time—"

"But he's here in Las Vegas," I accused. James's throat bobbed with an anxious swallow. "He's in this building right now, isn't he?"

James's eyes darted away and back again. Noting how young he was, I reined in my temper. He was only following orders, and I didn't want to get the guy in trouble. My problem wasn't with the messenger.

I flung up my palm. "Don't answer that. Just tell me where the casino's administrative offices are located, and I'll take it from there."

"I'm not sure—"

"Forget it." I spun on my heel and stormed back up the corridor. "I'll find him myself."

"But Miss Maxwell," he called. "The press conference!"

The tunnel vision was back, and I was on a mission. I was walking out of here a winner, dammit, and my prize wasn't a million fucking dollars. It was closure, and one way or another, I was going to get it.

I returned to the foyer of the casino, slowing my pace and schooling my features so I didn't come across as a raving lunatic when I asked a helpful concierge for directions to the corporate wing. She pointed to a wide hall that opened up onto a bank of sleek elevators, and after pausing to scan the electronic information board mounted high on the wall, I stepped into the first doors that opened and punched in the floor I wanted.

As I zipped high up into the building, I checked my appearance in the mirrored elevator walls. My braid was neat, and I'd dressed as if I'd be having my picture taken with my father—well-fitting pants, an ironed shirt, clean boots with a modest heel. It wasn't armour, and I didn't look like the daughter of a billionaire, but I was fired up enough that I *dared* anyone to try to stop me.

The doors pinged open, and I stepped out into a red-carpeted lobby, heading straight to the reception desk. A middle-aged woman with a "Rhonda" name tag and a headset over her brown curls watched me approach with a welcoming smile that quickly melted away at the murderous expression on my face.

"I'm Birdie Maxwell," I announced, a fluttery feeling in my gut as I heard the words at the same time Rhonda did. I never had reason to claim my name like that, and certainly not in a way that demanded deference and respect. "I'm here to see my father."

Rhonda's smile returned, though this time it wobbled with nerves. "Very well. If you'll take a seat over there, Miss Maxwell, I'll see if he's in."

"Don't bother," I snapped, stalking straight through to the hall behind her as she tapped urgently at her headset. It had the same impact as the sound of someone giving chase. I had to get to him before anyone got in my way.

Scanning the name on each office door as I passed it, I arrived at the end of the corridor and stalled at a set of enormous timber doors barring my way, the words "Seymour Maxwell" emblazoned across them in tall gold lettering. The familiar fire of a win burned hot under my skin, spurring me forwards. I set my hand on the knob and pushed the door open with a violent swing.

He stood behind his desk like he'd just got to his feet, lifting his suit jacket off the coat rack near the window. There was more grey in his auburn hair than I'd expected to see, and he was thicker around the middle than I remembered, but Seymour Maxwell took care of himself—if nobody else—and even nudging sixty, he was a handsome man. Confident. Rich. Powerful.

"Ah, Birdie," he said, not quite looking at me. "I'm just on my way out."

I blinked hard and fast, watching him swing his jacket onto his arms and settle it across his broad shoulders. He collected a wallet from his desk and tucked it into a pocket, then picked up his phone. It all happened in slow motion as I stood there, barring the door, barely daring to breathe. When he finally looked up at me, and our eyes met for the first time, whatever he saw there dropped his shoulders.

A rush of air escaped his lungs, and he clenched his jaw. "Let's not do this."

I moved into the cavernous room and closed the door behind me, wishing my hurt and indignation and rage still burned hot, but being in a room with my father doused it all. I was a little girl again. Angry, sure, but all I really wanted was for him to open his arms so I could run into them, and that was never going to happen.

"Do what?" I asked, creeping closer until I had a hand on one of the armchairs facing his desk.

He sighed again and sank into his chair, setting an elbow on the desk and pinching the bridge of his nose. "What do you want?"

I lowered myself into a seat and bit back a defensive retort. *What do you think I want? Money? An apology? A time machine so I could go back to the past and be a better kid so perhaps my dad might find something about me he loved after all?*

"I want to know why."

He raised his head slowly, and his blue eyes met mine. His nose wasn't the only thing we shared. "Why what?"

"Why you blame me for being trapped in a marriage with Cora." I called on every thread of control I possessed, every trick to keep my emotions from playing on my face. These were the questions I shied away from, even in my own head, but they were questions I needed him to answer. "I was a kid, and I didn't choose my parents. None of what was wrong with your life was ever my fault, and yet you've treated me like it was."

"Birdie—"

Resolve slipped through my fingers like sand. I had to leave here with something. Anything. "Just answer the question, and I'll leave," I promised. "I won't make a fuss, and you'll never have to see me again if that's what you want."

"If I answer your question, you'll leave?"

I swallowed the hurt at the relief in his voice and nodded.

My father shook his head and leaned back in his chair. "I don't have an answer for you. Not one that you'll like. I was never in love with your mother. She's a cold, manipulative bitch, and I only learned the depraved depths of her nature well after we'd married. When she fell pregnant with you, I was resentful. Still am, if I'm being honest. She knew a baby took divorce off the table for the immediate future—at least while you were still a child—but you aren't the only thing she's blackmailed me with over the years, so here I am, still with this fucking ring on my finger. I look at you, and all I see is—"

"Her," I finished, and his silence was all the confirmation I needed.

None of what he said was news to me, so there was no reason for it to make the wounds any deeper. But hearing it directly from him cut in a different way, and the pain seared fresh. I stared at my hands, where they were clasped in my lap. The tingling itch had dissipated, leaving my palms and fingertips numb.

"So, are we done?" my father asked.

"Just one more thing," I said hurriedly. "It's about Lauren and Anastasia—"

"Cora fucking told you about them, did she?" He chuckled humourlessly. "That conniving shrew. She couldn't help herself. What are you two playing at?"

"I'm not playing at anything," I barked, turning towards irritation where before there was defeat. It suited me much better. I was nothing like Cora, and I'd never *play* with her. Ever. "I figured it out for myself."

"And that's why you're here?" Seymour stood and buttoned his suit jacket, and his jaw feathered as he stared down at me. "Don't lose sleep over them. Your inheritance is safe. I've made provisions for Lauren and Asta in my will, but you'll get the lion's share."

I jumped to my feet, an appalled flush creeping up my neck and my fists clenched at my sides. "Screw you and your money. Your *other* daughter can have every cent for all I care!"

"Not going to happen," he muttered as he stalked towards the exit. "My lawyers advised against it."

I watched his back as he yanked open the doors and disappeared down the hall, my heart dropping fast and heavy all the way to my toes. It happened so fast. The moment I'd been waiting and planning for had just come and gone, and what did I have to show for it?

Nothing. Absolutely nothing.

Though I didn't feel like doing it, I deliberately straightened my shoulders and strode down the hall with my head held high. I attracted a few curious looks, but nobody attempted to speak to me. Good. I needed to get out of there. I wanted today to be over and done because I was finally ready to put all my childish dreams of having a real family behind me.

I rounded the corner approaching the reception area, and the sight of my father collecting messages from the front desk froze me on the spot.

I'd wait until he was gone before making my exit. Ducking back around the corner, I poked my head around just enough to watch him tuck a few slips of paper into his jacket pocket, then turn towards the elevators. As he passed the row of armchairs set against the wall as a waiting area, my father nodded politely to a blonde woman sitting there with a small child on her lap. The baby girl stretched her hands out to him, almost as if she knew who he was, but he pressed the button for the elevator and turned his back as the woman tried to soothe her squealing, squirming infant.

The woman turned her head towards me then, and recognition dawned.

As Seymour disappeared into the elevator, I took one slow step forwards, then another, picking up pace as I drew closer. I'd seen this woman before, but only in photos. She stood hesitantly at my approach and settled her baby on one hip, watching me warily. There was no question in her expression, and she looked at me like she knew me the way I knew her, but she nibbled at her top lip nervously.

"Birdie Maxwell?" she asked when I was close enough, holding out her hand for me to shake. "My name is Anastasia Hough."

"I know who you are," I murmured, taking her hand in mine.

A relieved sigh relaxed Anastasia's features, and she shifted her daughter again as the little girl wriggled for freedom. "And this is Emma. If you're not busy, I was hoping you'd let me buy you a coffee."

Emma reached for me, and I offered her my hand. She latched onto one finger, and I smiled. The wispy curls on her head were as red as mine, and as I glanced between mother and daughter, I realised all three of us had the same nose.

I tried to swallow, but my mouth suddenly felt dry. "No, I'm not doing anything. Let's go get coffee."

32

BIRDIE

"CALL ME ASTA," Anastasia insisted as we sat across from each other in a trendy cafe three blocks from the casino.

"Okay." I glanced at Emma, who had fallen asleep in her stroller. She had fair skin and ruddy pink cheeks, and I'd just learned she was six months old. "She's cute," I observed.

Asta glanced over at her daughter and love lit her up in a way that warmed me as well. "I think so, too," Anastasia agreed before looking at me from the corner of one eye. "I confess that I'm relieved we don't need to have any awkward conversations about hidden mistresses and their secret daughters."

I swallowed a mouthful of my coffee and tilted my head from side to side. "Eh, there are still plenty of ways this is going to be awkward."

Asta grimaced uncomfortably and shook her head. "You're right. I'm sorry. That was selfish of me to say."

"No, I get it. It's fine." The conversation stalled a moment as we flagrantly looked at one another. Really *looked*.

Asta had shoulder-length gold-blonde waves that shimmered under the overhead lighting. Her ivory skin was smooth and freckle-free, her large doe eyes a deep caramel-brown, her limbs long, lithe, and graceful. She wore makeup like a second skin, her nails were perfectly manicured, and her clothes screamed *money*. The only thing we shared was the nose we inherited from the man who fathered us both.

This woman was gorgeous and put together in all the ways I'd run far and fast to avoid. I'd never suffered from low self-esteem, but if I'd had to grow up with a sister who looked like this, things might have been different.

Fuck. Sister. I had a *sister*. I spared a look at the sleeping baby. A sister and a niece.

"I can't believe you're here," Asta said breathily. "I suppose you're wondering why I followed you to Mr Maxwell's office and why I was waiting for you in the foyer."

I blinked in surprise. "I didn't know you'd followed me or that you were waiting for me, but before we get to that, tell me why on Earth you call that man *Mr Maxwell*?"

A pretty blush bloomed on her cheeks, and she tucked her hands between her knees. "Force of habit. It's always been a rule to call him that everywhere but inside our private properties. At home, he's Dad. Anywhere else, he's Mr Maxwell—my husband's boss."

I snorted and shook my head, dropping my gaze to the table. "The nerve of that man."

Asta scrunched her shoulders then dropped them again, a resigned tilt on her lips, but then she glanced at the baby sleeping soundly beside her. A flicker of emotion played on her face, and when she turned back to me, she sat taller than before.

"I found out about you when I was twelve," she said, unnecessarily straightening the cutlery on the table. "I suppose I'd grown too old by then to be kept in the dark entirely. There was too great a risk I'd say the wrong thing to the wrong person, and he's a famous man, after all. He had a reputation to protect. So, my mother sat me down and explained that my father had another family, one that didn't include her or me. He had another home, another wife, and another daughter. Her name was Birdie, and she was the one he told the world all about."

"That's not—"

Asta reached across the table and grabbed my hand. Her fingers were cool. "Birdie, please. Let me finish, or I'll lose my nerve."

A rise of sympathy took me by surprise, and I nodded.

Asta gave my fingers a grateful squeeze before letting go. "I'll admit, there was a time in my life when I hated you." She grimaced apologetically. "I thought you had all the things he refused to give me. As if being a teenage girl isn't hard enough, I had to deal with the fact that my father considered me a shameful secret. He never came to my dance recitals. He didn't attend my parent-teacher conferences or my graduations. I wasn't allowed to tell anyone he was my father or call him 'Dad' in front of strangers. I had my mum's last name, not his. For a time, I genuinely didn't understand what it all meant, and when I found out about you, I thought it was as simple as he loved his real daughter more than he loved me. I resented you for it."

Asta looked at me through thick, dark lashes, and there was regret in her eyes. "I held onto that resentment for longer than I should have."

"He—" I cleared the lump in my throat and started again. "He loved you more. I promise you that."

She nodded, knowing it was true. Her agreement was both validating and devastating.

"When I was old enough to understand the politics of the situation, my mother explained it all in greater detail," Asta continued. "I didn't know before then that he was so distant with you or that your mother was very unlike my own. I didn't realise that he'd sent you away to boarding schools and that even though he spent so little time with me, I got more of his affection and attention than you ever had. And at least when he was with me, he was warm and loving to both me and my mother. What we have—when we have it—feels something like a real family."

I blinked back unexpected tears, and Asta rolled her glossy lips before clasping her busy fingers in her lap. "I'm sorry. I don't mean to make things worse, but I need you to understand that I haven't come out of this unscathed. Years of his mixed messages affected me more than my mother or I realised at the time. For obvious reasons, I struggle with low self-esteem. I have a hard time letting people in, and making friends doesn't come easily to me. On top of that, finding out the truth about your circumstances left me with a significant amount of guilt." She rolled her eyes and laughed quietly. "I'm so screwed up that I single-handedly keep my therapist in business."

"Don't do that," I whispered fiercely, and the heat in my tone widened her eyes. It was nothing new—I'd never liked listening to people talk about themselves so negatively—but hearing it from Asta, a woman I was quickly growing to like and knowing my father had damaged both of us, took my irritation to the next level. I dashed at the tears in my eyes. "Don't put yourself down."

The corner of her lip twitched. "Okay. Thank you."

"So," I said after an awkward pause. "Back to the part where you followed me today. Why?"

Her cheeks bloomed prettily again. "I've been talking this over with my therapist for six months, ever since Emma was born, but I've thought about it every day for ten years. And today, I suddenly felt brave enough to try." Asta sucked in a deep breath and blurted out hurriedly, "I was wondering if you might want to be my friend."

Surprise, followed by a flare of warmth, radiated through my chest. "Your friend?"

Asta smiled shyly. "Well, to start. Eventually, I hope you'll want to be my sister." In the stroller, the baby stirred, and as Asta set a gentle hand on her chest, she added, "As well as Emma's aunt. I can't imagine you living somewhere out in the world while Emma and I go on as if you don't exist. I *want* you to exist. I want you to exist in our life."

Emma squirmed a little, then appeared to return to sleep. Asta lifted her hand and fidgeted with the cutlery again, which gave her a reason to avoid my eyes.

"I understand if you need time to think about it," she added, "and if your final answer is no. I've sprung this on you out of nowhere. It must have come as quite a shock."

"I'm good at thinking on my feet," I replied, "which is why I have to ask—what's Seymour going to say about this?" I didn't particularly care about the answer, but I didn't want Asta doing anything that might make her relationship with the man more complicated.

Asta drew her teeth across her top lip. "If I know my father, and I think I do, he'll turn a blind eye to our friendship and expect me—us—to be discreet. He didn't bat an eyelid at seeing me in his office today, even knowing there was every chance you and I could run into each other. He simply doesn't look at what he doesn't want to see."

I chuckled humourlessly. "You don't have to tell me."

She closed her eyes and shook her head. "I'm so sorry. I keep putting my foot in it, don't I?"

"Don't worry about it," I reassured her. "I happen to agree with you. More importantly, I think I like you."

The hopeful smile on her face made Asta more lovely. "Really?"

"Yeah. So…friends." It felt weird to say, partly because history and blood made this woman more than a friend, and I already felt that kinship in my bones. But also, because I didn't have any friends.

But that wasn't true anymore, was it? I had Abbie and Jess and Emily and Tash. I had Will and Logan and Josh and Luca.

I had Isaac.

And with that brief lapse of self-control, I let myself think about him for the first time in more than a week. I'd expected it to hurt, but it didn't. It felt natural, and the warm glow behind my ribs pulsed a little more.

"Friends," Asta agreed, beaming as she pulled a notepad and pen out of an oversized tote bag tucked into the parcel tray under the stroller. "I'll give you my address and phone number. Oh, and email information." She printed her details across the paper in perfect lettering, then tore the page free and handed it over. "Here," she said, offering me the pen and pad. "Give me yours as well."

I accepted the stationery and wrote down my number and email address, then hesitated at the residential information.

Asta noticed the pause and tilted her head. "Please tell me you're not too far from Sydney. I'm not sure how much travel I'll be doing while Emma is young. We're only in Las Vegas for the opening of the casino. My husband, Jonathan, is CEO of The Maxwell Group, and he's been very much involved with this project. Otherwise,

I wouldn't be here at all." Her curious expression morphed into concern. "What's wrong?"

"What? Oh, nothing. It's just that I'm between homes right now. I travel so much with work that it's never made much sense to find a place of my own."

"Oh," she said with obvious disappointment. "I understand. We can always keep in touch via video calls. Families do that all the time."

Family. My gaze travelled over my sleeping niece, who was going to grow so quickly over the next few years. I'd like to be there for that, wouldn't I? Anxiety itched at my palms. And what about Asta, who wanted to one day be my sister in more than just name and genetics? Would we be able to work on this tentative bond if I wasn't around to explore it?

I handed Asta the pen and notepad. As she took it, her eyes swept across the tattoos on my bare wrist.

"Hold and fold," she read. "I know enough to guess those are poker terms, but that's about all I'm afraid."

I brushed *hold* with the pad of my thumb, the way Isaac had done before I got in that taxi and left him standing on the street in Valentine Bay all alone. Now I'd gone and thought about him twice in two minutes, and the response in my body was all warmth. Nothing about him or us felt wrong or risky. Even the memory of Isaac made me feel safe.

"It has to do with betting and how much you're willing to risk," I explained. "Hold means you're all in—you think your hand is enough to win. Fold means giving up—

cutting your losses to keep enough in your pocket to play the next game."

"I know nothing about poker," Asta confessed. "Maybe one day you can teach me?"

Her suggestion made me think of the love-coach arrangement with Isaac, and the memories tugged at my lips.

"What?" Asta asked with a smile. "What's so funny? I know, a grown woman who knows nothing about poker, but stranger things have happened."

"You're absolutely right," I agreed. "Stranger things *have* happened." Like Birdie Maxwell falling in love. Stranger still would be Birdie Maxwell running towards it, not away, and right now, I was fighting the impulse to do just that. Run right into a family that included not only the man I loved but this woman sitting across from me—a sister I never knew I wanted and a niece I never knew I missed.

On cue, Emma started wriggling again, squirming and mewling unhappily. Asta gently lifted the blanket that covered the baby and affectionately rolled her eyes before tucking it back in around Emma's chest and lifting it at the bottom. Underneath, Emma kicked her feet back and forth—one showed adorable, tiny pink toes; the other had a sock that had almost slipped off.

"I have no idea why, but she can't stand to sleep with bare feet," Asta clucked, searching for the missing sock and then dragging it gently over Emma's bare foot. Asta straightened the other one as well, and by the time she'd rearranged the blanket, Emma was almost quiet again. "Doesn't help that she kicks them off while she's dreaming. I've resorted to dressing her in onesies ninety percent of the time, but when the weather's warm, I prefer to put her in layers."

I grinned. "Some of us just struggle with cold feet, I'm afraid. Nothing a good pair of fuzzy socks can't fix." Fuzzy socks, or a man with the internal body temperature of a nuclear reactor.

Asta laughed a little. "That sounds like you speak from experience. Do you have cold feet too?"

"You know what? I think after today, cold feet won't be as much of a problem for me as they used to be."

Emma woke up hungry a few minutes later, so Asta and I said our goodbyes. As we hovered on the street outside the café, she seemed uncertain about what to do, so I scooped her into my arms and hugged her tightly for a good six seconds. She was taller than me with a lot less meat on her bones, but she fit. When I let her go, her eyes were glassy, but I took it as a good sign and promised to call her when I was next in Sydney.

I didn't tell her that time may be sooner rather than later.

I hailed a cab and went back to my hotel, plotting a return to Valentine Bay the entire ride, but by the time I was repacking my overloaded suitcase for the third time, I still wasn't set on a course of action. As much as I wanted to see where things might go with Isaac, I was not ready to move in with him. I'd need my own space if I wanted to invite Asta and Emma to stay with me from time to time, and agreeing to live with a man before we'd even made our relationship official was too much, too soon—for both of us. Love hadn't blinded me enough to believe that rushing into anything would have positive results. No, if Isaac and I wanted any chance of making it, I needed to do this in my own way and on my own terms. I just didn't know what they were yet.

I tipped everything out of my suitcase, prepared to start again, when my phone sounded with a notification. It was an automated banking update, followed swiftly by an email from The Maxwell Group. I opened the first to see that my prize money had been deposited into my account—all one million dollars of it. The email included remittance advice on official letterhead branded with the casino logo. It was totally impersonal, with no signature attached.

It felt like *The End* had been stamped underneath my relationship with my father.

I'd had no idea this would feel so freaking fantastic.

On a whim, I swiped through to my voice messages. It was the first time I'd dared to look at the list since I'd left the Bay, and after a quick glance, I realised Isaac had called me every day I'd been gone and left me recordings that lasted for as long as ten minutes each. With an anxious stutter in my chest, I sank onto the edge of the mattress, staring at the screen.

I was ready to give our love a shot—but had I waited too long? What I had to say to him needed to be said face to face, but would my surprise return to Valentine Bay be too little, too late?

I'd be the first to admit that I had some shit to work through, and Isaac could have decided it was all too hard. Maybe he'd given up, and could I blame him? Had I ruined everything before we'd even properly begun?

Desperate to know if I screwed everything up so I could start figuring out how to fix it, I tapped on the oldest message.

Isaac's deep voice exploded from the speaker, and I whimpered at the sound. Safe and sexy and *mine*—always mine. I registered not a single word he said in the first twelve seconds and scrubbed back to the beginning twice over before my confused adoration lifted, and I realised he was *reading* to me. Smiling to myself, I snuggled back into the pillows, turned up the volume, and listened.

Message after message followed, and tears rolled down my cheeks as Isaac narrated the happily ever afters of one romance story after another. Devoted heroes and their heroines declared their love over and over, leaning into what—who—made them whole.

Isaac's voice was confident and steady, and he signed off each one with, "I love you, Birdie. I'm holding for us and our happily ever after. You're it for me, and you always will be. Come home."

Just try to hold me back.

I jumped to my feet, tossed my phone onto the bed, and returned with renewed vigour to the disaster that was my pile of belongings. Poking out from where it was hidden under a mountain of clothes was the folder housing the paperwork and sales contract for the Valentine Bay house.

I'm not sure why I'd hung onto it, but without stopping to think twice, I snatched up my phone again and dialled the number printed on the business card stapled to the front.

Later, I ordered room service and repacked my suitcase—it gave me far less grief now that I wasn't taking out my frustration on my shoes—then took a hot shower and pulled on my pyjamas, including a pair of fuzzy socks that—no surprises—reminded me of Isaac and made me smile. I propped myself up in bed with a theoretical physics textbook on my knees, but I couldn't commit to solving any of the problems. I had other things to think about.

I had closure.

I'd always wondered who I'd be if my parents had been more loving, and now I had an answer. It was thanks to their emotional neglect that I'd grown into a person I genuinely liked, not a mathematical-brained automaton pushing papers and bending herself to fit the shape of a life she didn't want or a woman unsure of her place in the world. Without my parents' expectations suffocating me, I'd been free to be me. The difference now was that I finally realised the value of that.

My sense of self was priceless.

I'd known today would change my life, and I got what I came here for, but moving on looked nothing like I thought it would. I'd expected it to feel small and tight and contracted, as if finally cutting the ties to my parents would make my world smaller. Instead, it had opened up an ocean of possibility and loosened something in my heart that had been locked up tight.

Letting go of my old dreams had made room for new ones, but in all my life, my dreams had never felt quite like this.

33

ISAAC

NINE DAYS. THAT'S how long Birdie had been gone. Nine long days without a word, but I had to believe every hour of every one of those days brought me closer to the call that would change everything. She was coming back. I knew it. Things couldn't work out any other way.

My mother pushed a mug of tea across the island towards me, followed by a plate of brownies still warm from the oven. Leaning her hip against the sink, she took a sip from her cup and watched me with concern. "How are you holding up?"

"I'm fine," I said, taking a brownie and eating half of it in one mouthful as if a healthy appetite would prove that I wasn't totally fixated on where Birdie was right then and if she was thinking about me and when she was going to come home.

Mum raised her brows, and I dropped the half-eaten cake onto a plate before taking a gulp of tea that was still hot enough to scald my throat. I choked it down and pushed to my feet.

"It's all going to work out, one way or another," I said, not for the first time. It had become something of a mantra. "I'll see you at the surf rowing competition, right?"

Mum let me change the subject without any fuss. "Wouldn't miss it for the world. You boys are going to win this time. I can feel it in my bones."

"We'll see, but I have to go. I need to be somewhere in twenty minutes, and I have to swing past the store first to pick up a few things." I dropped a kiss on my mother's cheek. "Thanks for the brownies."

Mum sighed but thankfully refrained from saying anything more than a benign "Bye, honey."

I left the house with a small sense of relief. I hadn't lied to get out of there—I had a VBFYRRRBC meeting starting on the half-hour—but I would have made up an excuse to go if it were necessary. I loved my mother, but I was growing impatient with all the sympathetic looks being cast my way, and not just the ones from her and my sisters. There'd been a lot of those looks these last nine days, and they were everywhere.

Good news travelled fast, but bad news made the rounds a million times faster.

It was my turn to collect the pre-made baked goods for the meeting, and instead of making a last-minute dash to the supermarket, I'd planned ahead and splurged on a selection of French pastries from Raelene's bakery, *Le Gâteaux D'Amour*.

I pulled to the kerb along Main Street and had almost made it in and out of the bakery without incident when I ran into Dawn on the way back to my car. In fact, she was standing in front of it and waiting for me, so *ran into* was too generous. *Ambushed* was more like it.

"Good morning, Dawn," I said politely, hitting the central locking on my car fob and sliding the white bakery boxes onto the front passenger seat. "Can I help you with anything?"

"Oh, no, Sergeant. I'm fine." She scanned the boxes with inquisitive eyes but apparently thought better of asking who and what they were for. She had bigger fish to fry. "But how are you doing? Have you heard from Birdie yet? Nasty business, her leaving in the middle of the night that way."

I clenched my jaw to stop a frustrated growl. "It wasn't the middle of the night. It was close to sunrise, and she had an early flight."

I had no idea if she'd caught an early flight. It was entirely possible she left at the hour she had for the sole purpose of avoiding me, but I wasn't about to say so.

"And has she called? Can we hope to see her in the Bay again soon?"

"No, she hasn't called," I replied, trying to manoeuvre my way around a woman who looked to be made of sticks. I was quadruple her size, and yet she still managed to block my path to the driver's side door. "And I don't know when she'll be back. Birdie travels a lot for work. You know that."

"I do. And now, with the house for sale after all these years..." Dawn shook her head and *tsked* quietly. "Such poor timing, isn't it?"

"It's her parents' house to sell." I stepped this way, then that, as Dawn mirrored me. "Birdie didn't get a say in it." *And they haven't found a buyer yet,* I added silently. There was always a chance they wouldn't, and then Birdie would have a home to come back to. This wasn't all about me.

"I know you'd grown fond of her," Dawn commented with a sombre nod. "We all did. Nobody ever had a bad word to say about that girl, no matter that her parents weren't particularly pleasant."

"And I hope nobody's got a bad word to say about her now," I warned, giving Dawn the stern look I usually reserved for police work. "None of this is Birdie's fault. Everything will work out, one way or another."

Dawn flapped her hands. "Of course, it will, and of course, we're not speaking ill of Birdie behind her back. You're right, Sergeant. You're right. Well, I'll let you get to wherever it is you're off to with all those delicious sweets."

She left it hanging there, inviting gossip, but I simply laid a soft palm on her shoulder by way of goodbye, keeping her in one place while I stepped around her.

"Have a nice day, Dawn."

I slipped quietly into this week's VBFYRRRBC meeting, even though I'd started to wish I could skip it altogether. It was hard to remain positive when everyone behaved as though Birdie was gone for good and that my refusal to wallow was some sort of denial response.

Part of me was taken aback at how invested the town was in my happily ever after. My relationship with Birdie—if that's what you wanted to call it—had never really been made official, let alone shouted from the rooftops, and yet everyone seemed to instinctively understand that her absence was my loss.

I was determined to remain hopeful, but nine days of constant sympathy—and unreturned phone calls—would wear the most confident man down.

"Isaac!" Dot bustled out from the clutch of people brewing fresh paper cups of tea around the trestle table. No doubt their grumbles were all about the lack of baked goods. "It's good to see you, dear. The riffraff is getting vocal about the lack of sweets." As she drew closer, the creases in her forehead grew deeper, and her mouth turned down with a frown. "Oh, no. What's happened?"

I cleared my throat and tried to smile as I lifted the boxes in my hands. "Mind if I set these down?"

Dot spun around and stalked to the lectern, clapping her hands sharply before finding her gavel and cracking it against the sound block. I arranged the pastries on the tables while everyone divided their attention between the book club president and the array of croissants, cakes, and macarons.

"Order. Order!" Dot shouted. "This meeting's now in session. Please take your seats." Her eyes darted to me and away again, but not so quickly that everyone didn't take note and shoot me curious looks as well. "Sashes on. We'll skip the oath today."

I pulled my sash from my pocket and slung it around my torso before lowering myself into a plastic chair.

"Ah, my boy." Burt crossed his arms over his chest and swung his head from side to side. "It's not good news, is it?"

"It's not bad news either," I replied defensively. "I still haven't heard from her, but it's only been nine days."

Almost as one, everyone averted their eyes, and I rubbed my palms over the tops of my thighs.

"Isaac." Dot hesitated. "How can we help?"

I released a nervous breath. "I believe this is all going to work out in the end. Birdie wanted me to be confident, back myself, and know my worth. I can't throw that all away now—she wouldn't want me to—so you can let me hope, and you can hope along with me."

"Of course, you can hope," Dot said, all but glowering as she looked around the room as if daring anyone to disagree with her. "And as long as you believe in your heart that there's a chance for you and Birdie, we believe it too."

A murmur of agreement sounded, and just like that, my shaky grip on a future that featured Birdie front and centre firmed up again.

"Thank you," I said. "That means a lot to me."

"Can't say we'd be much good as a romance book club if we gave up on love just like that," Bill mumbled beside me, intent on the almond pastry on a plate in his lap.

"Thank you," I whispered again, and he gave me a solemn nod.

I left the meeting a little more than an hour later, my e-reader queued up with a dozen or more books about second-chance romance and lovers who come to their senses just when all the odds seem stacked against them. I was hopeful again, and I had another week's worth of stories I could read to Birdie's answering service. I'd find the words to get through to her eventually, as long as I never gave up hope. My focus was turned towards the future. Every hour that my phone didn't ring was an hour closer to the moment Birdie finally called.

But then I turned onto my street and drove past her house, and a hollow the size of an ocean opened deep inside my gut. There was her house, looking the same as it always did, except for the *sold* sticker on the *For Sale* sign out front.

34

ISAAC

MY LUNGS BURNED like fire, the sun hammered against the back of my neck, and a sheen of sweat slicked my skin under the splashes of warm saltwater. I rowed like a maniac, which wasn't a bad thing. It was the final race in the qualifying surf rowing competition, and we needed every ounce of power we could find. Lucky for the Valentine Bay boys, I was bursting with it. All the frustration and disappointment and hurt I'd kept on a tight leash the last two days had broken free, and the water beneath our boat took the punishment.

The Old Maxwell Place was sold. The only thing anchoring Birdie to this town now was me, and I didn't know if I was enough.

The day of the race had dawned clear and warm, but the waves were blown out—the swell manageable, even though it was windy, which made conditions a little rough. Still, we were on our home beach and knew the water better than any other team, which we'd used to our advantage.

The blades of our oars carved through the blue in perfect unison as Will, Josh, Logan, and I strained to conquer the waves. From my second seat in the bow, I watched the muscles in Josh and Logan's shoulders tighten and surge as our arms moved forwards and back, pulling on the oars and propelling us out to the gate can.

As expected, our biggest competition was the boys from Scarborough Cove, and they weren't giving up without a fight. All five boats in the qualifier had clean starts, but two had been pushed back hard enough in the opening seconds that the race was all but over for them.

Standing up front in the stern, Luca steered the boat with a steady hand and roared motivation loud enough to carry over the noise of the ocean. And behind me, Will bore the brunt of our speed as the bow ploughed into the face of the climbing waves. I welcomed every scream from Luca's throat, every impact from the sea, every sting in my muscles, and every jolt in my body. Anything felt better than the pain of giving up on the hope of Birdie ever coming home.

As our boat crested wave after wave, the swell soaking us with each break, we pushed on until we hit the clean water in the back, where the swell was heavy and undulating. Bearing down at the sight of Scarborough Cove half a boat length in front, we rounded the gate can with a smoother arc than our competition, making up the distance between us as both boats headed back to shore.

The swell of a wave lifted both vessels and propelled us forwards as a rush of adrenaline flashed through my veins, and as we shipped our oars and sailed ahead using the momentum of the ocean, Luca shouted, "We've got this! We're going to win it! Oars in, let's move!"

He was right. A quick glance at the Scarborough Cove boat showed that we'd gained a little, and as we powered into the whitewater, the momentum built underneath us. A quick check to my left confirmed that Scarborough Cove had slid off the soft edge of the wave as we coasted down the face of it and extended our lead by another boat length.

"We're going to fucking win this!" Luca shouted. "Pull! Fucking *pull*!"

My shoulders screamed, and my back burned as we leaned heavily into the oars, dragging the paddles through the water with renewed energy. We really were going to do this, and it felt fucking fantastic.

I sensed the determination rolling off the boys as we shot towards the beach. Heads down and strokes long as we hit the shallows, the cheers reached my ears just as the friction of sand dragged against the hull of the boat. We'd made it, and a darting look over my shoulder confirmed we'd left Scarborough Cove behind.

Luca was the first to punch the sky as he toppled backwards from the boat and into the water. As we slid onto the beach, Logan dropped his oar and turned to fling himself at Josh, and we all collapsed in a victorious scrum, laughing as hands grasped the boat and dragged us to a complete stop on the sand.

For a moment, thoughts of Birdie receded. This moment felt too freaking good. We'd worked hard, we'd earned this win, and I wasn't about to take anything away from the victory written bright and large on the faces of my friends. And fuck, it was a relief to feel good after nearly two weeks of feeling like total shit.

The first face I saw was my dad's. He put his arms around me in a rough embrace as we stood ankle-deep in the water, and I returned his hug with a few hard smacks on his back.

"Beautiful race, Isaac," he said, teeth flashing and chest puffed up proudly as he shifted to make room for my mother.

"Oh, honey!" she said, giving me a hug of her own tight enough to stop the breath in my lungs. "That was magnificent. Congratulations. You earned that win. I'm so proud of you all."

"Thanks," I replied with a grin as I followed the boys away from the boat and into the crowd. I swiped my board shorts from where I'd left them on the sand and dragged them up my legs as people whooped and called out their congratulations. It was easy to soak it all up in the flush of a fresh win, just like it was easy to believe that this was a good day, the best I'd had in too long...

But then I spotted Josh with Emily tucked under his arm as he shook his father's hand, followed by Logan and Jess a few metres away, his hands cradling her head as he kissed her upturned mouth, her body melting against his. And there was Luca, dripping wet and surrounded by his enormous family, Tash clinging to his arm and gazing up at him as if he were some kind of ocean god. Even Will had a girl, in his own way—Abbie waited for him with a bottle of water and a towel, and when he scooped her against him with an arm around her shoulders, she might have rolled her eyes, but she didn't object when he planted a kiss on the crown of her head.

Everyone had someone but me. I was alone. Suddenly, first place in a surf rowing qualifier was a pathetic consolation.

I forced myself to smile and accept the well wishes of my family, who were all there to watch me compete. I wrapped my arms around them when they ducked in for hugs, and though my smiles felt forced and my laughs sounded hollow, everyone seemed either too distracted or too excited to notice.

The collective energy buzzed across the beach as Luca, Josh, Logan, Will, and I circulated and shook all the outstretched hands. But the longer it took, the more mechanical it felt, and the heaviness I'd been able to set aside following the first thrill of a win settled over me again like a dozen wet towels.

It took forever to move much beyond the water's edge and up the beach, stopping every couple of steps to accept someone's congratulations. I tolerated it with as much good humour as I could find, but fifteen minutes later, I was over it. If I had to smile one more time…

"Sergeant Greene!" Dot's familiar voice sounded behind me, and I spun to find her standing there in a fluoro blue tracksuit, the VBFYRRRBC arranged behind her. Irena and Lorraine held a banner between them with "Go Isaac!" painted across it in dripping, bright pink letters. I did grin then—and it was real.

"Dot!" I jogged a few steps to close the distance between us and scooped up her slight frame. "I didn't know you were here." I set her down again and pretended not to notice that Agatha had sidled up beside her, obviously angling for a cuddle of her own. "Thanks for coming down. All of you. I really appreciate it."

"Oh, we wouldn't miss your big day," Dot replied.

"Mrs Spies pencilled this into the calendar a month ago," Burt muttered, a scowl on his face. "Says it's good to support the local community, but you don't see her writing down the dates for the quarterly library trivia night, do you?"

I coughed to hide my smile and tugged at my earlobe. "Days like today might explain why she's *insatiable*, eh, Burt?"

Burt scowled deeper, then shuffled off, mumbling to himself, no doubt to find his wife, who the last I saw had been admiring Will's biceps.

Dot chuckled, and as the group dispersed—Agatha giving me one last, lingering look—Dot looped an arm through mine. "Help an old lady along the sand, would you, Officer? I've had enough of this sun, and I'd like to go home."

I flashed her a grateful glance, and we began the short trek up to Main Street. "How did you know I'd had enough?"

"Oh, you live long enough, and you learn to read the room."

"Yeah, well. Thanks. I just—" I sighed, wondering why I'd hesitate to be honest with Dot. The old woman knew more about me than anyone in this town. The only person who understood me better was Birdie, and she was half a world away. "I wish I had someone to share these moments with, you know? All the guys have their girls, and then there's me—the friend."

"Oh, I can relate." Dot gave my arm a firm squeeze. "I've been thinking about looking for husband number seven myself. Life is lonely without that special someone by your side."

I swallowed my surprise and said, "That it is, Dot."

We walked in companionable silence until we reached the street, drawing to a stop at the kerb.

"My car is parked a block that way," I said, gesturing to the left. My house was only a short walk away, but I'd had too much gear to carry with me that morning. "Can I give you a ride home?"

"No, thank you, dear." Dot extracted her arm from mine and shook off her "old lady" stoop. "I have a date at Tony's Place in twenty minutes, so I may as well head straight there. Uh-uh!" She held up one knobby finger to stall my question. "I'll tell you all about it at the next meeting, all right?"

"Sure," I agreed, realising I didn't feel like talking about Dot's love life anyway. "Sounds good."

"Who knows?" she added. "Perhaps we'll both have good news by then."

I waved goodbye and waited until she'd crossed the street safely before walking the short distance to my car. Valentine Bay was a safe enough town that I'd left my phone in the centre console, and as I turned over the engine, I retrieved it to check for calls or messages. There was only one, and it was only a minute old, and I tried not to acknowledge the disappointed dive of my heart when I realised it wasn't from Birdie. I tapped on the notification to return the call.

"David," I said when my colleague answered the phone at the station. "Is there something wrong?"

"I doubt it," David replied, the sound of his pen clicking in the background. "Just wanted to let you know someone reported activity at the Old Maxwell Place. I know you're at the surf rowing competition, so I'm about to send Ross around to investigate, but I thought—"

"No need to send anyone." My pulse thundered as my fingers fumbled at my seatbelt. "I'm on my way."

I swiped to end the call before David could confirm and threw the car into reverse.

It took every ounce of willpower I had not to break the speed limit, and I spent every second of the five-minute drive swinging between the extremes of ridiculous certainty that the intruder could only be Birdie and the devastating belief that she was never coming back.

I shouldn't get my hopes up. If I walked into that house and found anyone there but her… Well, I wasn't sure how I'd bounce back from that, if ever.

I swung the car into my driveway and slammed it into Park, distantly registering that I was still half-naked and barefooted, my hair damp from the ocean and my shoulders pinkish-golden from the sun. Running across the lawn of Birdie's place, I leaped over the porch steps and tried the handle on the front door. It wasn't locked, which teased me with a sense of hope bigger and more insistent than before, and I let myself in, taking the stairs two at a time.

The door to the bathroom was closed, the shower running, and still, I tried to talk myself out of assuming it was her. But it had to be, didn't it? Who else broke into a house and took a fucking shower?

I stalled, not sure what to do. My blood thumped too loudly, and I wasn't thinking straight. Would she come back and not call first? Could this really be her?

The water shut off, and the shower door squeaked open and closed. I waited for someone—for Birdie—to appear, but when the door remained closed, I took a tentative step forwards.

My foot landed on a creaky floorboard, and I froze as the sounds of movement in the bathroom fell silent. The door remained shut, and I held my breath.

Without warning, the door flung open, and a heavy object came hurtling my way.

"Take this, you fucker!" Birdie screeched as her shampoo bottle smacked me square in the chest. I grunted reflexively as it bounced off muscle, then stepped over it, reaching the bathroom door in four long strides and smacking it wide with an open palm. Once inside, I wrapped my arms around the woman I loved, lifted her clean off the ground, and kissed her hard.

My Birdie was home.

She moaned against my mouth and wrapped her bare legs around my waist, tightening her arms around my neck as I pinned her against the tiled bathroom wall. I have no idea how long we explored each other like that, drowning in the knowledge that she was home, she was here, and she was mine. Her mouth was warm and wet and soft, and she clung to me like she'd never let go.

I was never going to let go.

Eventually, I pulled away. We were breathless, and I closed my eyes briefly, leaning my forehead against hers and inhaling the apple scent of her damp curls. Relief and devotion threatened to pull me under, and I gave myself a moment to find my balance.

"You came back," I whispered, nosing her hair and pressing my lips to the soft spot beneath her earlobe.

"I came back," she echoed, burrowing her face into my neck.

Between us, our hearts beat against each other, her breasts pressed against my chest, and I never wanted to move. "And this time, you're going to stay."

Birdie drew her head back and gazed deep into my eyes. Her lips brushed mine as she clenched her thighs around my hips. "And this time," she repeated, her fingers twirling into my hair as her blue eyes swam, "I'm going to stay."

35

BIRDIE

"THE HOUSE IS sold, you know," Isaac commented as we walked down my drive and past the *For Sale* sign on the lawn out front. He squeezed my hand as we paced past the bright red *sold* sticker on our way to The Salty Stop. "But don't worry. We'll figure something out. You can always move into my place"—he eyed me sideways, waiting for a rejection, but I held my tongue and enjoyed the anticipation buzzing under my skin—"but if you don't want to do that, it's okay. I bet Abbie would love a roommate until we work out where you want to live."

"That won't be necessary," I said, failing to hide my grin. "Isaac, I have to tell you something. *I* bought the house."

He stopped and turned to me, disbelief widening his eyes until a smile tugged at one corner of his mouth. "Are you serious? The house is yours?" He scooped me up in his arms and spun me around so fast it left me clinging to his shoulders. "Why didn't you say something, Red?"

I laughed, a little breathless, as he set me on my feet. "I'm saying something now, aren't I? Besides, we've been a little busy." I arched a coy eyebrow before lifting his hand and leading him further down the street.

It had been three hours since he burst in on me in the bathroom, and we'd spent every minute of that time getting reacquainted. I don't know how I ever thought I could go a lifetime without this man in my life and my bed.

"Yeah, we have," he said with a grin, pulling me closer to his body as we walked. "Fuck, I still can't believe you're here. I might never take my hands off you again."

"You'll get no complaints from me."

Isaac chuckled under his breath. "I never gave up hope, but I'll be honest—these last ten days have been the longest of my life."

"Just wait until I catch you up on everything that's happened to *me*," I replied, ticking items off on the fingers of my free hand. "I won a million dollars, then blew it all on the house. I confronted my father. I met my sister—"

"Hold on." Isaac drew us to a stop again, turning to face me. "I need to know what happened with your dad, of course, but your sister?" Concern wrinkled his forehead. "What happened? Are you okay?"

My smile grew wide enough that my cheeks ached. "Better than okay, but it's a long story, and today is all about *you*, Mr Surf Rowing Champion." I tugged on his arm. “Come on, hot stuff. The party can’t start until you get there.”

Isaac let me drag him to the corner, but like always, he stepped off onto the road before me and led the way across with a gentle hand on the small of my back. I’d been crossing roads on my own for a long time, no big man required, but his protectiveness didn’t annoy me. Not anymore. The way he took care of me made me feel safe in ways that had nothing to do with oncoming traffic, an empty stomach, or cold feet. I finally belonged somewhere and to someone, and I was going to watch out for him as fiercely as he watched out for me.

We finally reached Will’s bar, and Isaac pushed open the heavy wooden door. Inside, balloons and streamers hung from the ceiling in a rainbow of colours, and a band played soft rock music in the corner. People danced and laughed, but almost everyone looked over as we entered, heralded by a shard of mellow afternoon sunlight.

A high-pitched squeal cut through the noise, and I stumbled two steps backwards as Abbie barrelled into me, wrapping her arms around my neck and screeching again. “Birdie! You’re back! Did you win?”

I chuckled and returned her hug, too content to comment on the ringing in my ear. “I did,” I confirmed.

Abbie released me and winked. “Atta girl.” Picking up my hand, she dragged me deeper into the room. “We’re in our usual booth. Come on.”

The “usual booth” was crowded with people—Luca with Natasha on his lap, Josh with Emily snuggled under his arm, and Logan and Jess sandwiched happily in the corner. There was a delay in all their reactions at the sight of me, and I laughed when Jess gasped and scrambled up so quickly she climbed over Josh and Emily's laps in her rush to get to me.

I hugged her first, though she reached out an arm and pulled Isaac in on the action. I bit the inside of my mouth to hold back tears at the way the crew embraced me one by one. Will was last in line, and he grinned before giving me a kiss on the cheek. "Good to see you, Maxwell. Welcome home."

"Thanks, Kidd. Good to be home."

When I had space enough to come up for air, I realised Isaac was watching it all with a curious smile. I returned it and was about to ask what the sexy smirk was all about when he curled his broad hands around my cheeks, tipped my face up to his, and kissed me.

I mean, *really* kissed me.

I was vaguely aware of cheers rising up around us, feet stomping and wolf whistles too, but I was lost in Isaac. His lips parted as our kiss grew deeper, and I gripped the front of his shirt to keep myself from melting into a puddle on the floor. Applause sounded as he released me, and my vision swam with the picture of his pleased grin.

I never wanted to be without this man.

"Birdie!" Kris shouted as Isaac's parents appeared at my shoulder. As Rusty folded his son in a rough embrace, Kris dropped her head to one side, and tears filled her eyes as she looked at me. "Oh, come here, honey." Her soft, warm arms scooped me in close, and I wrapped my arms around her waist as she whispered in my ear, "Welcome to the family."

"Thank you for having me," I croaked, the overwhelm catching in my throat.

Kris and Rusty ushered me and Isaac to a long table on the other side of the bar. We found seats and shared a round of drinks with Isaac's family—his parents, his sisters, his brothers-in-law, and his eight nieces and nephews. To my surprise—and, I'll be honest, pleasure—Liam wasted no time reinstating our tutoring agreement before skipping out early to meet his friends at the beach.

Once the younger kids' bedtimes rolled around, the Greenes dispersed, and Isaac led me to a table where a group of oldies argued about something so secretive they clammed up as soon as we got within hearing distance. But for a group of people who I'd barely spent any time with, they seemed ridiculously pleased to see me. Old Burt Spies was grinning hard, his face red as a beet, and Lorraine Langley removed her glasses so she could wipe tears from her eyes.

"Birdie Maxwell!" Dorothy March took both my hands in hers, looking up at me from her seat. She wore an impeccable ensemble from the '50s or '60s—an original from her wardrobe, no doubt. She still had high tops on her feet. "We're so glad to see you back in the Bay. You and Isaac make a lovely couple."

"Well, thank you, Mrs March," I said, sharing a small smile with Isaac. "I think so, too."

Isaac leaned down to drop a kiss on the old woman's cheek. "Thanks, Dot," he said. "For everything."

Dot winked, and Isaac cleared his throat as Agatha Braverman wrapped her painted red lips around a straw in a move that was flagrantly unnecessary.

"What was that all about?" I whispered with an amused look over my shoulder as Isaac drew me away.

"Another long story," he replied. "I'll tell you another time."

The afternoon wore on into evening, and Isaac kept a hand on me or an arm around me the entire time. I wasn't mad at it. I hugged more people in the space of a few hours than I had in my lifetime, and I wasn't mad at that, either.

The hour crept closer to midnight, and the crowds in the bar thinned. Isaac and I danced a little, ate a bit more, drank a lot until Will closed the door behind the last paying customer, and it was just the ten of us left in the dimly lit room.

The conversation ebbed and flowed the way it does when you're with old friends. We laughed. I recounted the tournament in Vegas, playing up the scenes with Baseball Cap Guy but leaving out the details about my father and Asta. They regaled me with a detailed recount of the race, and I was sorry I'd missed it. I announced that I'd bought my parents' house, which called for a round of champagne, naturally, and then I somehow hired Logan to manage a complete renovation. I agreed to attend Abbie's yoga class the following morning—it was never going to happen—then settled back and soaked it all in.

It was new to me, but with Isaac's solid arm around my shoulders and his fingers twined in mine, I was able to breathe easily for the first time—maybe ever.

I had a real home and a real family. I had love.

Isaac gathered me closer and pressed his lips to my hair just as he inhaled the apple scent of it. I breathed him in, too, savouring the scent of leather and linen that was all him.

"I win," he murmured.

My lips twitched. "What?"

"The game. The bet. Whichever way this thing started between us. It's over, and I have you. I win."

I dropped my head back on Isaac's shoulder and turned my head enough that my lips brushed his ear. He was right, but he still had it all wrong.

"The game's over, but this isn't poker, Romeo. You've got me, and I have you. We both win."

SIX MONTHS LATER

BIRDIE

"NO, NO, NO," Abbie groaned, dragging herself out of her first-class pod long after the seatbelt lights had switched off on our commercial flight to Las Vegas. "*Please* don't tell me I have to get off this plane. These last seventeen hours have been the most luxurious I'll ever experience in my lifetime, and I want more of it." Abbie craned her neck to look for a flight attendant, then turned to Will, who was on his feet beside her. "Hey, babe. Do you think it's too late to order another glass of bubbles?"

He cocked a cute eyebrow and flashed his dimples as he swung his carry-on luggage across his back. "Everyone's disembarking, so it's safe to say that, yes, it's too late. Don't worry." He tapped the tip of her nose with one finger. "I heard a rumour that if you ask the right people, there are places that'll sell you alcohol in Vegas, too."

"Oh, yes!" Abbie's face lit up. "Starting with your casino, right, Birdie?"

"It's not my casino yet," I replied, giving Isaac an appreciative smile as he took a heavy bag from me and slung it over his shoulder. "But yes, there will be booze."

Stepping out from her pod and meeting me in the aisle, Emily wrapped her arms around me in a tight hug. I exchanged a smile with Josh, who hovered not far behind. "I can't believe you've done this," Em said as she let me go. "Ten first-class plane tickets and an all-expenses-paid trip to the States. It's too much—"

"Shh," Abbie hissed, sparing me a cheeky wink. "Don't say that. I can't afford the meal I just ate, let alone the airfare."

I chuckled as we gathered up our belongings, shooting Isaac a secretive look that he returned with a small, knowing smirk. "I wouldn't have done it if I didn't want to," I assured Emily, "so, not another word about the money, okay? It'll just ruin the incredible week I've got planned for us."

Logan looked back from where he and Jess were heading towards the front of the plane. "But seriously, Maxwell. It's beyond generous. Thank you."

"I appreciate you saying so," I replied, "but what I really want is for everyone to forget about it and just have fun."

We cheered loudly and probably inappropriately, given the venue, and it earned us filthy looks from a well-to-do middle-aged couple in the back row. For some reason, that only improved my good mood, and I laughed as we finally moved past the flight crew and through the plane doors.

I didn't say much as we made our way over the aerobridge to the terminal, through customs, and on to baggage collection. Isaac squeezed my hand a few times, and I knew we shared the same tension in our stomachs—that feeling you get when you're trying to repress excitement about a secret you're going to reveal in dramatic fashion any minute now. Luca kept an eye and a hand on Tash at all times—she was a little more than halfway through her pregnancy, and though they'd considered not joining us on this trip, Isaac had managed to convince both Luca and Tash that this was destined to be the experience of a lifetime. Who knew when, if ever again, all ten of us would be able to put our worlds on pause, jump on a plane, and party—just us, and just because?

Or at least, that's the story we'd told everyone.

"So, should we split up and hail a few taxis?" Jess asked as we stood outside the airport, a mountain of luggage piled behind us. We'd landed late into the night local time—the best time to explore the city, if you asked me—and Jess's head swivelled this way and that, betraying a little of her anxiety.

I checked my phone for confirmation that our transport was on its way, and like clockwork, a glimmering stretch Hummer pulled up to the kerb.

"Whoa, check this thing out," Will said, eying the sleek back car with appreciation.

Abbie squinted at the dark-tinted windows. "There are disco lights on in there."

The driver stepped out and paced around to the

passenger side, where I waited to confirm my booking.

"Car for Maxwell?" I asked, biting back a grin at the gasps behind me.

The driver nodded and opened the door, and I turned back to the crew, who waited in various states of stunned.

"Well?" I laughed. "Isn't anyone going to get in?"

"Hell, yeah," Abbie replied, flinging herself into the car without a backwards glance at her bags. At an impatient wave of my arm, the rest of the crew followed while Isaac and I coordinated the stowing of everyone's luggage. By the time we joined them inside, they'd discovered how to run the music and change the lights, and—no surprises—someone had located the minibar. As the driver closed the door behind Isaac, Abbie pulled out a bottle of chilled sparkling wine, then tipped her chin towards the row of glassware on the opposite side of the car. "Hand me one of those, will you? We cannot ride in this car without bubbles. We just can't."

The lights of Vegas slipped past us as we poured champagne for everyone but Tash, who took a flute of sparkling apple juice instead, and Luca, who was abstaining in sympathy.

"So, where to first?" Josh asked with Emily snuggled in tight against his side. "I suppose we should check in to our hotel?"

"Bor-ing," Will hooted.

Josh threw a balled-up napkin at his head. "Fuck off."

"The casino?" Logan suggested, one hand resting protectively on Jess's knee.

"Or food?" Luca added, glancing around as we topped up a second round of drinks. "I've got no idea what time it is or when we'll need breakfast, but you are all in for a rough morning very soon."

"Bor-ing," Will jeered again.

"Can someone punch him, please?" Luca asked wearily.

Abbie happily obliged, landing her fist hard enough in Will's ribs that he grunted. Luca offered Abbie a raised palm, and she high-fived it.

I risked a glance up at Isaac next to me, who pressed a kiss to my forehead. "Well," I said, taking his gesture as my sign to move to phase two of our plan. "There *is* actually somewhere we need to be in about twenty minutes."

Everyone exchanged suspicious looks as curious smiles pulled at their lips.

"What's going on with you two?" Jess asked, her eyes bouncing between Isaac and me. "There's something you're not telling us."

"Yeah, there is." Isaac gave me a questioning glance, and when I nodded, he cleared his throat. "This isn't just a party trip, and there's a reason we wanted you all here with us. Birdie and I are eloping. Tonight's our wedding, and this week with you all in Vegas is our honeymoon."

Following a heartbeat of total silence, Abbie was the first to scream. Shouts and whoops followed from everyone soon after. Everyone tripped and fell over each other to get to us, the confines of the car making it that much more difficult to reach the bride and groom.

The bride and groom.

Fuck, I was getting married.

I never thought this would happen, but then I never thought I'd meet someone I loved as much as I loved Isaac or trust someone the way I trusted him. Feel safe the way I did when he was in my life. I didn't know there was someone out there who could love me the way he did or understand me so perfectly that when I warmed to the idea of one day making our commitment official, *he* was the one who suggested we put our friends on a plane and run away to Las Vegas.

I could get married in sneakers, he'd said. We could say "I do" in front of a guy who looked kind of but not really like Elvis. Afterwards, we'd celebrate with a few hands of poker and a few more rounds of drinks, then top it off with a night of multiple orgasms, courtesy of the man who I could now call my husband.

I was getting married. And nothing in the world could have made me happier.

ISAAC

I STOOD AT the front of the chapel with a guy who looked kind of but not really like Elvis and waited for Birdie. My heart raced and sweat beaded on my hairline. I wasn't nervous. I'd just never loved anyone this much or wanted anyone so badly. The moment I said as much out loud with our friends as witnesses couldn't come fast enough. My blood pounded because I was impatient for the world to know that Birdie Maxwell was mine.

I knew she'd still be wearing the clothes she'd been in on the plane—jeans and sneakers—because we all were. I knew there was no logical reason for her to look different just because she walked down an aisle, but when Birdie stepped into sight, and our friends pushed to their feet in the pews lining the tiny Las Vegas chapel, tears stung my eyes. She'd found a bouquet of white roses somewhere and pulled out her braid, leaving her long copper hair framing her face in loose waves. Her cheeks were flushed, her freckles bright, and her plump mouth tilted upwards at the corners. I was peripherally aware of somebody crying—Jess, I thought, and perhaps Tash—but all my senses were trained entirely on the woman I was going to worship and adore for the rest of my life.

Birdie came to a stop opposite me, and I immediately reached for her hands, needing to feel her skin against mine as a reminder that this was real. Her face turned up, and she met my eyes, and impulsively I took her head in my hands and leaned in to kiss her.

"Well, that part usually happens at the end," Elvis drawled. "How about we start again from the beginning?"

The ceremony was quick, but we'd made sure there was time to recite our own vows. I'd spent the last month poring over the promises I wanted to make to Birdie. To begin, there'd been a hundred of them, each one a declaration of all the ways I'd make her happy and keep her safe. In the end, I realised that Birdie didn't need promises. She needed truth.

"I've loved you forever," I said, ignoring the crack in my voice as I tightened my grip on her hands. "I've never told you that, but it's true. I loved you all those years we were kids playing cards, but I never had the courage to tell you. Even then, you were brave and bold and selfless, and you created a safe space for me to be me. And all this time later, without knowing what I was missing, you burst into my life and did it all over again. We might not make much sense on paper, but in life, there'll never be anyone more perfect for me than you. I love you, Birdie Maxwell, and I promise to keep loving you for all the days of my life."

One tear, then another, rolled down Birdie's cheek, and I wiped away each one. The gesture made her smile, and she nodded before sucking in a deep breath.

"Once upon a time, I could never have imagined getting married. I thought I wasn't made for it. What I know now is that it's not about me being made for marriage—it's about me being made for *you.* You're the first person in my life to make space for the real Birdie—a safe space, I should say, because even when I was giving you all the reasons why we should never have given this a shot, you kept on loving me without ever trying to change me. I spent my whole life believing I wasn't enough, and then along came you. I'm not here today because I think we need to prove anything. I'm not marrying you because I'm supposed to or because I'm scared of losing you if I don't. It's just as you said. There's simply nobody in this world more perfect for me than you, and I want the whole world to know that I love you." Birdie grinned and cast an amused, sidelong look at not-Elvis. "I want to remember the exact moment we got our own happily ever after."

I didn't care if it wasn't the right time yet. I scooped Birdie up in my arms and kissed her again, and she threw her arms around my neck as our friends clapped and whistled and stomped their feet. Over the noise, Elvis shouted as he declared us husband and wife, and by the time I set Birdie down, we were both breathless and laughing.

The crew followed us down the aisle, directly to the waiting limousine, which whisked us to Birdie's family casino. We ate, we drank, we gambled until we fell into bed, and then we made love until the sun came up.

I fell asleep as the sky lightened outside, my wife curled up in my arms, her feet tucked in tight between my legs.

It wasn't traditional, but neither was Birdie. And perhaps, after all, neither was I.

BONUS SCENE

Isaac and Birdie's story doesn't end here! Visit my website at samanthaleighbooks.com/books/bonus-content or use the QR code to download a bonus scene set five years in the future...

UP NEXT: ONLY FOR YOU

Do you want to know why Will Kidd and Abbie Ellison keep playing cat and mouse? Here's what you're in for...

A single dad with a crush and an apartment with only one bed… These best friends are so screwed.

Abigail Ellison always had a reputation, but she's never let that define her. Confident and carefree, she's built her life on rewriting the script. All game, no shame. It's kind of her brand.

Will Kidd is an irresistible bartender with a reputation of his own. But when a baby wearing his dimples lands on his doorstep the same day his best friend comes begging for a place to stay, it's time for him to get serious.

And his overprotective daddy vibe? Seriously hot.

As they juggle the chaos of caring for a baby and fight the chemistry bubbling between them, Will and Abbie start rethinking everything they thought they wanted.

Could they really be cut out for marriage? Stability? A white picket fence?

Or will this former bad girl and reformed playboy miss their happily ever after?

Only For You *is a first-person, dual POV contemporary romance with lots of steam and a satisfying happily ever after.*

ACKNOWLEDGEMENTS

My gratitude and appreciation go to all those people who helped me get this book onto the page and into the hands of my wonderful readers. It wasn't easy, but we got there!

Thank you Dawn Alexander, Gina Salamon, Brandi Zelenka, Kate Farlow, Melanie Harlow, Stephanie Archer and Jenn Watson for your support, guidance and mentoring. Thank you to the long list of Harlot Authors who answered my questions or otherwise held my hand and might never realise what a huge difference they've made. Thank you to my enthusiastic and always supportive ARC team. Thank you to my LoveLeigh Readers group. And thank *you* for reading *Perfect For You*. I hope you enjoyed it.

And last but never least, thank you to my family—my husband and my children. I love you.

ABOUT THE AUTHOR

Samantha Leigh is an Australian author of steamy contemporary romance. When she's not playing matchmaker in imaginary worlds, Sam is reading books with all the feels and all the spice. In the tiny slices of time she has between word wrangling, Sam likes to hit her yoga mat, go for walks in the bush or on the beach, continue her search for the perfect poke bowl, drown herself in coffee and hot cacao, and binge-watch nineties television.

samanthaleighbooks.com

www.ingramcontent.com/pod-product-compliance
Lightning Source LLC
Chambersburg PA
CBHW050108120726
47904CB00004B/1264
* 9 7 8 0 6 4 5 5 7 0 3 7 3 *

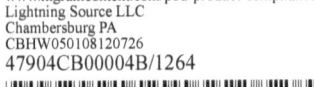